I0590102

Now I've Got You In My Space
The Latch Trilogy: Book One
Copyright 2025
Independently published by Briar Townsend
All rights reserved

Cover art and design: Hannah Christensen
Edited by: J. Brighton and Hayley Theobald

Print ISBN: 979-8-9923066-4-4

Now I've Got You In My Space

The Latch Trilogy:
Book One

By Briar Townsend

Content Guidance

Now I've Got You In My Space - as well as the entire *Latch* trilogy - contains allusions to, and mentions of, transphobia and homophobia.
There will also be instances of sexual assault, attempted sexual assault, doxxing, outing, a coercive sexual relationship, ableism (specifically in relation to autism), childhood bullying, racism, classism, familial rejection, grief, death of a family member, funeral, illness (influenza), and interactions with police.
This may not be an exhaustive list, and is provided as general guidance. Not all content listed will be mentioned in all three books, but will be found throughout the series as a whole.

One of the main characters lives with PTSD. The other main character is autistic. Along with the other identities portrayed, including multiple gender and sexual identities, these are written as individual perspectives and not intended to be understood as universal experiences. While Theo, Emir, and their friends offer one narrative of their identities, they are not representative of entire populations.

This book contains explicit sexual content. My style has been referred to as "comfort smut" and "homonormative." Be that as it may, if PG is your cup of tea, I am not the barista for you.

While I intend to handle these topics with both care and honesty, it's possible that reading about them may be uncomfortable or potentially triggering. Please take the space you need before, during, and/or after reading to look after yourself.

CHAPTER ONE

Wandering through his favourite hidden path on campus, Emir takes a few minutes to absorb his surroundings. It's one of his favourite times of year: when the air hums with excitement for the upcoming term, when the first year students are excitedly trying to navigate the expansive campus until they find their footing, when the last heat of summer makes the dance studios functionally unbearable while Emir sweats through his classes, and of course, when he's back with his favourite people.

This is his last year of education, his final chance to live the university life.

Emir ducks behind the library, sneaking away before a group of clearly lost first years notice him. That's certainly one advantage of his dance training: quiet feet and quick escapes when he wants to be alone. Which, to be fair, is most of the time he's not in class or performing. He's always been most comfortable with solitude, with the calm and quiet of being on his own.

Of course, there are exceptions to that: the people who understand him and whose presence is like a warm reminder of companionship rather than a drain on his energy. It's not that Emir's anti-social or doesn't love people, because he absolutely adores his friends and family. But he needs to be alone, to process the world around him at the hearth of his own mind.

He stops underneath an elm tree for a moment, a bird in one of the lower branches catching Emir's eye. It's a wren, its tiny round body hopping along near his head as if he isn't even there. Another bonus of his quiet feet and intentional movement: he can make his way through nature without disturbing much, a happy observer to the animals he encounters.

Maybe if Emir hadn't chosen his path long ago, he would've found himself as some sort of biologist, spending his days in fields and laboratories. His mum always calls him her "happy little nerdlet" when he gets excited about something, and he can't even argue. He loves to learn for the sake of learning, to pick up a book and enter a new world, or instead, learn more about his own.

Emir studies the wren until it hops out of view, eyes soft with an awed smile on his face. He truly loves this time of year.

He's taking his time walking back to his flat after dropping his technique shoes and other necessities in the dressing room next to the dance studios. Emir knows by now that if he doesn't claim his locker before classes begin, he'll be stuck with the spot closest to the toilets the entire year. Emir only got back to campus yesterday and he feels sincerely happy to be back.

His flatmate, Laurie, is one of his closest mates, inseparable since they were put together through a random rooming lottery by the university their first year. They're messy in the same way, both Capricorns (which says enough on its own to be honest), and they both value their independence. It also helps that Laurie is studying interior design while Emir spends his days in the dance studio. They always have someone waiting at home at the end of a long day that they can vent to without judgement.

More than anything, the two of them have bonded over the reality that they're both exceptionally gay. Well, Emir is bi, but gay in the broader sense of the term. In the way that bigots don't care about the difference as long as they can shove their hate in the general direction of a queer person.

Three buildings away from his flat, Emir's phone vibrates in his pocket, making him stop and decide if he's going to answer. Laurie's face is lighting up the screen, so he grins and hits accept, an honour given to only his favourite people. Anyone else can get what they need from him with a text.

"Almost home, Laur. Do we need anything while I'm out?" Emir could easily take a detour to the cafe or even jump on the tube if there's something they've already forgotten for their flat. He's not quite done with his walk yet and he wouldn't mind extending it.

"Nah, mate. Just making sure you're coming with me to Troy's tonight." Laurie sounds a bit distracted, out of breath even...

"I swear, Laurie, if you're about to have sex right now." Emir groans, knowing it's a very real possibility. It's happened before, more than once, because Laurie and his fiance, T, are insatiable.

"Unfortunately not. T is still unpacking at their flat. Now, are you coming with me tonight or not?" Laurie finally stops moving based on what Emir can hear in the background, and there's no *Laaauuur* being whined to get his attention, so Emir decides he's telling the truth.

"Yeah, alright. Classes haven't started yet. May as well let loose a bit. But I'm not sharing my weed. Those fuckers can bring their own." Emir rolls his eyes, his voice hesitant even as he agrees to go. The way everyone at parties expects him to have drugs has always felt more than a little racist. Something about the combination of his tan skin and preference for baggy clothes seems to tick their stereotype box. He only ever smokes weed or cigarettes, nothing harder than that, and only when performances are weeks away. And the fact he's half Pakistani has absolutely nothing to do with that. Bellends.

"Get off - no - " Laurie is back to sounding like he's struggling on the other end of the phone. Emir's starting to worry about what he's going to find when he makes it back to the flat.

"Right, well…I'm going to go. I'll see you in five anyway." Emir frowns down at his phone as he ends the call, barely waiting for Laurie to shout bye in the direction of the receiver before pocketing it and reorienting himself with his surroundings. Deep breaths.

It's just a party. He deserves to have some fun. And if Laurie is with him he'll be fine.

Crowds can be hard for Emir, but he's been to Troy's before for at least one other party, he knows there's a quiet balcony, and it's close enough he can walk home on his own if he decides not to stay. Emir's warming to the idea as he rounds another corner, hands in his pockets while he gazes up at the sky. Maybe a party is just what he needs to start the year.

***

"I'm not going." Theo steps away from Laurie as he ends the call with Emir, giving up on his attempt to stop the call since he's clearly already failed.

"You're going. You're my best fucking mate and it's our last year. You. Are. Going." Laurie climbs up to sit on his kitchen counter, grabbing the healthy snacks that T left behind for him to munch on. Thank god for his healthy partner or Laurie would survive on takeaways and spunk.

"Then I'm not going with *you*." Theo crosses his arms and glares at Laurie as best he can. The man is a human teddy bear, so even when he's grumpy, the best he can pull off is a pout.

"Well T and Ciaran are staying at yours to have a quiet night in, Gabe's flight doesn't land until tomorrow, and Lili doesn't go to parties after…" Laurie doesn't need to finish that sentence, gesturing vaguely to get his point across.

Theo's other best friend, Elizabeth aka Lilibet aka Lili, went to a house party a month into their first year where she had a bad high that put her in hospital. After that, she was more than content to find her entertainment elsewhere, and away from strangers handing out free drugs.

"Then maybe I'll just stay in with T and Ciaran. Quiet night at home sounds sensible." Theo shrugs as if he doesn't care one way or another. Ciaran and T are the perfect flatmates for him: quiet, considerate, tidy, and both drama free thanks to finding their soulmates within the first six months of uni.

"You and Emir need to just shag and get it over with. This shit is ridiculous." Laurie ignores Theo's immediate scoff and eye roll while tossing another cashew in his mouth. He can't believe those two have been fighting for two years already, despite being in almost constant proximity.

"Not fucking happening. Not ever. We *hate* each other, Lawrence." Theo throws out the last word, knowing it's barely even banter if the best he can come up with is using his full name. "We can't even be in the same room without supervision."

"You do *not* hate each other. You're both just fucking oblivious, honestly. Obsessed with each other." Laurie flings a cashew that hits Theo on the bridge of his nose and breaks through his stiff exterior as he drops his arms in surprise. Laurie is chaos, but like…lovingly. Maybe it was his fated personality with a last name like Tempest, but whatever the reason, he's a human whirlwind in the most positive way.

"We've been antagonists since before we even met. Rivals in more ways than one. He *knows* he's more naturally talented than me, even though I work harder. Emir never lets me forget it, always swanning around the place like he's god's gift to the dance programme. Not my fault you actually like the twat." Theo tosses a craisin in Laurie's direction in retaliation. They're both exceptionally mature when they bicker.

"That *twat* is my best mate, besides you. And it's exhausting being in the middle of this – " Laurie gestures through the air around them, " – whole thing. I thought a term abroad for the two of you might give it a rest."

Laurie hops down from the counter and heads towards the door. "And Emi will be back in less than a minute so unless you intend to fuck in the entryway and get this over with, I suggest you head home and get ready. Takes you ages."

"Not happening." Theo flips him off over his shoulder as he walks into the hallway. "I'm not walking to Troy's with you two. I'll meet you there after Emir inevitably finds his conquest of the evening and fucks off without you. And I'm having T pick out my outfit, so not a word from you about what I'm wearing or how long it takes. Argue with your fiance."

"Sounding awfully invested over there, Teddy." Laurie calls after him before closing the front door with a smile.

Step one of finally getting his two best mates together is in motion. First the party, then some other steps he'll figure out later, eventually true love. T would only entertain Laurie's plans so far, so his plan for now is essentially to encourage them to fuck and hope they decide to fall for each other along the way. Tonight, he needs to figure out how to make Emir look even more fit than usual without him being suspicious. Nothing like jealousy and undeniable attraction to bring two reluctant rivals together.

***

"Wanker." Emir grumbles the moment he catches sight of Theo in the kitchen of Troy's house. He gives Theo a thorough once-over, eyes travelling across his figure with absolutely no shame. Theo's fit. There's no denying that. If anything, that makes Emir resent him even more.

Theo's ridiculously toned upper body is clearly on display through his loose, sheer white vest, and his thighs are wrapped so tightly in a pair of dark wash jeans that Emir can see the outline of his dick. Of course Theo has to show off, even now, where the rooms are too dark to even ogle properly and everyone here has seen each other naked at least a dozen times. They're theatre people: it's just part of the whole thing. But whatever this display is? The muscles and the outfit together are a bit much. And is he flexing while he pours?

"Twat." Theo replies automatically without even looking up from the drink he's making. Laurie texted that he and Emir were on their way over, so Theo knew it was only a matter of time before they had to get this over with. T had insisted on steaming his top for him while he showered and even helped style his hair, so Theo knows he looks good tonight.

But there Emir is, effortlessly fucking beautiful, as per usual. As if he needed help to pull, the entire student body regularly throwing themselves at him with reckless abandon like he's Adonis reincarnate. The audacity to show up to a house party in a designer suit. Vintage, definitely. And are those tinted glasses? Absolute knob.

"Well, aren't we civil this evening." Laurie steps in behind Emir with a hand on his shoulder. "You two good? Good. I'm off to do the rounds. Take care of whatever this pissing contest is and find me when you're done."

As Laurie walks away he grumbles, "Eyes glued to each other's dicks and it's not even subtle."

"I heard that." Theo glares at Laurie's back but loosens slightly when Laurie turns to wink at him before joining the mass of people in the living room. Laurie can get away with anything thanks to his effortless charm and genuine kindness. It's a dangerous combination when he's also a tiny chaos gremlin, bouncing off the walls until T grounds him or he runs out of energy and collapses. God, those two are so gone for each other it's borderline embarrassing, but Theo's glad they're happy.

Emir walks over into Theo's space to make himself a drink, not so subtly bumping into him on the way. He smirks when he gets an annoyed scoff in response, tossing his hair to the side and out of his eyes. He can feel Theo watching his every move, eyes following the line of his arm and the way his fingers trail along the choices in front of him before making a decision.

"Could've just asked me to move, you know." Theo doesn't move though. He has just as much right as Emir to be at this party, in this kitchen, hovering by the drinks with a shitty excuse for alcohol clutched in his hand.

"But where's the fun in that?" Emir glances at Theo just barely while picking up the gin. Is a gin and tonic a drink for grandmothers? Maybe. Emir's never been bothered by that sort of thing. He loves botanicals.

"Is this going to be all night? You, butting into my space, literally, as if I'm not even here?" Theo turns to face Emir fully, taking a sip of his drink and wrinkling his nose. He must've been distracted when pouring because *eugh*. Theo can't even identify what's happening in his mouth right now.

"How could I possibly ignore you when your dick is saluting me through those jeans?" Emir glances down with a tilt of his head while he takes a sip of his own drink, eyebrow raised, waiting for an answer.

"Why are you even looking? My dick has nothing to do with you." Theo flushes as Emir sneaks out a hand and tugs at his loose vest, hand so close to Theo's abs that they contract, fingertips wrinkling the carefully steamed fabric.

"Maybe you'd rather it did..." Emir knows exactly what he's doing. He knows how to flirt with practically anyone, how to make their heart race and their palms sweat. He keeps his hand in Theo's shirt, letting his fingers be as close as possible to Theo's bare skin without actually touching him. And then he looks up at Theo through his thick eyelashes, golden irises glowing even in the low light of the outdated kitchen. "But unfortunately for you, I have a policy against the pursuit of heterosexuals. Not worth my precious time."

Theo looks genuinely confused for a moment before schooling his features back to an annoyed squint. How anyone could confuse him for a straight man is beyond him. Not that it's worth correcting Emir because, even though he's comfortably bisexual, he has a very concrete Emir Shah exception. "Just because you're fit doesn't mean you can have anyone you want, Emir. Takes a bit more than pretty eyes and a crooked smile to seduce me."

"And it takes a bit more than a wall of muscle and a thick dick to make me care, Theodore." Emir hasn't moved out of Theo's space even as they continue to throw their words around in the air between them. He's never minded Theo's presence. Theo's alright enough if you ignore the stick up his arse and his general pedantic behaviour. If Laurie can put up with him, Emir can be civil when needed. With that thought, Emir finally drops his hand from Theo's shirt but doesn't move away. If Theo wants space, he can be the one to take it.

"Are we done now? Can we go be at opposite ends of this party and pretend the other doesn't exist for the night?" Theo leans against the counter while turning his upper body to glance behind him into the living room. He sees Laurie on a coffee table, drink in hand while scream-singing along to some classic rock anthem Theo doesn't know the words to.

"Not yet." Emir sets his drink aside and leans to match Theo's posture, head tilting to the side and gaze intensely focused to meet Theo's. "This is it for us. Our last year.

And I don't particularly fancy spending the whole time arguing. I need my energy focused elsewhere."

"That might be the most intelligent thing you've ever said to me." Theo grins and this time it's genuine. "So what then? Some sort of truce? You let me focus on ballet and I leave you to your experiments?"

"Nothing that I do is experimental." Emir narrows his eyes, suddenly thinking a truce is both a bad idea and impossible. "You would know that if you valued any art form more recent than 1832, you pedantic fuck."

"I didn't mean it like that and you know it." Theo leans a bit forward now, but his manner has softened. He might not like Emir, but he can't deny his work is brilliant. Unfortunately. "I wouldn't have been choreographing for Boston Contemporary for four and a half months if I didn't value all forms of dance. Or did you not bother to learn where I spent my term abroad?"

"You were in Boston?" Emir leans back a touch, surprise colouring his normally confident tone. "BosCon is...they're incredible. Took a weekend trip to see their spring show. Not too far from Philadelphia and I wasn't in the mood for New York."

"And how'd you like it?" Theo tries to keep his face neutral, but if Emir wasn't aware that the show was at least partially his work, that means he did something right. He'd spent the term thoroughly pushing his boundaries as both a dancer and a choreographer, forcing himself into movements that felt as foreign as leaving his home country for the first significant portion of his life.

"Let me guess, you choreographed the street dance portion?" Emir's reply is absolutely dripping with sarcasm. If there's anything Theodore Palmer is allergic to, it's dance inspired by real people in the current century. And that had been the best piece of the show, something he would expect from the likes of Alvin Ailey's second company. It was a seamless blend of incredible technical skill and the freedom of House.

"I...I did, actually. How did you even possibly guess that?" It's Theo's turn to be surprised now, turning so his back is to the counter, hands braced to hold his body weight. It also has the advantage of flexing his arms, not that it was intentional. Emir definitely didn't notice...except he did, his eyes flashing to Theo's forearms before returning to his face.

"I was being a prat, but unfortunately you've won. A term away and I've lost my edge."
Emir is deflecting and they both know it. Especially when Emir gently presses a hand
to Theo's shoulder for a moment before letting it drop, halfway to a friendly side hug
or something. "Well, props to you, I suppose. I genuinely enjoyed the BosCon
show...So maybe that's how we start this truce?"

Theo studies Emir for a moment, trying to decipher if he's fucking with him, but he
seems honest, at least in this. "In that case, you were brilliant in *Firebird*. I tried to get
away to see it after it went viral, but I couldn't get the time off." Theo shrugs as if it
means nothing, that he had intended to go out of his way to see Emir's work outside
of their forced proximity here at uni. But he had genuinely wanted to see the show,
trying his best to ignore that Emir was the male lead for the sake of artistic
appreciation. *Firebird* has been done to death, but the clips he saw seemed like it had
been brought back from the ashes. There's a joke in there somewhere, but Theo's too
focused on the conversation to go searching for it.

Emir isn't sure which part of Theo's brief response to focus on, so he starts with, "How
do you mean viral? In a positive way?" He knew the show had been a success, and his
family and friends had all said he was wonderful, but they always say that. Was Theo
paying him a compliment? A real one?

"You and Cami were all over every single app for more than a week. Are you really
going to make me fawn all over you? I'd assumed the rest of the world doing so might
finally have tamped down that ego of yours, but I suppose it truly knows no bounds."
Theo's back to being annoyed. If there's one thing he can count on, it's Emir acting as
if he invented the concept of contemporary movement. The problem is that Emir *had*
been absolutely sensational as Prince Ivan in the Philadelphia Dance Consortium's
retelling of the classic work. And he clearly knows it.

"I, um –" Emir looks uncomfortable for the first time since they started laying into
each other tonight. They're inching towards one of his least favourite subjects. "I
haven't been on social media much in...well, in a long while. But viral? That's brilliant."
Emir seems to regain a bit of his brightness at that, standing up straighter and
situating himself in front of Theo so they can speak more normally. It doesn't *have* to
be a fight, even though conflict is their usual way.

"I had people asking me if I knew you every five minutes. Easy enough for them to find
out where you train and they obviously already knew I study here so..." Theo lets
himself trail off, not really sure what comes next. Their conversations don't usually

get this far without T playing mediator or Ciaran pulling one of them away to get a breather.

"Well...thanks. For the, erm, for admitting you know me despite-" Emir gestures vaguely between them, a habit he and Laurie share. "And for appreciating what you saw. Never worked so hard in my life."

Theo just shrugs while staring at his feet and decides to try his drink again. A mistake. He immediately gags and sets it down in the sink, reaching for a beer instead. At least that's palatable.

Emir watches him fuss about, comfortable in the silence. Not that it's really silent. The party is just a room away. The music is loud and the house creaks and groans from the weight of young adult hormones rubbing against each other in time to the beat. But this is the easiest conversation the two of them have ever had and neither of them seems to know what to do with it. No words have been said for half a minute, both sipping their drinks and occasionally glancing at the other. It's so fucking hot in the kitchen, between the lingering heat of the day and the sweat of the party. And maybe a touch of something else that neither of them is about to acknowledge.

"Whoops!" A loud, slightly less than sober voice calls from the doorway, followed by a giggle. "Didn't mean to interrupt."

Emir and Theo startle at the same time and turn to see one of their classmates with an empty cup, clearly on his way into the kitchen for a refill. They're still standing within a foot of each other, but the kitchen's small and they were trying to talk over the music. Emir pushes gently at Theo's chest to put space between them then turns away to talk to the newcomer instead.

"Believe me, you absolutely were not." Emir flashes a smile in his direction, completely ignoring Theo now. "Cayden, right?"

Emir recognises him from a few of these parties and from seeing him around campus. They might've even gotten off against a wall at some point early last year. He's pretty sure Cayden's an English literature student, but that hardly matters when he looks at Emir like that, as if they should already be halfway naked and working up a sweat together.

Cayden meets Emir a few steps into the kitchen, their bodies already attached from chest to knee as if Theo isn't still standing five feet away, watching whatever this mating ritual is as it unfolds. Emir shifts so their legs fit together and places a hand on Cayden's mid-back, clearly on board with the lust dripping from Cayden's eyes.

"Absolutely *unbelievable*." Theo picks up his beer and knocks his shoulder into Emir's on the way out, hard enough to make him spill his drink on his hand. "I'm going to dance with Laurie. Just leave me the fuck alone…Please." He adds on his way through the archway, determinedly not looking at them as he leaves.

Emir stares at his back for maybe a moment too long, feeling like whatever truce they just started is already on the verge of collapse. True to his word, Theo immediately makes his way to Laurie, mumbles something in his ear that makes Laurie look behind him at where Emir and Cayden still stand in the kitchen. Emir and Laurie lock eyes and Laurie gives a tiny nod. It's in response to whatever Theo is saying, but Emir can guess well enough based on the frown Laurie is sending his way.

Emir's attention returns to Cayden when he feels a hand brush against his face, turning him until their eyes meet.

"Alright?" Cayden asks, setting aside his empty drink and staring wide-eyed at Emir's lips. Well then. At least he and Cayden are on the same page. As an answer, Emir leans forward until their lips meet, waiting for Cayden to reciprocate. He's never had more than one conversation with this person, but he's fit enough and it's a party. Why not hook up with Cayden? Emir didn't intend to stay long anyway.

Fifteen minutes later, they're walking through the front door of Emir and Laurie's flat, clothes being dropped as they navigate the shit furniture on the way to Emir's bed. It's already messy and loud and desperate and fun and Emir is having exactly the night he intended. Cayden knows what he's doing, lubing himself up until Emir takes over with his own practised fingers. They kiss carelessly through a quick discussion of condoms and testing and boundaries before they stop talking and switch to moaning instead. They fuck hot and quick and more than once, and by the time they're done, smiling at each other in the shower, Emir feels relaxed, content with the way they'd both agreed before cleaning up that this was incredible and they never intend to do it again.

Emir doesn't do attachment, at least not like this, and Cayden was only interested in tonight. So when Emir sends him on his way and climbs back into bed, why is the only part of his body that's still throbbing the part of his shoulder that Theo slammed into?

***

Theo spends the rest of the party exactly as he said he would, dirty dancing with Laurie to whatever comes out of the speakers, getting just pissed enough to forget about the stress of his final year, and enjoying himself because he knows this is fleeting. This is the last start of uni party he is ever going to attend, and he sure as fuck is going to remember it.

"He left." Laurie leans his head back to get Theo's attention. "You can stop looking. Emi texted me that he's busy at ours and he'll let me know when to come back."

"I'm not looking." Theo says, annoyed, but his posture says otherwise. "He's free to fuck whomever he pleases."

"You still think he's a bellend, then?" Laurie tugs on Theo's hair. The dirtier they dance, the more fun they have. It's never been anything beyond platonic, but their physical boundaries are definitely blurrier than most friends.

"He wore a vintage suit to a house party, Laur." Theo frowns in annoyance, but lets Laurie guide him into a new position so they can talk more easily.

"Even though he couldn't stop devouring you with his eyes?" Laurie has one hand around the back of Theo's neck now, keeping him close while they multitask: filthy dancing and best mate conversation time. It's the only way to be heard above the screaming and the music, but it would look intimate to anyone who didn't know their context.

"Seems he found a snack he likes better anyway." Theo lets out a reluctant sigh. "Can we just...not tonight? Just dance with me, please."

Theo sounds incredibly tired so Laurie lets it go. They dance and grind and drink and sing until the dawn greets them as they wander home. They would normally split up once their routes diverge, but Laurie's going to spend the next few hours snoring on T so he follows Theo back to theirs instead. They whisper goodbyes once they're inside the flat, Laurie immediately curling up behind T in their bed. Theo slowly closes the door to his own room behind himself and leans back against it. He undresses and showers quickly to get all the sweat and alcohol off his skin before climbing into his own bed.

Theo doesn't often feel lonely in his own space, but tonight he does. This morning. Whatever ridiculous time it is. Theo feels an absence even though nothing's missing, like a shadow is filling half his bed where a light should be, like there's a handprint on his chest from the ghost of a touch. He groans and rolls over, trying to shove that thought from his mind so he can rest. But he dreams of honey sweet eyes and soft, wavy black hair, of delicate cheekbones and plush pink lips. When he eventually wakes a few hours later, the emptiness remains and he doesn't remember a single dream.

CHAPTER TWO

Theo opens the stubborn door to the dance building just after six on Monday morning, the familiar creak of its hinges echoing around the empty space. He drops his things in the dressing room, strips down to his joggers and a loose white tee, and wanders barefoot into the student practice studio at the very end of the hall.

This has been his favourite part of studying at Roseborough and one of the reasons he pushed to go here. International programmes were out of the question for him, and there was no possibility of the likes of the Royal Ballet School once he passed the age of about ten. But he was fine with that, his future career relatively secure without the prestige. Studying dance at the university level is still an advantage to have. Roseborough has more dedicated studio space than most of the other universities that he considered, and everyone in the dance programme takes it seriously, none of the "studying dance on the side before I start my real career" that you tend to see at other programmes.

Theo's not the only dancer here who has habits like this, where he starts his weekdays at half past five and dedicates about 80% of his time to the studio. Theo values routine and structure, and dance has always been that, no matter what else is happening in the world outside. That's probably why ballet has always been his preferred style. He loves and values his time doing jazz and tap and ballroom and modern, but for Theo, nothing could ever come close to his love for ballet.

Ballet is technical and full of rules and it can be studied and understood. But the best dancers, those remembered for centuries, they were the ones who took the rules and broke them, the ones who created a new space for themselves within the traditional structure of ballet. Of course there were the ballets themselves with their romantic plots and dramatic acting. The classics move Theo emotionally, both as a dancer and a fan, and he works incredibly hard to be able to perform a full length ballet, either in the corps or as a soloist, depending on what role he earns for each production.

Auditions for their autumn show are this week: Thursday evening for the preliminary auditions, Friday afternoon and evening for the call backs. The dance programme's production of *Alice In Wonderland* is a safe way to start the year, giving the first year dancers smaller roles to ease their way into a professional production, and leaving space for the third year students to start work on their dissertations. Theo intends to begin his final year with the best role he can secure in *Alice*. If things go to plan, Lilibet will be Alice, Theo will be Jack/The Knave of Hearts (the largest male, role due to being combined), and Emir will be the White Rabbit (the largest role outside of the main couple).

Theo waits a minute before connecting his phone to the bluetooth speaker, soaking in the silence while he stretches and warms up his joints. He pushes through his feet, rolls his ankles and his neck, and just generally wakes himself up. He feels a bit sluggish today on his first morning *really* back since Boston, so he puts on a soft sunrise playlist that Spotify made for him and decides to stretch on the floor for a few songs. It's chilly in the studio, but that won't last long before the late summer heat creeps in over the next few hours.

Switching to a barre warmup playlist, Theo puts himself through the basics, starting with plies but stopping after about a half barre. He doesn't want to tire himself out before the full day of classes, just get his body ready for the day. Once he's warm, Theo stretches again, packs away the things he'll need in the studio later, and heads to the gym to do a half hour weight set, taking his green juice from his bag to rehydrate between activities.

This is another thing Theo's meticulous about: while less serious dancers keep their training to the studio, Theo carefully plans and follows a weight routine that both maximises strength and minimises bulk. Professional companies are not interested in flashy muscle, only in sculpted, lean bodies that are as flexible as possible. Overdoing it at the gym would hinder Theo's flexibility, something he already has as a natural disadvantage and which he is very well aware of. Emir on the other hand is so naturally flexible that Theo spends hours gawping at the way he can bend while maintaining immaculate shape. It's incredible and Theo has envied him for it from their first class. Emir is such a natural talent in so many ways, something that Theo never has the luxury of. Theo isn't prone to being thin or flexible or articulate, but he is determined. And that determination and persistence always pay off, with Theo consistently performing well above most of his peers.

If Theo ever broke his concentration for a moment and looked outside the window while he went through his weight training, he would see that Emir is up just as early, running the campus every weekday to keep his cardio in check. He runs past the gym just as Theo is finishing up, but they're two ships passing, consistently following similar routines and both assuming the other isn't training nearly as hard. While Theo focuses on building muscle and pushing flexibility, Emir knows his weakness is endurance. If he wants to make it through entire shows as a soloist (or a principal someday, god willing), he needs to be able to run for hours as a matter of habit.

Emir's morning routine isn't nearly as orderly as Theo's. There's no green juice, but rather green tea with honey and lemon to warm him from the inside out. And where Theo has exact routines and schedules, Emir wakes early and lets his body tell him where it wants to run and what it needs to succeed that day. Sometimes he'll stop a half an hour into a run to doodle art on his phone, or the lake will call to him and he'll alter his running route for the morning so that he can catch the birds early while they twitter and flutter and float about while he observes. Where Theo focuses on pushing his boundaries, Emir focuses on balance, on maintaining his natural abilities and honing the aspects of his performance that are out of focus.

After his morning run, Emir returns to his flat to rehydrate and get a bit of reading or studying done, often taking notes on the videos of himself from days prior. Emir is a visual learner, and the way he improves is by watching videos of himself, in class and on stage, and noting where he's out of balance, where his musicality isn't being celebrated, places where he forgets to bring the audience's focus with his fingertips because he curled them away from the line of movement just a beat too soon. He watches his arches in every arabesque, checks his turnout to make sure it's starting at the hip and he's not cheating it because he can't afford another injury, and focuses on the way he interacts with the other dancers for synchronicity.

Emir's a perfectionist, but not in the ways that others would notice. He's introspective, a quiet learner, always incredibly demanding of his own abilities in private while wearing an easy smile in class. He's often told his dance looks effortless, that he floats and flies, ethereal and easy. If only any of them understood the effort. If only they saw how much he's sacrificed, what he and his family have gone through on his path to now.

***

Every weekday begins with a two hour technique class for the entire dance programme taught in their largest studio, usually just called tech hall. The only other time the space is used is for auditions, master classes, or full company rehearsals for productions. The dance programme only has 60 full time students, including all three years, and they barely fit in tech hall each morning. There are other students who take dance courses but not as their primary focus and therefore have only a handful of simpler, less frequent classes, and rarely interact with those in the dance programme.

Tech hall is the one class where all 60 dance students are on even footing, where they have the same instruction and the same chance to work. Technique is where it all begins before they branch out into their smaller, more specific coursework.

Monday morning finds tech hall filled with buzzing students. Everyone is early, eager to get started on a new year together, the older students already grouped into their friend circles and claiming their spots at the barre. The newer students are tentatively talking amongst themselves, looking around at the older students who, by now, they've at least heard of, and trying to find their own place in this environment. Technique class is taught on a rotating basis by the five dance professors, with occasional guest artists or visiting instructors.

Sean is teaching today, always taking the first class of the year, and therefore Monday in the rotation. He's the most approachable of the dance staff, with an open office policy and a reputation of going above and beyond to take care of his students. When Emir was injured during the final performance of *Coppelia* at the beginning of second year, he personally brought Emir to the hospital and checked in on him daily for the three weeks he needed to recover. And Sean was the one who sat down with Theo and designed his training plan, updating it with him as his strengths and needs changed over time, even over facetime while he was abroad in Boston. Sean was the first professor at Roseborough to proudly display pronouns in his email signature and to normalise gender neutral language when speaking with his classes. He even posted the contact information for Stonewall and Mermaids along with the other resources in his office, just in case they were needed. He's only been a professor at Roseborough for about eight years, but it's his passion, his students' trust and respect well earned.

Given that they're dancing at university level, the dress code for classes is fairly lax. As long as their teachers can see their body shapes as they move and it's nothing distracting or dangerous, the students are encouraged to wear whatever they please. Most of the older students are in a collection of layers built from cotton t-shirts, leggings, leotards, tights, dance belts, and a crew neck jumper or two for those who are naturally chilly. The younger students tend to stick with the classic leotard and tights combo or a white t-shirt with black dance tights, at least until they find more of their own style.

Theo's stretching at the barre with Lilibet, the two of them in their own little bubble in the sea of bodies. Theo's still in the joggers and white t-shirt from earlier, but he's wearing technique shoes now rather than dancing barefoot. Lili's wearing a semi-destroyed vest in the colours of the bi flag with worn-in black leggings and a red leotard underneath, skin tone canvas technique shoes set to the side for now. Their style could not be more different, Theo's clothes simple and well fit, Lili's outfits always loud and loose. But when you see the two of them side by side, you can immediately tell they fit together, complementary even.

"Stop staring, Teddy." Lili says it as nonchalant as possible while leaning into her calf stretch. Like Emir, Lilibet is wildly flexible, so flexible she has to be careful with her loose joints when en pointe. She's had issues with her knees on a regular basis since she was 14, but injuries are the norm rather than the exception in professional dance.

"I'm not staring. He's being...himself, and it's fucking annoying." Theo glances over at Emir again before leaning back over the leg he has in a front attitude on the barre, hip flexor fighting him while he grimaces. Annoying. Distracting. Infuriating. Emir is so many things, but Theo definitely *isn't* staring.

"It's not his fault he looks like that, mate. If anything, he seems a bit uncomfortable with the way it's the only thing people notice." Lilibet is always on Theo's side, but she's not going to let Theo be mad at Emir for something he can't control. This is how the first few weeks of class always are: new students flocking to Emir automatically until they realise he's a bit of a hermit. He's incredibly kind, but Emir keeps to himself roughly 90% of the time, even outside of the studio.

"But does he need to look like that?" Theo glances over again to take in Emir's black dance tights (that leave absolutely nothing to the imagination) paired with a soft, pale pink sleeveless crop and a lilac headband. He looks like something out of a wet dream. It's no wonder every new student is drooling over him while he tries to warm up for class.

"He looks fit." Lili switches to stretching out her back, talking to Theo upside down now. There are three first years at the other end of their barre, just taking it all in and watching the two in awe. Lili and Theo are the best pair in the programme, always put together for roles because they partner together so well.

"So he's fit. Doesn't mean he needs to remind everyone." Theo rolls his eyes and starts stretching his forearms against the barre.

"Oh and your outfit? Mr. Muscles is just dressing like this by accident? Please. You're too gay for that." Lili smirks before adding, "Almost like you're showing off for someone."

Theo doesn't even glance over, just swats her on the shoulder and stretches through his sides instead. The first years giggle and Theo turns to grin at them and introduce himself properly. He takes his role as a leader in the programme very seriously, and he always gets to know each new student personally, making sure they're aware that he can be a resource for them. Theo's familiar with what it's like to be left out, and he never wants the younger dancers to feel like that if he can do anything about it.

Across the room, Emir is trying his best to keep his nerves in check, to calm his breathing and focus on class, but like usual, every single new student is finding their way to him to say hello. They're very nice, and he's happy to have new faces around, but it's a lot and it's all at once.

Tech hall is hard for Emir. He can't always watch what he needs to in the mirror and because the group is so large, other less disciplined dancers tend to get distracted until the professor calls them out. So while Emir is smiling and greeting everyone he's also pounding his water because his throat feels desert dry. It's a lot of pressure to be in his final year, top of his programme and fresh off a successful study abroad term. People expect a lot from him, but no one expects more than himself.

The front spot on the barre furthest to the left is Emir's. It's been his since his first day of tech hall, and it will stay his until he finishes at Roseborough. It gives him just the right amount of mirror to see his angles and it's not in the middle of the crowd, influenced by the energy and distractions of the rest of the students. Emir's barefoot for now, but he knows he'll have to put on his canvas shoes once they're through tendus.

Even Sean will only stretch the rules so far for him, and they've been close since Sean found Emir crying at the end of his first week of class two years ago. He was sat in front of the mirror in the student practice studio, having pushed himself too far too fast, and he was covered in bruises from falling out of jumps he wasn't ready for. Emir had never had a teacher care enough to tell him to slow down before Sean.

Since it seems inevitable that he's going to be chatting a lot over the next few days, Emir decides to sit down with a theraband and just let them come to him. Class starts in ten minutes anyway, and his ankles could always use the extra conditioning.

"Alright, Emi?" Another third year takes the spot at the barre behind Emir with a smile and a nod. Emir relaxes because Alfie's one of his favourites. He's talented enough, a hard worker, and he's generally a good friend. They don't spend time together outside of class or rehearsal, but they've always gotten along. Alfie's the only Welsh dancer in the programme, with gorgeous auburn hair and a quiet, calm energy. Emir welcomes the presence of someone who already knows him. It's comforting to know someone nearby in a class this large. That sense of stability makes it easier to focus.

"It's good to see you, Alfie." Emir says it with a smile, genuine in his relief. "How was Sydney?"

"Incredible. Honestly, can't wait to go back." Alfie smiles bright and starts talking to Emir all about his own term abroad with the Sydney Dance Company. From what he's telling Emir, he has a good chance of getting a contract with them after finishing uni. Emir offers his congratulations just as Sean makes his way to the centre of the room to begin class. Finally. This, Emir can do. This is what Emir loves, what he lives for.

***

As class is coming to a close and they're finishing reverence, the four other dance professors file their way into the room and wait near the front with Sean as the class claps at the end. It was a good class with all the students pushing themselves and maybe even showing off a bit. It is the first class back, after all.

Sean introduces each of the other professors briefly to the first years before dismissing all but the oldest students. "Third years: stay behind for a few minutes. Quick discussion about your dissertations and then you'll set up your first individual meeting with your advisor."

This isn't news to any of the students, but it does make it a bit more real. They'll be working on their dissertation for the entire year. They're all required to choreograph and perform an original piece, accompanied by a thoroughly researched paper that should demonstrate what they've learned during their time in the programme and how it will be showcased in their choreography.

"Theo, Lilibet, Emi, Jordan, with me please." Sean waits for the four of them to gather their things and follow him off to the side so they can talk, the other students following their respective advisors. "I want to meet with each of you tomorrow so you can spend Wednesday preparing for auditions. You know when office hours are. Just send me a text or an email with what time works for you. I expect about 15 minutes each, since we're just discussing a general overview and expectations. I've already emailed you the requirements. Any questions about that, we can discuss in your meetings. That work for you all?"

The four of them agree easily, glancing amongst themselves. They're all excellent students, so Sean figures he'll have a relatively easy time advising them through the process. They're also worn out from class so they're not very talkative at the moment. Theo and Lilibet are leaning heavily on each other, sweat and energy mixing together while Sean gives them a few more instructions. The two of them have been discussing their plans together since first year, fully prepared for the work ahead. Theo knows exactly what he wants to do because this project means more to him than he can properly put into words.

Emir's to Theo's left, drinking from his Hydro Flask and using his shirt to wipe sweat off his forehead. He's also had his plans finalised for over a year, determined to make the most of this before he has to deal with the corporate dance world that almost definitely will not permit him to do anything like he envisions. This dissertation is just for him, but hopefully it could be important to other dancers too. While he often feels alone as a biracial ballet dancer, he knows he's not, and he wants to create something that speaks to his experience, beyond the dance studio. Deep in his thoughts, Emir doesn't have anything to add to the discussion, so he gives Sean a smile and a wave before heading in the direction of his next class.

"Emir, wait up." Lilibet gives Theo a kiss on the cheek before heading off after Emir. Their next class is just one studio over so she figures they may as well head over there together. She's been dying for an update on Emir's *Firebird* performance that hasn't been filtered through Theo, and this is her chance to get it.

Theo watches the two of them go with a confused expression until Sean calls his name to get his attention.

"You're with me again, I'm afraid." Sean smiles at him, clearly not actually sorry at all. "Small class this year. Just four of you. See you in twenty, up on floor two?"

Theo nods and heads to the dressing room, planning to run back to his flat and shower as fast as he can before his history of dance elective. Each dance student was required to take it for one year, but Theo chose to take it for all three. They only meet once a week, and since the class is so small for third years, it promises to be essentially an independent study, with Sean offering study guidance and grading papers occasionally.

As the rest of the students trickle out of tech hall, Sean turns off the lights to the studio with a sigh. Based on that first class alone, it should be an interesting year.

****

Tuesday early afternoon brings them to their first pas de deux lesson of the term. For everything except tech hall, they're separated by class, so it's only the third years in the studio. Since it's their final year, they're branching out beyond classical ballet into contemporary and modern, potentially more. They'll be practising partnering for any genre they choose, the students able to send suggestions to their professor, Lydia, as they go along, especially if it can be of use for their dissertation or one of their Roseborough performances. Theo and Lilibet are together, of course, but Emir is stuck with Georgia this term. She's competent enough, but she's definitely more than a little racist, and Emir suspects she's probably homophobic as well if the way she sizes up his outfits is any indicator.

Lydia starts them with the Knave of Hearts pas de deux, knowing that they'll need to perform it for the callback auditions on Friday. Theo and Lilibet are basically guaranteed the roles, but even the others, like Emir, who are auditioning for different parts, will need to perform it. The third year pas de deux class meets both Tuesdays and Thursdays, so Lydia's giving them an easy start to the term before they really push themselves in the coming weeks.

Class goes fairly well, Theo and Lilibet adjusting to partnering together again after several months abroad. Lili always dyes her pointe shoes fun colours (except for performances), and today the bright purple flashes through the air with practised grace, pulling the eye of anyone watching. But Emir and Georgia truly struggle, clearly not meant to work together despite their best efforts. Halfway through class, Lydia has them switch so that Emir is partnering Jordan and Georgia is bossing around poor Alfie. He's being a good sport about the whole thing but he's clearly no happier to be dealing with her than Emir was.

After class, both Emir and Theo head back to their respective flats to get ready to meet with Sean. They both have this hour open on Tuesday afternoons since they're in most of the same classes, and it turns out both Lilibet and Jordan are free now too. Lili and Jordan are flatmates so they arrive together, after Theo but before Emir, the four of them running into each other in the student lounge on the third floor. This is one of those things about such a small programme: you spend almost all of your time with the people you dance with, even without trying.

The third floor of the dance building houses the professor's offices, the dance faculty and student lounges, a dance library, and a small media room for the faculty to review performances, auditions, and whatever other film is necessary (the first floor is entirely studio space and the second floor is for their traditional classrooms). Theo's first to meet with Sean, having requested to go first so he could spend the rest of the hour getting some work done at his flat. The other three chat amicably in the lounge while they wait their turn, Lilibet's head in Jordan's lap on the sofa while Emir sprawls on the floor and stretches. He's always stretching.

"Theo...this is almost the entire written portion of your dissertation." Sean scrolls through the attachment Theo sent over this morning with his mouth open in shock. "I know you're always prepared, but a formal outline isn't even due until the first of October."

"I wrote it while I was abroad last term. I know it's rough and still needs a lot of work, and it'll inevitably change while we go through the process." Theo shrugs as if it's not a huge deal to have practically finished the portion of the process most of the dancers dread. "This project means the world to me, Sean. I'm not going to fuck it up because I'm underprepared."

"I can see that..." Sean turns away from his computer and back to Theo, clasping his hands together on his desk. "I guess I'm wondering where you see me fitting into this. You clearly don't need any help with your plans. And what I've read is more than sufficient for the requirements."

"Can I tell you a story?" Theo rubs his hand on the back of his neck, unsure how to answer Sean's question directly. He sometimes has a tendency to overshare, but there's no accurate way to answer without explaining his personal attachment to the project.

"We still have a few minutes. I don't see why not." Sean sits back in his chair and gestures for Theo to continue.

"My family are exceptional, truly. I should start with that." Theo waits for Sean to nod in understanding. "But they were not the problem when I was figuring out who I was. This project? Pushing a queer love story into the spotlight? Here's the thing." Theo takes a deep breath and resettles, crossing his leg over his knee. "There's a stereotype that all men who dance are gay, right? And because of that there's this insidious culture of trying to prove that wrong, or something. The internalised homophobia is taught to us so young, and before we even realise who we are. The obsession with body type, the way we're expected to dress and act, even the way we were divided up along gender lines during technique classes. Like when I was first training as a kid, any feminine or flamboyant traits were coached out of me by my dance teachers as early as I can remember. They tried to make me harder. Make me a manly man, whatever the fuck that means..."

He pauses again, his next point still hard to look back on even years later. "I took pointe for physio when I was 12 after I broke my foot, and I actually loved it. It was like strength training in a way I'd never been taught. I wanted to keep going, but the director made me switch academies just because I asked. My mum was furious. You should've seen her, honestly. She was incredible."

Theo smiles briefly and watches Sean's reaction. So far he's been carefully neutral. "But that never left me. I started realising I was bi when I was about thirteen, and I was terrified. Dance was my whole world. *Ballet* was my whole world. And all I saw were straight white people in pretty costumes performing on the world stage, like some sort of mockery of the dancers who hid their lives to get the roles. And it made me sick. Still does...And I guess that's why. I know I wrote at length about it in that-" Theo gestures at the computer. "But I didn't allow it to get personal. Because the cisheteronormativity and toxic masculinity of the dance world certainly isn't unique to me. It's a systemic problem. Oh and it's incredibly racist as well. I touch on that on pages twenty to twenty-two, but I plan to expand that section further. Queen Victoria can get wrecked."

Theo finishes his little speech with a huff, crossing his arms defensively across his chest. He didn't answer Sean's question, but he also answered much more than what was asked.

"I think I'm seeing where I fit in." Sean moves around his desk so he can sit in the chair next to Theo instead. "You need someone to fight for this, yeah? You need the advisor who's going to push it through if the Board worries about the public response to it as part of the dissertations. An authority in your corner to make sure this doesn't get stopped before it even starts. And I'm assuming that's where this almost completed written portion comes in as well. You've already done the research, you just need me to back it. Am I right?"

Theo's surprised to feel tears starting in his eyes because that is actually exactly what he needs. He chose Sean specifically because he knew Sean would never try to talk him out of this or ask him to tone it down. It's a relief to know he was right. "Yeah, I guess that's what I'm asking. I hope it doesn't come to that, but if you have my back, I'll make sure you don't regret it."

"You never even had to ask, Theo. I've got you." Sean places a protective hand on Theo's shoulder before letting it drop. "This is important and I'm behind you the whole fucking way."

Sean stands up, signalling the end of their meeting. As much as he loves chatting with Theo about this, he knows that sticking to a schedule is both necessary and important to Theo. "We don't need to meet every week, but I'll keep you on the schedule for this time slot just in case. That work for you? You can always just stop by to chat, even if it's not about this."

"That's...that's perfect. Thanks, Sean. Who's next? I'll send them in." Theo opens the door and steps into the hallway, running through his mental calendar and adding this standing meeting like Sean asked. He'll update his digital calendar later tonight. It needs to be adjusted anyway. The first week always wreaks havoc on his colour coding, but he's learned to expect that.

"Lilibet's next, then Jordan, then Emir. Thanks, Theo. And...thanks for trusting me with this." Sean gives Theo an understanding smile while he waves and walks away.

***

"I want it to dance through the centuries, different movement styles that evolve with the human story. Start as far back as I can find records and work my way up through the present, at least for the first song or two. And that journey through time, that evolution, is going to match the main character's development, which is essentially just mine." Emir gives Sean a sideways smile. It may seem a bit egocentric to use his own story for the narrative, but it's about so much more than just Emir. "About how I came to terms with who I am. My sexuality and my gender, but also how I relate to the world as an introvert. Where I fit in as a queer Muslim in this country. What parts of me I have to reconcile to be accepted as a non-white dancer. How I find my place in a world that wishes people like me didn't exist. It's a fight *and* it's a love story. A push and pull. I need it to show the tension of my existence. And I want it to hurt. It's not pretty, but it's real... that's all." Emir is clearly very passionate about this, his northern accent getting thicker and his hands fidgeting while he looks out the window to avoid the sincerity he sees in Sean's expression.

Sean waits for Emir to finish, chin in hand, listening intently. "I think what you're planning has a lot of heart, Emir. It's an important story. Seems like you're well on track for the written outline, and I assume you've already started on the choreography, knowing you. So my only question is, what's next and how do I help?"

"I need you to slow me down. Keep me...realistic. If you don't stop me, this is going to be a three hour production with an intermission and nine different sets. I need you to help me keep it focused and on a timeline. I can take care of the creative aspect. You show me how to make more than a gay mess." Emir laughs at his own joke, but there's a fire in his eyes. This is going to be the most important thing he's ever worked on and he can't have it getting fucked up because he pushes it too far. He needs someone to hold him at the edge of the cliff and let him dance his way along the precipice.

"You've given me a lot to think about. All four of you have." Sean makes a note for himself before finishing his meeting with Emir. "I'll keep this spot for you moving forward, but you only *have* to come to me once a month. You're welcome to come every week, but I think for you, I should probably see some rehearsals along the way as well, or at least a video clip every month. You need me to be annoying about the deadlines or do you have it?"

"I probably have it, but feel free to annoy me anyway. Can't hurt to have the reminder." Emir stands up and takes his bag with him, Sean bringing him into a brief hug, ruffling his hair until he cringes and pushes his hand away.

Sean laughs and steps back behind his desk. "Go relax for five minutes. You're already wound tight and it's only day two, Emi."

"Pas de deux was rough today. I might actually talk to Lydia about some options for me in the coming weeks since my piece is going to involve a significant amount of non-traditional partner work." Emir salutes Sean with two fingers on the way out of his office. "Captain."

Sean laughs again before sitting back in his office chair, thinking hard about all four meetings. His mind is spinning, wondering if what he's thinking is a great idea or the worst he's ever had. There's only one way to find out. Sean opens his email and drafts a message, but he doesn't send it yet. They have auditions and it can wait until after.

***

"Right, everyone dig in." Laurie says once T has placed the salad bowl on the table, the rest of the meal already waiting. Theo starts with the salad, filling his plate before passing it to Gabriel on his right. Ciaran and Laurie are currently fighting over the pasta, Laurie eventually winning but only because Ciaran gets distracted by the garlic bread in the middle of the skirmish. It's not a very healthy meal, but family dinner rarely is. It's not about nutrition, it's about being together. And they're at university, so a pasta dish or two isn't going to hurt them.

"So, who's first?" T smiles at all of them while patiently waiting for things to be passed around, a stark contrast to their impatient sprite of a partner

 Laurie's already three mouthfuls into his pasta while the rest of the table waits their turn. Some things never change. Like how Laurie gets moody if he isn't fed at regular intervals, or how Ciaran and Gabe have to keep their bodies touching even while they eat, legs and shoulders pressed together, or Theo always taking 80% of whatever vegetables are present because no one else really wants them anyway.

"How about you first, T? How's our favourite mermaid?" Theo smiles at T before taking a large bite of his dinner. His eyes crinkle as he waits for T to tell them about their first week back so far. Family dinner is Theo's favourite night of the week.

Since their first year, all five of them have gathered for family dinner on Wednesday nights, the time shifting around to match their schedules. Well, since a few months into their first year, once Laurie and T were together and a month or so after Ciaran started bringing Gabriel around. Family dinner is the only way to make sure they all keep up with each other properly, talking about their weeks, studies and otherwise, sharing updates on family members, and making plans for the weekends. Theo had a different flatmate in his first year who ended up transferring to another university after only a term, so he decided to move in with T and Ciaran, and they've all been family ever since.

T talks passionately about the study they're starting on an extant Regency era waistcoat for their 19th century European fashion course before sharing around pictures of Rusty the cat's most recent birthday party over the summer. Then it's Ciaran's turn to complain about how he can't stand the professor he's stuck with for his audio tech class because apparently he's "still in 1987, and as stubborn as Maggie Thatcher confronted with an Irishman." Gabe talks excitedly about a breakthrough he's had with his high notes thanks to one of the first years with a similar vocal range, then whines about still recovering from jet lag since he's the only one of them who spent the summer on another continent. Gabe's the token American of the group and they never let him live it down. Laurie doesn't have much to share about the new term yet, but he does tell them about how fast all of his siblings are growing up and how his mum is going to try her best to get the whole group to come to London to visit in December as an early birthday present.

"Theo, you had your meeting with Sean yesterday?" T always remembers these things, the meetings and important moments the rest of them mention, even just offhandedly. They're the most thoughtful person Theo has ever known, and he's so grateful that T is in his life, thanks to their relationship with Laurie. Nights like these he feels exceptionally lucky to call these people his best mates. And Lili, of course.

"I did and...he said exactly what I hoped! Even better than I expected if I'm honest." Theo is smiling so bright his eyes are squinting closed. "I sent Sean what I've written and he said he was behind me the whole way. I was worried he might say I'm being too ambitious, but he understood. I told him about why it means so much to me and he just listened and...yeah. I have some more research to finish the next week or two and then I'll be in the studio practically until the end of the year, between my own work, the three different dance programme productions, and classes. Oh and I still have one course for my business degree this term but that only meets on Friday mornings so it's not much."

"You'll need another dancer for your dissertation, right? And like - " Laurie pauses and darts his eyes at T before continuing. "Isn't the male love interest a fairly vital role?"

Theo isn't sure where this is going, but it's Laurie and he has that meddling glint in his eye so he figures he isn't going to like it. "Of course. The whole thing is a queer love story between two masc-presenting individuals."

"Are you going to have auditions? Or do you already know who it's going to be?" T seems genuinely curious, but Theo also notices them stomp on Laurie's toes when he opens his mouth to start again.

"I'll have the first years try out for the role. It's tradition to have them fill in for our dissertation work when we need dancers since they want the experience, the second years will be abroad, and we can't expect the other third years to find the time." Theo swallows down the rest of his water, eyebrows still scrunched because he can't see the trap he's about to fall into but he can feel it forming in the air.

"...and you think one of the first years should be your love interest?" Laurie is staring at him intently, his piercing blue eyes searching Theo's face like the answer is obvious. And - oh.

"No, Laurie. Absolutely not. No." Theo leans back in his chair and crosses his arms over his chest with a huff. Emir is *not* an option.

"Don't be daft, Teddy. He's the best dancer in the programme. It can't hurt to ask."
Ciaran leans across Gabe to finally insert himself into the discussion. Gabe seems
content to let them bicker without his input. A wise man, Gabriel Pereira.

"Not you as well, Jesus Christ." Theo stands up and starts to clear his plate, grabbing
everyone else's as he goes as a matter of habit. "We would fucking murder each other.
And he would *never* agree to it. I'll ask Alfie or James or one of the other lads. Anthony
even. Someone I can actually work with for more than ten seconds."

"But maybe–" Laurie tries, but Theo turns back around to face him and his expression
shares something deeper than just frustration. Laurie can't read everything held in
his eyes, but he can tell this is about more than just the dissertation. He gives Theo
shit, but Laurie doesn't want to make him genuinely upset. "Sorry. It's your project and
I know how much it means to you."

"It means...everything." Theo's arms are leaden at his side and he doesn't know why
this is bothering him so much. It shouldn't matter who dances with him, not really. It's
about the story more than anything. And anyone in the dance programme is capable
of helping him tell that story if he does this correctly. "I have to get this right. It has to
feel right. It's not even for me, really. It's for every queer dancer who ever has to hide
who they are in this fucking backwards world where we pander to the crusty old white
benefactors who just want to see *Swan Lake* every season and live their little
aristocratic hetero fantasies that don't leave any room for someone like me, or Lili, or
even Emir..."

Theo pauses for a moment and shakes his head, rubbing the stubble on his chin while
he thinks out loud. "I love ballet more than anything. But more of us have to fucking
pay attention or ballet is going to die. It's going to prune and shrivel under the
pressure of their bigotry until there's nothing and no one left to dance for. And I'll be
fucked if I'm going to sit around and let that happen when I *know* there's a future, for
me and for ballet. I can see it. I live it every single fucking day. So when I say this
means everything, it's...It's my future *and* it's so much more than that. And I can't ask
someone to be a part of it when he can't even look at me without–" Theo finally loses
steam, the fight completely leaving him as he falls back into his chair at the table with
a flop, laying his head on his arms.

As he wipes at his eyes, Theo feels T's gentle hands guiding him to stand back up and
into a hug. All at once there's four sets of arms hugging him close and sniffling away
their own tears. They're all very emotional people, so it's no surprise that a speech

like that would get them all going with the waterworks while they mumble how proud they are of Theo into the space they share.

"I don't really have anything to add...but I did bring dessert." Gabe says after a minute passes, his soft voice cutting through the tension like reflected candlelight across a draughty window. The others finish clearing up from dinner while Gabe lays out an assortment of biscuits, and when they pile onto the sofas and settle into each other, it feels like home.

***

Emir's been at the studio for two and a half hours already and he's reaching his limit. He's been recording on and off because his process is to put on music that fits the vibe and just let his body create, then watch the video back later to see what's worth keeping. Later, when he has the phrasing mostly worked out, he puts it to the actual music and works on the nuance. But it's just not happening tonight. He jumps and he turns and he tries to figure out floorwork, but none of it is right.

When he met with Sean yesterday, he was so *sure* that he knew exactly where to start. Emir already has a few chunks of choreography to work from, but there's no beginning or end and nothing that connects them. And what fucking good is a story with only disjointed scenes and no proper narrative? He's practically sweating through his clothes in the lingering heat of the late summer night, but he can't bring himself to care about the state he's in. There's no one around to see the mess.

"Fucking fuck." Emir groans when he glances at his phone and sees that it's already midnight. He should probably just give up but he's so frustrated and there's no way he'll get any sleep if he goes back to the flat right now.

Emi: *i'm staying a bit later at the studio. don't wait up for me.*
Laurie: *I'm up anyway. What's wrong?*
Emi: *it's not fucking working*
Emi: *nothing is working*
Emi: *i want to play in traffic i swear i'm fucking useless*
Laurie: *No you're not*
Laurie: *You're incredible*
Laurie: *What isn't working?*
Emi: *any of it*
Emi: *nothing connects and my body is just making gay shapes with no purpose*
Emi: *it's all off and i can't fix it*

Laurie: Gay shapes lmao
Laurie: Maybe just practise for the audition for a bit then come home
Laurie: I know you don't need to but
Emi: thanks laur
Emi: that's actually perfect
Emi: alright i'll do that for an hour or so
Laurie: Text me on your way back I'll fix tea
Laurie: T is sleeping over but they're already snoring away
Emi: you're my favourite
Emi: brb

Emir switches his music to the score for *Alice in Wonderland* and works through a scene or two, making sure he's paying special attention to the White Rabbit solo since that's the part he's most likely to get. He's quick and he takes on character work well, so it's the best fit of all the options available in *Alice*. Emir already knows Theo will be Jack since Lilibet is guaranteed Alice. Georgia's probably going to be the Queen of Hearts, and that thought makes Emir smile because how fitting? Maybe Alfie will be the Hatter. No matter how the final cast list plays out, it should be a fun show.

When he's relatively satisfied with his progress after running through the solo twice without incident, Emir packs up his speaker and Hydro Flask, bundling himself into a few extra layers for the walk home. As promised, he texts Laurie to let him know he's on his way then wanders back through campus, pausing to glance up at the sky while he tries to figure out what's missing.

The problem is, whatever's missing isn't just in his dissertation work. He can tell it goes deeper than choreography and he's not sure what he's supposed to do with that.

***

The auditions for *Alice* go incredibly smoothly and exactly as predicted. The professors take turns directing, with the others all choreographing at least a bit of each show, and it's Raphael's turn to direct. He's incredibly fair and encouraging, so by the time callbacks are finished, each of the soloists has been pulled aside and unofficially given their roles, with the official cast list to be posted Monday morning. Lilibet will be Alice, Theo will play the dual role of Jack and The Knave, Emir will be the White Rabbit, and so on. It gives them all a bit of breathing room for the weekend ahead, with rehearsals starting Monday afternoon. Since the productions are required aspects of their degree, the majority of afternoons and early evenings are scheduled rehearsal times, leaving their late evenings free for independent study or other pursuits. Everyone is in a fantastic mood as they relax into their weekends, Emir already planning to spend the majority of it outside and Theo texting Laurie audition updates on his walk back to his flat.

But an hour or so after call back auditions, just as they're settling into their respective flats, both Emir and Theo receive a joint email from Sean that confuses the hell out of them.

Theo and Emi,

I was hoping you could both meet with me on Tuesday during the hour we set aside for dissertation discussion. Together, if that's alright. You don't need to prepare anything, just bring yourselves and an open mind...

Have a nice weekend, and for the love of god please both of you relax for even ten minutes. I'll know if you don't.

Best,

Sean

CHAPTER THREE

Theo stands patiently outside Lili and Jordan's flat with his hands full, waiting for Lili to let him in for their Sunday morning best mate time. He and Lili spend hours together most weekends even though it has nothing to do with dance. It helps that they live in the same building, just one floor apart. Somehow they can always separate their time, work together for dance but also just do crafts or clean their flats together or whatever's on the agenda. Today it's laundry and baking, so Theo has a full basket of clean clothes ready to be folded and the ingredients they'll need to make vegan protein bars to share over the next week. He brought enough for Jordan too, of course.

"Do not judge me. I was up late." Is how Lili greets Theo, pulling the door open while rubbing at her eyes beneath her glasses. She's wearing a red flannel shirt over a pink bralette and green dance shorts, her feet covered in unicorn slippers that Theo gave her for her birthday last year. She looks a mess, and Theo couldn't love her more.

"That last night's makeup? Have to say, it looked better on snapchat, but you're still cute." Theo kisses the top of Lili's head while he shoulders his way into the flat and drops his haul on the kitchen table. "Why were you up so late?"

Lili ignores him and fills the kettle before reaching into the cupboard and pulling out whichever mugs are nearest. "Did you already have tea? I assume you already went through your whole morning *situation*, yeah?"

"Figured we'd have tea together, so no not yet." Theo carries the baking ingredients into the kitchen and sets them aside, reaching past Lili to get the oat milk out of the fridge. "Three mugs? Is Jordan baking with us?"

"Jordan is baking with you but first she needs a wee." Jordan yawns through her answer from down the hall, stretching as she wanders from Lili's room and into the bathroom, shutting the door behind herself while Theo turns to Lili.

"Elizabeth." Theo has his arms crossed, looking at Lili curiously. It's a two bedroom flat and he can do gay math. Or in this case, bisexual math.

"Hm?" Lili drops a tea bag into each mug, still ignoring Theo, but it's not exactly subtle. He knows her as well as his own sisters by this point.

"Did Jordan just wander out of your room wearing your favourite crop or...?" Theo's giddy now, realising there's metaphorical as well as literal tea about to be spilled in this kitchen.

"Yeah, suppose she did." Lili looks at him briefly before turning back around with heated cheeks to fill their mugs.

"Did you two share a bed last night?" Theo gently turns Lili to face him, his head tilted as he drops his hands. He's not sure why Lili is being so shy about this. It's not like he's going to judge her or anything. He's excited for her.

"No, she slept on the floor." Lilibet swats Theo on the chest, smirking at his offended huff. Theo relaxes though because this is the Lili he's used to: teasing him and bossing him around, but with love. "Of course we shared a bed, you numpty."

"And you shared a bed because..." Theo takes a sip of the tea Lili hands him, ignoring how it burns his tongue while he waits for an answer.

"Because it's easier to have sex if we're in the same bed." Jordan answers for Lili, joining them in the kitchen and holding Lili close from behind. Lili cuddles back into her and smiles when Jordan gives her a quick kiss. And that was officially the cutest most domestic thing Theo has ever seen from Lili. Her whole body relaxed as soon as Jordan's front met her back. They're absolutely adorable and Theo can't help the bright smile on his face.

"...Am I allowed to ask questions?" Theo holds his mug in both hands now, blowing gently at the steam fogging up his own glasses.

Lilibet lets out a suffering sigh as if Theo is her annoying little brother who wants to tag along to the shops. "I suppose."

Jordan moves herself away from Lili to grab her own tea and adds so much oat milk it may as well be a latte. Theo makes a mental note, because if these two are a thing now he should know how his best mate's person prefers their tea. Best to stay on her good side and all that. He learned that T prefers rooibos within a week of them getting together with Laurie, and Gabe whines often enough about the lack of New York coffee (apparently it's different from London in ways that have never been explained) for Theo to know his preference without effort. Theo has always been like this, a catalogue of the small things that make people happy. His mum likes to tell embarrassing stories of Theo when he was younger, like how he searched for a flower in his sister's favourite colour after she broke her finger, or the time his dad was away for work for a week and Theo spent hours in the kitchen with his mum making his dad's favourite meal for when he got home.

"Was last night the first time? Like is this new?" Theo watches the way they are together and his guess would be this is very much not new, but it's the first he's hearing about it so it's a fair question.

"No." Is all Lilibet says. Now that she's adjusted, she's back to being contrary, and she and Jordan are leaning into each other while the three of them gay bicker in the kitchen like an episode of *The L Word*. Theo raises his eyebrows waiting for her to elaborate but she just stares back and sticks her tongue out.

Jordan rolls her eyes before answering Theo properly. Those two are like children sometimes. "We've been official since mid July, after our term abroad, but we started shagging like a week after we moved into the flat last year, so depending on how you look at it, either a year or two-ish months."

"Elizabeth Grace." Theo sets his tea down so he can cross his arms again. "You've had a girlfriend for two months? Were you planning on telling me at some point? I think I'm supposed to throw you, like, a gay party or something."

"This is me telling you." Lilibet gestures between them with a scrunched forehead before crossing her own arms. "You've been told. Hi, hello, this is my girlfriend. Her name is Jordan."

"You two are ridiculous." Jordan shakes her head fondly and kisses the side of Lili's forehead. "I asked her not to tell you at first, Teddy. Not her fault."

"Oh, I mean, are you not out? I don't want to like...make you come out. We can totally just drop it. So, laundry? Let's fold laundry." Theo turns away from them without waiting for an answer and walks in the direction of his forgotten laundry basket. "I decided on a new way of folding my shirts that I think is really going to satisfy my inner Virgo."

Jordan and Lili follow him, sitting down at the kitchen table with their tea. Lili tugs on Theo's elbow until he drops the vest in his hands and joins them, taking his seat while Jordan slides his own tea back to him. He picks it up with a soft smile and a head tilt, waiting for them to talk about whatever they're comfortable with.

"No, I'm not out, Theo. Not to anyone Roseborough. But I told Lili last night that I'm fine with you knowing. I trust you." Jordan lays a hand on Theo's while she talks. "You're her best mate and I know you're not about to blab. That's why we were up so late. We were talking about what it means to tell someone after so long keeping it a secret."

"So, um...is that why you're still in a two bedroom? And why you act all platonic around the others?" Theo looks between both of them, realising this is a bit more complicated than he had originally thought. When he saw Jordan walk out of Lili's room so casually, he thought maybe this was new and they could be excited together. But he should've guessed it wouldn't be that easy. Lili would've told him before now if that were the case.

"My parents are raging homophobes. And racist as hell. And many other things besides." Jordan sighs and sips at her own tea, legs crossed on the kitchen chair while Lili plays gently with her hair, scratching at her scalp. They look so natural together and Theo can't stop his soft smile at watching his friend be so clearly in love. "We had a row just because Lili and I decided to be flatmates last year. I'm glad Lili didn't have to hear any of it because it was bad enough that I didn't talk to them for three months. They don't even know I'm a lesbian, so that argument was just based on being mates with Lili. I can't even imagine what's going to happen when I tell them the truth..."

"That's...I can't even say I'm sorry because it's inadequate. Fuck." Theo rubs at his face with both of his hands, the frustration he feels on Jordan's behalf making his whole body tense. "This is so fucking unfair. In the five minutes I've known about you two, I've never seen Lili so happy. And Jordan, you're great. Like, if I had to pick a first girlfriend for Lili you're just perfect. Your parents don't fucking deserve you. You and Lili are going to be so happy and honestly they can fuck all the way off."

Theo feels so angry, and so sad, and so many other emotions overlapping. He's starting to tear up the more he thinks about it. "Can I, like, be your new brother or something? Found family and all that. My parents would definitely adopt you in about five seconds if you're on the market. They've already unofficially taken in Lili and Laurie, and they both have fantastic families."

Jordan laughs even though she's starting to tear up a bit as well. "You can definitely be my brother, Theo. I always knew you were decent, but I'm starting to understand why Lilibet loves you so fiercely. I'm really glad we told you."

Lili's been quiet while she lets Jordan explain as much as she's ready to share, keeping in contact with Jordan to comfort her while she talks. "I wanted to tell you, Teddy. But it was Jo's choice. And, like...I'm just really relieved you know now because I'm so in love with her and it's been borderline impossible not to text you about it, like, every two minutes." Lili's looking at Theo in a way that almost seems like an apology, and he can't have that. None of this is her fault.

"I'm just really happy for you, for both of you." Theo smiles weakly at them before picking his tea back up. "I'm done asking questions because we're getting sad and I'm glad you told me and I promise I'll keep quiet."

"I know you will, Teddy." Lilibet reaches over to hug him sideways while they're still seated. "Now. On to business."

She shoves him gently away again and picks up one of his shirts, pushing her glasses up the bridge of her nose with her free hand. "What's this new folding technique and can you show me?"

Jordan laughs loudly at that, leaning over to kiss Lilibet with a hand on her cheek. "You two are so similar sometimes. How about I go grab that clean laundry you set aside so you can be little nerds together? I'm not helping though. My laundry is a mess and I like it that way." Jordan gets up from the table and walks back towards Lili's room, smiling fondly at them as she goes. It's nice to have someone know, and she's glad Lili can talk to Theo about it now.

"Love you, babe." Lili calls after her. And yeah, Theo is just really happy for them.

"I lied: just one more question." Theo turns to Lilibet again while upending his laundry on the table. "Who else knows about you two? Is it really just me?"

"No." Lilibet pushes Theo's boxers away from her with a crinkle in her nose. "My parents and brothers know and they adore her, of course. She came to stay with us for a weekend over the summer."

"That's amazing! I've always loved your family, even if they tease me worse than you do." Theo picks up the boxers that Lili pushed away and starts to fold them. Not a new technique though, just the same way as always.

"Oh and um...Emir knows." Lili says it hesitantly because she can predict the reaction coming and sure enough -

"Emir? As in Emir Shah? You trusted Emir before me?" Theo is genuinely shocked, dropping everything and staring at Lilibet, looking a bit hurt. "Sorry, I mean, you don't owe me anything, I'm just.."

"No, Teddy, it's not like that I swear!" Lili doesn't want Theo to be hurt for one second if she can help it. He's way too gentle of a soul and she would never want him to think that she didn't trust him. "I was dropping Jo off at the book club they're in together and he saw me kiss her goodbye behind a shelf at the library. He just said he's happy we have each other and agreed to keep it between us, which was decent, I have to say."

"Emir's in a book club?" Theo doesn't know what to do with that information. He assumes Emir does the amount of academia required for a degree with little extra. A book club? He likes reading? What kind of book club? And it meets in the library? Which one? How often? When does Emir have the time?

"Theo." Lilibet has a smug look on her face, apparently having said his name already more than once. "I have to say, that might be a record for the quickest Emir Shah distraction. I tell you he walks in on us necking in a library and your concern is his extracurriculars?"

"I just - " Theo's not sure how to answer that, his mind still trying to picture Emir in a book club, having earnest discussions of plot and character development, and for some reason he sees him wearing glasses? Is Emir a secret nerd?

"It's alright. He's as obsessed as you are." Lili kicks him gently with her unicorn slippered toes.

"I am *not* obsessed. I'm just in shock." Theo huffs and folds a pair of joggers a bit too forcefully. "As if...wait, what do you mean he's obsessed? You talk to him? Like properly?"

"Well that got your attention." Lili laughs and takes a long drink from her mug. "Yeah, I mean...we have a lot to talk about."

Theo picks up his own mug, the laundry forgotten for now. He raises his eyebrows at Lili, waiting for her to continue.

"Well, like, we have the whole queer in dance thing. And then the non-white dancer thing. I'm the first Black ballerina he's ever met and he's the first Desi dancer I've known. We were both the only non-white dancers growing up, at least past the nursery years. Even if we didn't get along we'd still have a lot in common. But we do. Get along that is." Lili shrugs, taking another sip. "And he brings you up in every conversation."

"Well, he can't be paying any attention because apparently he thinks I'm straight." Theo laughs at the absurdity of it, still not quite sure how it's even possible. It's not like he's ever hidden his sexuality at uni. "And he's Laurie's flatmate so, like, literally how?"

"He what?" It's Lili's turn to laugh now, cackling and trying to get her words out. "You? Straight? When did he say that?"

"When we were at that party last weekend and we had that kitchen truce that lasted all of 12 seconds." Theo checks his phone when he hears a soft ping, but it's just a reminder to call his mum later, so he snoozes it. "He was all up in my space, trying to like, I don't know, prove a point? And then he said something about not wasting his time on heterosexuals."

"Wait. Rewind. He was doing what exactly?" Lili is fully invested now, barely even noticing when Jordan rejoins them and takes the seat next to her after setting a basket of Lili's clothes on the floor.

"He was, like, hand in my shirt, body pressed against me and whatever. I'm not an idiot. I know he knows how to use his...appearance. But it's not like it worked." Theo rolls his eyes because he can already see *that look* on Lili's face. And there's absolutely no reason for it. "He fucked off completely the moment he found someone he was actually interested in. It was like I no longer existed. He shoved me away like I was a disposable distraction, and he didn't even react when I stormed out of the kitchen. We couldn't even hold a civil conversation for five fucking minutes, so don't get your hopes up."

"Theo, as an impartial third party...that sounds super gay." Jordan is trying her best not to giggle but it's getting pretty difficult. "There's no way you didn't react to that. I'm, like, the gayest person I know and even I find him unbelievably attractive. And if he's all up on you? Lili, how oblivious is Emir if he can't see that Theo is, like...extremely queer?"

"I thought he was just an introvert but...Theo, can I tell him?" Lili's eyes are practically sparkling with excitement. "Please please please please let me tell him. I want to see his reaction when he finds out. I *need* to see it."

"Absolutely not." Theo finishes his tea and sets the mug aside. "If he wants to think I'm a heterosexual, that's on him. Not that it matters. We hate each other, so he can think whatever he wants of me. It makes no difference."

"I...don't think you hate each other." Jordan says it cautiously but with a smirk, making Lili laugh, clearly in agreement.

"I'm going to let that one go on account of you making Lilibet very happy. But I promise you that we very much hate each other. We have for two years now. But you," Theo turns to Lilibet and tosses a pair of boxers directly in her face. He can't stop his laughter when she gags and throws them as far away as she can.

"Jordan, get out. I'm about to smother Theo with his own clothing and I can't have you as an accessory." Lilibet says it so seriously and yet she and Theo are sharing a knowing smile. This back and forth is how they've always been. Theo is happy for Lili in her new relationship, and Lili knows to leave the Emir situation alone, for now.

The three of them spend the rest of the morning folding and baking and laughing their way through Sunday. Theo calls his mum once he's back in his flat to catch her up on his first week of class, has a chat with his dad, says hello to his grandad for a moment, and by the end of the call all he feels is love: for his family who have never been anything less than 100% supportive, for his friends he's made while at university, and for the life he has here. Theo feels a twinge of regret that this is his last year before he has to leave and everything changes again, but mostly he just feels grateful.

****

Emir is having a wonderful morning so far. For the past hour he's been sitting beneath a Sycamore on his favourite green blanket, watercolour set in hand while he paints the lake in front of him. He hasn't seen a single person the entire morning, which is one of the reasons that he gets up before midday on the weekends, despite his love of a lie in. Most of the students sleep late to recover from the night before, so the campus is always quiet and calm until the afternoon. This tree is one of his favourites, hidden from the walking paths by the foliage nearby, and a perfect cover for the steady drizzle upsetting the water's surface.

He doesn't often include people in his art, usually focusing on the scenery itself with the occasional animal visitor. But today Emir finds himself adding a couple, strolling along the pond with their hands joined. They're off to the side, a similar height, and one of them is slightly broader so they can be told apart at a glance. Emir's kept them nondescript, more an afterthought of the scene rather than the focus. When he thinks about the figures he's painting, they feel the way he wants the couple in his dissertation piece to appear. Quiet, comfortable, private, gentle in the way they walk together. Or maybe that's just what he wants someday for himself and he's projecting. Probably the latter.

Emir still can't figure out what's wrong with his choreography, but looking at this, maybe he needs to start working with a partner. Maybe more than one. He doesn't necessarily need to actually cast the other half of the couple yet, but just for the sake of choreography, it's worth considering because he can only get so far on his own. He's thought about asking Lydia if he and one or more of the other lads can practise partnering each other during a few pas de deux classes since he has basically zero experience outside of traditional partner work. Not for lack of trying.

An excerpt of a Bach prelude breaks the quiet as his phone displays his older sister's face. Emir always keeps his phone on *do not disturb*, but he has it set to ring for his family and Laurie in case they call. Emir can already guess what this morning's call is about.

"Alright, Safiya?" Emir carefully sets aside his sketchbook and closes his watercolour case, settling in to chat for a while.

"Are you actually outside right now? It's pissing it down, Emi." Safiya has never been one for small talk, but it makes Emir smile to know she's fussing over him like always.

"I'm under my tree. The one I showed you last time you were here." Emir takes a deep breath and relaxes on his back with the phone above his face. "Been painting. I needed a break from the studio."

"Speaking of, did you manage to get your absence approved? And when are you turning up? You'll be staying at ours since we'll be at the hotel. I'm glad we decided on London for the wedding instead of back home. Shipley isn't nearly big enough for the whole family." Safiya is distractedly shuffling piles of papers while they facetime, clearly overwhelmed with her wedding less than a week away.

"All taken care of, Yaya. I'm staying at my flat Friday night, but I'll take the early train Saturday and be there in plenty of time. And I already let them know I'll be away until Tuesday afternoon." Emir is both dreading and excited for the upcoming weekend. His sister's wedding is going to have almost their entire extended family plus the groom's, and it's a three day event, starting Saturday midday and proceeding through the night on Monday.

But it's going to be a lot of people for him to deal with, and not all of them understand his multiple overlapping identities, which is why Safiya is having him stay at her flat rather than the hotel with the rest of the guests because she knows he needs the space. Plus, staying at the flat means he gets to look after her dog, which is a huge bonus in his opinion. God, Emir loves his sister so much.

"Right, perfect. Got a question for you, though." Safiya suddenly stops fluttering through the papers and focuses fully on the call and on her little brother's face. "Are you listening?"

"Yeah, yeah. Just glad I'm staying at yours. Thanks for that." Emir smiles softly at Safiya and waits for her question.

"You want to come to the mehndi party Sunday night? I saved a spot for you but...it'll be mostly aunties and I can't promise they'll leave you alone. Might be a few of the younger lads there, but you'd probably be the only one taking part. The cousins we like are going to be sparse, but Baba will be there if you want a human shield." Safiya really hopes Emir will say yes, but she knows it's a bit of a step for him. "You can say no. But...just wanted to offer. Not sure if that's too much? Or have I got it all wrong? You can tell me to fuck off."

Emir feels like his heart could burst as he sits up and smiles at his sister. He's *always* wanted to be included in the mehndi but he's never been given the chance. He used to steal the leftover henna and draw art all over his own skin even as a little kid, but because he was a boy he was never once invited to the actual party. "Safiya, I could scream. Of course I want to go! I've always wanted to. Can I sit with you and mum and the girls though because you're right that the aunties might be a bit much and most of them have never even heard of the term genderqueer and I really can't be arsed with fielding questions all night. I just want to spend time with you and the girls...maybe even Sashi and Nadira if they're not hiding."

"Perfect. And, like, if you want, you could just show up and decide if you feel up to joining in after we're all there. See how you feel." Safiya's happy she can include all her siblings in such a special part of her wedding. Even her dad will be there, so she'll get to have the whole family at the party. "You know I'm so proud of you, Emi? Like for all of it?"

"Thanks, Yaya. It's...hard a lot of the time. People are so fucking rude. The only people at uni I've told are Laurie and T. Oh - and Sean, but that's only because I had to tell him about it for the dissertation." Emir sighs, the frustration with his project at the edge of his mind. Maybe some time away with the family will help him figure out whatever's missing.

"You want to talk about that sigh or do you want to go back to your quiet time?" Safiya knows well enough that Emir *needs* his alone time or something in him just...breaks. It's not personal, he just needs time to be by himself. Glancing at the papers in front of her, she seems to remember something and smacks her forehead with the palm of her hand. "Oh, fuck! You're not bringing anyone to the wedding, right? Why didn't I ask that like three months ago before we finalised everything? I'm a bad sister."

"Safiya, shut up." Emir is laughing now because his dating life should be the least of her worries this week. "I'm bringing myself and my gay judgement and that's more than enough. You know I don't date, at least not properly. That would require finding someone I actually trust and want to spend time with. Ew."

Safiya sighs and gives Emir a look that's a bit too sympathetic for his liking. "I know you don't need someone to be happy, but Emi...it's so wonderful. Finding someone you trust with your...everything. The best feeling in the world."

"Yeah, alright. Get back to your fussing, I have a painting to finish." Emir turns away to hide his smile from his sister. It's not that he doesn't want that for himself, it just doesn't really seem to be on the cards for him. Maybe someday in some nebulous future, but for now he's content to have fun casual sex with fit people and save the feelings for later. Maybe one day it won't have to be one or the other, but...there's no rush.

"Alright, little nerd. I'll see you Saturday morning. Don't forget you have Buddy for the weekend." Safiya seems to have returned to her papers, finishing the call as an afterthought.

"I could never forget Buddy. He's my built-in excuse to leave whenever I want." Emir can't wait to have his own dog someday, but he's definitely giving it a better name than Buddy. Something related to a superhero maybe. Or name it after one of the minions. "Love you, Yaya."

"Love you too. Byeeeeee." Safiya hangs up with that, leaving Emir to the quiet rain and his drying painting. He looks at it for a minute before deciding it is actually done, the unfinished portions feeling correct somehow, like he's leaving space for something. But Emir doesn't want to go back to the flat yet so he lays back down and closes his eyes, letting himself doze off for a bit in the late summer rain.

***

Emir and Theo are both busy on their phones while they wait outside Sean's office for whatever this mystery meeting is. Well, busy is a generous term. Emir is texting his mum because he misses her and she's anxious about the wedding and Theo is practising French on DuoLingo.

"The owl is so mean." Emir mutters after a brief glance at Theo's phone.

"Hm?" Theo looks up at him with a raised eyebrow, his screen showing a passive aggressive grammar correction from an animated owl. "Oh. Yeah...it is a bit."

"Innit." Emir meets his eye briefly before going back to his own phone. Theo stares at him for another moment, wondering if he's supposed to keep the conversation going. They're ostensibly in some sort of truce, so he figures he should make an effort.

"Lili and Jordan told me that you, um, that you...at the library." Theo struggles to find the words, both because it's Emir and because he's not sure who could walk by and overhear them. "That was, uh, thanks. For like...because she's my best mate and...yeah." Theo's phone is still in his hand, the screen going dark from lack of use.

Emir takes his time finishing a text before tucking his phone away so he can turn to face Theo. They're a few feet apart leaning up against the wall, so Emir tilts his head with a smile. "Cute, right?"

"Yeah, but...also sad, because...I don't know how much you know. Nevermind." Theo still hasn't moved, but Emir reaches over and gently presses on the phone clutched in his hands until he lets it drop to his side.

"Relax, Theodore. I know too much, honestly. I was the only one she could talk to, so I know enough." Emir lets himself look at Theo, like really look at him, and he notices how tense he is, how it seems he's holding every muscle in his body as if he's ready to bolt. "It's fine. I'm not telling anyone."

"No, I know. You and I are enemies or whatever, but I trust you." Theo won't meet Emir's eye, finally tucking away his phone and rolling his ankles as if it's incredibly important for them to be warmed up for him to sit in a chair for an hour. Emergency grand allegro might happen.

"You...trust me." Emir repeats the sentiment to make sure he heard that right. He doesn't believe Theo, but that's beside the point. And it's not that Theo shouldn't trust him, it's more about not understanding why Theo would volunteer that information. Quieter, Emir adds, "Enemies is a bit dramatic..."

Theo laughs and crosses his arms while finally facing Emir. Banter he can handle. "Is it? We can't even hold a conversation for longer than ten seconds."

Emir just shrugs and adjusts his jumper. It's not cold or even remotely chilly, but he wants to feel cosy today. Like a portable hug, even if it is a bit warm. "We seem to be doing alright for now."

Theo follows the way Emir's fingertips trace absentmindedly along the neck of the fabric. This is one of those things about Emir that he can't help but notice. Every movement, from the brush of a finger to the angle of his body, seems so intentional, so considered. Emir has a presence in a way that can't be taught, a gravity that draws people in automatically. Even if he wasn't gorgeous, every eye would follow him. But he is, and they do. And Theo has never known what that's like, to be able to hold attention so gracefully. As if Emir was born with poise as the default setting.

Emir notices the way Theo's eyes are fixed on his hand so he lets it drop away from his neck. He knows it's innocent, but everywhere he goes he's always being watched. He's like a magnet for attention, despite his need for quiet and solitude, and he has been for as long as he can remember. His mum calls it his burden of light.

She used to read him this bedtime story about a little boy who was born too close to the sky, way up at the top of a mountain, so his skin would glow as gold as the summer moon, even during the day. And the little boy would try to hide or cover himself but the light would always show. And as he grew, he learned to share his light, to be proud of it.

Emir's not sure why he's even thinking about that story right now. Maybe it's because of the way Theo looks at him differently than the others, not with an expectation but rather like he's trying to solve a puzzle. Or maybe not as calculating as that. Maybe Theo's trying to see him past the glow.

"You earned a fair few points with the Lilibet situation, so I suppose we could have another go at the truce." Theo finally breaks the silence and shifts a few inches closer to Emir against the wall. He looks more relaxed than he did a minute ago, which Emir takes as a good sign.

With a shouted apology, Sean comes barrelling down the hallway, arms full and in a rush. "Sorry, sorry. Raphael and I were chatting about the Cheshire Cat choreo and I lost track of time. Could've let yourselves in, you know. I only lock it at night."

Sean opens the door and drops his things on his desk with a huff. "Sit, please. And thanks for stopping by even though I didn't really *need* to meet with either of you for another few weeks. At least not for this."

Theo takes the chair on the left, closest to the door. When Emir walks behind him, he lets his fingers trail along Theo's shoulders in passing, ending with a tap on his right elbow that makes him look up. Emir grins down at him and winks before taking the seat on the right. Theo just stares back because what the fuck was that? But as Sean puts away his things, Emir leans closer to Theo to mumble, "Let's see how long we can make it last this time."

It takes Theo a moment to remember what they were talking about. Right. The truce. Whatever that means. Basically just not being antagonistic would be his guess. Orbit each other but leave the other person be, give each other space, that sort of thing. Theo doesn't have any objections so he just nods and gives Emir a small smile in return, hoping that's enough of an agreement for now.

"So...I hope my email didn't come as too much of a shock. There's a few things I wanted the three of us to discuss together." Sean tries to keep his voice light. Maybe if he treads really carefully the two of them will manage to keep this civil.

"About our dissertations?" Theo sits back in his seat with his legs crossed and his arms folded over his chest. "Why both of us?"

"Well, how about we start with this: Theo, could you explain in a few sentences what your plans are for your piece?" Sean takes a swig from his water bottle and settles in, ready to listen.

"Oh..I suppose so." Theo keeps his posture how it was, closed off and a bit defensive. This is a really personal project and he trusts Emir but he's also not thrilled about opening his ideas up for criticism so soon. "Basically, it's a gay love story. Two male presenting dancers and how they find each other. Like I start with their separate stories, their separate struggles, and then their stories come together, and we get to watch...no, we get to *experience* their love. How they grow together. I know it sounds basic, but that's the premise."

Emir scoffs loudly and rolls his eyes, crossing his own arms now and openly glaring at Theo. He doesn't understand why Theo would choose that topic, other than for the clout of doing something "different". And Emir will *never* be okay with cisgender, heterosexual people taking ownership of queer narratives. They've stolen enough. But he doesn't say that out loud because he respects Sean too much to start tearing Theo a new one in front of him.

"Thanks for sharing, Theo. I know it's more complex than that, but I did ask you to keep it short." Sean turns slightly to Emir and hesitates when he sees the fire blazing in his eyes. Which...this is not off to a great start. "Emi, could you also share what your plans are? Briefly."

"Why?" Emir says it before his mind can even catch up to his emotions. Theo doesn't need to be part of this discussion. "Sorry, I just meant why are we doing this? My project is my project, and frankly, I don't care about what Theo's working on, despite my objections."

"Objections? It's my work. How can you have objections to it? You don't even know anything about it." Theo turns to face Emir, confusion and annoyance fighting dominance right now.

"If we could just take a breath please." Sean waits for both of them to simmer for a moment before continuing. "Let's start with sharing the basics and then I'll explain a bit more. Emir, if you would."

Emir sighs before turning away from Theo. If he's going to talk about this it's to Sean and only because Sean asked. "Queer love story. I plan to travel through the historical dance record as the characters move through their own story. Start with pedestrian movement, work my way up to contemporary dance. It's about more than my sexuality, but I don't feel comfortable being more specific in present company."

He didn't mean it as an insult to Theo specifically, but it certainly feels that way. Theo flushes at the comment, feeling hurt for some reason, as if he's betrayed Emir and he didn't even know it. They've always fought, but neither of them has ever crossed a line that would warrant that kind of flippant dismissal. At least not that Theo's aware of.

"Thank you for sharing, Emi. That's plenty." Sean gives Emir a searching look, making sure he's alright to continue. He knows Emir isn't out as genderqueer to anyone at uni besides his flatmate and his flatmate's partner, and he wouldn't expect him to out himself in this context. "Now, after hearing that, do you both understand why I sent that email?"

Neither of them says anything, staring back at him with expectant eyes and furrowed brows. "I'm just going to say it, and please just let me finish what I'm suggesting before you object."

"...Alright." Theo mumbles, while Emir just sighs again and nods.

"Right. So remember the choice is entirely yours, but I think you should combine your dissertations - Wait - " Sean holds up a hand because they've both already tried to cut in. "Hear me out before you start on each other. Please."

Sean gives it another few moments, seeing they're both trying their best to hold back their immediate reactions. "Theo, I know yours is already written, but the written portion would still be separate, and I think the tweaks would be relatively minor compared to what you've already done."

Emir chances a quick glance at Theo because how in the fuck does he already have the entire written portion done? What kind of overachieving bastard even does that? And when did he have the time? They're in almost every class together and most people use an entire year to get that done. Theo doesn't seem phased though, as if reworking parts of his written portion is the least of his concerns, which is fair enough.

"Emir, I think this could be just what you need. You mentioned concerns about the time limit? If you combine them, you would combine your time. You'd have a full thirty minutes for your performance if needed, and you could potentially work in more of those side stories you mentioned." Sean knows he's just played his ace because Emir was already pushing the limits based on the number of scenes he'd outlined for Sean last week. He'd been very hesitant to consider cutting any for the sake of time.

"I think this goes without saying, and I'm not meant to have favourites but," Sean pauses for dramatic effect. Maybe he's not above playing into this rivalry they have. "You two are the best dancers in the programme. The best dancers we've had in years if I'm honest. Your work will be incredible on its own, but think of the possibility of working together. Theo," Sean turns to him and waits until they lock eyes, "You are the best student choreographer I have ever trained. And Emi."

Sean waits for Emir to focus on him, "You capture an audience in a way that we could never teach you...If the two of you combined your work, which, if I'm honest, has far more in common than you're willing to admit," Sean smiles knowingly after saying that bit, "Think of the power of that piece. This competitive thing you two have going on, it's always pushed you both to be better, to work harder and get creative. I just...I know how much these projects mean to both of you. And I think if you open your minds a bit you'll see the answer is sitting in the seat beside you."

Sean's finished his speech, content that he's given them more than enough reason they should work together. But he knows it has to be their choice. No one could force them to collaborate on something this important. And even if they could, the result would be a disaster. They have to decide this on their own. "I'll support your decision either way, obviously. But after meeting with you both last week, I had to at least get you in the same room and present the option. What you do with that opportunity is up to you."

Theo isn't sure what to think. It seems so obvious to everyone else. Laurie and Ciaran, and now Sean, and probably Lilibet if he were to ask her. But working with Emir doesn't seem like an option. Not just because they don't get along, but Emir seems inherently offended by what he has planned...but Sean's right that their work has more than a passing similarity.

And what does it mean that they both came to the same place independently? Theo readjusts in his seat and shifts into a more relaxed posture, dropping his arms onto the armrests of the chair and accidentally brushing his hand against Emir's elbow before quickly retracting it. "I'll...I'll think about it. When do we have to decide by?"

"By the time the outline is due, so just a few weeks." Sean is shocked, to be honest. He thought he would get much more pushback. But then he looks over to Emir and sees he's still visibly upset. "Emi?"

Emir is practically fuming. He doesn't know how to process the conversation, because Sean's right about how obvious it seems, but he absolutely cannot work with Theo. How do those two things fit together? This is going to be his last independent work for a long time, potentially forever. Once he starts with a company, it will never be up to him, and he may never get the chance to tell a story like this again. He can't compromise on anything that isn't absolutely necessary.

"I don't have anything else to say right now. I need to...I'm taking a walk before I say something I'll regret." With a nod to Sean while very obviously ignoring Theo, Emir picks up his bag and walks silently out of the office.

As they hear his footsteps fading, Sean turns to Theo again. "Maybe he just needs some time. I really think it's worth considering, but that's up to the two of you."

"I'm not on board either, at least not yet. This is so personal to me, and it must be to Emir as well...but you're not the first person to tell me to consider it, so I suppose I should. I respect your judgement, even if I don't really think it will work. For a dozen reasons." Theo holds his breath for a moment before letting it out with a sigh. "Honestly, I can't tell you what I'm going to decide. But I will consider it. Of course, none of it matters if Emir says no anyway, so."

Theo stands up from the chair but he isn't sure what he's meant to do next. He and Emir don't talk. He doesn't even have Emir's phone number for fuck's sake. They don't acknowledge each other in class, just glare and occasionally bicker when something comes up. But Theo has to decide what he wants first, he supposes. Then he'll have to figure out a way to have an actual conversation with Emir, whichever choice he lands on.

"I'll, um, I'll see you in rehearsal in a bit, yeah?" Theo looks at Sean with a weak smile.

"Course. Let me know if you need to chat, Theo. That's what I'm here for." Sean watches Theo go, not quite sure what he expected. He anticipated Theo would be more resistant and Emir would be slightly less so, but it could've gone worse. So now he waits and he watches and, if asked, he can be a sounding board. This is one of the hardest parts of being a teacher: knowing what's best for your students but understanding there are things they have to figure out for themselves. But he has faith in both of them, in Theo's earnest trust and Emir's soft heart. They could be spectacular together, if they only give it a chance. Sean hopes they give themselves that chance.

***

Emir doesn't even bother going back to his flat after rehearsal on Tuesday night. Instead, he heads straight to the student practice studio, blares Tchaikovsky (the canon blasts are very cathartic sometimes), and throws his body around the studio in frustration. He's tired and he's hungry and his body is screaming at him to take a break, but he can't think and the only thing to do when he can't think is to dance. So here he is: pushing himself way too far and hoping for the best.

As he's launching through Gamzatti's variation from *La Bayadere*, Emir stops halfway through the manege portion when he sees two sleepy figures standing in the doorway. Emir's chest is heaving from the overexertion, but he feels a smile spreading across his face at the sight of Laurie and T in their comfiest snuggle clothes, arms full and clearly here as emotional support.

"That was incredible, Emi." T is completely sincere as they step into the studio to set their stuff down just beside the door, dutifully sock footed, their Adidas trainers left in the hall. "I don't remember that one. Is it for *Alice*?"

"It's absolute shite, but I learned it in Variations last year. *La Bayadere*. I'm not even doing it en pointe and I'm barely making the doubles for the piques." Emir shakes his head at himself and holds his arms above his head, still catching his breath from the, admittedly, famously difficult variation.

"Don't know what any of that means, mate." Laurie walks across the Marley covered floor and ruffles Emir's sweaty hair before retracting his hand with a nose scrunch. "Come on. Time for a break. We brought food."

"Not hungry." Emir mumbles, turning his back to them and setting up to practise some pirouettes a la seconde. They've always been his weakest pirouette even though he practises them every day. Emir tries spotting himself in the mirror, but his vision is cloudy and he falls out of the turn after just four revolutions with a curse.

"I don't give a fuck if you're hungry or not. You're taking a break to eat with us." Laurie walks over to him again and brings him into a tight hug, Emir hugging him back automatically with a sigh. "You need a break or you're going to hurt yourself. All I'm asking is that you pause and eat some fucking food."

"And I made you your green tea!" T adds while trying out a few balances in the mirror, not warmed up enough to do more than fall out of a retiré with a smile. Emi has gladly spent a handful of bright Sundays in the studio with T teaching them the basics because, as it turns out, they love ballet, despite never having the chance to really study it. Laurie even got T a practice outfit for their birthday last year so they could really look the part.

Emir turns out of the hug to smile at T because tea is the magic word. T knows how to make it almost perfect: green tea with extra lemon and just a hint of honey. With grabby hands, Emir waits for T to hand it over from where it sits on the floor, sighing happily as he takes his first sip. "Thanks, T...alright. I suppose a short break won't kill me."

"Put on your warmups or we're not going anywhere." Laurie crosses his arms over his chest and stands in front of the doorway. He's the one who sat with Emir while Sean gave him a very necessary lecture on keeping his body warm after time in the studio. Emir's had enough injuries over the years that he could've prevented with basics like that, but Sean was the first one to really pay attention enough to his habits to help him take care of himself properly.

Emir rolls his eyes but picks up his red joggers and black PDC jumper while following them to the stairwell. They walk quietly up to the student lounge and claim the oldest, comfiest sofa to share, a tangle of legs as the three of them lay across each other and start eating. T made them healthy rice bowls packed with veggies and with tofu added for protein. Laurie generally frowns at something like tofu, but if T made it, he's not about to complain. And sure enough, Laurie enthusiastically starts in on his food after a quick kiss to T's cheek.

Thanking T as he starts eating, Emir feels how badly his body needs this, moaning around his fork and closing his eyes while he chews. Thank fuck for his friends or he would be a shriveled, overworked prune by now.

"So...this about the Theo thing?" Laurie asks, never one to sidestep the issue at hand.

"What *Theo* thing?" Emir says, putting special disdain on Theo's name. He's not in the mood. Clearly.

"Come on, mate. He texted me about it hours ago. I was waiting for you to do the same, but I see you've been...busy." Laurie waves his fork around in the air while he talks. "You ask me, Sean makes some good points."

"Is that why you're here then? To talk me into this?" Emir retracts into himself, pulling his knees into his chest and glaring at Laurie. "Not fucking happening."

He reaches out to take a sip of his tea, hoping that will calm him down a bit. If dancing about it didn't help, he doesn't see how this will.

"We're here to make sure you don't get too in your head and also because we never get to have dinner together." T adds, speaking slowly as if they're scared of making it worse. "We care about you, Emi."

Emir softens at that because he could never be mad at T. They're the most genuine, kind person he's ever met. "I know, it's just…" Emir pauses to take another bite of food and chews slowly. "This is *my* story. I don't want to share it with anyone, but especially not Theodore Palmer. Ugh."

"You two have got to get over this shit, honestly. Neither of you can even tell me why you're always fighting." Laurie shakes his head in frustration. "I'm not saying you have to work together, but whatever this is, it's holding you both back. And I know you know that. You're fucking smart, Emi. You know this is an opportunity, whether you like it or not."

"Can we just…tell me about your plans for the wedding or something, I don't know. I don't want to talk about my dissertation right now. Please." Emir's voice has changed to a quiet, soft spoken hum. He doesn't like that his friends are in the middle of him and Theo. It's never on purpose, it's just that Laurie and T are basically the only people he trusts outside his family and Theo has always been part of the friend package with them. So are Ciaran and Gabe, but Emir has zero issues with them besides the occasional gratuitous foreplay in common areas when he's trying to get his coursework done.

"I can *always* talk about the wedding." T's voice is so bright it's practically visible. "Right, so I talked Lucy into officiating for us. Finally. So my sister has until summer to figure out what she's going to say. I even told her she could wear anything she wanted so long as she doesn't look prettier than me." T laughs softly, lost in Laurie's eyes.

Emir relaxes with them in the lounge for another half an hour, letting them bicker about table settings and floral arrangements while he just absorbs their joy. He's so excited for them and he's honoured to be included in their wedding as one of the wedding party. They say it's because he's the reason they met, but he knows that they would've found each other anyway. Proper soulmates, if Emir believed in that sort of thing.

Laurie and T leave Emir back in the studio with the promise that he'll only stay another hour before coming home to the flat. They're planning to stay at T's place tonight, but they still ask him to text on his way home so they know he got there safely. Emir shrugs and nods as he watches them leave, but runs to catch up to them before they get too far. He gives them each a hug and mumbles a thank you. He hopes they know how sincere it is, how he's grateful for more than the food and the company. Emir doesn't know what he would do without them.

***

Wednesday night family dinner arrives and Theo feels like he can breathe again. He's been consumed since the meeting with Sean, unable to focus properly on anything besides what in the hell he's supposed to do. Because as much as he hates to admit it, Sean's right. Laurie and Ciaran are right. If he wants his choreography to have the best chance to tell the story, he needs Emir. So now it's a question of how he gets used to the idea and how he asks Emir. Based on yesterday's reaction, there is no way in hell Emir is even considering it.

It's Ciaran and Gabe's turn to make dinner, and to their credit it looks great. Theo's helping them carry the pesto pasta and roasted veggies to the table when the front door to their flat opens and three people walk inside. Theo glances with half a wave, sets the bowl he's carrying onto the table, then does a double take because Laurie and T are there as expected, but walking through the door behind them is Emir. He glances at the table, sees it's set for six, looks over at Ciaran refusing to meet his eye, and realises this is his friends' idea of an intervention. Great. Fucking fantastic. The least they could've done is warn him. They know he doesn't do well with surprises.

Before he thinks of how it will sound to say aloud, Theo asks Laurie, "What's he doing here?" Emir flushes immediately and glares at him just as his brain finally catches up to his surprise. "I just meant...family dinner."

"It's dinner and he's family." Laurie says with a shrug as if he doesn't know exactly how big of a deal this is. "You two have a problem with that or can we eat? I'm fucking starved."

"No it's...I'm fine...Hi, Emir." Theo is still standing in the same spot, feet unmoving beneath him while he tries to process the scene in front of him. This has never happened before and he has no clue what the protocol is. Where is Emir going to sit?

Emir gives him a shy smile before taking the seat between Laurie and T, putting him across from Ciaran and diagonal from Theo. Emir feels incredibly self conscious right now, like he's intruding. They've been doing family dinner for years, but this is the first time he's been invited. Well, that's not technically true. Laurie has made it clear he has a standing invitation, but he never thought he was truly welcome. Which, based on Theo's initial reaction, he was probably right. But he and Theo have to figure out how to exist in the same room, so he accepted Laurie's suggestion of coming along almost immediately. This is the best buffer the two of them are going to get.

No one seems to know how to start the conversation tonight, the elephant in the room metaphorically trumpetting from the centre of the table and drowning out all other thoughts. They pass around the food to take what they want and start eating without more than a brief mumble of thanks between them. Eventually Theo can't take it anymore so he clears his throat and starts with something simple.

"Gabe, I like your nails. Did you do them today?" Theo smiles at Gabe across Ciaran, hoping this is a safe enough topic.

"Yeah. T helped me since we both felt like procrastinating this afternoon." Gabe holds his hands up and stares at them for a moment. "Not sure if the colour suits me but T did a great job."

"You look perfect, sweetheart." Ciaran leans over to give Gabe a kiss to the side of his mouth between bites.

"Emi, didn't you want to try minion nails? I have some new nail art tools we could try for their little eyes and goggles and stuff." T turns to Emir, trying to invite him into the conversation.

"Erm...yeah. Just have to, like, plan it around performances." Emir takes a huge bite of pasta and chokes a bit before swallowing and recovering with a few sips of water. God, he's so fucking nervous and for what? It's just dinner.

"But you'll be in gloves for the Rabbit." Theo says once Emir's recovered, not expecting the intensity of Emir's stare in response. "Sorry, I just meant, like...your nails would be covered, even if they're...minions?"

"Yeah, but just in case, I suppose." Emir holds eye contact for another moment before looking away again. The silence settles back in quickly despite Theo's attempt, but Laurie takes pity on the whole situation, encouraged by the small exchange.

"Haven't gone through our weekly updates yet." Laurie adds as casually as possible. "Ciaran? You get your recording situation settled or are you still waiting for the email?"

Ciaran starts into a lengthy summary of his struggle with fighting to get time in the recording studio since everyone else in his programme is also trying to book time for their own projects. Gabe's in a similar situation, but vocally rather than with production. The conversation flows smoothly from there, Theo contributing to their updates as normal and Emir completely silent while they finish eating. They catch each other's eye a few times before quickly looking away again, not sure how they fit in this environment yet.

The conversation *was* flowing smoothly, that is, until it's Theo's turn. Everyone seems to realise the problem at the same moment as Laurie finishes his update on the fabric samples he finally found in storage. Quietly, everyone turns expectantly to Theo who glances at Emir, over to Laurie, back at Emir, then at T, and finally at his own hands before standing up to clear his plate.

"You finished, Laur? I'll take yours," he says as he walks away and into the kitchen with both of their plates. Everyone left at the table watches him go before Laurie shakes out of it.

"Theo, get back here." Laurie's eye roll can be felt through his voice. "Or if you're going to faff about in the kitchen at least bring the biscuits back with you and we can move to the sofa I suppose."

Theo turns back around but keeps his eyes on his feet. "I just...didn't want a fight. It's been...nice so far." But he walks back to the table empty handed and takes his seat like Laurie asked.

"Think I'll head home..." Emir stands up immediately when Theo sits down, but Laurie's faster, tugging him down before he's even out of the seat.

"Fucking hell. You," Laurie swats Emir gently on the back of the head. "And you." Laurie glares at Theo, only breaking it when Ciaran swats Theo on the back of the head. "Thanks Ciaran – "

"No more smacking, please." T singsongs across Laurie, making Gabe giggle and mumble, "Unless it's for fun."

"Right, I'm off to have a smoke. T, why don't you come with?" Laurie stands up from the table and pulls on T's arm without waiting for an answer. "Ciaran, don't you two have somewhere to shag?"

"We haven't made a mess on my couch for a week or so. May as well." Gabe grins as he and Ciaran stand up, Ciaran's hand already finding its way beneath Gabe's shirt. They're out the door in record time, the anticipation of a good fuck enough to engage gay walking speed.

"I'll just - " Emir tries to get up again but Laurie pushes on his shoulder to make him fall back into his seat with a huff.

"You'll stay right here until the two of you talk about this." Laurie lets T pull him away then, content when he sees Theo and Emir both glaring at him with their arms crossed but making no move to stand up this time. "See you in a bit. Don't get any blood in the carpet."

Laurie and T close the door to the flat after them and the silence left behind is thick, the air filled with years of contempt and more than enough reluctant energy. Theo knows he has to be the one to start the conversation, but he honestly has no clue how. He doesn't *want* to fight, at least not this time. He's spent the past day and a half realising that the end product he both wants and needs is for both of them to agree to this.

Emir has never been alone with Theo at this flat. He'll occasionally stop by with T, or even Ciaran, but it's never just him and Theo. It's not awkward, but it is tense. They don't know how to act around each other without fighting. But why change a good thing?

"Wanker." Emir finally says, but there's no poison in it this time. He just wants to push a bit of the stillness out of the air, and if there's one thing they know how to do, it's argue.

"Twat." Theo adds automatically, and Emir thinks he sees a hint of a smile cross his face.

They glare at each other for another moment before Theo starts giggling, and once he's started he can't stop. And nothing's actually funny, but Emir starts laughing too, unable to help it because this is a bit ridiculous, the two of them put in time out like school children.

"We should – " Theo does his best to stop laughing, arms now uncrossed and his hands relaxed on the table. "I think we should work together."

"Well that was fast." Emir stops laughing immediately and hunches down further in his chair. "Please, do continue." He doesn't hedge his sarcasm because he knows Theo is going to whether he asked him to or not.

"Jesus, Emir, I'm trying to have a conversation." Theo's annoyed now because he really is trying, but it takes two people to bury a hatchet that's held tight in both of their hands.

"No, you're not." Emir says it evenly, making sure he's being clear. "You don't start in with your decision before you've even asked the other person's opinion."

"Alright, that's...that's fair." Theo was trying to get this over with, but Emir's right. He does have a few questions anyway. "Maybe you could start by telling me what about my work is so inherently offensive to you?"

Theo can't help how defensive his question sounds because it certainly feels like Emir's issue is personal.

"Are you going to actually let me answer or are you going to argue?" Emir still hasn't moved, arms firm across his chest, ignoring the hair falling into his eyes because he's too focused on the argument to fix it.

"I asked, didn't I?" Theo sits back in his chair and waits, watching Emir with his full attention. Most of the time he averts his gaze, but for the sake of this conversation, he makes himself return Emir's eye contact. It takes a ridiculous amount of effort, but Theo's used to that by now.

"Fine: I'm tired of straight people getting clout for gay roles. No, tired isn't the right word. I'm furious." Emir sits up taller because he could go off about this for hours. "If I never have to see another straight white man win awards for the audacity of pretending to be gay it's the bare minimum. We should get to tell our own fucking stories because they don't belong to you. It's our pain and our joy and whatever else.

And if you're doing this project to pull your career out of the fucking dark ages you've dug yourself into, I want no part in it." Emir finishes with a glare at Theo, but loses a bit of confidence at the look on his face.

"You have got to be absolutely fucking kidding me." Theo stands up now and starts to pace, barely controlling his anger because he's about two seconds away from walking out and never speaking to Emir again. "How fucking dare you. How- no, you know what? I need a moment. Just like...don't look at me for a minute because I swear to fucking fuck, Emir."

Theo walks into his bedroom but he doesn't shut the door. He faces the mirror and tries to calm himself down but it isn't working. He would *never* try to pull something like what Emir is implying. And if Emir thinks so little of him that he believes he would...

"He doesn't realise," Theo mumbles to himself before holding and releasing all the tension in his body three times over so he can walk back out into the common area with a semblance of calm.

"Are you done?" Emir asks when he reappears, as if Theo's being dramatic or something. Emir knew he wouldn't like being called out like this, which is why when they were with Sean he didn't even bother. Sean doesn't deserve to be collateral damage when he's been nothing but supportive.

"Am I *done*? No I'm not fucking done, you absolute swan." Theo is standing in the entrance to the hallway, stuck in place with the weight of his emotions. "I used to think it was a bit of a joke, but no. You're actually serious. I'm not fucking straight, Emir, and I honestly have no fucking clue what ever gave you that impression."

Emir doesn't say anything for a moment, trying to decide if Theo's being honest or if he's just angry and saying what he thinks will get him out of this conversation. But Theo asked him a question so he may as well answer it. "You've never told me otherwise, so how was I supposed to know?"

"Oh, so if someone doesn't shag you that makes them straight, does it?" Theo walks past Emir and into the kitchen, turning on the kettle because the only thing he can think to do right now is make tea.

"I didn't say that. And anytime I made a pass at you, even if it was to annoy you, you seemed disgusted by the concept, so I'm not sure what you expected me to assume."

Emir stands up now too so he can argue properly with his whole chest. "Besides, you had that bird. The one with the hair and the legs."

"What the fuck are you on about?" Theo turns around to glare at Emir again. The only person he really spends time with besides his flatmates and Laurie is – "Lili?!"

"No, not fucking Lili, you bellend. That one you were all over first year. I don't know her fucking name. You're the one who dated her." Emir waves his hand around in the air while he talks, trying to get his point across but mostly just looking exceptionally camp.

"Valerie? What the fuck, Emir. I haven't even spoken to her since like November of first year. We were together barely three awkward weeks before we called it off. And I'd hardly say I was 'all over' her, seeing as we went on exactly two dates and she only stopped by the studio once." Theo gets out two mugs because even if they're arguing, he's not rude enough to not offer Emir tea as well. But he's giving him the shit mug with the chip in the handle. "So what, now you're saying that I can't be queer because I dated a woman? You seem to have no problem hastily removing your trousers for all genders."

"No, I'm obviously not saying that. As you've so brilliantly observed, I'm a chaotic bisexual. I understand multi-gender attraction." Emir rolls his eyes and shoves Theo out of the way so he can pick which tea he wants out of the cupboard. T usually makes sure there's a box for him tucked away, even if Emir is rarely here.

"So it's just me then? I have to be actively gay in front of you or I'm straight? I'll make sure to bring my queer card next time we hang out. Maybe snog a lad or two while mid conversation to really get the point across. That seems to be your method." Theo grabs the oat milk out of the fridge for himself and sets it on the counter with a little more force than is strictly necessary before rubbing his hands across his eyes. They're shaking slightly with all the adrenaline coursing through him from this argument. "Fucking hell, this is the worst coming out I've ever had."

"Yeah, I suppose that's on me, to be fair." Emir tosses a green tea bag into his mug, searching the cupboard for the honey. It is a bit shit of him to have assumed Theo is straight just because of lack of evidence to the contrary and he's a big enough person to admit that. "So like...sorry about that...shouldn't have assumed." But he doesn't sound *that* sorry. At least now they're being honest with each other, even if it's very loud and sarcastic.

"It's fine. Just…" Theo sighs and turns to look at Emir with tired eyes. "This project is personal to me because it *is* my story. It took me years to come out to anyone outside of my family because of all the shit they put us through. I'm sure you know what that's like well enough, unfortunately…And hearing you come at my story as if I don't understand what it's like to be queer in ballet just…set me off."

Emir looks Theo up and down, literally not a subtle bone in his body.

"I can see that." Emir smirks at the flush that covers Theo's skin from his high emotion and tilts his head. It's a good look on him, the passion and the honesty. "We should probably work together then."

"What – " Theo splutters and sets the kettle back down before he can pour the water into his mug. "It was that fucking easy?"

"How do you mean?" Emir takes up the kettle instead to fill his own mug, seemingly unbothered. The problems he had with the collaboration have been resolved, so in his mind, they can move forward.

"I've been torturing myself since yesterday trying to figure out how to get you to agree to this and all it took was you finally realising I'm bi?" Theo watches as Emir pours water into his own mug too, leaving room at the top without having to be told. It's surprisingly generous of Emir.

"I was only upset because I thought you were exploiting the community." Emir really doesn't have much more to add because if Theo's in the alphabet mafia, then the stories they're trying to tell are more similar than they are different. At least based on how little he knows about Theo's plans. "Right, my turn to ask questions, then."

Emir gently pushes Theo's mug in his direction, waiting for him to accept the offer. He watches as Theo realises in real time that Emir is making an earnest effort. Is he usually that much of a twat? A rumination for a later time. Tonight, probably. "Why do you even want to work with me, Theo? Clearly we can't fucking stand each other."

"Simple. You're the best dancer in the programme and I know you understand the message I'm trying to get across." Theo shrugs, both hands holding his mug up near his face. The familiar smell calms him down a bit even if it's too hot to drink yet. "You?"

"I need direction. Focus and structure, mostly. Someone with more choreography experience." Emir blows the steam off the top of his tea. "And unfortunately, that means you. I can hate you and still admit you're fit – I mean smart. You're competent."

Emir takes a sip of his tea without thinking and promptly spits it out into the sink. "FUCK! That's boiling."

Theo tries his best not to laugh but that was...something. "You alright there, Emir?" Theo sets his tea back down and adds another dash of oat milk to hide his amusement.

"Fine. So, like...what now?" Emir watches Theo move around the kitchen while his tongue throbs, a reminder of whatever the fuck that was. Theo seems significantly more relaxed now that they've somehow agreed to work together, or maybe Emir just doesn't want to choke him anymore. Unless...nope, not the time to realise that Theo looks fit as fuck tonight. He *cannot* be attracted to someone he has to work with on his dissertation.

"Suppose we should clear up from dinner since we basically chased everyone away with our fighting." Theo walks over to the table and picks up the rest of the plates left behind in a neat stack.

"No I meant like with us– I mean our project. Don't we need some sort of plan?" Emir clears the leftover food while they continue their conversation, wondering where these three keep their tupperware.

"Oh. Well, I suppose I could send you my write-up. It'll have to be modified of course, but that should explain the rest to you." Theo sets the plates in the sink to wash later, grabbing storage containers from above Emir's head, remembering that they don't have each other's contact information and thinking it'd be pushing it to ask at this exact moment. "I could have Sean email it to you?"

"Yeah, I'd like to read it. Thanks." Emir tries to sound as genuine as possible, but he's worried it sounds forced despite what appears to be their first actual truce of the year. "I have dozens of choreography clips that I could have Sean send you. It's a gay mess and it's out of order, but my process tends to be...chaos, mostly."

"I've noticed." Theo smirks at Emir while storing away the leftovers in the fridge. He'll come back and label them later. "You and Laurie share more than a flat."

"Glad to see that working together doesn't mean getting along." Emir smirks right back while adding the rest of the dishes to the sink.

Before Theo can respond his phone vibrates in his pocket. "Shit, one sec. It's Lilibet - Alright, Lili?"

"Are you two done? Can I send your gremlins back?" Lili sounds annoyed and whoever is in the background is being loud. Theo thinks he recognizes at least three voices.

"Which ones? Wait, what's happening?" Theo covers his other ear to try to hear her better over the excited background noises.

"Your gremlins. The Laurie one and his tree of a partner. I caught them listening at the door while you had your gay domestic and I made them come with me instead and now they're bonding with Jordan or something. Outfits are involved. So are you done? You two banging it out on the kitchen floor yet?" Lili's voice has more than a hint of exasperation, but Theo still flushes at the thought.

"We are absolutely not 'banging it out' but yes you can send my gremlins back. Thank you for babysitting." Theo rolls his eyes and glances over at Emir to see him lift an eyebrow at the implications. "Tell them we made tea."

Emir turns around and refills the kettle at that, a soft smile warming his face. Things feel different now. They're on a similar page for once. So instead of immediately leaving once Laurie and T get back to the flat (Gabe and Ciaran are definitely busy for the rest of the night), the four of them settle onto the sofas and watch an episode of *Bake Off* before going their separate ways: Emir to the studio, Theo to his coursework in his room, and Laurie and T for a visit to the other flat for something wedding related.

Emir's time in the studio is short that night, only about an hour and a half. But for the first time in weeks he makes progress. Finally, it's starting to work. But instead of letting himself dwell on that, he packs up his things and heads to his flat, snuggling in bed with *Boyfriend Material* for the next book club meeting and falling asleep early. It's a nice change.

CHAPTER FOUR

Theo can't stop watching. He's seen every clip half a dozen times by now, and he even annotated a few of them in his choreo notebook. At both of their requests early this morning, Sean had sent Theo's written work to Emir and Emir's video clips to Theo with only a brief, "Excited to see where this collaboration takes you!"

And so here Theo sits, spending the Thursday evening time that he sets aside for coursework watching Emir instead, headphones in and snuggled on the sofa with his laptop open. Theo watches and processes the almost thirty minutes of choreography clips as best he can out of context. And based on the studio spaces and hairstyles in the videos, Emir has been working on this for at least a year.

There's roughly six different dance styles that he's identified, so he's sorted the videos by that for now, making a note to clarify with Emir if he intended it to be a historically accurate timeline of movement or if he wanted it to be more freeform. The music in the background doesn't seem to matter, with Theo noticing everything from Taylor Swift to Bollywood, so Theo notes another question for them to go over together. He has *so* many questions. It's hard to know where to start.

But Emir is just...sensational. There's no other word for it. This is only practice, and some of it seems like complete improv. He's always known Emir to be a talented dancer, but this is like watching his mind in action, as if he's free with his movement in a way Theo hasn't seen before. It's mesmerising. And the way he's showing complete mastery of multiple different techniques shouldn't surprise Theo, but it's still fascinating to see it like this, unrehearsed and raw, but somehow closer to the truth.

Theo isn't even making sense to himself anymore, eyes tracking the movement of Emir's hands as they trace an outline in the air seemingly between his own body and a missing partner. It's clear that some of what Emir's recorded needs a second dancer to complete, his weight shifting in a way where he should be caught or readjusted or supported but has to pull himself out of it instead. Maybe they can work with that, use this version earlier in the piece and enhance it later to show how they grow together, how Emir's character is still himself, but now with the person to lean on that had been missing. Something to think about...

"Alright, Teddy? What're you - " T sits down next to Theo and leans their head on his shoulder, sitting up again once they see Emir on the screen. "Oh!"

"What? Um, I was just..." Theo removes his headphones and looks at T out of the corner of his eye. "Since we're going to work together, we had Sean share what the other's been working on, so I'm...doing research."

"But Ciaran...he said you haven't moved since eight." T glances down at the screen again before meeting Theo's eyes with a curious head tilt.

"Yeah, but it's only about ten." Theo shrugs and sets his notebook down, stretching his neck side to side. His whole body is stiff, but he hadn't noticed until he was interrupted.

"Theo, it's almost midnight." T sets a hand on Theo's laptop and carefully closes it, setting it aside and taking Theo's face in his hands. They move the back of their hand to Theo's forehead as if checking for a fever. "Are you poorly? You're flushed and up past your bedtime on a school night."

"Oh, I'm...no, I'm alright, T." Theo gives T a weak smile but feels something strange in his chest, like he's keeping a secret. "Just been working, I suppose. I let time get away from me while hyper-focused on my dissertation."

"I'm putting you to sleep. You have a long day tomorrow. When's the last time you hydrated?" T looks around and sees no signs of a water glass or snacks or anything. This is so unlike Theo. "Are you sure you're alright?"

"It's later than I thought. I should probably have some water and go to sleep." Theo starts to stand up with a groan, his joints protesting after so long in the same position. "You staying here tonight?"

"Yeah, Ciaran left for Gabe's a few minutes ago, but Laurie should be here soon. You want to talk with Laur about...anything?" T glances briefly at Theo's closed laptop as if it's incriminating. "I could make you some tea?"

Theo yawns wide and leans forward to meet T in a sleepy hug. "I'm going to sleep, but thank you. Got a lot on my mind, but it's not bad, just..."

"Need time to think?" T is still hugging Theo back, arms warm around his middle. They've always given good hugs.

"Yeah, suppose so." Theo yawns again and breaks the hug to ruffle T's hair before heading down the hallway to his bedroom. "Tell Laur I said goodnight."

"Course." T watches him leave with another head tilt. "If you can't sleep you know where to find us."

Theo snorts at that because there is no way in hell he's opening that bedroom door tonight. It doesn't matter if it's a school night, Sunday morning, or a bank holiday, those two are always on top of each other, inside each other, whichever they fancy. Theo's not judging them, just thinking *I don't want to see my best mates fucking without it being a pre-approved group situation.* Theo gives a soft little wave before closing the door to his room. "I'll let you know if I need anything. Night, T."

"...Night." T mumbles back even though Theo's already closed the door. Thinking for a moment, they take out their phone and text Laurie.

T: *Theo's been watching Emi for hours*
T: *Not like that*
T: *He's not like stalking Emi*
T: *I meant he's watching videos of Emir*
T: *DANCING*
T: *Innocent, work related dancing*
T: *But still...for four hours*
T: *Are you coming soon?*
Laur: *hehe coming*
T: *Laurieeeeee*
Laur: *I'm already on my way love*
Laur: *Be there in five*
Laur: *Then you can tell me the gay tea*
Laur: *Emi isn't home from the studio yet but I texted that we're staying at yours so he doesn't worry*
Laur: *You know how he worries*
T: *Emi's a good one*
T: *We're keeping him*
T: *...it's been five minutes*
T: *Oh :) I just saw you walk past the window :) :) :)*
T: *Love youuuuuuu*

***

Emir's morning jog around campus on Friday is perfect. The weather is finally cool in the mornings and he woke up a bit early, meaning he only saw a few tiny animals and one overly exhausted first year for the entire run. He chose to leave the headphones at the flat this morning, listening instead to his own breathing, his own heartbeat, the sound of his shoes against the ground and the way it changes from one surface to another. By the time Emir gets back to his flat it's just turning seven and he has plenty of time for what he has planned before class.

Sean had emailed what they each requested the day before, but Emir was too busy to read Theo's writing yesterday, knowing that he would need to actually focus. He knows Theo well enough to realise it'll be an intense, well researched document that requires a clear mind. The flat is empty, Laurie staying the night before with T, and it's peaceful, if a bit messy. Emir takes his *Mandalorian* mug off the drying rack and fills the kettle, deciding to take a quick shower before settling in on the sofa for a few hours.

While towel drying his hair, Emir thinks about what he wants to do to it after *Alice*. Or maybe over winter break would be better. He hasn't done anything fun with his hair in months, but between productions he should have time to do...something. For now, it's the length he likes and he has his sister's wedding this weekend so nothing wild before then. He can't believe he's leaving in just over a day to go to Safiya's wedding. When did they get so...grown up?

Once his tea is ready, perfectly hot and just the right balance of earthy, sour, and sweet, Emir sits cross-legged on the sofa in his comfiest jumper and joggers and pulls his computer onto his lap. He already has his contacts in for the day, but maybe he should've thought this through. It's a 60 page document and his eyes are definitely going to be strained. Emir sets his laptop aside again and switches back into his glasses before actually settling in, much more comfortable now.

Emir reads and he rereads and he makes a few notes and by the time he's ten pages in he feels like shit. He's guilty and impressed and overall realising he's a proper bellend for that fight on Wednesday. But he keeps reading until the end, sighing when he realises it's time to get ready for tech hall and knowing that he owes someone an apology. He still might not be wild about the idea of working together, but he seriously misjudged Theo. What he's written is better than Emir could have predicted, and not just technically. Theo is *clearly* personally and emotionally invested, and he's smart, like actually truly intelligent, making connections and properly researching in a way Emir's never learned. And personal differences aside, Theo doesn't deserve a lot of the things Emir has said to him.

Laurie stumbles back into the flat just as Emir is leaving, smiling at each other in silence until Laurie seems to wake himself up enough to pull Emir into a hug.

"Morning, mate." He squeezes Emir tight before letting him go again. "Will I see you again before you leave?"

"Think so, yeah." Emir readjusts his bag on his shoulder. "I'm staying the night and leaving early in the morning. I'll make sure I say goodbye before I head out."

"Right. Off to class with you then." Laurie waves his hand in dismissal and turns around to head to his own room, calling over his shoulder, "Love you!"

"Love you too, Laur." Emir smiles as he leaves, feeling significantly better than he did a few minutes ago.

***

Theo and Lili are stretching at the barre before class, which is basically what they do every day, making their plans for the weekend and deciding if it's worth the time to make homemade bread or if they're destined to muck it up. Lili smiles over Theo's shoulder just before he feels a gentle hand on his forearm, making him turn around. Theo's more than slightly shocked to realise that the person so carefully getting his attention is...Emir? He doesn't think they've ever intentionally had a conversation in tech hall before.

"I was wondering if we could talk? Just for a minute." Emir retracts his hand slowly, watching the surprise gradually wear off of Theo's face as he asks.

"Yeah, of - of course. What about?" Theo lets his eyes study Emir, trying to determine if he's about to get yelled at again. He hopes not but it might be tradition at this point.

"In the hallway?" Emir tilts his head behind himself, smiling softly when Theo nods and leads the way. "Alright, Lili?"

"Love the shirt, Emi." Lili grins at him, making him smile sideways and wave her off before turning back around to follow Theo out of the studio and into the hallway. He's wearing a Black Lives Matter shirt with the sleeves cut off, never one to shy away from making a statement.

"So…" Theo faces Emir from a few feet apart and waits for him to say something. The way he's looking at Theo is not an expression he's familiar with. At least not from Emir.

"I need to apologise." Emir runs his fingertips through his fringe and pushes it back, looking across at Theo uncertainly. "And I didn't want to make it everyone's business."

"You what?" Theo visibly flinches, scrunching his eyebrows together and staring at Emir with more than a little suspicion. Since when does Emir Shah apologise to Theo? For anything? Neither of them has ever really crossed a line that he can remember. Then again, Theo's not amazing at noticing social cues despite literal decades of effort.

"Please don't make this a fight. I'm genuinely trying here, alright?" Emir drops his hand and waits for Theo to relax a bit. Maybe he should've started with some sort of intro rather than straight into the apology. Straight. Ha. Ironic. "I read your dissertation this morning and I realised I've seriously misjudged you. You're…extremely intelligent. And you see more of the world than I thought. And *maybe* that stick up your arse is actually just caring a fuck tonne about the people around you in a way I misunderstood. Also you're, like, exceptionally queer, and that's on me for not noticing. So…yeah."

Theo shakes his head in disbelief, trying to reorient himself in this conversation. "I don't…I don't understand. I mean, thanks, I guess. But you don't owe me an apology? Well, besides the thinking I'm straight part. That is a bit offensive. Imagine being straight? In this economy? Eugh." Theo laughs, unsure what else to say.

The two of them don't really do sincerity. At best they do sarcasm, and occasionally tolerance. "Thanks for, um, for reading it. But really, it's alright. It's not a big deal."

Emir didn't realise how uncomfortable Theo would get from an apology, practically squirming in place as if he's itching to leave. And Emir can't have that.

"Theo…" Emir reaches out a hand and places it carefully on Theo's cheek, waiting for Theo's wide eyes to meet his own. "It is a big deal, and I do owe you an apology. So can we just…if you forgive me, we can move on from this, alright?"

Theo feels like he's on fire, the heat from Emir's hand and his amber eyes holding him in place, no longer listening to a word he's saying. He's looked at Emir before but never like this. Usually they're glaring at each other, a veil of frustration blocking anything else from passing between them. But this Emir, this open, sincere person that's doing an incredibly decent thing with absolutely no prompting? Theo feels a burning in his chest and his mind has gone completely blank. What had they been talking about?

"Theo?" Emir removes his hand but doesn't step away. He wonders vaguely if Theo is having difficulty processing this. It's certainly a lot of emotions and Emir did pull him out of his routine without warning. Is that...is Theo neurodivergent? Maybe. Emir doesn't want to assume, though. It's possible he's just in shock.

"What? Sorry, just - missed that last part." Theo flushes but can't look away. Those fucking eyes. And is that an eye freckle? How has he never noticed before?

"Am I forgiven? Can we move on?" Emir tilts his head again, hair falling in front of his eyes because he hasn't put his headband on yet.

"Yeah - yes. Let's move on." Theo is the one who steps back and takes a deep breath. "That was...it just caught me off guard. I'm not used to, like, actually having a conversation with you...does this mean I'm not a wanker anymore?" Theo finally smiles at his own joke, relieved when Emir laughs. His joy feels so bright it's blinding, and Theo wonders why it's taken so long for him to notice.

Emir shoves at Theo's arm gently and shakes his head. "You're still a wanker. Don't worry. We don't have to get along just because I was wrong about something."

"Good, because you're still a knob. What even was that outfit yesterday?" Theo leans against the wall and crosses his arms over his chest with a grin. This feels nice, teasing without the venom for once.

"Excuse you, I have excellent fashion. Practically a model." Emir turns and starts to walk away before stopping himself. "Oh, that reminds me. Rehearsal is done early today. Should we?"

"Should we...?" Theo hasn't started following yet, busy watching Emir walk away. But only out of professional curiosity, of course. Also, he could use a moment of transition time after all that.

"In the practice studio. Spend some time working together." Emir lets a first year walk past him and into tech hall while he watches Theo make his decision. Now that he's paying attention, he can read Theo and all the processing that goes into his decisions. Emir knows now that he's not brooding. He's thoughtful.

"Oh. Suppose we could. After an early dinner? Around six, maybe?" Theo doesn't have any plans for tonight, at least not yet, so they may as well get started.

"Right. Six it is." Emir doesn't have anything else to say so he walks back into the studio, Theo following a moment later and rejoining Lilibet for the last few minutes before class starts.

"What was that?" Lilibet asks Theo, tying her electric blue pointe shoes that match her sports bra of the day.

"Nothing. Well, not nothing. But it's fine. We're going to work together tonight and see how it goes." Theo picks up his water bottle and takes a long drink, suddenly incredibly thirsty as if he's in the middle of a workout.

"And if I bring popcorn and watch from the doorway?" Lili smirks up at Theo before accepting his hand to stand back up.

"You might have to invite our other friends as well. Pretty sure Laurie and T have a bet going about how long until we unalive each other." Theo picks Lili up briefly by the waist to spin her around. They've always been very tactile together, gay besties who are more like siblings than anything.

"That's not what the bet is about." Lili laughs and presses on Theo's hands so he'll keep them in place while she practices a few balances before class gets started, staring at herself in the mirror to adjust her placement.

Theo pointedly ignores that comment. "You and Jordan have plans tonight? I'll probably go to bed early since I was up late, but maybe we could have a picnic brunch tomorrow? Weather's supposed to be decent."

"Only if there's mimosas. Jordan's book club got moved for the weekend so she's free." Lili turns around to get her girlfriend's attention. "Oi. Jordan. Brunch with me and Teddy tomorrow?"

"Perfect. I've been neglecting my posh upbringing so I'm overdue to make a cucumber sandwich or two." Jordan winks at Lili before turning back to the barre. Theo's amazed at how well they keep their privacy, but now that he knows about them he picks up on the little things, how Jordan glances down at Lili's lips when they're talking, how Lili's eyes are softer when looking at Jordan than anyone else. Theo squeezes Lili's sides pointedly so their eyes meet and he can give her an understanding smile.

"Good morning everyone. Sorry I'm late." Margaret walks into the room, coffee in one hand and a random costume piece in the other. "We all got a bit caught up at the costume shop, but I think you're going to like what we've decided on for *Alice*."

Theo lets Lilibet go so they can start class, Lili reaching over to adjust the collar of Theo's shirt before turning to face the front. So far, it's been a good day.

***

Emir heads straight for the practice studio after rehearsal, stopping to refill his water bottle but otherwise without taking a break. He turns on a playlist and stretches for a few, letting his heart rate calm down after a rather intense solo practice with Raphael. The Rabbit is an incredibly aerobic role and Emir is grateful for his daily runs.

Once he feels rested enough and stretched out, Emir decides to try some of his choreography en pointe, something he's mostly avoided until now because he wasn't sure he would find someone for this project that *could* safely partner him. But Theo is definitely strong enough, and with more than enough experience to keep them both safe in the process. Emir rolls through his feet and tries a few practice balances before getting into it. Switching to his *gay but quiet* playlist, Emir warms up the basics then runs through some of the choreo he's sure he wants to use, seeing if it'll need to be adapted if he's en pointe. But then he realises he can't really do that alone anymore since it's not a solo project and he stops, hands on his head while he thinks.

That's how Theo finds Emir once he arrives, fifteen minutes before they agreed because he was a bit anxious and figured it'd be better to be early than late. He wants to respect Emir's time, even if he doesn't have any plans for himself tonight.

"I didn't know you did pointe." Theo comments from the doorway, startling Emir a bit in the process.

"You're early." Emir walks to his things to take a drink from his water bottle, stalling for time because this is a whole other conversation, but it's one he supposes they need to have.

"I figured you might have plans tonight and I didn't want to make you late." Theo shrugs as he walks inside, sitting down and pulling his bag into his lap. "I think we should chat a bit before we get started, if that's alright?"

"About pointe? I've been doing it since I was a teen. Lili's never mentioned it?" Emir takes a seat but leaves space between them, pulling his own things toward himself to grab his phone.

"Why would she?" Theo starts rustling through his bag, taking out about half a dozen things while they talk.

"Because I'm in Variations with her? I just figured it would have come up in conversation, with how close you two are." Emir lowers the volume on his speaker so they can talk easier. "Is it a problem?"

"No, not at all." Theo stops what he's doing to give Emir a bright smile. Potentially too bright, giving away that he's overcompensating. "I think I'm a bit jealous, but that's not new when it comes to you. I'll manage."

"Why would that make you jealous?" Emir drinks more water, a bit tired already and they haven't even started. Maybe he should've taken a break.

"Did you eat anything? Or did you come here straight from rehearsal?" Theo ignores Emir's question and reaches in his bag again. "Here." Theo hands over a Tupperware container and waits for Emir to take it.

Emir holds the container in his hands but he doesn't open it. He stares at Theo like he's suddenly sprouted wings. "What the bloody fuck is this?"

"Shit. Do you have allergies? I should've asked. They're vegan protein bars that I made with Lili and Jordan last Sunday. I have more than I could ever eat because we accidentally tripled the recipe while distracted by Gogglebox." Theo watches Emir watch him, confused by the expression on his face. Shit. Is this about more than just skipping dinner? Is this like *a thing* for Emir? Like a food thing? There's so much he doesn't know. "They're good, I swear. But like, it's okay if you don't want one. I won't be offended."

Emir blinks at Theo for another moment before cracking the lid of the Tupperware, glancing inside at a passable excuse for a snack. They're small, about two bites each, which makes them perfect for a mid-rehearsal snack. Before taking one for himself he holds it out to Theo. It'd be rude if he was the only one eating while they talk. Theo takes one from the top and waits for Emir, smiling as he reaches inside and picks one up for himself before setting the container aside.

"So...why are you jealous?" Emir takes a tiny bite of the protein bar, surprised that it's actually incredibly good. Theo can bake?

"I always wanted to do pointe. I did, actually, for a bit. When I was 12. As part of strength training after breaking my foot." Theo can't make eye contact now, taking his time talking between bites and staring at the food in his hand like it's absolutely fascinating.

"That's about when I started too. Not because I broke anything, just around that age." Emir starts stretching while he sits, finishing the snack in his hand before bending over his leg. "Why'd you stop?"

"Oh, well...bit of drama with that, actually." Theo clears his throat and takes a sip from his own water bottle. "I wanted to keep on, but the school I was at actually kicked me out because I asked. I had to transfer to a different academy across town. I suppose it worked out because I had excellent training at the new studio, but...yeah. Never really got over that, if I'm honest." Theo chances a glance up at Emir, surprised to see something resembling pain in his eyes.

"You were just a kid. It's not like I never heard bigoted comments about doing pointe myself, but I can't imagine my studio telling me no, nevermind kicking me out for it? That's...fuck, Theo. I'm sorry." Emir shakes his head, another new piece of information about Theo proving just how wrong he'd been. He always thought things had been so easy for Theo, but apparently not.

"Did you - were you the one who taught Lili how to dye her shoes?" Theo would rather change the subject, all things considered. It's not something he enjoys talking about.

"Yeah, first year. I taught her the fun colours and she taught me how to pancake mine to match my skin. It's how we started talking because you and Lili were already close and...well." Emir shrugs and takes another bar from the Tupperware. Why the fuck are these so delicious?

"Why don't I ever see you performing en pointe, even for fun? And like you haven't auditioned for any pointe roles that I can remember." Theo starts looking through his notes now. They have a lot they have to figure out for this project, but this is good.

Learning how to have conversations without fighting is going to be essential moving forward.

"I audit Variations so I don't have to worry about any of that. It's...I love pointe but there's a level of self-preservation that I need to maintain." Emir stands up now so he can keep his body moving, Theo watching him from his spot on the floor.

"Do you...is that something you want to talk about?" Theo sets his notes aside but stays on the floor, trying to gauge what comes next. Do they keep talking? Do they try to dance together? Separately? He has no clue how they're meant to start working on this.

"Not particularly." Emir rolls through his feet, waiting for Theo to join him so they can get started.

Theo tries not to take that personally, but he remembers what Emir had said in their meeting with Sean. *Present company,* and Theo had been the only one in the room, so what the hell else would that mean? But then again Emir is being remarkably civil and he even apologised to Theo this morning. "I have a lot of notes and like...dozens of questions after watching your video clips."

Theo holds up his notebook for Emir to take a look over.

Emir waits for Theo to nod his permission before starting to read, eyes scanning one page, and then another, and eventually just flipping because he realises Theo wasn't kidding about the quantity. "Theo, how did you even have time for this? Sean sent those yesterday afternoon."

"I watched them last night and annotated the ones I thought we should start with. Then I organised the clips by style for reference, and the list of questions is near the end." Theo flushes, a bit embarrassed by how much effort he's put into this already. And obviously Emir's read his written portion so he has a window into how important this is to Theo. It's not that Theo's ashamed of being overprepared and responsible or whatever, but Emir's like a proper cool person and this kind of analytical tendency feels decidedly uncool in moments like these.

"Impressive and all that but...well there's no way in hell we can get to this tonight." Emir hands the notebook back to Theo and waits with a hand outstretched to help him stand up. Theo takes it at first but drops it almost immediately, standing to the side with hesitancy in every inch of his posture. Emir might find it a tiny bit endearing. Turns out Theo is surprising once you get past whatever it is that Emir seems to have gotten over. "Let's just...get used to sharing space, yeah?"

Theo can't argue that, so he shuffles forward a bit and turns to face the mirror, but he isn't sure where to go from there. "Did you want to try a few of your sections but with a partner instead of solo? Seems like some of them were created with one in mind."

"Why not?" Emir can think of a hundred reasons why not, but he's more of a *do first, ask questions later* personality when it comes to dance. Not that he doesn't think things through. He'd rather follow his instincts and adjust as needed rather than force anything. "Anywhere in particular you wanted to start?"

"There was that section with all the weight transfer. Seems simple enough to start with - not simple - I just meant nothing too acrobatic." Theo feels like apologising already. He doesn't want to slag off Emir's work, especially since he was genuinely impressed by it. "But we haven't worked together before. Shouldn't we like...ease into it?"

Emir smiles in Theo's direction, already anticipating that question.

"Catch me," he says before flinging himself across Theo's path, knowing that he will. And sure enough, Theo catches Emir midair with a huff of surprise before setting him down again. Theo didn't hesitate for a single moment, hands reaching out to grab at the safe part of Emir's waist, careful not to drop him too suddenly. Having Emir in his space is definitely going to be an adjustment if he's planning to throw himself through the air without so much as a warning. Not that Theo minds, he just doesn't want anyone to get hurt.

"I think we'll be fine." Emir turns around in Theo's arms and lays his hands on Theo's shoulders for a moment. Theo's hands are still on Emir's waist out of years of partnering habit. It's one of the first things they teach you when you learn to partner someone en pointe: keep yourself stable near your partner in case you need to catch them.

"You can let me go, I'm done jumping." Emir doesn't actually want space, but they need a bit of distance to work on the segment Theo mentioned. But why is Emir disappointed at having to carve space between them again? Just two days ago a continent didn't feel like enough. But Theo's hands are so strong and sure, and now that Emir knows he isn't a bellend, at least not entirely, maybe he doesn't mind the proximity. He's trying not to overthink it, and yet...

"Actually," Emir does step away now and back towards the front of the room where they left their things. "Let me take these off. I know you can partner me just fine, but we shouldn't start there. I haven't even decided if I want to use them for the piece yet."

"You should." Theo says automatically before backtracking. It's not actually his choice, even if he does have a preference. "I mean, whatever works best for you. But I think...I think you're really brave for being a male pointe dancer and I'm sure you're, well...you're probably brilliant, based on what I've seen."

"Thanks, mate." Emir grins up at Theo from the floor, unsure where all of this sudden support is coming from. "Who knew you'd be such a softie once you stopped fighting me? First snacks and now compliments? Slow down or we'll be in bed before the night is over."

"Christ, Emir. Is it really that easy for you?" Theo slides both of his hands down his face and groans. "Surely someone, at some point in your life, has turned you down. That wasn't even a line, honestly. All you did was suggest getting horizontal. Then again, based on - " Theo waves his hand vaguely in Emir's direction, "it probably is that easy...Also, you argued right back so I'm not the only one who stopped fighting."

"Honestly? Yeah, usually all I have to do is ask." Emir shrugs and stands back up, pointe shoes set aside for now. "People make assumptions about me, so sometimes I let them think I'm all dark and mysterious and whatever, even if I'm really just a quiet nerd who enjoys a good shag. It's easier that way."

"We're getting off topic." Theo definitely does not want to talk about this. He does *not* need to know Emir's sexual history and they're getting dangerously close to that territory. Just thinking about it has Theo ready to bolt. "Does the music matter? I noticed in the videos that it seemed fairly random."

Emir picks up his phone again and scrolls for a moment with a smug look on his face before making his choice. Theo groans when he recognises the opening notes of *Teenage Dream* by Katy Perry, but he feels a little flutter in his stomach when he hears an adorable giggle from Emir's direction that he assumes is in response to his reaction.

"Literally any other song, I am *begging*." Theo puts his hands on his hips, but it's hard to be annoyed. Honestly, Emir's laugh is pretty infectious.

"Begging, hm? Noted." Emir looks back at his phone with a smirk, changing to one of his favourite playlists, assuming Theo won't recognise any of it since it's mostly tiny artists that he found randomly and the songs have about half a million streams combined. "So I'm thinking I should work through a sequence or two and you should just do what feels natural. If I lean you lean, that sort of thing. Yeah?"

Theo shrugs but holds his arm out, waiting for Emir to take his hand like Lili (or any other partner) would to begin. Emir walks over to him calmly enough, trying not to laugh at the way Theo is wanting to be so formal about all this. Maybe, just maybe, by the end of this, Theo might actually loosen up a bit. That doesn't mean Emir can't have some fun along the way.

Taking Theo's hand, Emir laces their fingers together and moves right into Theo's space, pulling him close by their joined hands. He feels Theo catch his breath and try to react, but Emir doesn't give him enough time, pulling himself away again and letting their arms stretch in the open air, joined only at the fingertips until Emir loosens his grip to trail along the palm of Theo's hand, making him shiver. Theo doesn't remember any of this from what Emir shared, but maybe he missed this part or doesn't recognise it. He's sufficiently distracted just trying to react because Emir moves quickly, as if on instinct.

"Keep up, Theo." Emir teases, turning away from Theo and throwing himself through the air in a barrel turn then landing in a side lunge, rolling out of it and away from Theo. "You're meant to be following, remember?"

"But I don't...I don't know the choreography." Theo feels completely out of his depth; Emir's confidence as he moves through the space is something Theo can't access. He's used to counts, steps, knowing exactly what comes next, the entire sequence decided before he even starts moving. But Emir is just...dancing. Just like that. Feeling more than thinking, responding to the music in fluid motions that never once seem to falter.

"Neither do I." Emir rolls his body back up to standing for an entire eight count, moving his head to look over at Theo on the beat. "It's not about knowing, it's about feeling. Show me what you feel, Theo."

"I don't...know how to do that. As a choreographer, sure, but not as a dancer. It's a different skill." Theo keeps watching Emir, trying to match his movements in some sort of strange pantomime. But that's not partnering, that's mirroring, and it's not what they need to be working on.

"Do you want help?" Emir stops moving, one arm still in the air above his head that slowly deflates to fall back at his side.

"...Alright." Theo holds out his hand again, and this time Emir takes it properly, keeping Theo close so he can lead him. Ironic, really, since Theo's meant to be the traditional male role in this scenario. Emir smiles again at that, thinking that they're already throwing those rules out the window and fuck does it feel good.

Emir brings Theo close, swaying them for a moment before using his own body to guide different parts of Theo in time with the music. Turning Theo's face with fingers to his jaw, moving one of his legs out with his own knee so he can circle Theo and get behind him, pulling him back by the front of his shoulders to lean onto Emir who then pushes him forward again, using their weight to move them both around. "That's better. You know how to dance Theo. I've seen you."

"That's class. I know what to do in class." Theo catches Emir's eyes and it gets easier to follow him then, able to anticipate his next move the closer he pays attention. Or it was, until Emir turns around and Theo's met with Emir's exposed back muscles where his vest slips as he leans and all Theo can think to do is grab him from behind and pick him up. So he does, taking Emir in a cradle hold to turn them both around and setting him down to do a penché, Emir knowing where he was headed with this because it's fairly standard choreography, but at least they're moving together.

"Not in class. I mean at parties and shit." Emir turns himself in Theo's hold to let Theo support him through a backwards fall, and sure enough Theo's hands guide him the whole way, safe on the small of his back while he lets himself suspend before pulling himself upright again.

"That's different. That's just with Laurie. We don't give a shit what we look like or who sees us. It's for fun." Theo turns around so their backs are together, waiting for Emir to lean over him and he does, pushing Theo forward while he uses his back as a support to seemingly float for a moment.

"It's just me, Theo. And who says we can't have fun?" Emir surprises Theo by moving around his side and beneath him, meeting Theo's eyes and using a soft hand to push him upright again, turning them around to face the mirror.

"You're not *just* anything, Emir." Theo sighs and stops moving, frustrated with his own limitations. "I think I need more practice before we try improv together because I keep reverting back to the classics and I know that's not something either of us has planned for this."

"It's just because that's your body's vocabulary." Emir shrugs, not especially concerned because the classics are going to be at least a portion of the final product. There's no removing that influence from their training. "Besides, what the fuck did you spend all your time learning at BosCon, hm?"

"That was still choreographed ahead of time, though." Theo holds his hands on the small of his back while they talk. "I can't just...I don't have that instinct like you do. I can feel the music or whatever but I can't do it without thinking."

Emir stares at Theo for a moment, considering what he said. It's a fair point, but also... "Isn't this part of why we decided to work together?"

"How do you mean?" Theo decides to take a break, drinking from his water bottle to give himself something to do. They've barely started dancing so he's not exactly desperate for hydration.

"I needed structure, which is you, right? And you need my dancing, which is why I'm here. So instead of fighting what comes naturally to you we just have to find a way to use it." Emir drops himself to the floor to drink from his Hydro Flask, watching for Theo's reaction.

Theo sits down as well, a soft smile in his eyes as he reaches out a hand to tap gently at Emir's knee. "Didn't know you were so smart, Emir."

He stares at his own feet, thinking about what Emir said. And he's absolutely right, of course. They weren't meant to be fusing into one unit. The goal is working together and offering what each of them is best at.

"Always have been, Theodore." Emir's voice is...too soft right now. He's not used to Theo being so calm and quiet. Normally he sees him from across a room, laughing with Laurie or showing off in class. But like this? Quiet and contemplative and cooperative? Emir much prefers this Theo. He's definitely easier to spend time with. "I want you to try something for me, alright?"

Still looking at the floor, Theo nods. This whole experiment so far has been so different than what he could've predicted or planned for but it seems like Emir knows exactly what he's doing. When Theo looks up again he sees Emir watching him, a warm confidence in his eyes. "What did you have in mind?"

"Well, I'm assuming you're not a complete knob and have in fact been exposed to some pop culture." Emir grins when Theo scoffs, but this is banter and not an argument so he continues. "Which, knowing as little as I do about you, means you memorised the choreography from any dance movie you watched and probably even wrote it down in one of your notebooks."

"It's helpful, alright? I mostly studied ballet and modern growing up so I had to learn the rest myself." Theo crosses his arms over his chest defensively. He's tried his best to branch out, but it's not that simple when he was constantly being shoved back into a box.

"Relax, I'm not judging. It's cute to picture little Theo scribbling away while watching *Footloose*." Emir nudges Theo with his toe since they're still sitting facing each other. Theo might be flushed again, and he's definitely smiling, which Emir considers as a win. "I'm hoping we can use that to get you out of your comfort zone. And it would be choreography you know so it'd be about figuring out how we move together and not focusing so much on the content yet...what do you think?"

Theo sets aside his water and stands up, waiting for Emir to join him. "I grew up with two older sisters. Chances are I've seen whichever film you're thinking of."

Emir smiles at Theo again and feels something like excitement growing in his chest. Maybe this really can be fun. At least for today. "Well, since *nobody puts Baby in a corner...*"

Emir trails off, picking up his phone yet again and quickly typing what he needs in the search, pressing play as he stands up.

"Dance with me, Baby." Emir does the little finger *come hither* motion just like Johnny, laughing as Theo huffs but steps closer.

"Let's stick with Theo, and I want no comments about the fact that I prefer to dance Baby's role in this scene." He waits for Emir to join him, his stomach dropping when Emir runs his hands along Theo's waist to hold him by the small of his back and pull him close. Fuck.

"You continue to surprise me...*Baby.*" Emir adds, having a bit too much fun teasing Theo. But Theo seems to take that as some sort of challenge, running his hands along Emir's forearms to get them in position, clearly having practised this exact moment dozens of times. Emir wonders who he practised with before remembering he needs to dip Theo. And oh. The way Theo lets himself be moved, completely submissive and dropping his head back, which of course exposes his neck, and Emir forgets the context for a moment, staring without shame at the tawny brown birthmark at the base of Theo's throat.

Theo brings himself back up and laughs at the look on Emir's face. "Keep up, Johnny."

They're *so close* right now, their bodies completely connected. Neither of them had really thought through how close their faces would be since they're the same height.

Emir seems to remember himself after Theo's joke. He moves behind his partner, guiding Theo's arm up so he can trail his fingertips along the skin of his tricep then down his side, face turned so he's breathing softly against Theo's cheek.

Theo can't stop his responsive shivers and Emir can't help the way he kisses the tip of Theo's nose before spinning him away, just like in the movie. Theo lets himself be spun, his movements matching his thoughts because this is maybe a bit too much.

To both of their credit, once they start actually dancing, respecting each other's dance space and catching smiles as they do, it's remarkably fun. They laugh every time the dance brings them significantly closer than a platonic distance apart and they forget that this is work or research or whatever as they get lost in the steps. This is what Emir has always loved about dance, how it can take any moment and give him freedom from his surroundings while he moves through space. And this is the most he's enjoyed it in a very long time. They make a few mistakes, of course, but generally keep up, their talent and years of practice making up for any missteps. Emir even kisses Theo's knuckles on cue, making Theo smile so wide his eyes crinkle.

The two of them keep going until it would be time for Johnny (or in this case Emir) to jump off the stage, but as there's no stage to jump from and they're both getting tired already, Emir goes for a knee slide and collapses on the Marley, laughing and breathing heavy with his face to the ceiling. Theo flops down next to him to catch his own breath, turning his face to look at Emir. He's never seen Emir like this, happy and smiling and free. He's stunning.

Theo can't understand how he feels too far apart, already wishing they could've kept going. He scoots his hand over until their fingers meet and gives Emir's hand a gentle squeeze. Emir turns his head to catch Theo's stare with glowing eyes, waiting for Theo to speak. "This was perfect, Emir. Thank you."

Emir doesn't drop Theo's hand, instead squeezing his fingers back and smiling while continuing to catch his breath. "That was the most fun I've had in years. No one can ever keep up with me like that." He takes in the sight of Theo laying beside him, disarmed for once and looking truly happy. He's never looked at Emir like this before.

They stay like that on the floor until they're breathing evenly, eventually getting up to rehydrate when the song ends a few minutes later. Sitting down near the mirrors with their things, it's clear that they've finished "working" for tonight even if it's only been about half an hour.

"So...that was great, but not exceptionally productive." Theo is the one to bring them back to business, of course. But Emir doesn't mind. It's why he wants Theo here in the first place.

"I think it was though. Think of where we were two days ago." Emir takes another drink of water, and when Theo nudges the protein bars in his direction again, Emir gladly takes one.

"Point made." Theo picks up his notebook and flips through before starting to pack his bag one item at a time, everything exactly in its place. "I'm happy to do that again literally anytime. But I think we should do some more research. Together."

"I spend exactly as much time in the library as I'd like. Do we absolutely have to?" Emir feels comfortable being dramatic. If they're going to work together Theo has to get used to it. Emir throws himself back on the ground with an arm over his eyes, sneaking a bite of the protein bar between dramatic sighs.

And now Theo is finding it difficult to stay on task. Who is this person and what has he done with Emir Shah? "Well, lucky for you the research I have in mind is mostly visual and can be comfortably completed at our flats."

"I'm too tired for a shag tonight, Theo." Emir jokes, giggling to himself. But then he chances a glance at Theo and sees that all of the colour has drained from his face. "Fuck, I'm only joking. Deep fucking breaths, mate."

Theo doesn't know what just happened. He's usually quick with the banter but Emir just said that so casually after...well, after dancing together like that. He felt like he forgot how to breathe. Probably just overtired after a long week. And he didn't get much sleep last night. But then again, Emir's the reason for that too, technically...Fuck, he really needs to get a grip. He clears his throat and takes another sip of water before continuing.

"I was thinking like films. Recordings of classic ballets, dance scenes like that one -" Theo gestures at the room around them, "Variations from our favourite dancers that could be inspiration. That sort of thing."

Emir considers Theo carefully. His tone just switched back to pompous arsehole as if that could undo any of the past half hour. But Emir knows better now. He knows it's a front or masking or whatever this is. He sees the real Theo behind it, so instead of getting defensive, he responds calmly as if nothing has changed. "That makes sense. We draw inspiration from what's come before so we have a clearer idea of what we're working towards."

"Yeah and like, I think we need more practice with...supervision before we try to choreograph together again." Theo was hesitant to say as much, but it's true. Neither of them has experience in a same sex dance partnership and they could use all the help they can get. "I don't mean that to sound - it's just...we have time. And I'd rather we get some technical help so we don't get hurt or plateau. But in the meantime, we can research."

"And get more used to each other." Emir thinks tonight has gone remarkably well, but that's no indication that it will always be this easy with them. "So, start research next week? That work for you?"

Theo pauses before answering. He was sort of hoping they could start this weekend, but it can wait a few more days if that works better for Emir.

"Alright...so I guess I'll just - " Theo stands up, straining a bit from sitting in one spot a minute too long, and taking his bag with him.

"I'll walk with you. I think I'm done for tonight. I have an early morning so I should probably head home too." Emir gathers his things while Theo waits, throwing on his joggers and the same jumper he's been wearing for walks home to his flat all week.

Once they have their bags on their shoulders and they've closed up the studio, they start on the familiar path back towards their flats. They walk in silence, the early evening still warm, but there's a breeze and it's overcast so it cools them both off after the heat of the studio. Emir never feels the need to fill the silence with noise, happy to listen to his surroundings. He thinks it sounds nice, hearing another person walk in step with him. His siblings and his friends aren't quiet like this, always wanting to gossip or make plans or just generally fill the air. But it seems that's not the case with Theo. It's refreshing to be calm, and together.

Theo would normally feel like he's under some obligation to start a conversation while they walk side by side, but he gets the sense Emir is perfectly happy as is. It's not something Theo's used to, just walking in silence as if it's already enough. But maybe Emir has the right idea because Theo can hear so much he normally misses: the sounds of speakers playing through a nearby open window, the street noise in the distance, the awareness of Emir beside him, their steps in sync while they walk on.

They part ways at the appointed spot, Emir to his flat and Theo to his own, waving goodbye and mumbling goodnights, unsure where this leaves them. Usually one of them would be storming off or pulled away by one of their friends. But this amicable parting feels empty, as if there's something they should be saying but they both forgot the script. Emir turns to glance at Theo walking away, feeling some sort of pull to hold him back. Before he can overthink it he calls, "Theo?"

Theo stops and turns, confused while Emir walks straight up to him and brings him into a tight hug. He's in shock for a moment but Emir is a proper cuddler, arms firm around his shoulders and face tucked into Theo's neck. So Theo relaxes, hugging Emir close, one hand on his lower back and the other holding Emir's head in place. Theo can smell traces of Emir's cologne this close, mixed with what he assumes is some sort of hair product and just a hint of sweat. And Emir can feel as Theo incrementally calms down the longer they hug, his firm muscles losing their tension beneath his arms, Theo's neck soft against his cheek. They hold onto each other for a moment longer before Emir steps away with a sigh.

"Have a good weekend, Theo." Emir says before he walks away again, hands in his pockets and a contemplative smile on his face. Theo watches him go until he's out of sight, shaking his head and following the familiar path back to his own flat. His stomach knots while his mind tries to solve the puzzle that is Emir Shah. Theo's having a difficult time putting together the Emir he's known for over two years and this new Emir that he's only just meeting. He wonders if Emir's feeling the same, grappling with a foundation of animosity that seems to be crumbling, and hoping there's enough there to build a new one from something a bit less toxic.

Theo feels exhausted. It's good they finished early because he definitely needs to sleep and get himself back on track. When he doesn't get enough sleep it can really throw him off. But Theo spends the rest of the night thinking about that hug and how it feels to have Emir in his arms. And when he's not thinking of that, he's wondering why it seems to matter so much anyway. He knows he's quieter than usual and that his friends definitely notice when he goes to bed before ten on a weekend. But he needs to be alone. He needs space to process the week he's had.

How is it possible that, just two days ago, he and Emir were fighting in a kitchen while passive aggressively making tea? And now they're what, exactly? Colleagues? Partners? Theo doesn't find any answers that night, but he does fall asleep almost immediately once he's in bed. Maybe the weekend will give him the time he needs to figure it out.

CHAPTER FIVE

"Teddy, this is the gayest thing we've ever done." Lilibet sips her champagne out of the charity shop glasses they've brought along, legs draped across Jordan's lap.

"You have an entire girlfriend. This is definitely not *the gayest thing* you've ever done." Theo isn't in the mood for champagne at 11 in the morning, so he's drinking lemon water instead, opening the various containers of snacks and setting them out on the gingham blanket between them.

"There aren't even any rainbows, darling." Jordan adds, taking Lili's glass to taste the champagne and wrinkling her nose. She's a bit of a wine snob, but Lili doesn't mind. It sort of comes along with having a posh girlfriend who summered in Provence growing up.

"That's what makes it gayer. Trust me, babe. Only the straights trying to prove something drape the scenery in rainbows." Lilibet looks at Theo, waiting for him to agree.

"Actually...you have a point." Theo pauses to think, an open container of grapes in his left hand. "Unless it's made by a queer artist or something, the gays usually only have rainbows as, like, an act of defiance."

"But I like rainbow things." Jordan pouts until Lili kisses her cheek. It's so sweet Theo laughs quietly to himself. He's never seen Lili like this and he's just glad to see his friend so happy.

"That's different, babe. For you they're always an act of defiance." Lili reaches out to grab one of the Tupperware containers still in the basket. "Theo, where did you even find a proper picnic basket? We're uni students for fuck's sake."

"Borrowed it from T of course." Theo settles in facing the other two with the lake to his right side. "They always have these sorts of things. I think it goes with the whole vintage, fashion history thing."

"Did Lili tell you that we're friends now? I met them on Wednesday when they were eavesdropping on whatever that homoerotic dinner argument was." Jordan shifts Lili's legs off her lap so she can grab a few snacks for herself, and maybe add enough juice to her champagne to make a passable mimosa.

"That was *not* homoerotic. And we're fine now. He even apologised for it." Theo can feel them both watching him, hoping he'll continue. Theo and Emir gossip is better than reality television.

"That was three days ago and somehow you're fine now?" Lili knows Theo a bit better than that. "The two of you have driven the rest of us up the wall for two fucking years but now all of the sudden you're just...friends?"

"Also, it was definitely homoerotic." Jordan adds with a knowing smirk.

Theo averts his eyes and drinks his water so fast he chokes. "Why are you helping her? Is it always going to be two against one now?"

"Yes, of course. Why else would I want a girlfriend?" Lili takes another sip of her champagne and lays her legs back in Jordan's lap. They're in a private enough area that there's no other people walking by and they can be more open than they normally are in public.

"I think the frequent sex is probably a benefit as well." Jordan tilts her head to catch Lili's eyes, as if they talk like this everyday. Which they probably would if they didn't have to be so private.

"Should I leave? Give you two a proper date or whatever?" Theo's only mostly teasing. But he also thinks it's probably hard to have actual dates in their situation so if they did want him to go, he would.

"No, I want to hear about last night. All of your limbs appear intact so it must've gone better than I thought." Lili hands Jordan one of the containers of fruit and a fork, knowing she'll refuse to eat it with her fingers.

"What's there to know? We met up in the studio, talked a bit, tried to dance together, and decided we needed to do some more research first." Theo shrugs, trying to get them to drop it. He gets why they're curious, especially Lili, but it feels like something he doesn't really want to share.

"With you two? No fucking way. Not a single fight?" Lili sincerely doesn't believe that, from either of them. Theo is practically family and Emir is...well, they know each other and see each other almost every day and have conversations sometimes. She loves them but she also knows they argue on a regular basis, even if there's nothing to argue about.

"I mean...no?" Theo tucks his legs up to cross in front of him, putting his chin in his hand. "He apologised for the whole 'assuming I was straight' thing, and honestly, he's like..."

"What's that look?" Lili wiggles her fingertips in Theo's direction.

"There's no look." Theo frowns and stares back at Lili, eyebrows creased in confusion.

"There's definitely a look. Even I can tell there's something happening on your face." Jordan glances at Theo over the top of her mimosa glass before finally giving up and setting it aside for Lili to finish.

"He's just...not what I expected. And I'm having a hard time understanding that the person I danced with yesterday is the same person I've been fighting with for two years." Theo tries to play it off, picking up one of the cucumber sandwiches that Jordan made and taking a dainty bite. He's not as posh as Jordan, but he's posh enough for most of his friends to make fun of him for it.

"I'm going to need a bit more than that." Lili is giving Theo her full attention now, and for reasons that go much deeper than gossip.

"Well...I always thought he was arrogant. Huge ego. That sort of thing. But...I think he's maybe just shy? And, like, when we walked home he was just...smiling, like, enjoying the quiet and whatever. And he apologised to me yesterday morning even when I told him he didn't need to. But he did...and to be honest, last night was fun. Like genuinely enjoyable. We spent as much time laughing as we did dancing." Theo's been staring out at the water while he talks, trying to sort through his thoughts while answering Lili's question.

"He's actually alright, if I'm honest. Like, I'm sure we're still going to fight sometimes, but I feel like I know who he is now. I can see how wrong I was and how smart he is. I always knew he was talented, but he's actually sort of brilliant. The way he dances when it's how he wants, it's like nothing I've ever seen." Privately, Theo thinks that Emir is entirely wonderful, but that's far too much to admit to anyone besides his innermost self.

Lili and Jordan don't really know what to say to any of that. They've always known how incredibly talented Emir is, but whenever Theo's mentioned the fact, it's always been begrudgingly, as if it was another reason to resent him. The way Theo's talking about

Emir now is almost fond, like he's watching Emir dance across the water in his mind's eye. When they don't respond for several seconds Theo turns to look at them and deepens the crinkles in his forehead at the way they're staring at him.

"What? You asked for more. That's more." Theo crosses his arms over his chest defensively.

"Yeah, that's...that's definitely more." Lili clears her throat and bites into a strawberry, still staring at Theo. She isn't quite sure which buttons to press this morning.

"Tell me about the dancing together part." Jordan is the first one to say something useful again. "Did you both partner each other? And like, whose choreography did you use?"

"It was sort of a mess at the start. He's read my paper and I've watched his video clips, but it wasn't exactly obvious what to work on first. But eventually Emir sort of...guided me, or at least tried to. But I'm shit at improv." Theo laughs at himself because he really is shit at improv. Always has been. "But then Emir...well he had a good idea and it made it so we could dance together because I knew the steps already, but it wasn't traditional partner work. Like I said, brilliant."

Theo shrugs and finishes the cucumber sandwich before picking up another one. They're absolutely delicious and they should definitely make picnic brunch a regular thing.

"...And?" Lili waves an empty strawberry stem at him, waiting for the rest of it. "What was the brilliant idea?"

"We, um...*did the final dance from Dirty Dancing*." Theo mumbles, flushing and taking several large drinks from his water glass.

"I'm sorry, you officially need to confirm that I just heard you correctly." Lili sits up and crosses her own legs so she and Theo are practically face to face with only a few snacks between them. Jordan's content to sit back because this seems like best mate business.

"We didn't do the lift or anything. Just the first few minutes, like until Johnny jumps down to dance with the ensemble. And then we called it a night and walked home." Theo won't meet Lilibet's stare, suddenly needing to try a bite of every single snack they brought with them.

"Let me get this straight - nope, no I heard it too. Now's not the time." Lili smirks at Jordan's immediate laugh, then stares back at Theo. "Theodore George Bisexual Palmer, you're telling me that you let Emir Shah be the Johnny to your Baby and that it was *fun*? That you laughed about it and then walked home together afterwards?"

"Yeah we did, and then he hugged me goodbye and I got home and went to bed early and now I'm here with you asking me a dozen questions for some reason." Theo stuffs an entire sandwich in his mouth after that sentence in an attempt to stop the interrogation. Why is Lili making it seem like such a big deal?

"He. Hugged. You. Goodbye." Lili enunciates each word, both hands on her cheeks while she stares at Theo. "Nope. No. You're lying. You think it's funny and you're taking the piss because there is no way in fucking hell that the two of you not only danced together while, like, touching and stuff, but then also hugged goodbye after a quiet walk across campus. What the fuck, Teddy."

"It's not a big deal! We're just, like, friends now or whatever. Colleagues. Dance partners. It's fine. We're just getting used to each other, alright?" Theo huffs and takes the entire container of yoghurt parfaits so he can decide which one he wants, claiming the tiny, sensory friendly spoon that he knows T packed just for him. It only takes Theo approximately five seconds to choose the one with strawberries and granola. Blueberries are a no for him. Something about the way they pop makes him shiver.

"Okay, well you're right that this isn't the gayest thing we've ever done. Reenacting *Dirty Dancing* alone in the studio is, like...Teddy, it's *so* gay." Lilibet sits back a bit and picks up her own sandwich, still staring at him intensely.

Theo doesn't really want to talk about it anymore. He thought it had been nice, really, great progress towards their working together, but now it feels weird, like he missed a chapter and he was the one who was there. He normally wouldn't, but he takes out his phone and scrolls through his notifications, not actually reading a single one of them. Maybe if he's quiet for a minute they'll move on to a new topic. It doesn't help that he still hasn't answered Laurie's text about how it went last night, so the notification is just sitting there, reminding him that he's going to have to have this same conversation all over again. Theo sighs and turns off his phone, picking up his snack as if it can explain any of this to him.

"Theo?" Jordan's voice is very gentle as she moves to sit closer to Lili again. "Can I ask you something? Or maybe a few somethings? I'm just curious."

"Only if you're not going to yell at me like Lili is." Theo pouts again while starting on his yoghurt, one carefully composed spoonful at a time: half with yogurt, then two pieces of granola, and one slice of strawberry.

"Could you describe Laurie and T to me? Like if I didn't know them, how would you describe them?" Jordan tilts her head, genuinely curious and still speaking as if she might spook Theo.

"Erm, sure. Laurie has like this tiny chaos energy with the biggest heart I've ever met. He's, like, sort of short but don't tell him I said that, and with light brown hair and blue eyes. Messy as hell, which is why we could never be flatmates. And T is the absolute kindest person I've ever known. They're generous and definitely the best thing that's ever happened to Laurie. And T is tall with dark brown curls, curlier than mine, and green eyes. Oh and an absolute fashion diva." Theo can always talk about his friends. He's so grateful for all of them, and he's not sure what he would do without them.

"From what I know of them, I would agree." Jordan smiles softly at Theo. "And Emir? How would you describe him?"

"Oh – " Theo stares out over the water again, thinking hard. The same question two days ago would've been easy to answer, but now? "Well...I still don't know him very well. But I would say he's shy, quiet, prefers time to himself. He doesn't have many close friends but he gets along with everyone. He seems to forget his own importance sometimes. Like, I brought snacks yesterday because I figured he would skip dinner to rehearse and I was right. And he only ever drinks green tea, and it has to have honey and lemon or he'll just go without. He's potentially the most talented dancer I've ever known, even after studying abroad. He has this light, you know? Something about him that just draws you in. And for the longest time it annoyed me because I thought he was putting it on, but...he's not. I don't think he actually has any idea how remarkable he is. Like...he knows he's talented but I don't think he understands, like truly comprehends it. I will *never* be able to have that."

Theo pauses and sighs, still looking into the distance. There's so much he could add, but he supposes he should mention Emir's general appearance as well since he did for T and Laurie. "And his eyes are, like, this honey golden colour, and I think I noticed an eye freckle. His hair seems to be important to him. Its natural black colour suits him, but sometimes he does fun colours or shaves part of it, so I think it might be how he expresses himself since we have so many restrictions as dancers. But honestly he's just, like...he's pretty. I can't think of a better word. Everyone who knows Emir can see that. It's just how he is. And again, I really don't think he understands. I used to think he flaunted it, but now I think he assumes he's average and gets by on his charm. Which he does, of course. But those fucking eyes..."

He's still staring out at the water but he pauses to take a bite, chewing slowly while he thinks. It's not just the eyes, it's his plush lips, his constant stubble, his arched cheekbones and long eyelashes...After a moment he turns to look at Jordan, who has an almost sympathetic look in her eyes. "Did that answer your question?"

"It did, Theo." Jordan nods and reaches out to grab Theo's hand for a moment with a small head tilt before letting it drop again. "Very thorough answer."

"I've been thinking about it a lot the past few days, especially since that apology. He's never apologised to me for anything. And he doesn't seem very interested in fighting with me anymore so I don't really have anything to argue with him about. So now I just...I don't know what we are. Because I don't think we can call ourselves friends. Like you two? Definitely my friends. We're having a gay picnic by the lake." Theo laughs and looks around at the carefully arranged containers of food between them on the blanket.

"How did it feel to dance with him?" Lili is back to sipping her champagne, wondering if Theo is going to actually figure this out or if they're all about to pretend it's nothing and move on.

"I don't know? Why?" Theo shrugs and readjusts on the blanket to be more in the sun. If the sun's out he's definitely going to take advantage.

"You dance with me every day. You've danced with Jordan. You've partnered probably dozens of people. How was it with Emir?" Lili's trying not to force Theo to open his own fucking eyes, so this question is the closest she can get right now. It's even related to the questions they've been asking about the two of them working together, so it should be safe.

"With you it feels easy. With him it feels...natural." Theo is so confused, but that was the most honest answer he could give. "Like...I know how to partner you - or really anyone - but especially you. We've worked together for so long we just have physical shorthand. Like, I know when you're favouring a certain side or if you have an injury, right? But with Emir, it was like I didn't need to think...and I don't know what that means. Like, I'm worried one of us will get hurt, honestly. I think we need to ask one of the teachers for some advice. It's not like he's too heavy or tall or anything, but it *is* different since we're both AMAB. There's weight distribution to consider and training techniques. But...once we were dancing it made sense. Not the improv of course because I'm terrible at that. But letting him lead was so fucking easy. It felt like things were just falling into place...And when I was supporting him, I knew where to put my hands, and at one point he just, like...threw himself in my direction? I caught him, of course. But it just felt..."

"Natural." Lilibet answers for him. Their posture is mirroring each other right now, both with their chin in their hand and sitting cross legged. Jordan smiles to herself because without their obvious physical differences, anyone would assume they're siblings. They even talk alike sometimes.

Theo and Lili sit like that for a few moments, looking at each other in silence until a group of students runs past and both of them turn at the sudden noise. It seems to wake Theo up, suddenly a lot less contemplative and more his normal posture.

"Anyway, we're starting research next week, probably Monday or Tuesday after rehearsal. It'll be a week or so before we should even try to choreograph together, I would guess." Theo uncrosses his legs and stretches them out in front of him, but there's still tension in him, like talking about it hasn't made any substantial difference.

Jordan lays a gentle hand on Lili's arm before she can respond, instead adding herself, "You'll keep us posted, yeah? Let us know if we can help?"

"Sure. But you have your own to be working on so I may have you look at some choreography later on, but for now I think we're...I think we're good, honestly." Theo leans back on his hands and lets the sun catch his face for a minute. It feels nice to spend some time outside while it's not either boiling hot or torrentially raining.

***

Emir can't stop staring at his hands. They're beautiful, covered in intricate designs, patterns that loop and join and tell a story. He feels adorned, like his body has been honored through the tradition. Emir thinks about how the art reminds him a bit of choreography, the way everything comes together, but the tiniest details make the most impact. He's been so patient, letting the henna artist work while he sat with his sisters and mum, chatting and laughing and smiling so bright. It's a memory he's always wanted to create, but wasn't sure he would ever get the chance. It feels fragile, so important to him in a way he's scared to admit sometimes.

Safiya needs the longest to have her mehndi applied, of course, so while Emir is done with just his hands and wrists, Safiya remains seated as they complete her wedding look. Emir leans over from her right and kisses her cheek because he can't exactly hug her right now. It'd ruin an exceptional amount of hard work.

"What was that for?" Safiya tilts her head, exactly like Emir always does when he has a question, and he feels safe knowing that he's surrounded by his family for the next few days. Classes only started a few weeks ago, but he's missed them.

"Thank you." Emir moves his hands around in the air to show her all the different sides. It's gone so well, honestly. Not a single nasty comment to deal with so far. The relatives have basically left him alone, and both his cousin Sashi and his Aunt Nadira have stayed nearby. He's not sure how much of that is interference by his parents, but whatever the reason, he's grateful.

"Oh, Emi..." Safiya wishes she could hug him tight right now, give him a proper cuddle like she's done since he was just a tiny little thing in her toddler arms. But the best she can do is give him an understanding look with tears starting in her eyes. "It seemed right to have you here. I'm *happy* you're here. I wouldn't want you anywhere else."

"You two done?" Saima groans from Safiya's left. "Yeah, we love Emi. The golden child. Yawn. I'm fucking starved."

"Pardon?" Natalie leans across Amina with a raised eyebrow to gently chastise Saima. Her daughters are certainly growing up if they're using that sort of language around the extended family. "There are sensitive ears around."

Saima rolls her eyes but settles back in her chair. "Should've eaten more while I still had my hands."

"Baba has free hands." Emir looks around, searching the room for his dad, and finally finding him surrounded by a group of Aunties. "He'll be back soon enough and you can bat your eyelashes until he brings you food."

"As if you don't pout until you get what you want." Saima says with a scoff. It seems she's really in a mood tonight. As fun as weddings are, they can be a bit much. Emir is *so glad* that he isn't staying at the hotel with the rest of the family. When they're done here tonight he gets to go back to decompress with Buddy on a nice walk around the block before cuddling up to sleep. Tomorrow is going to be a long day.

"Emi, can I stay with you tonight?" Amina asks, her own henna complete so she can move around as well.

"Course you can." Emir glances at Safiya, since it is technically her place. "As long as Yaya says it's alright."

"You lot stay wherever you please. Just be on time tomorrow." Safiya smiles gratefully at their dad as he walks over to them, a glass of water with a straw already being held out to Safiya. She takes a sip with a quick thank you before turning back to her siblings. "Actually, best you do stay with Emi tonight, Mina. Make sure he wakes up."

"It's not my fault that your dog is basically melatonin. He's. So. Fluffy." Emir says with bright eyes. Buddy always sleeps plastered to his back, warm and soft and comforting, like a sleeping draught. He's also the size of a small bear and constantly sheds fluff no matter how well he's brushed. They all love him so much.

"Yes, well, why do you think I chose him two years ago?" Safiya replies with a smile and a tinkling laugh. "It certainly wasn't for all the tricks he's never learned."

"Oi. Don't talk about my grandson that way." Saleem finally joins his children's conversation, carefully handing over a small food plate to Saima, not wanting to ruin the art on her hands. "Buddy's my favourite."

"Thought I was your favourite." Emir pouts up at his dad, and it would be incredibly effective if Saleem didn't have decades of experience resisting it at this point.

"It's a toss up. You learn to play fetch in the park, I'll consider moving you up the list." Saleem rubs his chin thoughtfully, the same glint in his eye that Emir and Saima get when they're being funny.

"Emi probably could, if we're honest." Amina laughs and elbows Saima. "Remember that time we scared him and he jumped on the table? Impressive, that."

"Not ashamed of that." Emir huffs, tossing his hair out of his eyes, annoyed. "Self-preservation, innit."

"They were half your size, Emi." Safiya laughs without restraint. She was the one who caught the prank on camera a few years ago around Christmas time. Their family doesn't really celebrate Christmas, but they still get the time off to muck around and make memories.

"But there were two of them." Emir says with another huff. "And I *thought* I was home alone that afternoon."

"Obviously." Saima giggles. "That's why we caught you doing that silly dance from *Love Actually* in only your boxers and Baba's old shirt."

"My little Emi. Always so sweet." Natalie leans over again, looking at Emir with her softest, proudest motherly look. She's adored having all of her kids in one place for an entire weekend. It's so rare now that two of them are grown, except for the main holidays when they're able to make time. "We miss you, you know that?"

"What about me? I'm in London, too." Safiya huffs now, just like her little brother. "*And* I'm getting married."

"Not a contest." Saleem adds, wanting to keep the peace. He can tell his kids are all getting tired at the end of a happy, but very long day. "We miss you both and we're more proud than we could ever tell you."

Saleem stands behind Natalie as he stares at his kids with love, hands on her shoulders and pressing a soft kiss to her temple that she leans into.

"Your Baba's right. I'm so proud to be your mum. Always." Natalie smiles at all of her kids and nuzzles back into her husband's steady presence until he lays his arms across her chest for a hug. "We probably won't see everyone together again until Emir's autumn show. Are you enjoying this one, Emi?"

Emir shares a proud smile as he tells them all about *Alice* and his role as the Rabbit. He spends the next few minutes catching them up on all three of the planned shows for the year, as well as a brief mention of his dissertation. He doesn't really want to get into it and pull the focus from Safiya, but he's grateful they all care so much about what he studies, always reminding him how proud they are of him and how they can't wait to see his next show. Natalie and Saleem even made a trip to Philadelphia to see one of his *Firebird* performances earlier this year. They'd had to save for months to afford the trip, and he knows it was an enormous sacrifice, even if they'd never dream of making him feel guilty about it.

The six of them chat comfortably as the party finishes, Emir soaking up the new memory like a welcome breeze on a summer day. He loves his sisters, his parents, even the extended family (when they behave). Sometimes he gets a bit too dedicated to dance, gets lost in the rehearsals and the productions and the routine of the studio. But when he gets a chance to step away, it's a much needed space to reset. And his family has always been that: the place he can be safe and loved, no matter what.

***

Theo: *Is Emir alright?*
Laurie: *Far as I know*
Laurie: *Something happen?*
Theo: *He hasn't been to class all day. I've never known him to miss class.*
Theo: *And I haven't seen him since we tried to work together Friday.*
Theo: *Which I thought went well...*
Theo: *But he's not been in class.*
Theo: *And I know it's not about me, but also maybe I was a dick without realising?*
Theo: *But I thought we got on, actually.*
Theo: *Or is he ill?*
Theo: *Sorry, none of my business.*
Theo: *But tell me if I fucked up? You're always honest with me.*
Laurie: *Fucking breathe Teddy*
Laurie: *He's been gone for the weekend with family*
Laurie: *Emi gets back tomorrow sometime*
Laurie: *I'm fine by the way thanks for asking*
Theo: */eye roll emoji/*
Theo: *I saw you this morning. Saw a bit too much of you this morning.*
Theo: *T is practically a nudist and yet they were clothed.*
Laurie: *I had boxers on*
Laurie: *What more do you want from me?*
Laurie: *T woke me up far too early for a Monday*
Theo: *You barely made it to class on time.*
Laurie: *I don't see your point*
Theo: *You're lucky I love you.*
Laurie: *Gay*
Theo: *Thank fuck for that.*
Theo: *You coming over later?*
Laurie: *Nah we're staying at mine since Emi is out*

***

"Honey, I'm home." Emir walks back into his flat mid-morning on Tuesday, proceeding directly over to where Laurie is working on the sofa and dropping his things to the ground so he can flop on top of him. Laurie groans as Emir wraps him up in a tight bear hug.

"Get *off* me, you lump." Laurie grumbles, begrudgingly hugging him back while being squashed into the sofa cushions.

"Mmm but you missed me. I know you did." Emir sits up and lets Laurie get readjusted, leaning back to relax for a minute himself.

"Absolutely not. I don't even know you. Who are you?" Laurie picks up his scattered things that Emir dislodged with his hug, glasses slipping down his nose while his hands are busy.

"No clue. If you figure it out, let me know." Emir grins with his eyes closed and lets out a sigh. "You here most of the day?"

"Just til noon. Lunch with T, then I have to go see my advisor." Laurie gives up on the work in front of him for a few minutes, setting aside a portfolio of fabric samples. "How was it?"

"Incredible, of course." Emir smiles at him and shows off his hands, fingers spread wide to expose all the tiny details. "And look!"

"That's class, that." Laurie takes one of Emir's hands in his own, admiring the designs, flipping each hand over to see what's on his palms as well. "How long does it last?"

"A week or so. Depends. I haven't had it before to know, really." Emir shrugs and reaches for his things on the ground. Pulling open the front of his rucksack, Emir hands a package to Laurie. "Here. Don't think I forgot you. I brought one for T as well. Ciaran and Gabe have to share but I think they would anyway."

"Natalie make these?" Laurie opens the package to a selection of goodies inside a tiffin, trying to decide what to start with. He chooses gulab jamun, his fingers sticky just from the first touch. "Your mum always makes the best stuff."

"Of course she did. Safiya had caterers for the whole weekend, but mum made some things herself. She says she likes it. Likes taking care of us." Emir decides to take one as well, even though he usually avoids something so sweet this early in the morning.

"You're covered in dog hair, mate." Laurie brushes a bit off of Emir's shoulder and sits on his own foot, leg tucked under while they chat. "Looks like you rolled around in a Furby factory."

"I don't mind. I spent as much time as I could with Buddy. Best sleep I've had in months." Emir smiles bright and brushes a few more hairs off his jumper.

"You know, your boy was worried about you. Did you forget to tell him you were leaving?" Laurie smirks at Emir, eyes piercing even behind his glasses.

"I don't have a boy. I don't have an anyone." Emir closes his rucksack and turns to face Laurie again in annoyance. This feels like teasing for some reason. "What are you on about?"

"You do, but we can fight about that another time." Laurie pats Emir on the knee like a big brother, as if he's sympathetic or something.

"Are you going to explain in English or have you learned Urdu while I wasn't looking?" Emir waves a hand expectantly towards Laurie before crossing his arms over his chest.

"Theo texted me, wondering why you weren't in class. Apparently someone never misses class and might've been ill." Laurie squeezes Emir's knee before closing up his tiffin to return to later.

"I was only gone for one day of class. Day and a half. Whatever." Emir looks off to the side. Since when does Theo care enough to check up on him when he's absent? Friday was fun, but does this mean they're like...friends or something? It's not that he minds, he's just surprised.

"Well, your absence was noted. Maybe he just wanted to work together, but he was worried he scared you off or something. Didn't you say things went well on Friday?"

Laurie pushes his glasses up his nose again and tosses his fringe out of his eyes. It's getting a bit long but he likes the way it sweeps up when he styles it.

"Better than I thought. But we didn't actually set a time to work together again so he was probably just anxious to get started." Emir shrugs, brushing it off as a work related concern. "I've got rehearsal in a few hours, so I'm going to rest for a while. I'm worn out from all the socialising."

"Go eat a snack first. And drink some water, or at the very least tea." Laurie turns back to his work while acting the mother hen. It's second nature with how many little siblings he has running around back home.

Emir sighs but grabs a banana from the kitchen and makes himself a cuppa before turning in for a few hours. Five minutes later, he's snoring facedown on his mattress.

***

Theo stops outside the dance building, staring at the door and letting out a sigh. Why is he here? Genuinely, why did his brain tell him to do this and let himself walk all this way? It's almost ten at night, practically bedtime. Emir might not even be here. But he probably is. Theo already walked across campus, so he may as well commit to...whatever it is he's doing.

He walks quietly through the corridor until he reaches the practice studio, the melody of the *Firebird* score accompanying his steps. Peeking around the open door, Theo watches as Emir finishes the choreography, which by now must be second nature to him. It's likely important to Emir if he still returns to it even months after the final performance. When the music ends, Theo knocks gently on the doorframe to get his attention, giving him a shy smile when Emir turns in surprise.

"Theo?" Emir has his arms resting above his head, wrists crossed while he catches his breath. "What're you doing here? It's late."

"Do you mind?" Theo tilts his head while toeing off his shoes. He doesn't technically need Emir's permission since it's a shared space, but he feels like he's intruding.

"I don't own the studio, Theo. You're free to barge in at your leisure." Emir teases, but he smiles, letting his hands drop back to his sides. "Isn't it past your bedtime?"

"Almost, yeah." Theo laughs softly while walking over to meet Emir. Holding out a thermos and waiting for Emir to take it he adds, "Here. Laurie said you weren't sick, but I figured just in case. It's only tea. So even if you aren't sick. Which, you don't look sick. But...tea."

"You...brought me tea?" Emir reaches out a tentative hand to take it from Theo, letting his fingers graze along the back of his hand before taking the tea in his grasp.

"You don't have to drink it. I just...Laurie said you were with family but, obviously, he didn't give me details. And I didn't know if it was happy or, like, a funeral or something else, but I didn't ask because it's none of my business, but either way I figured...tea?" Theo is talking very fast and staring at the ground. He's starting to feel like a complete arse for doing this. Emir never asked him to.

Emir watches Theo, the way his shoulders start to hunch and his eyes dart away, like he thinks he's done something wrong. Emir's surprised but he's certainly not upset. On instinct, he leans forward and kisses Theo's temple before moving away again, smiling gratefully as Theo looks up to meet his eyes, finally. "Thank you."

"It's nothing." Theo shrugs and puts his hands in his pockets. He can feel himself flushing, which happens at the slightest rise in emotion.

Theo's definitely not adjusted to how tactile Emir is yet. And maybe he's embarrassed, but this is just how he is. He likes taking care of people, doing little things to make them happy. It feels automatic for him, to try to take care and keep warm and make snacks and bring extra blankets. Or in this case: tea.

"I tried to make it how you like it but I wasn't sure." He's only seen Emir make tea for himself the one time, and they were technically fighting.

Emir pouts his lips before taking a careful sip, feeling like this is some sort of test. But surprisingly it's perfect, exactly how he prefers it. Even better than when T makes him a cuppa. "Mmmm. You guessed right."

"So...you're alright then?" Theo feels like he needs at least that much before he can leave. He doesn't want to waste Emir's time, but it was unusual for him to miss even a moment of class. Their differences aside, Theo knows how dedicated Emir is and he wouldn't miss class for something trivial.

"Brilliant." Emir smiles wide and it feels like Theo can breathe properly for the first time since entering the studio. Emir's joy warms the space, reaching into every corner and brushing away the tension. "My sister got married. Desi weddings are sort of...they take a few days. That's why I was gone past the weekend."

"Is that from...?" Theo glances down at Emir's hands before meeting his gaze again. He could spend hours studying the art he glimpsed, but staring isn't polite. He doesn't want Emir to feel like an exhibition. "Sorry, you don't have to tell me."

"You brought me tea. You're allowed a few questions, if you'd like." Emir sits down near the front of the studio, tapping the floor nearby and waiting for Theo to join him. "And yeah, it's a wedding tradition."

Theo sits down cautiously, crossing his legs and resting his hands in his lap. He wasn't really planning on staying but this is another one of those things they should be doing if they're going to be spending more time together. "Which sister? You have three, I think?"

Emir grins at Theo before answering. He knows they've never talked about their families, or really anything personal, so Theo must've figured that out just by paying attention when they're in group conversations with Laurie and T. How did Emir used to think he was so conceited and self-centred? "Safiya. She's the oldest. Right pain sometimes, but I love her."

"And she's the one with the dog?" Theo thinks he's heard Emir mention it before when talking to Laurie, and the joggers he left on the ground are covered in dog hair. So if he's putting context clues together...

"Buddy!" Emir pulls his phone out, always wanting to show off cute pictures of the dog. Really any dog, but especially one he's related to. "Look at him this morning. He's absolutely brilliant, Theo."

Theo loves seeing Emir excited like this. It's like standing in the sun early in the morning, refreshing and bright and calm. "Are you sure that's a dog? Looks a bit like a polar bear, mate."

"Nah, he's a softie. He just wants cuddles and walks." Emir smiles at the phone in his hand, laughing when he finds a picture where Buddy was mid-sneeze and showing it to Theo. "I had him all weekend so he's been a bit spoiled."

The conversation peters out as Emir puts his phone away and picks up his tea, Theo looking at his feet again. Emir doesn't mind taking a break or sitting in silence, but it seems Theo isn't ready to leave yet. And he does have to start working again in a few minutes.

"So...what'd I miss?" Emir nudges Theo's foot with his toe, thermos warm in his hands.

"Just class. I think they planned around your absence for rehearsal since we didn't need you for the scenes yesterday. And then today was only solos so you were on your own. But I suppose you're here rehearsing because you hate to miss and get behind." Theo sits back on his hands, chest opening while he answers Emir. It's nice to feel like he can take up a bit of space.

"I'm usually here every night, at least during the week. But you're not wrong about feeling behind." Emir unfolds his legs so he can stretch a bit. He doesn't want his body to get cold while they talk. "But I wasn't talking about class. I missed four entire days of gossip. Fill me in."

"And why would I be the one to ask about the gossip?" Theo teases, head tilting to the side while he stretches his own legs in front of himself to get comfortable. If only himself from a month ago could see what's unfolding.

"Please. You're gay and observant. Spill." Emir gestures vaguely in his direction before bending over his left knee to stretch his hamstring, tea still held in his free hand.

"It's been pretty quiet. Gabe and Ciaran had a fight about getting a fish. T is trying to get Laurie to do yoga so he'll relax about all the wedding stress. Lili and Jordan are pretty much the same, but we had a very gay picnic Saturday which was nice. Sean and Raphael are arguing about the sets for the winter show, but they're both pretending they're *not* arguing which made rehearsal interesting yesterday. Beth and Anthony scarred a few first years by necking in the student lounge after tech hall. Georgia accidentally cut her fringe too short and cried about it until Alfie told her she looked French. Now she's pretending it was on purpose, even though I'm pretty sure Alfie just wanted her to stop making it everyone's problem." Theo laughs at the memory as he finishes, Emir smiling up at him as he does.

"Sounds fairly tame. But most of the drama hits just before we go on break, so I shouldn't be surprised." Emir stretches back, hands on his bum and arching away from Theo, exposing his neck. Theo watches him, eyes following the line of his throat and down his arms, flushing when Emir sits back up and catches his eye. He wasn't staring. He wasn't. Except he was.

Emir's fit. Theo can admit that. But they're barely friends. It's been less than a week of getting along. Theo doesn't need to fuck this up by confusing it for more than it is. It's just that Emir's made more than a few passes at him, and while Theo knows they were to annoy him or whatever, that Emir thought he was straight until recently, it's not as if Theo receives that sort of attention very often. The feeling of Emir in his space back at the party was...memorable. And Theo's remembering it too well at the moment.

"I'll...um...I'll let you get back to work. D'you have time to get together tomorrow?" Theo stands up from the floor, hand running through the hair at the back of his head while staring at the ground again.

"Your place or mine?" Emir let himself tease Theo, delighting in the way he flushes at the innuendo. But he knows Theo will ignore it and pretend it was a strictly professional question. Maybe one day Emir will crack through that carefully maintained composure, but not tonight.

"Um...mine?" Theo glances at Emir with a furrowed brow. What's that tone? "If that's alright? What time d'you think?"

"I know you need your beauty sleep, so I won't keep you up too late. Let's say eight?" Emir takes one last sip of tea before setting it down near his Hydro Flask. "Do you want me to bring anything or did you already have something planned?"

"I have everything planned for the next three months, but I can be flexible." Theo starts pulling his shoes back on in the doorway, careful not to step on the Marley with his trainers.

"I'll bet you can." Emir mutters to himself, eyes catching the curve of Theo's arse as he bends over to tie his laces.

"Hm?" Theo stands back up with another questioning look. There's a vibe happening, but he's not sure what flavour.

"Nothing. Just said I'll be there." Emir watches him nod and start to leave before he calls out. "And thanks for the tea!"

He smiles to himself looking over at the thermos nestled amongst his other belongings. That was...sweet. Caring. Something a real mate would do to check up on him. T and Laurie have shown up often enough to bring him things, to worry about him while he spends late nights in the studio, but they're the only ones who've ever bothered. Until now.

***

Theo's just finished in the shower, towelling himself off when his phone vibrates with a text from an unknown number.

Unknown: *you didn't get my number*
Unknown: *bit rude if I'm honest*
Unknown: *make plans for tomorrow then fuck off without even asking*

Theo's confused reading the first two, until the third text comes through and he laughs out loud, stifling it behind his hand once he remembers his flatmates. He walks across the hall and into his bedroom before typing his answer, narrowly missing the doorframe as he does.

Theo: *Who are you and how do you have my number?*
Unknown: *how many lads have you made plans with tomorrow?*
Unknown: *i thought I was special*
Unknown: */broken heart emoji/*
Theo: *So dramatic. Is this a Capricorn thing?*
Theo: *I'm used to it with Laurie but I figured that was more a twink drama kid thing*
Unknown: *call laurie a twink to his face and let me watch. it's been a while since i've seen him destroy someone. i'll be the one with popcorn and a first aid kit.*

Theo pauses to save Emir's number to his phone with a grin, sitting on the edge of his bed with the towel wrapped around his waist. At least he won't have to bother Laurie next time he's worried about Emir. Not that there will be a next time, of course. But just in case.

Theo: *But how is it you have /my/ number?*
Emir: *you gave it to me you bellend*
Theo: *Did I? You'd think I'd remember that.*
Emir: *first week of first year. you sent it to all the first year dance students at the bottom of that email*
Emir: *nerd*

Emir: maybe i'll finally update how i have you saved in my phone
Theo: What am I saved as? Wanker?
Emir: /screenshot of Theo's contact, including phone and email, with the title: dance daddy tongue emoji/
Theo: You're a menace.
Theo: What was it actually?
Emir: Laurie's favourite white boy with an eye roll emoji
Theo: Have you forgotten that Laurie is also white ™?
Emir: he's /my/ favourite white boy. but i have him saved as Tempest unless T gets hold of my phone and changes it to something disgustingly sappy
Theo: What about Ciaran and Gabe?
Emir: nah they've got proper names in my contacts
Emir: except that weekend I walked into your place with T and found them at it on the sofa
Emir: i had them marked as hoe 1 and hoe 2 for about a month until I forgave them
Emir: the least they could do is use Ciaran's room ffs or give us a warning
Emir: they didn't even invite us to join. rude.

Theo tosses aside his towel to keep getting ready for sleep, moisturising and pulling on a pair of boxers and a Green Lantern t-shirt while they banter via text. He climbs into bed and plugs in his phone so he can keep typing for a bit. He usually reads before sleep, but he can spare a few minutes for whatever this is.

Theo: All four of them are so far gone for their person that they're absolutely beyond help.
Theo: You'd think they'd calm down two years into it but no. I wasn't even surprised when Laurie proposed to T last year, even though we're so young.
Theo: Happy for them though.
Emir: don't encourage them. i'm pretty sure they'd just shag in the open if we didn't remind them to at least go behind a door
Emir: and i know way more than i ever wanted about all four of their sexual preferences
Theo: I suppose it's just part of uni. T and Ciaran both joke about becoming naturists so I think we've been relatively lucky so far, if I'm honest.
Emir: you're the one who chose to live with them
Theo: Oh and Laurie is such an angel, is he?
Emir: yes. my messy, dramatic, rainbow angel. maybe more like a pixie
Emir: whatever he is has wings
Theo: And T is a mermaid. Match made in heaven?
Theo: Nah that doesn't seem gay enough.
Emir: match made in wonderland, maybe?

Theo: *We can workshop it. Do a survey.*

Theo is starting to get sleepy, snuggled into his pillows and smiling at his phone, glasses a bit crushed against his face from how he's laying. He yawns and scrolls back up to reread what they've said so far, his chest warm and light. They've always bantered so immediately, but this is the fun kind. No venom being thrown, just...easy. Nice. They're a match intellectually, their energy feeding off each other, and for once it's positive. It feels so fucking freeing.

Emir: *isn't it past your bedtime, princess?*
Theo: *You're the one keeping me up?*
Emir: *you want to rephrase that?*
Theo: *Woof*
Theo: *Goodnight. See you in tech hall.*
Emir: */gif of minion waving goodbye/*

Theo smiles at the little yellow wave before turning off his phone and rolling onto his side, glasses set beside the water on his nightstand. He yawns and snuggles into his sheets, letting out a happy sigh before drifting off to sleep.

CHAPTER SIX

Emir shows up to Theo's flat just before eight, rucksack over his shoulders and his mind swirling with uncertainty. Is he supposed to knock? Or does he text now that they do that? Nothing seemed off in class today besides sharing a smile occasionally, which they wouldn't have been able to accomplish more than a week ago. God, was it really just last week that they were fighting in this exact flat after their friends abandoned them to their argument? This is silly. Emir's been here hundreds of times before. He'll just knock. Why is he overthinking this?

Tapping gently on the flat door, Emir's surprised when it opens immediately to Ciaran's bright smile and a, "Good, you're early!"

"Ciaran?" Emir hugs him back as he's pulled inside, door clicking shutting behind them somehow. "Were you expecting me?"

"Course I was. Teddy's been stress cleaning for an hour." Ciaran grins as he steps away again, Emir barely recovering before Gabe pulls him in for a hug as well.

"Hi, Emi. Glad you're here." Gabe seems to have been waiting just behind Ciaran. What is with the welcoming committee?

"Hello?" Emir moves back from the hug with a confused smile, looking around the flat behind them as if that would explain what's happening. "Are you two, like, working with us tonight or something?"

"Nope!" Ciaran is practically chirping, way too excited for a Wednesday night. "We missed you at family dinner, though."

"I needed to catch up in the studio. Can't fall behind." Emir shrugs off the concern, and his rucksack with it, dropping it near the door with his trainers. "But maybe next week."

"Emir?" Theo pokes his head out of his room, clearly in the middle of something. "You're early."

"Yeah, I – " Emir stops himself from continuing because... "Why are you naked?"

Emir only got a glimpse, but there were bare shoulders and a broad chest on display, which wasn't exactly where he thought this night was headed.

"I'M NOT NAKED!" Theo hides behind the door frame again, face absolutely on fire while he hurries to pull on the shirt in his hand. It's only green but it'll have to do. What should he even wear to research with his recent antagonist turned friendish person? He wants to be comfortable, but not too comfortable, and look like he made an effort but not enough it'd be weird, and Emir usually sees him at the studio so really anything besides dripping sweat is an improvement.

"He gave up cleaning ten minutes ago and ever since he's been trying on his entire wardrobe." Gabe stage whispers to Emir, definitely loud enough that everyone in the flat can hear. "You see, it takes a while because he has this whole folding technique and every shirt that went on and back off again had to be refolded properly."

Emir giggles at that because he barely had time to jump in the shower and throw on whatever was nearest to rush over here. Looking down at himself, he sees he's in Laurie's joggers, an inside out pink jumper with a white vest underneath, and fuzzy black socks. Not exactly winning any fashion awards, but he's cosy.

Theo's still flushed as he walks out of his bedroom to meet Emir, Ciaran and Gabe standing together and watching them interact as if they're at the zoo.

"Sorry. I thought I had a few more minutes, but I'm ready now." Theo stands in front of him awkwardly for a moment until Emir pulls him into a hug. It'd be weird if he didn't, seeing as he already hugged both Ciaran and Gabe. Also, he has a hunch that Theo doesn't get enough hugs.

"Didn't know you wore glasses." Emir mumbles near Theo's ear, pulling back again after just a moment. He still isn't quite sure where their boundaries are, and he doesn't want to make Theo uncomfortable. But Theo was still adjusting to the hug, his arms barely settling around Emir before he was moving away again. His hands don't disconnect from Emir right away, lingering on his waist before letting them drop.

"Just at night. My eyes get tired watching telly or staring at the computer for too long." Theo shrugs, hands in his pockets now as he looks down at his bare toes. "Did you have time to eat after the studio?"

"I'm fine." Emir ignores his question and turns to Ciaran and Gabe. "So are you two staying? I think we're going to be watching a fair amount of videos, so if you need quiet we could wear headphones or something."

"We actually wanted to watch the Derby game Ciaran missed." Gabe pulls Ciaran into his side. "Is it alright if we use the big screen out here? I'm going to work on some sheet music while we watch and it helps to spread out."

"Yeah that's...we can use my room. We'll just use my laptop." Theo glances up at Emir to see a slow smile growing across his delicate features. Why does he look like Laurie just before he gets up to mischief?

"Never been in your room before." Emir grins, leaning down to pick up his rucksack again and starting to unzip it. Ciaran and Gabe finally shuffle away to get settled on one of the sofas, whispering between themselves, Theo still waiting on Emir before doing anything else. Emir opens the top pocket and reaches inside, fishing out the thermos that Theo had given him yesterday and holding it out to him. "I believe this belongs to you, princess."

Theo can't help but smile at the nickname, taking the thermos back and heading toward the kitchen. "You can go ahead into my room and get comfortable. Not like - fuck, why did I say it like that?"

Emir laughs as he closes his bag again, already walking toward Theo's room. "You're the one who greeted me in the nude, mate."

"I didn't - " Theo sighs and runs a hand through his hair. "Nevermind. Be there in a minute."

Theo watches Emir wander into his room with what appears to be an unhealthy level of excitement. Sure, he's never been in Theo's room before, but it's not exactly noteworthy. Theo sets down the thermos, reaching instead for the fridge to take out the leftovers he already set aside for Emir. He'd expected Emir at family dinner now that they were...not fighting. So really he's just following through on an expectation, or so he tells himself as he places the stir fry in the microwave to reheat.

While Emir's food is in the microwave, Theo takes the thermos to the sink to wash. But when he opens it up there's a note inside. Theo looks at where Emir is hidden from view in his room, presumably snooping. Quietly, because the last thing he needs is to alert the two loveable meddlers on the sofa, Theo takes the note in hand to see what Emir left him (and notices the thermos is thoroughly cleaned already). It's a piece of cardstock, seemingly ripped from some sort of sketch book, and there's a pencil drawing of a cup of tea, delicately shaded and with a steam cloud with words in a language he doesn't know. But before he can google what it says the microwave beeps at him, making him jump. He'd forgotten what he was doing. Theo carefully tucks the note away in his pocket and stows the thermos back in the cupboard where it belongs. He can figure it out later.

Theo finds a tray, lays it with cutlery and a napkin, two glasses of water, a bowl of mixed nuts for himself to snack on, and the reheated stir-fry for Emir.

"Keep the door open, young man." Ciaran calls over, not even taking his eyes off the game.

"Fuck off, Ciaran." Theo shouts back, laughing as he does. He knew his friends would be like this, but they're showing a level of interest in this working relationship beyond his expectations.

Emir hasn't exactly been snooping, but he's spent the last few minutes looking at his surroundings. He's *never* been invited into Theo's space before and it is...a lot to process. This is far and away the neatest flat he's been invited into during his time at university. It's not like it's sterile; the room actually looks exceptionally comfortable. But where Emir has possessions strewn about, dance shoes and art notebooks and more literature on every surface than he could account for, Theo clearly has a spot for everything. He doesn't want to open any drawers, but Theo's bookshelf is just sitting there across from his bed and Theo couldn't blame him for scanning the titles.

The top shelf seems like uni materials, though not for any courses required for a dance student. But the bottom three shelves are like a trove of queer literature, the classics like Wilde of course, but also independent authors Emir hasn't even heard of, mixed in with a bit of modern romance, some of which Emir has read for his book club. Emir glances around at the neat desk, every cord secured with an organising clip, Theo's laptop charging on top.

And then there's the bed, which Emir assumes is where they'll sit to watch whatever Theo has planned for them. It's neatly made, all soft pillows and pressed linen. Theo must make his bed every morning when he wakes up. And there's a candle lit on the bedside table, some sort of soft, woodsy smell filling the room. It's neat, neater than Emir could ever hope to be, but it's warm. It's...well, Emir thinks it's a lot like Theo. At least a lot like the Theo he's just starting to know.

"Should I be expecting to find all my trousers inside out tomorrow?" Theo walks into his bedroom, setting the tray on the corner of his desk and turning to Emir.

"Laurie?" Emir is all too familiar with Laurie's little pranks.

"Laurie." Theo laughs softly in confirmation, hands back in his pockets, fingertips brushing over the note still kept there. He doesn't think he's meant to bring it up. Emir seems like the type who would want him to figure it out first. "I think we can watch everything on my laptop. I'll take notes, but you don't need to. I'm not sure what your learning style is, to be honest. But I like notes."

"I've noticed." Emir sits cautiously on the side of Theo's bed, not wanting to invite himself any further without permission, but also hoping Theo will sit down so they can get started. It wasn't a coincidence that Emir hid a note in that thermos. He figured that would be the way to connect with Theo, to thank him properly for the gesture and the consideration behind it. "Are you not only studying dance?"

"Hm?" Theo moves to unplug his laptop from the charger and set it on the bed.

"Top shelf. Those aren't for dance." Emir nods towards the bookshelf, pulling his legs up so he's cross legged near the foot of Theo's bed now. There's a soft red blanket folded next to him and Emir sort of wishes he could snuggle up inside of it.

"Oh." Theo looks up to meet Emir's gaze, once again realising how little they know of each other. "I study business, too...just in case."

"In case of what?" Emir's genuinely curious. He expected Theo to say he just liked it or something, assuming that Theo had some sort of side interest in the business part of dance companies. Plenty of people study broadly while they have the opportunity. But that didn't sound like genuine interest.

"I'm not unrealistic, Emir. I know there's a good chance that I'll graduate and never dance again." Theo's turned away from Emir, picking up the tray to sit between them while they start work.

"You're telling me that you study business because you think you won't have a career in dance? After all this?" Emir actually can't believe that. Theo is more dedicated to dance than almost anyone else he's ever known. Even when they were fighting, the reason they always pushed each other to be better is because they were working against each other to be the best in the programme. And it was never a foregone conclusion, both of them excelling in different ways. "Theo, that's daft."

"It's just how it is." Theo sits cautiously on the edge of the bed, trying not to upset the things he's just set down with any sudden movement. "I work hard and I'm moderately talented, but that's not enough. I'll never have what you have, Emir."

"I'm not even sure what that means, but I'm starting to think that you may be delusional." Emir changes how he's sitting so that he's facing Theo fully, even though Theo still has his back to him, staring at his hands in his lap. "Theo, please look at me."

Theo sighs but turns so their eyes meet. He's genuinely not trying to be a downer, but he's more than aware of his chances at a professional dance career. It's unlikely that he'll get a contract with a company in London. He has a much better chance working as a choreographer, but even that requires connections and an unreal amount of luck, and even then most companies want their choreographers to have professional experience as a dancer first. It doesn't matter how hard he works if he doesn't happen upon someone willing to see his work.

"Do you want a career in dance, Theo?" Emir is staring hard, his eyes blazing amber and seeing right through Theo's veil of caution.

"Of course I do, it's just - " Theo stops when Emir sets a hand on top of his, effectively silencing him. The henna captures Theo's attention, drawing his gaze while he gets lost in the patterns.

"If you want a career, you'll have one. I'm not saying don't have a backup. I'm saying, as someone who is unbiased and used to resent you quite a bit, that you are more than moderately talented and that your work ethic will count for far more than most dancers' ten minutes of stage presence. If you want to dance, or teach, or choreograph, or whichever path feels right to you, it *will* be an option. And I'm not blowing smoke up your arse. I can't believe you don't understand how important you are."

Emir feels something inside him twisting when he sees the doubt in Theo's eyes. He's never thought of Theo as overconfident. Pretentious? Sure. A bit insufferable at times? Definitely. But he had no idea that Theo thought so little of his own abilities, that he thought so little of himself.

"You don't have to feel sorry for me or whatever." Theo turns to face him better, keeping his hand under Emir's. It's comforting. "I was just being honest about why I study business. We really don't have to talk about it."

"Theo..." Emir sighs and withdraws himself, getting up from the bed and walking around it until he's standing directly in front of Theo.

Laying his hands on Theo's shoulders, Emir gives them a gentle squeeze and makes sure he has his full attention before continuing. "You say you can never have what I have? I feel exactly the same. I will never have your clarity. You have this...direction. This constancy. Everything you do has depth. Most people spend their whole lives searching for that sort of grounding and you just...have it. I've always been envious of that, since the first day we met. I can fly, but you? Theo, you're the fucking sky. You don't even see the way you cradle the world around you, and everyone in it."

Theo's stunned, unable to process what he's hearing. He's shocked, honestly. Emir looks entirely sincere, his eyes giving everything away. He's looking at Theo with something close to wonder, and Theo's trying to figure out how that's even possible. He's...the sky? To Emir fucking Shah?

"Emir –" Theo's breathless, completely unsure of what to say, his stomach falling further after each earnest word Emir spoke. "That's the kindest thing that anyone has ever said to me. I don't even know what to do with that."

Emir moves his hands from Theo's shoulders to tug at his forearms instead until he's standing again. He folds Theo into a hug, just like Friday night, holding him and waiting until he feels Theo relax against him. Emir's said enough for now. He wonders how often people take Theo for granted if no one has ever made the time to remind Theo of how integral he is. Emir has always seen the way that every single student looks up to Theo, the way the teachers default to his leadership at rehearsals, the way their friends have always admired him and the comfort he so readily offers.

It used to bother Emir, like an itch for something he couldn't have. He would never lead others the way Theo does on instinct. But maybe what Theo needs is someone in his corner who sees that, even if it's natural, it's not easy for Theo, that all the effort and commitment has a cost and that someone acknowledges it. Maybe Theo needs someone who doesn't have expectations for him. And he definitely needs more hugs.

Theo holds Emir, breathes him in and shares his space, reciting his words over and over in his own head like a mantra. It's not that his friends and family don't say they're proud of him or remind him he's good at what he does, but this is different. Emir had no motivation to say those things, no reason to be so earnestly kind and reassuring. He could've just brushed it off and moved on. But he didn't. He stopped Theo and made sure he heard those words. And then he hugged him again, as if it was the most natural thing in the world to cradle Theo's head on his shoulder and keep him close. Theo's never felt so seen. Protected, even.

They hold each other close for what could be an entire minute, neither of them wanting to pull away from each other. A moment so poignant changes things between them, Theo offering up one of his deepest vulnerabilities and Emir soothing it away with grace. But of course they do eventually end their embrace, slowly pulling away from each other and creating space, but not nearly as much as before. Emir quietly returns to the side of the bed he was on and Theo sits across from him, reaching for the tray to get them both settled before opening his laptop to work.

"Didn't you already eat with the others?" Emir asks when Theo scoots the tray closer, careful not to spill the water from the glasses.

"It's for you, of course." Theo smiles, taking his own snack off the tray and pushing the rest toward Emir. "I thought Laurie would invite you tonight, and then, when you weren't there, I felt bad because I should've known you wouldn't be since you said eight when we talked last night. And as you being here now means you aren't eating back at your place..."

"You're, like, a proper good person, you know that?" Emir reaches over and pinches Theo's cheek. It's a tease but it's also sincere.

Emir's starting to understand why some of his favourite people are so devoted to Theo. He cares about his friends, and not in a way that's put on. And maybe Emir is starting to see himself as one of those friends, especially as Theo continues to go out of his way to think of Emir, like how Laurie makes sure he puts on his warmups, or T reminds him to take naps when his head is swimming. Now he has Theo looking out for him as well, and he's becoming one of Emir's safe people. It probably helps that the people Emir trusts most already adore him, so Theo has built in references. Emir's really glad they've moved past their feud and can start figuring out how to be friends.

Theo scrunches his nose at the pinch and swats Emir's hand away gently, opening his laptop to get them started on their actual goal for the evening. "So I figured tonight is *Swan Lake* - "

But before he can explain any further Emir groans, mouth already full of stir fry. Apparently the drama can hit at any time.

"Theo, *why?*" Emir shakes his head before stabbing a piece of tofu with his fork. Who knew simple utensil movement could hold so much gay judgement? "I know it's a classic but it's so - the straights are *exhausting*. Like, *Romeo and Juliet* is even worse, but *Swan Lake?* Even *Black Swan* couldn't make it properly queer."

"Oh how little faith you have in the process." Theo scoots back against the headboard, placing the laptop beside him and waiting for Emir to follow his lead. "I never said it was *only Swan Lake.*"

"That's literally the Royal Ballet." Emir glares at the screen as if he's personally offended. Theo can't help but laugh at the way that Emir was holding him close just moments ago and now he's being all dramatic and gay and fun. How did Theo ever think he was shallow? Emir might contain the most depth of anyone he knows, layer upon layer of personality and life beneath potentially the most fit exterior Theo has ever seen. Not that the last bit matters, of course, except in the way that most people brush off everything else about Emir to focus on his appearance.

"We're only watching the romance scenes. For reference. We have to know what the audience is expecting if we intend to perform a love story. You know how important audience response can be. Just look at what you did with *Firebird.*" Theo presses play, knowing they can ignore the beginning part of this scene. He reaches for one of his notebooks in his bedside table and grabs a pen to go along with it, opening to a blank page and dating it in the top right corner as he sits back up.

"Quite a view..." Emir mumbles as Theo leans over the side of the bed, his arse practically bulging at Emir through his tight joggers.

Theo turns his head and catches Emir staring, swatting him softly on the chest when he does. "Stop ogling and focus. My arse can be admired later."

"Is that a promise?" Emir tilts his head, staring at Theo's lips now before meeting his eyes again. He's a shameless flirt when he wants to be, especially with his friends. Laurie and T are so used to it now that they usually flirt back without hesitation.

"Finish your dinner and watch the dancers, Emir." Theo laughs, making a note to tell T no feathers for their costumes, no matter how much either of them beg him at some point.

Emir chews on a carrot, still ignoring the ballet to watch Theo. He's so sweet like this, glasses and soft clothes and hunching over his notebook to scribble whatever comes to mind as he watches. And Emir can tell he's really analysing what he sees, not just passively viewing the scene.

"You're staring." Theo smirks while writing a note about the transformation trope that they're going to see repeated in so many of these classic ballets. He wonders if that's something they should incorporate or at the very least hint at...

"You're more interesting than the video." Emir shrugs, shifting on the bed so he's leaning back against the headboard too. There's a tray between them and Theo's laptop, but Theo doesn't have people in his bed very often. Lili, Laurie, and T (and if the other is out of town, Ciaran and Gabe) are the only ones who make a habit of it, but this is decidedly different. He's conscious of the space, of how it feels both like a canyon and like the heat of Emir's skin is pressed against his own.

"Find me fascinating later. We have to distil which parts of these scenes we care about, and I can't decide that on my own." Theo glances over at Emir and sees him still staring, happily enjoying his dinner with a sparkle in his eye. It's very distracting. Theo's only taken about six lines of useful notes so far and they're almost five minutes into the video.

"Tell me when you switch to Bourne's version. There's this one lift in the final scene that we should try." Emir has seen the original *Swan Lake* enough times that he could probably dance it from memory, and he'd much rather spend a few minutes entertaining himself instead of watching it yet again.

"Are you going to pay attention if I switch to that?" Theo asks, reaching out to pause the video partway through Act II's pas de deux. It's a beautiful scene, but it's literally the blueprint. Maybe Emir's right that they should switch to watching something they haven't already studied to death during their training.

"Are you going to sit next to me and not halfway off the side of the bed?" Emir glances down at Theo's lap and how he's so close to the edge Emir could unseat him with barely a nudge. "I won't bite."

"Not even if I ask nicely?" Theo surprises himself with that, but it just flew to the front of his mind. There's something about how playful Emir is, some combination of serious artistry and endearing mischief that Theo can't help but lean into.

"I'm learning so much about you tonight, baby." Emir grins, dropping his fork to tug on Theo's arm until he scoots closer. "Maybe I *should* be taking notes."

"Are you always such a ridiculous flirt?" Theo scoots closer with a smile, picking up his laptop to set across their legs instead, empty tray forgotten at the foot of the bed.

"It's part of my charm." Emir scoots himself closer as well, their sides touching now. If someone were to peek around the open door they'd look like proper mates, not two people who loathed each other just a week ago. "Please show me the gay swans. I promise I'll be useful."

"I'm glad you'll be paying attention, but I hope you know you're worth more than the utility you offer." Theo isn't looking at Emir, instead he's scrolling through his bookmarks for the scene Emir mentioned. "And you're not just useful, Emir, you're integral. This is both of our work, not just mine."

"Who the fuck are you and where is that wanker I've been arguing with for two years?" Emir still has his dinner in his hands which is good because he just had the overwhelming desire to run them through Theo's hair. What the hell is happening to him? They stop arguing and all of the sudden Theo's this endearing, soft, golden retriever of a person who says things like *you're integral* as if that isn't exactly the sort of thing that no one says aloud because from anyone else it would sound pretentious. And Emir used to hear it that way, too. But not anymore.

"You were busy thinking I was straight." Theo finds the clip he's looking for and resettles, laptop shared between their laps awkwardly so the screen is at a bit of an angle. "Now, gay swans. Is this the scene you meant?"

"Yeah..." Emir glances towards the screen, doing his best to actually focus while finishing the food Theo made for him. He can hear Theo scribbling notes beside him, the two of them comfortably quiet while the story unfolds before them. The final scene isn't very long, but there's a whole intro to sit through before it gets to the partnering. But then it's just the two leads, both 'injured' and – "There! That one."

"Want me to rewind?" Theo looks toward Emir and sees his eyes fixed on the screen, tracing the shapes of the dancers as they support each other through space. He picks up the laptop so he can control the video again.

"Go back a bit and then watch how they both use their weight to support the lift." Emir sets his empty plate aside on the tray at the foot of the bed, picking up the red blanket while he does. He's not chilly, but he likes to be cuddled up in soft blankets. Always. "And the arms. It just...something about it."

"It feels intimate, but not sexual." Theo states, understanding exactly what Emir means. "Even without the context of the scene, the choreography makes it clear that the moment is an emotional bond between the characters."

"I want that." Emir says, clear and with intense focus on the screen. Theo replays the short clip again, both of them watching the moment they come together and the Swan cradles the Prince. "That feeling. I want people to see that when they watch us."

"That's perfect, honestly. That gives me a direction to follow while we work on this." Theo pauses the video, the frame stuck on the characters' embrace. "I want us to review the classics and the works they inspire, but it helps to have a goal in mind, right?"

Emir opens the blanket so he can burrow under it, getting comfortable and laying down a bit further on the bed. He looks up at Theo, face partially hidden beneath the red fluff, his eyes wide. "It's not only about me though. I want that, but if the story you need to tell isn't that, we'll find a way to fit them together."

Theo smiles down at Emir, cuddled up in his blanket beside him. He slides down a bit as well, taking a sip of his water and ignoring the screen for now. "I want that too. I don't want it to be a parody of a traditional romance, and I also don't want it to do what so many others do. Even Bourne's *Swan Lake* if I'm honest. Most of it is almost...it's like he was timid when it came to allowing the male dancers to have femininity. At most they lean towards neutral. Like, there's no dancers en pointe, and they're all bare-chested as if to prove *'look it's all lads, we promise'*. And in interviews he never explicitly stated that it was queer. Which, I think in the moment it was created made a lot of sense. But..."

He rotates so he's facing Emir better, their eyes level and gaze connected. "We're in a different moment and I want to tell a more nuanced story. One with room for masculine and feminine and both and neither to all work together, and for the story to be both sensual and sexual, if that's something we're both comfortable with. I don't mean for shock value. But I'm a bit sick of queer stories either shying away from sex entirely or focusing only on shagging, because real life and real love is never that. It's shades of grey, or rainbow if that's more your thing, overlapping and intertwining, and it's a disservice to queer people to only tell a portion of our truth...Sorry, that was a bit of a ramble."

"Theo?" Emir stays cuddled under the blanket, soaking up Theo's words like water in the desert. He's never had someone echo his thoughts back to him so completely.

"Too much?" Theo scratches at the back of his head, already planning to clarify and apologise in case he crossed some sort of line.

"Actually, I was going to say that I'm really glad we're doing this together. Even if our methods are different, I think we're on exactly the same page." Emir opens up the blanket from around his shoulders so he can get up and clear away the tray from earlier. "Can we watch Ballet Trockadero next?"

"How'd you know they were on the list?" Theo watches Emir tidy up their snacks, leaving behind both of their water glasses and moving towards the bedroom door.

"Because I'm starting to know you and you definitely appreciate an entire drag ballet." Emir wanders out and into the kitchen before Theo can respond, quickly taking care of his dish and setting the things out of the way to be put away properly later.

"How's it going?" Ciaran asks from the sofa, Gabe's head in his lap while he plays with his curls.

"Mostly gay." Emir turns to them with a bright smile. "What happened to sheet music?"

"Not gay enough." Gabe answers from Ciaran's lap, watching Emir upside down with a grin. "Need anything?"

"Nah. Theo's got us covered. Thanks though." Emir walks over to them for a moment to kiss each of them on the tops of their heads. He spends more time with T and Laurie, but these two are just as loveable. He's really going to miss them next year if they do end up moving to New York like they keep hinting at. It's Gabriel's hometown, so it makes sense, but he's still sad to think of them so far away.

While Emir is in the common area, Theo takes the notecard out of his pocket and hurries to open Google. At first, nothing. But after a minute he thinks he figures out what's written there. Apparently it's Urdu (which Theo didn't know Emir wrote or spoke until now), and it says, *the adventure begins with tea. thank you, princess*". Theo just stares at his phone for a moment feeling emotional. It's just a little drawing with a scrawled quote, but it's so...delicate. And he's starting to like his new nickname far too much.

He's never felt especially feminine, but something about the way Emir calls him princess feels sweet, like he's one of Emir's people now. And Emir seems to keep his circle pretty small, just T and Laurie, with Ciaran and Gabe a step behind them. But now Theo has a nickname, and a little drawing, and Emir said all those lovely things about how he's the sky, and Theo isn't sure where to store any of what he's feeling.

But he hears Emir leaving the kitchen so he opens his bedside table to tuck the card safely inside. If they're taking turns, it's definitely on him to offer the next olive branch, but he thinks he'll wait a day or so. Tonight seems comfortable and he doesn't feel any need to push Emir. They've already made an incredible amount of progress in just a few days.

"Act II? And I want to watch the dying swan." Emir walks back in and straight to the spot he left, picking up the blanket and tossing it across both of them, laptop included.

"So we can compare it to the Royal Ballet, is that it?" Theo frees the laptop from under the blanket and gets comfortable, tucking his feet under and feeling decidedly cosy. He could lay in bed and watch dance all day. Or at least most of the day. He and Lili have spent entire weekends just like this, with snacks and blankets and laptops either in one of their rooms or sprawled across a sofa. So even if this is technically work, it mostly feels like downtime, and he finds he doesn't mind having Emir here at all. He's so bright, and Theo can't help but cuddle a little closer.

Theo finds the video they're looking for and starts it, still marvelling at its existence even after all these years. He remembers the first time he discovered Les Ballets Trockadero, amazed by the fact that there was an entire internationally famous ballet company where men danced en pointe and did it in drag. "You know, *Swan Lake* was the only time I've been able to see them live. When I was about 15, I think."

"You've seen them?" Emir turns to Theo, snuggling further into the blanket with his hands bunched up near his chest. "What was it like?"

"They're incredible. Every single one of them, honestly." Theo's still watching the six swans on the screen, laughing as one of them goes to the wrong side of the stage. He's always loved the way this company combines comedy with actual ballet. Because when they do it, they're not making fun of queer people, they're embracing the comedy as part of the whole. "I've always wanted to meet them but never got the chance."

"They're doing shows in London this season. We should go." Emir is watching the dancers now too, giggling at the ensemble. Watching this is like a serotonin boost, honestly.

"Field trip?" Theo smiles when Emir nods, that glimmer back in his eyes as he watches the swans. So Theo relaxes beside him, both of them watching and laughing and sighing through the second act. When the video ends, Theo starts to put his things away because these three versions were the ones he had in mind for tonight. But Emir stops him with a gentle hand on his wrist.

"I want to watch the dying swan. It's my favourite." Emir waits for Theo to release the laptop, letting Emir find the video he wants.

"It's not part of *Swan Lake* though." Theo also loves that variation, and really it'd be impossible to find a single dancer who didn't grow up dreaming of that moment: alone on stage, moving the audience to tears in the space of a few short minutes.

"But it's impacted every single performance of *Swan Lake*, so... Also, I don't care. I just want to watch it." Emir smiles at Theo and starts the video, stars in his eyes as he hears the first few notes. Theo keeps his gaze for a moment longer, sharing he isn't exactly sure what, but maybe there's some string of understanding being passed back and forth tonight, a window into each other's interests that feels remarkably like a mirror.

"Plisetskaya's version?" Theo's always been partial to this one too, even though he has a few favourites. But the way Emir connects to this video seems fairly personal. Theo doesn't bother taking notes since it's not partner work and he doesn't really need to analyse it in the same way.

"This video is the reason I started pointe." Emir takes a few moments to answer Theo's unasked question, sighing as he watches Plisetskaya cambré back towards the audience. "It's my favourite song in the world."

Theo would usually be focused on the video, but he can't take his eyes off Emir right now. He looks so content, eyes shining and the softest smile that Theo has ever seen. He follows every movement as if it's brand new to him, and Theo wonders what he's thinking about. He wonders if Emir's ever had the chance to perform this, especially since it means so much to him.

When the video ends, Emir replays it, ignoring Theo's soft laugh as he does. He'll never tire of this or stop admiring how beautifully simple it is. It's not easy but it *is* simple, just a series of bourées and arms movements really. The emotion is what matters, the stage presence and artistry overpowering any technical requirements. But after watching it twice through, Emir's content for tonight. He glances up at Theo and catches his eye, realising that Theo didn't take a single note or really pay much attention at all. But he doesn't look bored, he just looks...happy.

"Call my phone." Theo says, confusing Emir who just stares back at him with a question in his eyes. "Just...you have your phone on you, yeah?"

Emir nods and slides it out of his pocket, unlocking it automatically to do as Theo said. He dials Theo's number and waits, a soft melody muffled against Theo's bedside table that quickly comes into focus, the same song that was just played twice over while Plisetskaya floated across the screen.

"*The Swan* is your ringtone?" Emir asks, hanging up the call because now he understands the purpose of the exercise.

"It's *your* ringtone. I set it when I saved your number to my phone. It just...it sounds like you." Theo shrugs, flushing slightly at the way Emir is staring between the phone in his own hand and Theo's face. "I pick a different song for all my friends and family. And when you texted me, that one just seemed to fit."

Emir doesn't know what's happening inside of him right now, but his chest feels tight and his face feels hot and overall he's a bit numb and there's something happening low down in his gut that feels warm and squirmy. There's no way that Theo could've guessed how he connects to that song, to that performance specifically, but he chose it anyway. And he said it sounds like Emir. *It sounds like you.* Does he even realise how much that simple comment means to him? When things have been really bad and the world was too loud and he felt alone and broken and wounded, he would listen to *The Swan* and let himself swim through his emotions, knowing that someone, somewhere, understood what he felt.

Theo feels a hand grab his, warm and soft and gentle as their fingers link together. He finally looks at Emir again, wondering if he's overstepped or misunderstood and he really should've just let it go. He shouldn't have told Emir about the song. Not that he explained it. But looking at Emir now, or when he's performing, or when he sees him sitting quietly somewhere just existing, it's like he can hear the notes in the back of his mind, Emir every bit as graceful and striking as the dancers he admires so dearly.

Emir's as inspiring to those who know him as that song has been to the recent history of Euro-centric dance. Choosing that song for Emir was automatic, something Theo didn't even have to think about.

Emir watches and waits for Theo to settle in beside him, both of them still underneath that soft red blanket but barely touching except for where Emir moulded their fingers together. Theo hasn't shied away from the hand holding, letting their fingers intertwine without resistance or hesitation, as if he expected it. "I'm not sure what to say"

"You don't have to say anything. I shouldn't have even brought it up, I suppose." Theo looks down at the screen, still frozen on the folded body of the dancer. Maybe they should just watch the video again.

"I'm glad you did, I just...I don't know, Theo." Emir is searching his face, not sure what answer he's expecting to find there. "Are we done with the work part of tonight?"

"Yeah. I just planned for the original and then Bourne and Trockadero. I know it's getting late, if you want to head home." Theo starts to sit up but Emir squeezes his hand to ask him to stay.

"I'm in no rush, unless you want me to leave." Emir isn't heading back to the studio tonight, already having finished what he planned to work on earlier. "It's your space and you can boot me anytime."

"I don't want you to leave, I just figured you may have places to be." Theo doesn't really know how Emir spends his time outside of class, besides in the studio most evenings. But he assumes he has friends or social obligations, or at the very least he may want some quiet time at home to relax. Maybe do some reading for that book club he's in with Jordan.

"Actually, we have another classic to watch, and I'm shocked you didn't start with it." Emir grins at Theo, that hint of teasing sliding back into his tone.

"There is? I mean, I'm sure there is. We're barely scratching the surface, honestly." Theo mentally runs through his catalogue of performances related to *Swan Lake* and the only thing he can come up with is *Black Swan*, but that's not really about dance and it sounded like Emir didn't really like it.

"There absolutely is, Theo. I thought you were cultured." Emir scoffs and he has the laptop back in his hands now, releasing Theo's hand so he can type and find what he's looking for.

Once he does, he hides the screen from Theo, laying back down and waiting for Theo to do the same. As Emir turns the laptop, Theo laughs so loud he's certain that Gabe and Ciaran are going to come check on them. Emir found *Barbie's Swan Lake*, the full version, and *fuck* why is that so adorable?

"Now cuddle and watch *Barbie* movies with me like the princess you are." Emir puts his arms around Theo's shoulder and tugs until Theo settles with his head on Emir's shoulder, letting himself be cuddled while the movie starts. The CGI is truly appalling but a wave of nostalgia washes over them both.

"You're a good pillow." Theo says, yawning and trying to hide it behind his hand. It is getting close to his bedtime as it's about nine at night already. And the blanket is so fluffy and Emir is so warm and he always gets sleepy watching videos in bed. "Never knew you were such a cuddler...not complaining, of course. Just...didn't know."

"Mmm...I am with people I'm comfortable with." Emir glances down at Theo, realising that he really is very comfortable with him already. Maybe Laurie was right and they weren't ever really fighting about anything at all. Nothing about this feels forced or awkward, at least not to Emir. It's just as normal as cuddling with T and Laurie on the sofa, or with his sisters back home while they watch telly together.

"Is this alright?" Emir probably should've asked that before just squishing Theo into him.

"Yeah." Theo yawns again, not sure what to do with his hands, so he lets one rest just beside his face on Emir's chest. "Why do you smell all nice? You get dressed up for this?" He knows he's teasing, but it's only fair that he pays Emir back for all of his teasing from earlier.

Emir laughs and Theo feels it from his spot on Emir's shoulder, a shared movement. "Hardly. These are Laurie's joggers and my shirt's inside out. But I did shower after the studio. I was disgusting."

Theo snorts in disbelief. "Well now you're just lying. You barely even sweat. Used to make me proper annoyed. Ask Lili. We'd be at the end of a day of tech and you'd be fucking glowing like some sort of dance angel. We'd all be haggard and you'd just be glistening like you were coated in shimmer dust."

Emir laughs again, bringing his hand up to cover his mouth while he does. "That's absolutely ridiculous, Theo. I get sweaty just like the rest of you. Trust me, you'll find out soon enough since we'll be working together all year. We're going to be all up on each other."

"Hm. Guess we will. So this is basically practice." Theo lets out a sigh, eyes fixed on the vibrant pastels that are practically blasting his eyes through his glasses. Barbie's movies are great, but they're certainly a specific visual experience. He can feel his eyes getting heavy already.

They watch the movie quietly, occasional soft laughs and steady breathing as they stay snuggled up under the blanket. Emir starts playing with Theo's hair from where his hand is lying nearby and neither of them thinks anything of it. They're both so comfortable right now, relaxed and happy and distracted by Barbie and Ken's swan drama. Emir's other hand rests gently across his own stomach, the designs from the wedding still bold after just a few days. Theo cautiously reaches out, taking Emir's fingertips to rest on top of his own so he can look at the patterns. Emir can't hold back his smile at Theo's fascination. He knows the feeling well enough himself.

"Pretty hands." Theo says quietly, letting Emir's fingers out of his grasp so he can flip his hand over slowly and admire the designs on the other side as well. Emir lets him trace the lines with his fingertips for a minute until Theo sighs and his own hand drops.

It takes Emir a moment to realise Theo's asleep. It's only about twenty minutes into the movie, Odette just getting started on her journey, and Emir's princess is fast asleep on his shoulder. He isn't even surprised, honestly, with the amount of yawning and eye rubbing during the past hour. Theo's like an overtired puppy who doesn't want to take a nap.

But Emir's in no rush, and Theo definitely needs the rest, so he just keeps watching, turning down the volume so it won't startle Theo awake.

***

A few minutes before Barbie finishes telling Kelly about her swan adventures, Emir hears the front door of the flat open as Laurie and T come back home for the night.

Laurie had already texted that he was staying the night with T, saying they'd pop in and say hello if he was still here working with Theo. Well, he is still here, but work ended quite a while ago and it's now well past ten. Theo's barely moved since he fell asleep, Emir shifting as little as possible. He'll wake Theo up when the movie's done, unless one of the other four decides to be loud in the meantime and he wakes up on his own.

Soft green eyes and a mess of curls peek around the doorframe of Theo's room before the rest of T appears. Emir presses the pointer finger of his free hand to his lips, gesturing down at Theo until T nods and smiles. They watch the way Emir is still running his fingers through Theo's hair, how Theo's face is nuzzled into Emir's upper chest, hand loosely on Emir's abdomen from where he was drawing the mehndi patterns as he dozed off. But then T grins and pulls out their phone, taking a picture which Emir assumes is about to be shared with the other three who must be chatting in the living room.

And sure enough, about twenty seconds later, a very loud, very Northern gay waltzes into the room (followed shortly by an American giant, a grinning Irishman, and a slightly apologetic T) before flopping himself across both of their legs with a, "Well, well, well."

"Oi!" Emir grumbles at Laurie, bringing his free hand up to cradle Theo's head protectively. He hisses in a terrible whisper, "Let him sleep. He's exhausted."

But it's too late. A chaotic Laurie Tempest is an effective alarm clock at any time of the day, but especially when he lands quite harshly across your legs. Theo groans and turns himself further into Emir before realising the weight across his bottom half.

Squinting, Theo looks down and groans, "You're not Emir," at Laurie.

"No, princess, that would be me." Emir smiles down at Theo, sitting up again and letting Theo readjust to the land of the living.

"I was trying to let you rest, but *someone* - " Emir glares at Laurie, sparing a glance at the other three who all look like it's fucking Christmas morning, "Decided to ruin the last ten minutes of the movie."

"Brilliant, what are we watching?" Ciaran slides onto the bed, shoving Laurie until he makes room. At least he has the foresight to pause the movie and move the laptop out of harm's way.

"Barbie - Swan - gay - wait no - " Theo rubs at his eyes underneath his glasses, stretching through a yawn as he sits up, *"Barbie Swan Lake."*

"I love those movies!" T tries to sit in Laurie's lap, but the bed already has four occupants, so they're mostly doing a very convincing squat near Laurie's seat. If Gabe decides he needs to join the pile, Emir fears for the bed frame.

"If we're having a slumber party," Theo yawns again, Emir smiling at him and rubbing the top of his back to help him wake up, "Could we at least move to the sofa? This is generally a single occupant bed."

"Well, it clearly holds at least two." Gabe winks at Theo, not so subtly tilting his head over at Emir. He's standing next to Ciaran, both hands on Ciaran's shoulders absentmindedly rubbing away any tension.

"Did you remember to use protection at least? I'm not ready to be an Uncle." Laurie tugs on Emir's toe through the blanket. The kick he gets in response is well deserved.

"He made me dinner first like a proper gentleman, but a lady never kisses and tells." Emir squints his eyes before trying to shift himself out of this mass of limbs. T has somehow manoeuvred their way between Laurie's legs so it really is getting quite crowded.

"Boring." Laurie sing-songs, tickling T's sides and making them squirm in his lap. "T finds you two in bed together and there isn't even anything gay happening. How are you two my best mates?"

"You and Theo? Not sure. But I snogged your partner at a party before setting the two of you up, so I think you kept me around as some sort of thank you." Emir's gathering his things now, rucksack retrieved from its spot on the floor once he managed to work his way around all the people in the way.

"Similar, actually. Laurie and I met at a party early on and it's been true love ever since." Theo gently moves T out of the way so he can tackle Laurie and mess up his hair.

"Off! I'm delicate!" Laurie and Theo wrestle, effectively pushing everyone else off the bed as they laugh and watch the skirmish. Laurie flips Theo over and pins him easily, surprisingly strong, as always.

"Please." Theo huffs and shoves at Laurie to let him up. "I'm at the gym every day and you're still more fit. You're not delicate, you're just dramatic."

"So I guess I'll just..." Emir gestures at the door as he turns to go, feeling like he should leave the five of them to their...whatever this is.

"You don't have to leave." Theo gets up from the bed, following Emir as he walks out and towards the front of the flat. "They're your friends too. I didn't mean to like - "

"You didn't." Emir stops and turns to Theo near the dining table. "I would've woken you up in a few minutes anyway so you could actually go to sleep."

The other four file their way out of Theo's room too, Laurie carrying T on his back before they all settle on the sofas.

"I didn't mean to fall asleep. Sorry if that was weird. You could've woken me up, you know." Theo has his hands in his pockets again and his shoulders hunched. Emir's learning this must be his nervous, self-conscious posture. And he really doesn't want Theo to feel that way around him.

"Theo." Emir tugs him forward with a smile, bringing him in for a goodbye hug. "If I'm uncomfortable, I'll tell you. Besides," Emir pulls back and glances over at their friends in the living room, "These lot are a bit loud for me sometimes. I love them with my whole arse, but I always need quiet time. Watching Barbie with you sleeping on my shoulder was the highlight of my night, alright?"

"Yeah?" Theo looks at Emir shyly, a hint of pink on his cheeks. "...me too."

Emir breaks into a brilliant smile, running his hand through his own hair before letting it drop again. He actually can't wait to do this again tomorrow. "I'll sneak out before Laurie convinces me to stay."

"You're always welcome here, Emir. I'm sorry if I kept you from coming round all these years. Even when we didn't get along, I never wanted you to feel unwelcome. I know you love these gremlins too." Theo glances over at the four of them bickering on the couch, deciding on what they want to watch before they all head to sleep.

"It was both of us, Theo. I'm sure you felt the same at our place, even if it was never intentional. I never wanted to come between you and Laurie. You're a good friend to him." Emir sort of vaguely turns towards the door, getting ready to leave and searching for his shoes amongst the pile on the ground. "You should get some sleep though. Don't let those four bully you into staying up on a Wednesday. You need your rest."

"Should we meet up tomorrow or take a night off?" Theo is still focused on Emir, watching him slide into his trainers for the walk back home.

"Why don't you come over to ours tomorrow? Only fair, I think." Emir stands up again, finally ready to leave. "If you come over around seven, I'll plan to go to the studio after so you aren't up as late. Our working together shouldn't interfere with the rest of your life."

"Sounds perfect." Theo holds the door open for Emir who slides past him with an arm around his waist and a hand that trails along his back. It seems Emir actually isn't uncomfortable being a human pillow so Theo can relax a bit. "And thanks."

Emir nods with a smile as he leaves, Theo watching him go until he's out of sight.

***

Laurie: *Multiple choice question for you*
Laurie: *Is Theo: a) sleeping beauty b) the princess and the pea c) Belle or d) Snow White*
Emi: *let me guess. the four of you are sitting around gossiping like a bunch of old hens*
Laurie: *Yes, obviously*
Emi: *we've fallen asleep together plenty of times, laur*
Emi: *we've done a lot more than fall asleep together, actually*
Emi: *it's not weird*
Laurie: *But you call him princess and he's all shy around you*
Laurie: *Also that picture T took*
Laurie: */picture of Theo asleep on Emir's chest/*
Emi: *is there a point somewhere in here?*
Laurie: *So defensive*
Laurie: *Almost like*
Emi: *lawrence.*
Emi: *be nice*
Emi: *we're adjusting to being friends and i don't want to scare him away. he's actually really decent and i have to work with him the rest of the year.*
Emi: *so even if what you're implying is true it's a non option*
Laurie: *So you've thought about it*

Emi: *goodnight laurie*
Emi: *tell T and the others goodnight for me*
Laurie: *Get some rest?*
Laurie: *Theo's not the only one behind on sleep*
Emi: *love you*
Laurie: *Love you too*

CHAPTER SEVEN

"So we were wondering if next week, maybe, we could give it a go?" Theo is still a bit out of breath at the end of class, he and Emir needing to talk to Lydia to get her permission before they scurry away to their next class. Using pas de deux to work on partnering each other is the most logical way to get a bit of experience under the watch of a professional, so here they are: asking.

"We've tried to dance together already, and it was fine, but Theo thought it might be a good idea to have some supervision." Emir has a hand on Theo's shoulder, taking sips from his Hydro Flask between sentences. "To make sure neither of us gets hurt."

"Just for a few classes. We should be good on our own after that since we have so much experience otherwise." Theo turns to look at Emir briefly and he nods.

"Well, I don't see why not." Lydia smiles at the both of them while packing away her things so Raphael can take over the studio for his next class. "Did you already talk to Lilibet and Jordan, since they'll be without pas de deux partners?"

"Hi hello that's us." Lilibet speaks up from her spot on the floor where she and Jordan are removing their pointe shoes. "Actually, if it's alright, Jordan and I would like to give it a go as well. It could be good experience to have."

"Well then," Lydia gazes off in the middle distance for a moment. "You know...maybe I should have all of you give it a try. At least those of you who want to. Might be fun for everyone."

"So...is that a yes?" Theo smiles, looking between Emir and Lydia and waiting for confirmation.

"Why not? I'll think it over this weekend just to be sure I can actually be helpful." Lydia smiles back at both of them. "I'm glad you two are actually going through with this. It could be spectacular."

"You sound like Sean." Emir laughs and moves his arm around Theo's back to give him a side hug, both of them still sweaty and warm from class.

"Thanks, Lydia. You won't regret it, I promise." Theo squeezes Emir back before ruining his hair. Emir scoffs and brushes his hand away, rolling his eyes.

"I know I won't. Honestly, the two of you could ask to do pretty much anything and we'd all say yes." Lydia laughs too, the three of them heading to the door with Lili and Jordan just behind them.

"What about us?" Lili asks, jogging to catch up. Lydia waves them off with another fond laugh, stepping into the adjacent classroom to get set up for her next group of students.

"Nah, you're a troublemaker." Jordan teases Lili, smacking her bum just enough to make her jump and turn around with a yelp. Theo and Emir catch each other's eye with a grin, glad that their own need to work together might give Lili and Jordan an excuse to explore as well.

"See you three in rehearsal?" Theo asks, turning to walk down the opposite hall as Emir, Lili, and Jordan all stop next door for Variations.

"No, we're all skiving off but you weren't invited." Emir answers while fixing the hair Theo mussed using his reflection in the window of the classroom.

"Wait, actually?" Theo stops and turns back to the three of them, looking genuinely confused. That doesn't sound like them.

"No, you numpty." Lilibet laughs, "We're the other three leads. It'd be a sorry rehearsal with only you to entertain everyone."

"Are they always this mean to you?" Jordan asks, scolding Lili with arms crossed over her chest. Lili rolls her eyes but places a hand on Jordan's waist momentarily before letting it drop. Jordan softens and turns back to Theo, "We'll see you in rehearsal. Plus, if we were ditching, you'd definitely be invited."

"Yeah?" Theo smiles at that, hands in his jogger pockets and glancing across at Emir who takes pity on him.

Emir walks the few steps back to Theo, grazing his cheek gently before moving his hand down to smack Theo's chest with a grin. He's met with warm muscle that his hand would like to explore, but Theo's muscles are nothing new. It's Emir's proximity to Theo that's changed.

"Ow?" Theo looks down at the spot Emir swatted, rubbing it with his own hand.

"I'd need your help to plan something that interesting...Wanker." Emir smirks up at Theo, taking the hand that Theo has on his chest and giving it a squeeze while stepping back. "Go rest, princess. We'll see you later."

"Oh...okay." Theo holds Emir's stare for a moment, trailing off as their fingertips lose contact and Emir turns away. "Bye..."

Theo watches him follow Lili and Jordan into the studio, staring at the empty hallway for a few moments before remembering what he was doing and walking away to head to his flat.

***

Theo lets himself into Emir and Laurie's flat, per the text Emir had sent ten minutes prior saying that Laurie was busy with something for class and Emir had his hands full. He still knocked first, because it felt odd not to, but Theo didn't wait for an answer before opening the front door.

"Emir?" Theo asks into the air around him, feeling like the world's least notable burglar.

"In here!" Emir shouts back over the music he has playing. Theo doesn't recognise it but he's learning that Emir's music taste is excellent while also being very obscure. Theo follows the sound around the corner to Emir's room, the only room in this flat he doesn't know inside out and back to front after years of being Laurie's best mate.

"You're just in time!" Emir smiles up at Theo from the floor once Theo reaches his doorway, and his hands *are* actually occupied. Moving a strand of hair off his face, Emir manages to leave quite the streak of charcoal on his cheek.

"You've just - right there." Theo drops his bag and points at his own face where Emir has a mark. But Emir waves him off and waits for Theo to join him on the floor, tilting his head to the space beside him so he gets the message.

"Well?" Emir sets aside his charcoal in the storage tin and uses his messy hands to pick up the picture he'd been working on before Theo got there. Impressive, considering rehearsal only ended about a half an hour ago. Theo holds his hand out, asking to take it to examine closer.

"It's...it's incredible, Emir. I didn't know you could do this. This is like proper art, you know?" The drawing in his hand is a beautiful swan, blurry and almost in movement with the way Emir used his fingers to shade it. "Is this because of last night?"

"A bit. Hold on. I've got another to show you." Emir wipes his hands off on his joggers, reaching under his bed to pull out an art portfolio. Theo's eyes widen as Emir casually flips through a dozen or so pieces of art before stopping and carefully taking out another drawing by the edges, trying not to smudge charcoal on the watercolours.

Emir watches as Theo takes the second drawing, setting aside the swan as he does. His face is full of wonder, like a kid opening a present on their birthday, and Emir feels warm all the way to his toes. Sharing his art with people isn't something he does lightly, usually showing only his family and a few friends. But Theo said that Emir reminded him of *The Swan* and then Emir had a dream that he was the swan, only instead of dying he was learning to fly, embraced by the sky while he spread his wings. Emir had waited all day to finally get the chance to draw her.

"Is this that one lake on campus?" Theo asks, pointing out a few of the more distinct landmarks. When Emir nods, Theo looks down at the painting again, ready with another question, "Who are they?"

"Oh...I suppose they're me. Well, not both of them. But I was having complicated feelings about my dissertation when I painted this one, and needed a way to capture how I wanted it to feel." Emir scoots next to Theo and lays his head on his shoulder so they're looking at the picture together. "It was the weekend before last."

"Do you...I don't want to read into things that aren't there." Theo looks at Emir again, shy and soft, and Emir feels a very fond smile warming his face. He didn't know that Theo would be so interested. Really, he just wanted to show him the swan because he inspired it, at least indirectly.

"I think we'll save that for another day." Emir reaches out and wipes a bit of charcoal on Theo's nose with a giggle, his own nose crinkling and eyes sparkling at the shock on Theo's face. "But I wanted you to see it. The swan, that is."

"Why do you keep them all hidden away?" Theo looks around the room and only sees a few things on the walls of Emir's room, and in doing so he notices how messy it is. But it's not like it's dirty or uncomfortable, it's just very lived in, all the things that are important to Emir scattered about like some sort of chaotic nest.

There are dozens of books covering almost every surface, Emir's place kept with notecards and post-its but nothing looks dog-eared (thank god). Theo sees more blankets than he can count, which makes sense with the way Emir always seems cold and like he needs a cuddle. And his dance things are all over, different colours of pointe shoes laying around, tucked out of the way as if they've been removed from circulation.

But there's none of Emir's art on the walls, just a few pictures of Emir with their friends, and some with people Theo assumes are Emir's family. There's one rather small portrait of Emir in *Firebird* from last season, set atop his desk between notebooks and a half sewn pair of pointe shoes. Theo keeps looking for a single one of Emir's drawings or paintings on display, but it seems they all live in that folder under the bed.

"I don't know, really." Emir shrugs, tucking both pictures back into the portfolio and hiding it away again. "They're just for me, I suppose. I show them to people sometimes, but it's not as if they matter."

"They what?" Theo puts a gentle hand around Emir's forearm as he sits back again to keep his attention. "What do you mean they don't matter?"

"Just what I said, princess. They're just little sketches and paintings for when I'm feeling creative. They're not, like, deep or intellectual or whatever." Emir uses his free hand to rub at the charcoal still on his face, smudging it even further and earning another shy smile from Theo before he reaches up and wipes it off himself. Theo's thumb is soft against Emir's cheek, gentle but firm as he wipes away the mess.

"Just because they're casual doesn't mean they don't matter, Emir." Theo holds his gaze, and Emir can't help but listen when he looks at him like that. "Just the few I've seen are beautiful, and if they matter to you then they matter. End of. I firmly believe that we decide what matters, that where we put our attention and energy is how we decide that. And clearly your pictures are *you*."

Theo glances down at where the art has been tucked away again, already deciding he's going to display his small tea note quite proudly once he gets home, especially knowing what he does now. "Thank you for showing me."

Emir ducks his head then rubs the bit of charcoal off of Theo's nose. It's only fair after Theo helped him get it off his own face. Theo scrunches his face as he does, like an annoyed puppy or something. "...You're a bit sappy, you know that?"

"Oh, I'm well aware." Theo laughs, starting to stand up again and taking Emir with him by the hand. "The teasing is unbelievable. Especially from Laurie."

"Why does that not surprise me?" Emir watches Theo reach for his bag again before turning away and back towards the hallway. "Wait - you're leaving already?"

"We're making dinner." Theo answers over his shoulder with a proud, confident posture. Emir's glad to see him more comfortable in their interactions, at least outwardly. "Multi-tasking. Think you can handle it?"

"Depends on what the tasks are...but I've been told my hands are very talented." Emir trots after Theo and into the kitchen without a backward glance, surprised but not in any way upset to have an activity to do while they watch videos tonight.

"Noted." Theo flushes slightly, and Emir kind of loves how easy it is to make him look all pretty and pink. "Now, T said you should have some basics lying around since they go to the shops with Laurie and make sure you two eat on a semi-regular schedule."

"Honestly, thank fuck for T or Laurie and I would both survive on tea and rubbish. Like, literal refuse. Laurie talked me into bin diving once, but not even to save money, just to say fuck you to capitalism or whatever." Emir moves behind where Theo is standing at the sink, ready to wash up, and he puts his hands fleetingly on Theo's waist in passing, as if reassuring him that he's there. "He was in some phase where he really wanted to help the environment and he was watching a bunch of those YouTubers, but they're all American and we realised it wasn't as much of a thing here. But." Emir shrugs and pushes up his sleeves.

"That sounds exactly like Laurie. I'm surprised he didn't invite me or T along." Theo soaps up his hands and blows some of the suds at Emir, laughing at how he bats them away.

"You were asleep and T was sick. This was first year when they had bronchitis...actually thinking back on it, maybe Laurie needed an outlet since he'd been arguing with nurses all day about getting a new breathing treatment for T. He really does love them, doesn't he?" Emir nudges Theo out of the way so he can wash his hands as well, bumping his hip with his own.

"More than should be humanly possible. Those two are like actual soulmates, honestly." Theo smiles to himself as he opens up the fridge, surveying the admittedly bleak contents and trying to come up with a plan. "So...what would you usually make on a weeknight?"

"Honestly? Nothing healthy. Something microwaveable, or if I'm really adventurous, maybe some beans on toast." Emir stands next to Theo staring into the fridge.

"You and Laurie are so similar. I'm surprised I never noticed before." Theo takes the few vegetables present out of the fridge and sets them aside, reaching for his bag again. It's a university flat, so the kitchen has about enough countertop space for a cutting board and nothing else, but it'll work. "If we make roasted veg, we can get all the prep done and work while it's in the oven. That alright?"

"You're the chef." Emir smiles so bright when Theo pulls an apron out of his bag, accompanied by a few Tupperware. He really thought about this. "Do you just...travel with that?"

"Of course not." Theo laughs while tying the strings behind his back. "I brought a few things that I figured we both liked. Planned ahead. I'm good at that, you know."

"Yeah, I know." Emir finds the few actually useful knives that he and Laurie keep around, setting them beside the cutting board that T picked out for them last year. "It's one of the reasons everyone likes you so much. You're...thoughtful."

"And are you one of those people?" Theo opens up the Tupperware, revealing pre-cut potatoes, brussels sprouts, and onion. He spent his own time after rehearsal agonising over which vegetables he thought Emir might fancy then dicing them while listening to a podcast.

"Getting there. If you behave." Emir takes the carrots to the sink to clean before adding them to the mix.

The two of them spend the next ten minutes preparing and seasoning everything until it's ready to go, Theo showing a comfort in the kitchen that reminds Emir of his mum. He reaches for spices and tools automatically, clearly experienced and enjoying himself at the same time. And that fucking apron, honestly. Emir never knew that a Batman apron existed, or that Theo would have any interest in one, but he can't stop smiling and joking along. And Theo doesn't miss the way Emir's eyes sparkle, or the times their hands brush accidentally and it makes him flush. By the time dinner is in the oven, he thinks the space feels something like home.

***

"This shit is depressing." Emir's finished eating, so he's folded himself under one of his many blankets on the sofa as if it's practically freezing in the flat (it's not). They've been watching *Giselle* on the telly together, Theo taking notes (of course) and Emir mostly complaining.

"I think that's sort of the whole point." Theo doesn't look up from his notes, drawing a small figure next to his latest costume question. Is there space for some semblance of a romantic tutu in their work? Probably not, but it should be on the list. "Like, knowing the historical context and the general trend of romantic ballets, it's definitely intentional."

"The fact there's no modern adaptations for us to watch should tell us something." Emir is definitely grumpy. But Theo had given him the choice of *Giselle* or *La Sylphide* and Emir had barely needed to think it over. So here they are.

"I think it could tell us many things, but this is one of the classics for a reason." Theo glances at Emir and finds himself smiling at the way his grumpy eyes are barely visible over the purple blanket. "We're already into the second act, so the worst is over."

"She literally killed herself with a sword and now she's fighting her ghost friends to save her boyfriend. Oh, and they're about to drown her other boyfriend and it's not even a fun polyamorous situation." Emir emerges from his blanket to sip at his tea. The gay judgement is palpable.

"But it's so…Emir, they're gorgeous. I know the story leaves a lot to be desired, but aesthetically this is incredible. Literally nothing else has ever compared." Theo turns his notebook around to show Emir his little drawing. "You could definitely do this better than me. Please?"

"Fine. But only because I can barely tell that's a person you drew." Emir takes the pencil and notebook in hand, quickly drawing one of the Wilis, full romantic tutu and somehow perfectly shaped hands. Theo watches in awe as Emir demonstrates an artistic skill he's only ever dreamed of having himself.

"Here." Emir huffs and hands the notebook back before huddling under the blanket again. The effect of the huff is downplayed somewhat by the fact the blanket is decorated with cartoon huskies.

"I think I have to frame this…" Theo stares at Emir's sketch for a minute, completely ignoring the telly for now. "How'd you do that?"

"Told you I was good with my hands." Emir grumbles from underneath the fabric, scoffing at the screen as Hilarion makes another brief appearance. He hates every single one of these characters, regardless of how beautiful the choreography is.

"Actually, um…that reminds me." Theo sets his notebook aside and turns completely sideways to face Emir. This is as good an opening as any. "Can I ask you a question?"

"Maybe…" Emir looks at Theo suspiciously, his intense focus seeming very pointed.

"You don't have to answer me and you can tell me if it's way too personal or if I'm being a twat for even asking. But at this point it'd be weird not to ask because I've seen multiple things that make me wonder and I don't want to be insulting you by accident especially now that we're friends and – " Theo stops suddenly when one of Emir's hands comes up to cover his mouth.

"…Sorry." He manages to mumble from beneath Emir's palm, eyes blinking as he waits for Emir to either be annoyed or worse.

"Just ask the fucking question before you explode, mate." Emir takes his hand back and waits for whatever this is about to be. Theo looks more hesitant than Emir is entirely comfortable with.

"Well…so I looked up the art on your hands because you said it was from your sister's wedding and I wanted to educate myself a bit more, but what I was reading said it was…for women?" Theo glances at Emir but he doesn't seem keen to interrupt so he continues. "Which I know doesn't have to mean anything. Obviously. And you do pointe, which again, I know doesn't have to be gender related at all, but we grew up learning it was, so…but then in your art folder I thought I saw a painting of a genderqueer flag. I swear I wasn't snooping, it was just there and I recognised it. And, like, that painting could be for someone else, of course, but there's also a chance it's for you? So I guess I'm wondering…um…I don't mean to, like, make you come out to me. But I'm also worried I've been misgendering you or maybe you prefer Emi because now that I think back on it that's what Sean usually calls you and so does T and…yeah."

Theo finishes what he wanted to say with a rush of air as he deflates, waiting for…he doesn't even know what. "Sorry."

"What are you sorry for?" Emir asks, focusing on the last part first, because Theo's not wrong, but he didn't know they were going to have this conversation so soon. Or at all.

"I'm scared I've made you uncomfortable. It's possible I'm crossing a line. I would never want to do that. Or maybe this is something I should've noticed years ago but because we spent so much time arguing I wasn't paying close enough attention and missed it." Theo fidgets with the hem of his joggers where his legs are crossed in front of him on the sofa. *Giselle* is still playing in the background, but neither of them seems very interested at the moment.

Emir lets the blanket down from around his shoulders as it pools across his lap. He sighs and takes Theo's hands in his, always surprised at how warm they are. "I'm fine with either Emir or Emi. And no you haven't been misgendering me. He/him pronouns are preferred, but...I don't mind they/them either. I like it, actually, in some contexts. And she/her are okay in some cases in private, but it's not validating in the same way, just like, not offensive to me, I guess." Theo looks up at that, searching Emir's face with an earnest expression. "I am genderqueer, Theo. But I also have reasons I don't share that identity outside of a very select circle."

"Oh - of course. I didn't mean to - thank you for telling me. Trusting me." Theo squeezes Emir's hands and keeps staring into those gorgeous amber eyes that he's becoming so familiar with. "We really don't have to talk about it if you don't want to. And I'll make sure to keep this private...actually, who else knows?"

"At uni, it's just T and Laurie. And Sean. I had to tell Sean for the purposes of this." Emir tilts his head at the telly, indicating their dissertation. "But I trusted him enough for it to be alright...Other than that, just my immediate family."

Emir pauses and takes a deep breath, "I'll just say that besides the people listed, anyone else who I told did not take it well. To put it mildly."

"Fuck, Emir, I'm so sorry." Theo has really never understood bigotry, and obviously he doesn't know specifics, but the look on Emir's face is enough to tell him that whatever happened was bad. Painful in a lasting way. "Can I - would it...hug?"

Emir smiles weakly, dropping Theo's hands to bring him into a hug. It's awkward at first because of how they're sitting, but they both settle into it, Theo holding Emir on his chest as if he could protect him from all the pain in this world. Emir lets himself be held, feeling relieved that Theo asked, actually, because he never would've brought it up and he sort of needed to know, if only for the sake of their collaboration. Emir wants his full identity to be present in their performance, and since they're working together it would've been a bit impossible if Theo didn't know.

"Do you want to talk about it?" Theo mumbles somewhere near the side of Emir's head. Emir is so cuddly, and Theo is still getting used to it, but it's also really nice, like something Theo's been missing.

"Not particularly. But if you have questions, it's alright to ask. I know you're not a bellend. Well – I know that *now*." Emir laughs softly against Theo's chest before pulling away from the hug. "I wasn't so sure a few weeks ago."

"Neither was I." Theo agrees easily, picking his notebook back up automatically. "But...I'm really glad we're past that. You're sort of wonderful, you know? You have all these talents I never knew and you're really cuddly and you make gay jokes at least as much as I do, also you're very pretty and I enjoy spending time with you."

"What was that?" Emir smirks at Theo, back underneath his purple dog blanket while they finish watching the film.

"I enjoy spending time with you?" Theo asks, striking through a note from earlier because it needs to be rewritten. "I would've thought that was a given with me volunteering to do so."

"No, before that." Emir doesn't miss the flush working its way back into Theo's cheeks. But Theo looks ethereal when he's shy, and Emir can't help but tease him just to see him glow. Like some sort of pink angel.

"You know you're gorgeous, Emi." Theo is pointedly avoiding his eyes, pretending the Wilis have his full attention on the screen. "That can't possibly be news to you."

"It's not...but you're cute when you're flustered." Emir scoots closer on the sofa until he can lay his head on Theo's shoulder, tucking his legs to the side and yawning, but hiding it with a blanket covered hand. "How much longer are we in pretty ghost lady land?"

"Mm...I think about twenty minutes or so. You can make it. I believe in you." Theo glances down at Emir, at the way the light from the telly brushes his eyelashes, the way he's curled himself up against Theo. He shakes his head at himself because he's romanticising his own life and for what? All of these ballets are getting to him.

"There's only like one scene left with partner work and it's definitely not the most important or interesting part of this." Emir lets his hand out of the blanket to take Theo's notebook and pencil to draw Giselle and Albrecht, but in their costumes from the first act. "Act One has heterosexual drama, but it's also the only solo or pas de deux worth watching...in my opinion. Second act is all about the Wilis."

"As it should be." Theo lays his head on top of Emir's and watches him draw. They finish the film like this, Emir huddled under his blanket leaning into Theo's side, Theo watching Emir doodle and sketch until it's over. When the performers are taking their bows, Emir stretches and yawns, getting up from the sofa and helping Theo to stand up as well.

"Prince Charming? Or is that too...?" Theo looks down at where their hands are linked.

"Well if you're the princess, then I suppose I must be. Because as much as we used to pretend, I don't think I've ever been the villain in your story, pumpkin." Emir smiles when Theo giggles at yet another nickname. It is *so easy* to make him smile, but Emir still delights in it every single time.

"Should we take the weekend off? Wait until pas de deux on Tuesday to make more plans?" Theo asks as Emir drops his hand.

"Probably. I'll be in the studio of course, and I'm sure you will be as well, but we can get together next week." Emir walks Theo to the door now that he's packed up the few things he brought with him.

"I'll text you?" Theo stops to put his shoes back on, not quite wanting to leave, but knowing they both need to get on with their nights. As much as he's enjoyed their time working together, they both have responsibilities outside of their dissertation.

"I'd like that. And it doesn't have to be about work you know." Emir adds, steadying Theo with an arm while he wobbles into his shoes. "You can just text me about whatever. Can't promise I'll answer right away, but I'll answer."

"Okay. I will." Theo pulls Emir into a quick hug before heading home, taking the long way because he's in such a wonderful mood and for some reason he really wants to enjoy the walk.

***

Emi: *what's princess doing on friday night?*
Emi: *laurie hasn't tried to drag me to any parties so I assume you aren't drinking your body weight in cheap beer while wading through a sea of hormones*
Theo: *Hush, you.*
Theo: *I'm with Lili and Jordan of course.*
Theo: *Laurie and T are "busy".*
Theo: *I did not ask for details. And left the flat quickly.*
Emi: *smart*
Emi: *usually about a three minute window from warning text to naked moaning*
Theo: *You get three minutes? I usually only get one.*
Theo: *I'm sure the wedding stress is contributing to that.*
Emi: *the studio's boring tonight*
Emi: *look*
Emi: */picture of himself in the studio mirror pouting/*
Theo: *No. Absolutely not. You don't get to send thirst traps without warning.*
Emi: *i wasn't aware i had*
Theo: *Yes, you were.*

"Who're you texting?" Lilibet tries to peer over Theo's arm to get a look at his screen. "You're all smushy."

"I am *not* smushy." Theo says defensively, with an added huff. "I'm just texting Emir. We do that now. Proper adults and all that."

"I thought I recognised that face." Jordan adds oh so helpfully from her spot at Lili's feet. They're having a quiet night in, painting nails, face masks, the works.

"There is no face." Theo frowns at Jordan, but then Emir sends him that gif of Joey from *Friends* saying "I'm sorry" and he giggles. So. "We're getting on, is all. He's a laugh when he wants to be."

"We're well aware, but since when do *you* know that?" Lili is still trying to wrestle Theo's phone away from him, but he's locked it so even if she managed she wouldn't be able to read anything.

"Since we stopped fighting and started getting to know each other." Theo gives up and lets Lili tackle him. She exclaims with glee once she has his phone in her hand, raising it up in triumph until she sees it's blank, still crushing him into the sofa.

"Open it." Lilibet holds it out to him like he has any intention of listening to her.

"No. It's private." Theo smiles seeing yet another text come through. He can't help it. But he can gently shove Lilibet off now that she's distracted.

"Ooooo your boyfriend texted you again." Jordan says, raising her eyebrows at Theo while she files her nails.

"Not my boyfriend. He's just a friend who's..." Theo stops himself from adding 'not a boy', trapped because he can't out Emir but he also doesn't want to misgender him. Holding his hand out to Lili he whines, "Gimme. Pleeeeease."

"Fine. But you're definitely smushy." Lili sits back in her corner of the sofa with a humph, crossing her arms over her chest.

Emi: */selfie with his face scrunched in a wink/*
Theo: *And what is that one proving?*
Emi: *i'm bored*
Emi: *or weren't you paying attention last time*
Theo: *Then leave? You've been there for hours.*
Emi: *no. i need to work. get better. be a better dancer than you*
Theo: *You already are.*
Theo: *Why do you think I used to hate you so much?*
Emi: */side eye emoji/*
Theo: *Go work on the solo Raphael blocked for you this afternoon.*
Theo: *Not rabbity enough yet.*
Emi: *i hate that you're correct*
Emi: *bye princess*
Emi: */gif of Jensen Ackles in a princess crown/*
Theo: *Okay first of all Dean Winchester my bisexual king we stan*
Theo: */gif of Batman saying goodbye/*

***

Theo is having a wonderful weekend so far. His sister Barbara is visiting, here to leave him her old car since she and her husband bought a new one. Theo tried to pay her for it and she laughed, making jokes about uni student budgets and the fact that it's basically worthless anyway. In addition to loving his sister's company, Theo has always revelled in this time of year, obsessed with sweater weather, the actual weather and the song, like the raging bisexual he is.

"So when's the show again? You know we all want to see it." Barbara is walking next to Theo across campus, glad to have actual alone time with her younger brother which rarely happens these days.

"Couple months. Late November. It only runs for two weekends this time, though." Theo shoves his hands further in his pockets, regretting leaving the wool mittens that T knit for him back at the flat. "It's going to be great. The sets are incredible."

"And what about your dissertation? You've been losing it over that for years and it's finally time to work on it." Barbara and Theo sidestep an abandoned bike to keep on their path. It looks fairly similar to the one she used to ride around Leeds during her own uni days, the nostalgia bringing a smile to her eyes.

"Actually...it's not just mine anymore." Theo glances up and he can't believe the timing. "Shit."

He not so subtly fixes his hair (it looks the same) and brushes off his jumper as quickly as he can. Because Emir is walking in his own world right now, directly towards them, but he looks unreal, his cheeks rosy from the cold and his hair perfectly windswept and what the fuck honestly? How does he always do this?

Emir sees them only a moment later, lighting up when he sees Theo, but his face goes immediately stormy when he notices Barbara at his side. He's glad to see Theo, especially on a brilliant Sunday afternoon, but not if he's on some sort of date or whatever. And he can tell the two of them are close, walking and chatting with that casual intimacy that only comes with time.

"Emir!" Theo rushes forward and pulls him into a hug, surprising Emir because he's usually the one who initiates the cuddles. Theo's genuinely glad to see him, an anomaly that's becoming a habit. "We were *just* talking about you."

"You were?" Emir is clearly skeptical, glancing at Barbara over Theo's shoulder with more than a little suspicion. "Why?"

"Oh, well, not technically. But Barbara asked me about my dissertation. And...well." Theo releases Emir, letting his hands rest on Emir's waist for a moment before they drop. "That includes you, of course."

"Oh. Right. We're working together, yeah." Emir shrugs and rubs his hands together, trying to warm them up a bit. It's chilly and he really should've planned ahead. Although he usually doesn't notice the cold as much when he's spending his walks lost in his thoughts.

"So you're Emir then?" Barbara stands there staring between them, and Theo ignores the look he gets in response to that knowledge. Why does everyone insist on giving him that look? "It's nice to finally meet you. I've been hearing about you for years."

"You have not, Boo." Theo rolls his eyes and shoves his hands back in his pockets. "*Anyway*, as I was saying, Emir and I combined our projects. We started working together the week before last and it's going really well...or, at least *I* think so."

"It is." Emir smiles at Theo, but it's not his normal, bright smile that would blind anyone a kilometre away. It's uncertain and soft, because Emir isn't really sure where he fits into this conversation.

He hasn't even been properly introduced so he just stands there like a Sim, waiting for Theo to do so. The breeze blows a strand of hair across his cheek and Theo follows it with his gaze, itching to tuck it back behind Emir's ear, but also just admiring the way it looks. And Barbara doesn't miss the way her brother can't stop staring.

"I'm Barbara by the way." Barbara holds her hand out to Emir, who takes it with a half-hearted shake before letting it drop. "I'm only here to visit for the day. I could leave you two if you need to...whatever."

Her eyes dart to Theo who gives her another eye roll and a sideways smile.

"There's no need. I would hate to interrupt your date - I mean day - I mean...it's nice to meet you, Barbara." Emir actually flushes, which so rarely happens he could almost convince himself he's coming down with something. "I'll just - "

Emir turns to leave, but stops when Theo's voice cuts in.

"Oh my god, NO." Theo starts laughing so hard that Emir puts a hand on his lower back to stop him from falling. "Barbara's my - "

Theo loses his sentence in the middle of another laugh. It's infectious, Emir starting to giggle along even though he doesn't get the joke yet.

"Big sister. And Theo's the baby. Little bitty baby brother." Barbara clarifies, and Theo miraculously stops laughing to pout and cross his arms, which really isn't helping his case.

"I'm an entire adult, Boo." Theo misses how Emir has completely changed, his smile genuine now and with zero intentions of running away from this interaction.

"Calm down, princess, no one said you weren't." Emir's hand is still on Theo's lower back, but now it's just to keep Theo close. "Now that you mention it, I do vaguely remember seeing you at a few of our performances. Usually with a whole gaggle of people."

"That would be the rest of the Palmers. We can be a bit much." Barbara smiles, eyes darting down to where Emir's hand has made its way to the far side of Theo's waist. And to the fact that Theo hasn't even reacted. She's about to have so much gossip to share over the phone with their other sister, Jayna, on the train back to Stafford. How else is she meant to pass the time? "You want to join us, Emir? Theo's just been giving me a bit of a walk around the place since I'm so rarely able to visit."

"I better get back. I could use some hot tea to warm my hands." Emir smiles at Theo, still holding him by the waist. "You forget your gloves?"

"Yeah. T make you a pair as well?" Theo is basically ignoring his sister at this point, but she really doesn't mind getting to watch whatever this is. Her brother looks happy.

"Of course. Mine are purple. My favourite." Emir smiles again, his eyes so warm that Theo forgets summer has passed. "Just finished book club. Jordan says hi, and Lili was...occupied but I assume she says hello as well."

Theo smirks at that, the two of them sharing a knowing look. Lili and Jordan are still very much a secret, but sometimes it's a wonder no one else has put it together yet. "I'll text her later. She was going to join me and Barbara for dinner, but if she's busy..."

"She's not *that* busy. Lili always has time for you." Emir finally releases Theo with one last squeeze to his waist, letting his hand trail along his back as he steps away. He holds out his other hand to Barbara with what she assumes is his signature charm. "Lovely to meet you, Barbara. I'll see you at one of the *Alice* shows, I presume?"

"Wouldn't miss it." Barbara shakes his hand and lets him walk a few feet away before turning to Theo with her arms crossed over her chest. "You didn't tell me you were dating!"

"I am *not* dating. What are you on about?" Theo bumps into his sister while they continue their walk, ignoring the way his stomach falls when she asks the question.

"Alright, but Emir wanted me dead before he knew I was your sister, and the second he found out, he had you in his arms. Also, you look at him like the sun shines out of his cock. So." Barbara holds her hands out palms up, as if presenting evidence to the court. "Princess?"

Theo is so red that there's no pretending it's from the cold. Why did Barbara have to choose today to be observant? "What? We just stopped hating each other like two weeks ago, alright? We're, like...friends now."

"Mhm. And your point is?" Barbara links her arm with Theo's, pulling him close to steal some of his body heat.

"The point is, we're working together and we're still learning to be friends. Is that so bad?" Theo shrugs as best he can with their arms connected, hands and cheeks both plenty chilly, even with the sun out.

"That depends. Would it be bad if it was more? He was clearly jealous, and maybe even a little hurt before he realised. It was written all over his face." Barbara looks up at her brother, trying to read what he's feeling in his expression. He's usually such an open book to her.

"I don't really date, Boo. You know that." Theo looks down at his feet now, scuffing his toes on the path as they slow down, weighed down by their conversation.

"That's not, like, a rule. From what you've told me, you just have to have a connection with someone first, right?" Barbara waits for Theo to nod before continuing. "I'm just suggesting you keep the option open. If it's a no, that's fine, but he's unbelievably gorgeous, Teddy. You could do so much worse."

"It's not about his looks, though." Theo answers before he can stop himself. "I just meant...he's really talented, and not only at dance. He's shy and quiet, even though he could have the entire world at his feet. And we get along really well now that we're not fighting anymore. And he calls me nicknames and cuddles me. I just...I don't know."

"It's alright not to know. Take all the time you need, baby brother." Barbara is glad to see Theo smile at that, his posture relaxing again with the teasing. "But I would be really happy for you. You've been banging on about him for two years now, so maybe you're finally figuring out why."

"I absolutely have not been. You're dramatic." Theo elbows his sister gently, just enough to make her annoyed. "Now, what else did you want to see before we go back to the flat? We didn't wear enough layers."

***

Theo: /selfie with Lilibet and Barbara/
Theo: The girls wanted to say hello.
Theo: You have a new fan. Barbara says you're gorgeous and have nice hair.
Emi: those are just facts, pumpkin
Emi: did you know your eyes are hazel? the green jumper really brings it out
Theo: I've always thought they were just brown.
Emi: they're not "just" anything. trust me, i'm an artist.
Emi: you can even sing that kelly clarkson song
Theo: I do enjoy a good karaoke night.
Emi: of course you do
Emi: /princess emoji/
Emi: having a nice time with your sister?
Theo: The best. I miss my sisters. And my parents. Also my Grandad is one of my best friends. I just really love my family, and I don't care if that's uncool or whatever.
Emi: me too :)
Emi: go focus on sibling time
Emi: tell my new admirer thank you and get to sleep
Emi: can't have you up late on a school night
Theo: /eye rolling emoji/
Theo: Because you're going to bed so early?
Emi: actually...yes
Emi: /selfie from bed, glasses on and huddled under three blankets/
Emi: sleepy
Theo: Go to sleep Emi! You look exhausted.
Theo: I didn't mean that to sound rude.
Theo: You look great.
Theo: Your hair's doing that swoosh thing.
Theo: But like you also look tired.

Theo: *Objectively.*
Theo: *Also I like your glasses.*
Theo: *That's a lot of blankets.*
Theo: *Are you cold?*
Emi: *how am I supposed to sleep with my phone getting a dozen notifications a minute?*
Theo: *SORRY*
Theo: *Goodnight <3*
Emi: *goodnight, teddy :)*
Emi: */gif of minion snoring/*

CHAPTER EIGHT

Tuesday's pas de deux is the most fun that the entire class has had in years. True to her word, Lydia asked that all of the dancers find a partner of their same gender, mentioning that Emir and Theo need to practise for their dissertation and she wanted to take the opportunity to give everyone the experience they might not get elsewhere. It's exciting and the studio is glowing, the air full of giggles and "oops" and an overall vibe of new things and adventure.

"You're so squirmy. Hold still." Emir has been partnering Theo for the past hour already, both of them having the time of their lives and actually doing quite well despite their initial reservations.

"That time was on purpose." Theo catches his breath after a series of giggles, and when he looks up at Emir he sees that glint of mischief in his eyes.

"It's not my fault you're so ticklish." Emir lets his fingertips wander again, sliding beneath the open sides of Theo's vest to tickle at the skin there.

"Emir!" Theo doubles over again, laughing and squirming harder, but Emir is holding tight to his waist to keep him close. Maybe he likes teasing Theo. He's cute.

"Everything alright over there?" Lydia is walking along the pairs trying to give advice, but mostly just letting them have a bit of fun and correcting anything that seems dangerous.

"Grand." Emir answers for them, tickling Theo once more and grinning wide. "We'll be ready for the stage by next Tuesday."

Theo pokes at Emir's stomach, making him lean forward with an "oomph", but he catches Lydia's eye and Theo can tell they're not actually being scolded for anything. She looks to the ceiling momentarily to gather herself but they can both tell she's holding back a laugh before moving on to the next pair.

"On Thursday we're definitely switching." Theo straightens back up and waits for Emir's hands to find his waist again. He's surprisingly strong given how dainty he manages to look sometimes. An enigma, as in most things. "You're a menace."

"I'll have you know that I don't have a single tickle spot on my entire body." Emir takes Theo's hands, setting him up for a practice turn.

"Is that a challenge?" Theo turns himself one and a half times so he can stare at Emir instead of the mirror and Emir almost falters before remembering that providing support is basically his entire purpose right now. Not that Theo needs it because his balance is perfect. But their faces are very close, and they would be just inches away if Theo wasn't on demi pointe and slightly taller at the moment.

"...Maybe it is?" Emir doesn't know what to do with that look Theo's giving him, so he moves his hands to Theo's waist and keeps turning him back to the front, setting him up to practise the other direction as well.

"Let's hope you're ticklish somewhere interesting." Theo leans back to say, and what the hell is Emir supposed to do with that?

"I hope you like my feet then." Emir turns Theo's head back to the front with his fingertips. He's not used to being the one making sure they focus, but he's glad Theo's actually enjoying himself and not being a wanker about this. Could've gone either way, if he's honest. But Theo's been surprisingly willing to let Emir take over for the class.

"Oi!" They both turn and look at Lilibet who's currently in the process of partnering Jordan, with only mild success. "Watch your knee, Jo."

"You watch your torso. It's in my way." Jordan's significantly taller than Lili so it may have worked better the other way around, but it's fairly entertaining and both Theo and Emir have been fondly watching them all hour. They certainly seem to have no issue bickering like an old married couple, even if the others think it's platonic.

"Try it slower, just a quarter turn at a time. This is why I said no pointe shoes yet." Lydia walks over to adjust them, just as she has for so many of the "lady" pairs. The "men" are much more used to moving out of the way of a turning body, so their challenge has been on the other side. Some of the guys aren't willing to let another dancer guide them after so many years practising the other way around.

"Princess?" Emir pats his side so Theo will come off balance and turn to look at him again.

"Emi?" Theo wipes at his forehead with his vest and messes up his hair in the process. Emir fixes it for him with a smile.

"We should talk about pointe. Like with our piece." Emir swings their hands between them, eventually bringing them above Theo's head and letting him twirl like a music box ballerina. He's quite good at it.

"That's up to you, though. I wish I could do pointe, but I can't..." Theo meets his eyes in the mirror and Emir can tell he's still sad about it all these years later. Emir files that information away to figure out later because he can't immediately do anything about it.

"But we should talk about it. If pointe fits, where it fits, logistically how I might get in and out of shoes mid performance, that sort of thing." Emir walks over to the side to take a drink from his Hydro Flask, glad when Theo follows so they can continue their conversation.

"We should. But maybe later?" Theo takes a long drink from his own water bottle before setting it down again. "Tomorrow after family dinner? You should come...I want you to come."

"You do?" Emir pauses what he was doing to search Theo's eyes. They look darker today, reflecting his black vest...he's getting sidetracked. It's one thing for them to spend time together, but family dinner is a bit sacred for those five. And the last time Emir attended it hadn't gone very well. Was that really only two weeks ago?

"Definitely. But only if you want...and then we could talk and watch some other videos after." Theo shrugs and starts fidgeting. Emir sighs because Theo was doing so well, having fun and teasing and acting a bit more self confident for the past hour. But here he is, unsure and making himself small again.

"I'd like to, Theo, but I don't want you to feel obligated." Emir glances at the rest of the class to check for eavesdropping, but they're all still very absorbed in their own work at the moment. "I can always come by after if you'd prefer."

Theo reaches out and gently grasps Emir's arm. "I wouldn't have asked if it wasn't a sincere invitation. And not just for tomorrow. For all of them...I'd like you to be there." Theo doesn't know how to explain what he means any clearer than that. The conversation with Barbara has been bothering him for days, but more than anything he enjoys Emir's company, even when they just sit in silence together. He feels calm with Emir, like they understand each other.

Emir believes Theo, but he doesn't know what his own reaction means. He's glad Theo wants him there, but is it just because they're working together? Because Theo is trying to make nice after so much time spent antagonising each other? And why does it matter so much? An invite is an invite, and if he wants to go he should just accept. All his favourite people will be there. "Alright. I'll come for family dinner and plan to stay for a few hours. And…thank you."

"Wait to thank me until after. Laurie's in charge of cooking this week and T swore they wouldn't help this time." Theo sets his water bottle back down and holds his hand out to Emir, waiting for them to rejoin the others and get back to work for the last few minutes of class.

It goes smoothly from there, Emir only tickling Theo by accident (and once on purpose). Theo ensures they both get done what they need to under Lydia's guidance. At the end of class, Lydia announces that on Thursday they'll stick to the same arrangement but try basic lifts, which gets a wide mixture of reactions from the students. Jordan picks up Lili making her yelp in surprise, and Georgia looks like she's seen a ghost. She's never been very good with change.

***

"Right. Everybody dig in!" Laurie insisted on bringing everything to the table himself while everyone else sat down and chatted. It's quite the spread, but it's also…unconventional. "Come on, it's not that bad."

Laurie looks around at them when no one has reached out to grab anything, sharing silent gazes with one another.

"No, it's not bad." T takes Laurie's hand and gives it a kiss. "It's just interesting, honey."

"I get the fruit salad." Theo takes the entire bowl and sets it on his plate, leaving the others to fend for themselves. He's had more than enough experience with what Laurie calls cooking.

"Pasta." Ciaran is next to Theo just like last time Emir was here, and it shouldn't be a surprise to anyone that he'd claim the carb option. Luckily there's enough for a few people so he fills his plate while the others decide before setting it back in the centre.

"Uh…" Gabe eyes what's left, weighing his options before reaching for the cereal and oat milk. "I suppose I'll start with breakfast, and then maybe some soup later."

"Can't I just have you for dinner?" T stares at Laurie with the most intense combination of lust and love, sliding a hand onto his upper thigh under the table. Upper thigh might be a generously innocent description.

"Emir told me no sex in the common areas unless it's preapproved, so no." Ciaran answers between bites. "Choose a food option or you're cleaning the dishes."

This was something they'd all decided on years ago. No matter how sad of an attempt someone made for family dinner, everyone had to at least try it or they got the cleanup.

"Ciaran's room was wide open behind you. If you want to shag in public, at least ask first." Emir doesn't actually seem bothered, reaching for what appears to be some sort of pancake stack, but the shape of each one is reminiscent of an amoeba.

Laurie piles a bit of pasta on his own plate, adds dry toast on the side for some reason, and sits back to enjoy the chaos. "T, I made you an omelette. Did you see it?"

"Oh, I didn't...I'm sure it's perfect." T cautiously takes the clearly scrambled egg which in no way resembles an omelette. It looks to be topped with a bit of cheese which should help. They try the tiniest bite and look at Laurie in surprise. "This actually isn't bad. When did you learn how to cook eggs?"

"You can share some of this if you'd like." Theo offers Emir, who's seated across from him instead of diagonal this time. Apparently, their friends decided they didn't need a physical buffer anymore. "I promise I don't have diseases or anything."

"Thanks, princess. Maybe save me some melon for later?" Emir smiles at Theo before taking another bite of pancake. "Laur, these pancakes aren't half bad. A bit dry, but with the butter they're almost good."

"Wait a minute..." Theo looks at Laurie, comprehension dawning with each edible surprise. "Laurie, that poor woman is busy enough. Tell me you did *not* make her stay on Facetime with you the entire afternoon."

Laurie flushes immediately, chugging his water as if he's dying of thirst. He loves his mum and he's never going to apologise for it. He was technically supposed to do this on his own, but she's his mum. If he isn't allowed her help, he wouldn't know who he is in this world.

"I should've known." T shakes their head fondly and kisses the side of Laurie's head. "I didn't have time to help today, but Sara will always make time for her boy."

"She didn't mind!" Laurie stabs his pasta a bit too forcefully and it doesn't even make it onto the fork. "Gave us time to chat. Catch up. I haven't seen her in weeks."

"Your mum is so sweet." Ciaran adds. He's only met Sara a handful of times, but she's one of the warmest people any of them have ever known. "Proper saint, she is."

"Laurie, you're so – " T drops their fork so they can kiss Laurie properly, holding his face with both hands to smush their mouths together. Laurie moans far too loud for the dinner table, and definitely too sexually for someone who was just talking about their mum.

"Oi." Emir tosses a piece of pancake at them because now Laurie's kissing back, and if someone doesn't interrupt it's about to get blue.

"Ooo are we having a food fight." Gabe picks up a handful of dry cereal and drops it on top of Ciaran's head. Ciaran throws his head back and laughs, the cereal falling to the ground around him.

"Sweetheart, that was the most delicate food fight I have ever seen." And now Ciaran's kissing Gabe, so more than half of the people at the table have stopped eating to snog instead.

"What is even happening right now?" Theo has a piece of pineapple halfway to his mouth that he drops back in the bowl. This is a new level of horny, even for this group. "Hello! Family dinner time. Orgy later. At least let me and Emir eat something before you get spunk all over the food."

"That would *not* go well with these pancakes." Emir looks down at his plate while considering it. "Too bitter."

"What does – " Theo turns scarlet when Emir looks up to meet his eyes. "Nevermind. Should we just...take this to the sofa? Or my room? Let them get it out of their system?"

Theo glances briefly at the others to confirm they're still connected at the mouths. It's not properly indecent yet, but they don't seem to care that anyone else is around. Or that they're literally in the middle of a meal.

Emir's still trying to determine if Theo was about to ask what spunk tastes like, and based on the way he flushed he absolutely was. Interesting...but Theo asked him a question. "If we go in your room, can we watch something that isn't work?"

"Literally whatever you want. Just don't leave me alone. Please." Theo throws a grape at T's head that bounces off and makes them giggle, but they don't stop, so. "And I am *not* cleaning up this mess when you lot are done."

Theo gets a dismissive hand waved at him from Ciaran and a thumbs up from Laurie, so he rolls his eyes and stands up.

The two of them grab their plates, or in Theo's case, the bowl of fruit, and shuffle over to Theo's room, shutting the door most of the way behind them. Theo grabs his laptop from where it was charging on his desk and the two of them settle on his bed, Emir grabbing the fluffy red blanket automatically as if it belongs to him now.

"So...what are we watching then?" Theo turns the laptop towards Emir to let him choose, picking up his fork again and wincing when he hears something clatter back out in the common area.

"Well, it's autumn, so – " Emir has Netflix open to *Gilmore Girls*, scrolling through to find an episode that looks fun. "Oh we *have* to watch the Bracebridge Dinner. I don't even care that it's not snowing."

"Alright, but first a very important question:" Theo pauses while Emir settles his pancakes across his lap, "Team Jess or Team Logan?"

"No Team Dean option?" Emir raises his eyebrow at Theo, grinning when he shakes his head no, still waiting for an answer. "Team Paris, obviously."

"Right? Okay, thank god you see it too. Those two are *so* gay for each other. Even in this episode!" Theo scoots closer to Emir until their knees are touching, facing the screen together with their legs crossed. Emir reaches over and steals a piece of cantaloupe with his fingers, Theo tilting the bowl to give him easier access.

They eat their food quietly while the show starts, laughing at Lorelai and Sookie and falling into the world of Stars Hollow like every other time before. But a few minutes in, Emir sets his empty plate on the floor and clears his throat, trying to make this as non-awkward as possible.

"You don't have to be embarrassed about that, Teddy." Emir taps Theo's knee softly with his fingertips. It's an unimportant part of the episode so he doesn't feel bad making Theo ignore it.

"About what?" Theo tilts his head at Emir while finishing a strawberry. It makes his lips shiny and pink when Emir glances down at them before meeting his eyes again. Not the time.

"Not knowing what cum tastes like. That's what you were going to ask, right?" Emir figured Theo would flush, but maybe not quite so severely. He could give that strawberry some competition.

"I'm not embarrassed." Theo mumbles, setting his fruit on the bedside table and folding his hands across his lap, staring at the screen without really paying attention. He definitely *is* embarrassed, even if he knows he shouldn't be. He never minds talking about sex, but he is admittedly insecure about his own inexperience.

"But you're curious?" Emir waits for some sort of reaction, but Theo just shrugs and keeps staring anywhere but at him. "You haven't asked Laurie or one of the others?"

"It'd be weird to ask one of them." Theo glances at Emir quickly before turning away again, heat continuing to pulse through his reddened face. "I know their partners. It's too...personal."

Emir considers that for a moment. Theo makes a good point. He wouldn't necessarily want to know that about his friends either, even if he already does know in a few of their friends' cases. "I could see that. But lucky for you, I know the answer and it's not partner specific. So if you're curious I don't mind answering."

Theo feels like he's on actual fire right now, and he can only imagine how red his face is. He's also a little surprised that Emir is being so nice about this. Clearly this shows that Theo has basically no sexual experience, at least not with anyone with a penis, or if he did it would be minimal. He has absolutely none, but Emir doesn't know that.

Emir could so easily be laughing at him or making it awkward, but he seems to be treating this like...a sexual health situation? "You don't have to. That's personal, too. I shouldn't have even – "

"Theo." Emir sets his hand gently on Theo's knee again, but this time he keeps it there. "It's a perfectly normal question and one I've definitely answered before. I hope no one has made you embarrassed to talk about these things?"

"I've never asked. And it's not like school would've taught me." Theo glances at the door, sees that it's still partly open, and hopes that the others don't choose now to unglue their mouths from their partners. "I can't always trust the internet, either."

"Well, if you want to know, it depends a bit on the person. Like generally it's bitter, sometimes vaguely...metallic. Some people say it can be sweet but I've never thought so. Bit salty sometimes too. And it can be different from the same person at different times. Lots of reasons it might taste one way or another." Emir talks slow and quiet, watching Theo process what he's hearing one word at a time. He has a feeling he wishes he could be taking notes right now, and that thought makes Emir smile. "I've never minded how it tastes, but the texture can be a bit much for some people."

"What does it, um, feel like?" Theo starts fidgeting with the edge of the red blanket that's across Emir's lap, trying to be even a fraction less self conscious right now. He's failing.

"In your mouth?" Emir waits for Theo to nod before answering, wanting to reassure him with more than just words, but settling for what's allowed. "It's warm. Reminds me of raw egg whites a bit. Sort of gloopy? That's probably why some people spit it out. Or they just don't get it near their mouth to begin with. Everyone has their own preference."

"It's not that...I just...I don't..." Theo isn't sure exactly what he wants to say. Obviously, if things were easier for him and he could just...find out for himself, he wouldn't be having this awkward conversation right now. But Emir's not making it awkward, even though it's potentially the most intimate conversation they've had.

"There's no rush, Theo. If you want to find out someday, I'm sure you'll get the chance. People think everyone is so experienced so young, but I don't think that's true." Emir smiles softly when Theo looks up at him, finally. "Sure, some people start shagging as teens, but a lot of people wait til university or later. Whenever is right for them. And if it hasn't been your time yet, that's fine. Or if you never want to...if you aren't interested in sex that's fine too. It's okay to wonder, even if you don't want to experience it."

"I do." Theo returns Emir's gentle smile, not wanting to get any more into it than that right now. He's barely managing to stay put, his only escape blocked by four naked gays in the living room. "I want to. But um…you're right. I haven't yet. Not…not with anyone actually."

"That's alright." Emir takes Theo's nearest hand and gives it a gentle squeeze. That's not surprising, now that he knows Theo, but admitting as much is a huge show of trust. "But you want to, someday?"

"Someday, definitely. I do feel a bit embarrassed sometimes." Theo glances down at their hands and links their fingers together, grateful for the reassuring comfort of it. "It feels like all my friends found their person so young and I missed the train. Or like…you aren't with anyone, at least I don't think you are?"

Theo turns his head to Emir for confirmation. He doesn't want to assume.

"I'm not. Just me, for now." Emir squeezes his hand again to encourage him to continue talking if he wants.

"Right, but I know you have multiple partners. I don't mean all at once, but if you do that's fine too." Theo shrugs, and Emir appreciates Theo's acceptance of however he chooses to live his life. "But between my friends - and even my sisters both got married young…I just worry it's not going to happen for me. I can't do casual, and I'm in my final year of uni so like…I'm supposed to have it all figured out. The partner and the job and all of it. And I just…don't."

"Teddy." Emir reaches over to pause the show. Neither of them has been watching for several minutes, but Emir wants to make sure Theo hears him. Maybe he should be shocked that Theo is always so willingly vulnerable around him, but he feels a similar way. They just seem to understand each other.

"It's alright. I didn't mean to vent at you like this." Theo sniffles, trying to hold back his emotions because this is one of his deepest vulnerabilities - that he's too difficult to love or too uninteresting or that he missed "The One" at some point and now it's too late. Even if he's always wanted a partner someday. Wanting someone doesn't matter if no one wants him.

"You're putting a lot of pressure on yourself, princess." Emir brings their joined hands into his lap while he talks. "No one expects you to have all the answers, right now or ever. And finding a forever partner like those four idiots in the other room did? At our age? That's astronomically unlikely. You just happen to have chosen four of the biggest lover bois as friends, and then you have Lilibet and Jordan who are living up to the sapphic stereotype of moving in together immediately. But Theo, your story doesn't have to look like theirs. And being inexperienced sexually, with or without a romantic partner, that's nothing you should feel insecure about. Really." Theo glances up at Emir again with a small smile. "Believe me, I've been with enough people to know."

That makes Theo laugh quietly, nudging his shoulder into Emir's with a grin. "Thanks for that. Who would've thought that a conversation about spunk would lead us here?"

"Me." Emir lets go of Theo's hand to scoot back on the bed and get comfortable, picking up the laptop to set on his own lap. "You're a very deep well, princess. Lots of layers. You think things through and make connections, so I figured there may be more to it."

"Remember how you thought I was straight?" Theo snuggles under the blanket where Emir's holding it open for him. He fits himself onto Emir's chest, just like last week, honestly needing a bit of a cuddle after feeling so open and vulnerable.

"Ugh, don't remind me." Emir gags and uses his right hand to rewind the show to where he interrupted it for this conversation. "I'd much rather you get weepy over spunk than whine about heterosexual drama."

"You're so strange..." Theo feels warmer with every brush of Emir's fingers over the outside of his arm, soothing him. "I like it. We match."

"You're visually the poster child for conformity, princess." Emir laughs and hits play again. "All muscles and schedules and capsule wardrobe and meticulously folded socks – "

"How do you know about my socks?" Theo shifts so he can look at Emir again, pushing up slightly off the bed. Did he snoop more than Theo realised last week?

"That one was a guess, but I'm assuming if I open the top drawer on the right hand side there would be folded socks." Emir tilts his head in the direction of Theo's wardrobe.

"How did you - ?" Theo doesn't know how Emir could possibly know that. Is he really that predictable? "Are you...am I boring?"

Emir laughs, ruffling Theo's hair fondly. "Pumpkin, if you were boring I wouldn't give you the time of day. If you haven't noticed, I barely talk to most people."

He doesn't even mean it as an insult to other people. It's just that only certain people capture his attention enough to make him want to interrupt his quiet, and even fewer turn out to be decent. "It's more like a yin yang. My room is covered in half-finished art projects and yours has an inventory system. You're not boring, you're centred."

"Why do you keep being nice to me?" Theo resettles on Emir's shoulder with a sigh, only partially paying attention to the show even now.

"Would you rather I was mean to you?" Emir laughs at Michel who is easily one of his favourites. He had a feeling that Theo would be a *Gilmore Girls* fan too. He's glad he was right.

Theo doesn't answer Emir but he certainly thinks about it. It's not that he ever enjoyed fighting with Emir, but there was something about the way they would argue, how they were always on the same level, pushing each other towards the same goal. It was fiery and exciting, even if it was also exhausting and sometimes in the way of their friendships. "After this episode, can we make tea? I don't really feel like working tonight, if that's alright."

"If you tried to make me focus on work tonight I think I'd overturn that fruit bowl on your head." Emir grins when he feels Theo laugh quietly in response. "Now shhh. It's almost time for the ridiculous costumes."

***

"Unbelievable. Absolutely unbelievable. We gave you an *hour!*" Emir picks up one of the cushions from the ground and tosses it at Gabe and Ciaran while Theo turns on the light. The fact that one of them had the foresight to turn it off before getting fucked in the living room is borderline impressive. Because they've definitely all been having sex, which Emir realises as he looks around at the evidence provided.

"At least they moved to the sofas." Theo adds from the kitchen. When they left his room to check on the others, he decided to let Emir deal with the four writhing figures in the darkened living room.

"We kept our clothes on...most of them." T sits up with Laurie on their lap, rubbing at a huge love bite on the side of their neck. They both look wrecked.

"Well I'm *so sorry* to interrupt, but we're having family tea since the four of you fucked your way through family dinner. Get up and clean up the table while we fix tea and meet us on the sofas when you're done." Emir throws another cushion at the back of Ciaran's head because he's still biting at Gabe's neck. "Up!"

"Jesus, Emir. I'm up." Ciaran rubs at the back of his head and scoots off of Gabe, but neither of them looks even slightly apologetic. Gabe has to pull up and rebutton his jeans and Ciaran is down to his undershirt, his jumper discarded back at the table next to a knocked over chair.

"But isn't my new bra so cute? It's all frilly." T stands up and twirls, their hair an absolute disaster, but they have that well-loved glow. It suits them.

"Did you go shopping?" Emir steps past Theo to the fridge to get out the different milk options for everyone. With a vegan, a vegetarian, and four omnivores, their fridge is an organised, but cluttered storage vessel.

"Laurie picked it out. Said he wanted me to feel pretty." T twirls again and knocks into Laurie who steadies them before pulling them into a hug from behind.

"I'm ordering a pizza." Laurie's voice is extremely hoarse. Theo decides not to ask any questions about that. He already knows too much.

"Fine. But only because you're one fourth of the reason we're all starving." Emir, despite his little speech, goes to the table and starts clearing it up. Which means that Theo joins him, and in less than five minutes, the six of them are settled on the sofas, Emir curled up in Theo's red blanket with Theo sitting on the floor at his feet.

"Why are we watching *Gilmore Girls*?" Gabe asks after a sip of his tea. He's sitting next to Ciaran, their legs crossed together as they basically share a lap. At least the soft core porn has stopped for now.

"Not a single complaint from any of you." Emir grumbles, setting the remote aside and holding his tea in both hands. "Drink your tea and appreciate Stars Hollow."

Theo's wearing what feels like a permanent smile on his face. Emir didn't even want to come tonight, but here he is, bossing everyone around while huddled in his blanket like a grumpy kitten. He lets his head rest on Emir's knee until the pizza arrives, Laurie plopping it on the coffee table before resettling next to T. It may not be the family dinner anyone planned for, but it's definitely family.

***

Laurie: *Gays*
Laurie: *This is an emergency*
Laurie: *What are we wearing*
Laurie: *We can't clash*
Ciaran: *This is already the gayest conversation we've ever had. How is that possible?*
Laurie: *My homosexuality is infinite /rainbow emoji/*
Gabe: *We have a group chat now?*
T: *Laurie if you don't let me choose your outfit we're getting a divorce*
Laurie: *We aren't married yet?*
T: *As if that matters???*
Theo: *Are we all going to this party?*
Theo: *Laurie, you only asked me two minutes ago.*
Theo: *I haven't even decided if I'm going yet.*
Gabe: *You're going.*
Ciaran: *We didn't go out for my birthday so*
Theo: *Am I being guilted into this?*
Laurie: *Is it working?*
Emir: *i'll wear whatever i want /painted nails emoji/*
T: *I'm thinking if we all stick to an autumn colour palette we should be fine*
Theo: *Won't it be...dark? No one will even see us.*
Theo: *Also I'm thinking the closest I can get to that is green.*
T: *Hush Teddy I'm dressing you*
Ciaran: *Isn't this just another house party?*
Laurie: *What's your point?*
Ciaran: *Well four of us already know who we're going home with*
Ciaran: *And Gabe prefers me in my birthday suit*
Ciaran: *Although I should always keep the option open that we might bring someone else home. Wouldn't be the first time.*
Emir: *hoes*

Emir: (affectionately)

Emir: too hot to wear a turtleneck?

Theo: Please wear a turtleneck.

Laurie: Are we meeting there?

T: Probably easiest. You and I have to leave early since we're out of town this weekend

Emir: i also have to leave early. well...before one preferably.

Theo: Does that mean you finally chose a venue?

Laurie: I chose a lovely place in Darton called my mother's home

T: Not this again

T: Your mum has quite enough on at the moment

Emir: this is why my sister just used a venue in the city

T: I am not getting married in London

Laurie: I am not getting married in London

Gabe: See? You agree

Ciaran: Careful, sweetheart. Last time I tried to help I was kicked out of the flat

Laurie: You went to Gabe's and fucked for hours so it wasn't exactly a punishment

Theo: I'm going to sleep. It's a school night.

Laurie: But the party's TOMORROW

Laurie: And what are we going to WEAR

T: I'll take care of it

T: Everyone send me your options and I'll make sure we don't clash

Theo: Emir, where are we on that turtleneck? Yes? I said please.

T: Need a distraction from this fucking assignment

Emi: goodnight, princess. i'll wear the turtleneck.

Emi: /selfie from the studio, sweaty and with his vest riding up his abs/

Laurie: ...what the fuck was that?

Ciaran: Do you often send Theo thirst traps?

Emi: why does everyone keep saying that?

Emi: i'm gross. i'm at the studio. what about that is thirsty?

T: Do we really have to go through this again

Laurie: Emi, I have zero interest in you but you're the hottest human alive

T: Zero is not the correct percentage, Laur

Laurie: Not helping

Gabe: Feel free to send more. None of us are complaining.

Ciaran: Damn I think Teddy is actually asleep

Ciaran: Yup. Already asleep. Snoring away.

Emir: princess doesn't snore

Laurie: Wake him up and show him that picture and tell me what happens

Emir: /eye rolling emoji/

T: Excuse me no one has sent me their outfits for tomorrow

Emir walks to the party with Laurie and T, more than used to being a third wheel after two years of it. True to their word, T told everyone what to wear, and Emir was more than happy with their choice for his outfit: a soft brown turtleneck, vintage maroon suit trousers, and T even told him to wear his glasses for a sort of "hot librarian" vibe. Overall, Emir feels very comfortable, which is great because he has a busy day tomorrow.

Every few weeks, the dance department holds a master class with one of the many touring dance companies that visit or are based in London. It's usually on a Saturday and always early. While Emir definitely wants to be at this party, he also needs to be responsible and if he goes home with someone, it'll have to be early. He's not even sure he's in the mood for that tonight.

Once they arrive they head straight for the kitchen, Emir grabbing water to sip on, T digging a bottle of wine out of somewhere and opening it up, and Laurie taking two shots of vodka in under a minute. By the time they're "hydrated" the other three have found them, Gabe and Ciaran both making mixed drinks from what's left out and Theo grabbing water, like Emir.

"Dance with me, Teddy." Laurie grabs Theo's hand and physically drags him out of the room laughing. Theo was sort of hoping for a low key night, but this is their tradition and they always have fun.

T and Ciaran head outside to sit under the stars and chat about music and life. They'll check in on their partners occasionally. Gabe is more than happy to dance on his own or with strangers, a few feet away from where Laurie and Theo are grinding like they're being paid for it, which leaves Emir to meet someone, or at the very least, wander around and hear the gossip to pass along to everyone else later.

Just like all the other times, this party is a bit much for Emir. He's actually glad to be wearing what he is because every single person he passes seems to feel the need to touch him, so at least he's covered by fabric. It's exceptionally loud, even for a uni party. Emir's relieved that he won't be staying late because he's already feeling a bit overstimulated and he's only been here about ten minutes, including their trip to the kitchen. He wonders if Theo's feeling the same. Emir hasn't asked Theo outright, but he has a few reasons to wonder if he's neurodivergent, too. With his PTSD, Emir's neurodivergency came later in life, but it's as inherent to his being as if he'd grown up with it.

"So you're Emir Shah." Emir's been wandering on his own when he turns around to see a pretty, petite woman standing against the wall. She lets the beer bottle fall out of her lips slowly, leaving zero mystery about what she's interested in, especially when she looks him up and down, then tilts her head.

"And you are?" Well, that was faster than Emir planned, but he's not going to complain about the ease. He leans against the wall next to her, waiting for her to initiate something. Emir would never touch someone without their explicit consent, and until he knows that they're at least mostly sober, he's happy to flirt from a few feet away.

"Mary." She answers, reaching out to tug on his turtleneck with her bottom lip caught between her teeth. Her lips are thin around a diminutive mouth, but it suits her. Emir wouldn't be surprised if the worst sorts of guys take one look at her small...everything, and make her into a fantasy.

"Is that your real name or is that just for tonight?" Emir stops her hand as it wanders down his chest. There's no need to rush this. And for some reason he's not feeling it. Not tonight. His mind flickers to a memory of huddling beneath a blanket with Theo while watching *Gilmore Girls*, and any potential interest Emir had in Mary's offer evaporates.

"Smart, too." Mary smiles at him and moves closer, leaning into him. "I've been trying to get your attention since last year. Finally got the chance to talk to you."

"Mary, you seem lovely." Emir steps back, bumping into the person behind him and apologising. "I'm actually just here with my friends tonight. Maybe another time?"

Mary scoffs at his rejection and pushes him away by the chest with a sneer. She went from dripping in invitation to staring at him with disgust in record time. "I should've known. So what's their name then?"

Emir isn't sure what that's supposed to mean, but he's losing interest in Mary by the second. She seems to assume a lot about him, and that's his least favourite flavour of stranger. She won't even tell him her real name and she thinks he's so easy that the only reason he won't go with her is because there's someone else?

"Have a nice night, Mary." Emir turns around, deciding that maybe he'll go find Ciaran and T.

On his way outside he sees Theo and figures maybe they can chat for a bit since they both have to leave early anyway. But Theo's not alone. Well, good for him, meeting some new people. Maybe he'll be tired tomorrow if he gets wrapped up in the party, but Emir decides to return to his previous plan of finding T. He makes his way through another dozen people, wishing he'd thought to stay with one of their group so he wasn't in this situation.

Emir glances again at Theo again and oh. That's not...friendly. Theo is practically underneath the guy now, and Emir immediately changes direction again. He couldn't even explain why, but he doesn't like it. He's seeing neon green, a combination of envy and panic so strong it's distracting.

But as he keeps moving through the crowd, slowly because the room is overflowing with people, his heart stops and falls through his feet. Theo is still across the room and he's not alone, which is whatever. But Emir knows the guy making a pass at Theo and Laurie is nowhere in sight. Which would be fine, except Emir will have to deal with this without backup and if he doesn't, Theo's going to get hurt.

"Fuck. Not again." As casually as he can, Emir hurries across the room, hoping that Laurie is coming back soon. He probably just stepped into the kitchen for another shot.

Before Emir even reaches the two of them huddled in the corner, he can hear that dickhead laying it on thick, and Theo doesn't seem bothered. But Theo probably doesn't know him yet, and he's definitely too trusting, unaware of what some people are capable of.

"Josh." Emir slides in between them on the wall, gently nudging Theo back and squeezing his hand before letting it drop again. He didn't plan on being a human shield tonight, but this is an emergency. "Never thought I'd see you again. I planned on it actually."

"What do you want, Emir?" Josh rolls his eyes and tries to lean around him to get to Theo, but Emir gets in his way again. Absolutely the fuck not. "We were having a conversation."

"And now you're done." Emir may be shorter than Josh, but his glare more than makes up for it. It's a miracle Josh is still standing, honestly. "Goodbye, Josh."

"You don't get to tell me what to do, bum boy." Josh spits his words at Emir, as if they mean nothing. As if he himself isn't queer and should know better than to use that sort of language. Ever.

"Emir, what's going on?" Theo tries to get around Emir, but he holds Theo back with his arm. He'll explain later.

"Go home, Josh. You shouldn't even be here." Emir really wishes Laurie were here right now, because at least he understands. He knows exactly what breed of monster Josh is. "And if I ever see you speaking to Theo again, I'll put you through a wall."

"Didn't know you had yourself a boyfriend, Shah." Josh leans back against the wall, not in any rush to go anywhere apparently.

"He's not mine but he's also not yours." Emir turns to glance at Theo and sees he's confused as hell. But that can wait. Priorities. "Leave or I'll make a scene. Your choice."

"Fucking hell." Josh rolls his eyes again but walks away, Emir watching him until he's out of sight. He can't follow him, but he hopes he actually does leave. He walked in the direction of the front door, so hopefully. Maybe in a few minutes he can double check...

"Emir...what the fuck was that?" Theo's voice brings Emir back to reality and makes him turn around. Even in such a loud room, Theo's voice focuses him.

"What were you doing talking to Josh?" Emir crosses his arms over his chest, suddenly very protective of Theo. He shouldn't just be talking with some random guy he doesn't know, especially without one of their friends around. Emir can hear how angry his voice sounds, but he doesn't really know any way to change that right now. The panic hasn't entirely receded.

"We had a business class together last year. He was just making small talk." Theo starts walking away. He needs some fucking air. He doesn't understand anything that just happened, but he doesn't want to be in this room anymore. It's stifling.

"No he wasn't, Theo. He was practically on top of you." Emir follows, trying to continue their conversation while they get jostled around walking through the crowd. "You can't just go chatting up any random stranger who's nice to you at a party."

"Excuse me?" Theo turns around abruptly and Emir's surprised to see he looks genuinely upset. "What is that supposed to mean?"

"Exactly what I said. You're too trusting." Emir tries to reach for Theo but he steps back. "I'm just looking out for you."

"Why were you even trying to find me in the first place? I can talk to whoever I want and I don't need your permission." Theo starts walking again. He's not some child that Emir can boss around, and he has some nerve saying something like that when he usually goes to parties with the express goal of going home with a stranger. Theo's seen it firsthand plenty of times, so what the fuck?

"Theo, slow down. Where are you going?" Emir reaches out and grabs Theo's shoulder, but he shrugs his hand off.

Theo just wants to be somewhere quieter. Maybe find their other friends. It's too fucking loud and he's reaching his limit.

"I don't know yet. I need a break. Just...why do you even care so much? It's a party. Go find someone to take home. You were chatting with that girl earlier, go find her." Theo is in some sort of hallway, Emir right behind him. It's not crowded, but it's also not exactly where he meant to go. He was hoping to end up outside. Clear his head.

"I don't give a fuck about that right now. I'm trying to talk to you." Emir finally gets in front of Theo again, waiting for him to stop walking before continuing. He needs Theo to understand. "Josh is dangerous. I don't want you to talk to him anymore."

"God, now I remember why we used to fight all the time. You don't own the world, Emir! And you don't get to decide who I talk to." Theo throws his hands up, suddenly on the verge of anger. This is ridiculous. Can he not have a conversation with a classmate? "I can talk to whoever I want, and you don't get any say in that. I'm not a fucking child."

"He's a fucking predator, Theo." Emir says it quietly, but Theo hears him all the same. Words this heavy hit hard. "He tried it on me, and he's done it to others. I was genuinely trying to protect you from him."

"...Oh." Theo deflates, looking at Emir with surprise, then concern. Is Emir alright after seeing him? That might partially explain why he's being such an arse right now. "I...I didn't know."

"No. You didn't." Emir sighs and holds his head in both hands. He has a sudden need to pull his own fucking hair out, but at least Theo understands now. "Just...you have to be more careful."

And now Theo's angry again.

"Oh, like you are?" Theo crosses his arms over his chest and glares at Emir. "You barely bother finding out most people's names before you leave with them. I don't care who you sleep with, but you have some nerve telling me to be careful when you're one bad decision away from - "

"Shut up!" Emir shoves at Theo's chest, not even wanting to hear the rest of that sentence. He's barely keeping it together, and he doesn't need judgement about his sex life piled on top. "I know what I'm talking about, Theo. Why can't you just listen to me?"

"Don't tell me to shut up. You don't get to tell me one thing and then do the opposite. I understand why you don't want me talking to Josh, but beyond that, I can do whatever I want. Talk to whoever I want." Theo's on the verge of tears from how frustrated he is. What even is this conversation? "Just *once* I want to be the person who goes to the party and has someone want to take me home. Just once, I want someone to choose me. People don't even fucking notice me. And you're telling me that I shouldn't even be talking to people."

"That's not what I'm saying. Fuck!" Emir slides a hand down his face, pushing his glasses up and away from his eyes. He's not saying anything he means right now. The adrenaline is still too high for him to make any actual sense. "And how could you possibly think no one notices you? You have no fucking idea."

"I don't even know what that means, Emir." Theo rubs at his own temples, feeling like he has a headache looming. "Why do you even care? Two weeks ago you would've happily let Josh do whatever he had planned. You wouldn't have even noticed."

"How fucking dare you." Emir is the one raising his voice now, but the noise from the party is loud and only one person even bothers to look in their direction. "I would *never* let him do that to anyone. That's the first time I've seen him in a year. I thought he finally got kicked out of Roseborough. I didn't exactly plan for him to be all over you, Theo."

"And what if it hadn't been Josh? There's no way you recognised him from where you were." Theo crosses his arms again, facing Emir with fire in his eyes. "Does every person I see have to pass some sort of Emir Shah inspection before I'm allowed to speak to them? You about to make a list of who's allowed to talk to me?"

"Why should I care?" Emir throws his hands in the air again, confused about where this conversation is heading. He's trying to keep Theo safe from people like Josh. What about that is so hard to understand? "We're talking about you, not me."

"Well you seem to care a lot. Telling me I can't be chatting people up at parties and *I need to be more careful*." Theo glares at Emir, waiting for him to apologise for being a dick. "Like I said: I'm not a child. And who I talk to doesn't affect you."

"This isn't about me, Theo. It's about you getting hurt. You shouldn't be wandering around alone at a place like this." Emir runs his hand through his hair, trying to calm down. Why are they fucking yelling at each other in a hallway?

"And what about you then? You going to stop? Or is it only me that needs to worry?" Theo knows he's making at least a little bit of sense because he can tell Emir feels guilty. Hopefully for the right thing and not just for arguing.

"You trust people too easily. I know what to look out for. You don't." Emir is trying to make Theo understand, but now he just looks hurt. Fuck, that is not what Emir wanted. That's the opposite of what he wanted. How did they end up here? Emir doesn't want Theo to ever know what he knows, to live with pain and fear and trust issues so strong he barely opens up to his closest friends.

"Is this about how I'm....how I haven't...I'm not stupid just because no one wants to shag me." Theo starts to walk away again, hunched over and looking defeated, but Emir stops him with a hand on his arm. "I may be awkward, but I'm not stupid."

"You're not either of those things. Theo, please just talk to me. I'm sorry I've been yelling. Can we go somewhere and just talk? Please?" Emir tries to get Theo to meet his eyes, but he won't. Emir's never seen him this upset. Angry? Yes. But not this. This is so much worse. He looks like he's shutting down, and shutting Emir out in the process.

"I don't want to talk to you right now. You're being mean and that isn't like you." Theo turns to Emir but still won't look at him. His voice is small and sad, like he's lost something. "I told you about my inexperience in confidence. You don't get to use it against me as some sort of control thing. That's fucking cruel."

Emir doesn't even know what to say to that, because Theo's right. He didn't mean it like that but he's also being a dick and he knows it. He doesn't like himself right now, and he can't unsay any of that. This is all so fucked up and it's at least partially his fault. "I'll leave. Please go find Laurie. He's your best mate and he'll understand about Josh. And...I'm sorry. I'll give you space."

"You don't have to leave, Emir." Theo sounds about three inches tall right now, and Emir wants to punch his own face. He never meant to hurt Theo like this. He was just worried and it spiralled and they're both too emotional to have a productive conversation about it. But it doesn't matter if he meant to hurt Theo or not because he did.

"I'll – " Emir clears his throat and wipes at his eyes, in the process of bolting. His vision is clouded in shades of icy gray. "I'll see you tomorrow."

Before Theo can respond, Emir walks off, disappearing into the crowd again. And when Theo goes to see where he went, he's gone.

***

Laurie: *Where are you and why is Theo holding back tears??*
Emi: *i was a jealous tit*
Emi: *but then Josh was involved and I panicked*
Laurie: *Where the fuck is he I'll knock his teeth out*
Emi: *he was with theo*
Emi: *on theo*
Emi: *i got him to leave but then i sort of lost it*
Emi: *i said some things I shouldn't have and i definitely hurt theo without meaning to*
Emi: *is he alright?*
Laurie: *I'm taking him home*
Laurie: *Are you alright?*
Emi: *he didn't touch me. i'll be fine.*
Emi: *just...please let me know when theo's home safe*
Emi: *that fucking scared me. i thought that fucker was gone*

Emi: *and theo's too trusting. he could've been hurt.*
Laurie: *Well according to Theo you were a controlling twat*
Laurie: *And based on what he's told me he's correct*
Emi: *i said i was a jealous tit*
Emi: *i'm sorry*
Laurie: *I'm not the one you owe an apology to*
Emi: *i'll talk to him. but like...maybe in a few days*
Laurie: *Emir what the hell*
Emi: *i was scared*
Emi: *i know that's not an excuse but i need to get over this or its going to happen again*
Emi: *im not myself when i panic and theo didn't deserve any of that*
Laurie: *Jesus fuck emi*
Laurie: *You two are fucking stubborn as shit, but I'm glad you're both safe.*
Laurie: *Theo's home.*
Laurie: *I'm letting T sit with him for a bit to make sure he's alright. We're staying here tonight since we leave early.*
Laurie: *You sure you're alright?*
Emi: *i'll be fine. as long as theo's safe it's fine.*
Emi: *just...check on him again for me?*
Emi: *i said i would give him space on account of acting like a massive bellend*
Laurie: *He's in bed*
Laurie: *You have to fix this Emi. He's fucking hurt.*
Emi: *i will. i promise.*
Emi: *love you*
Emi: *and i'm sorry*
Laurie: *Love you too*

***

Emir doesn't sleep the entire night. He spends hours obsessively cycling through thoughts of what he needs to say, how he needs to apologise, and how he ended up here in the first place. And what he realises is that Theo was right in more ways than one. Before he even knew it was Josh, before his PTSD spiked his adrenaline and made everything worse, he wanted to put himself between Theo and whoever was with him. He made the choice before it escalated. And he didn't make that choice from a place of platonic concern. The way he lost control afterwards only confirmed that for Emir. He was completely out of line and there's no excuse for it. No one deserves to be yelled at like that, treated as if they're incapable of making their own decisions.

Laurie's been right this entire time. All he's ever wanted was Theo's attention, and for years he thought the only way to have it was through competition and constant fighting. But spending the last few weeks letting Theo into his life has shown him another way. It's probably what he's been wanting all along if he's honest with himself. Emir's learned that Theo is everything he's always wanted to be and exactly the type of person he would hope to find. Theo is kind, considerate, funny, intelligent, warm, and he respects Emir's boundaries. He has the most adorable laugh and his eyes crinkle when he's truly happy. He's an incredible friend and an encouraging partner to those he works with. Theo's the sort of person whose presence is a comfort, someone Emir would want to come home to at the end of the day.

He's fairly certain he's ruined any chance of what he now realises he wants, but what's indisputably necessary is an apology, and showing Theo that he means it. Theo should never be as hurt as Emir made him feel, especially when he did nothing wrong. So even though Emir's had this revelation, even though he knows he wants to be with Theo, he can't do fuck all about it. So he stays awake until he finds every inch of his own culpability in that argument, ready to take responsibility and make sure it never happens again.

***

The next morning dawns slow and cold. Emir and Theo put themselves through their morning routines before showing up early at the studio for the master class. As Emir hoped, they're the first two there. This doesn't need an audience.

Cautiously, Emir walks up to Theo and sits beside him, leaving plenty of space in between them this time.

"Emir." Theo sounds so monotone, as if any spark behind his usual warmth has been snuffed out. And that apathy is so much worse than any fight they've ever had.

"I'll just say this, and then I'll leave you alone." Emir watches Theo, wishing he could do literally anything more right now. "I owe you an apology. A real one. But we both have to get through today, so I'm going to stay far away and give you your space and let you be with Lili. I know I fucked up and I know I hurt you and I'm going to fix this."

Emir pauses. "If you'll let me, that is. You have every right to change your mind and stop working with me and go back to how things were before. I would respect that. But for today, I wanted to let you know I'm not ignoring you or upset with you. I'm just respecting your space until I can make this right."

Emir stands up without another word and heads back into the hallway, planning to spend some time in the practice studio until the others show up and Theo can put space between them if he wants. Theo watches him go, still so fucking hurt, but feeling like there's hope they can fix this. But not today.

Theo goes to the barre and fusses around until Lili shows up with Jordan. Lili doesn't know anything about last night, but she knows Theo. Without saying anything, Lili wraps him in a very tight hug, only stepping back when Theo squirms away. Theo knows he can get through today, glad for the distraction from his turbulent heart, but he can't help how often his eyes find Emir.

When their long day is over, Emir rushes out of the dance building before anyone else. He hurries back to his flat and makes himself scarce. Laurie's gone for the weekend with T so it's just him and his thoughts. Around 10 that night, Emir gets a text from Theo.

Theo: *When you're ready to talk, I'll listen.*
Theo: *I'm not making any promises, but I'll hear you out.*
Theo: *Goodnight, Emir.*

Emir doesn't think he's meant to respond, at least not over text, so he goes back to his rumination. Meanwhile, Theo turns off his phone and tries to sleep. Their fights have never felt like this before, to either of them. It means something more now. There's real hurt, real pain being tossed around. They both have to fit themselves around that new reality. No one can do that for them. So they sit in their own minds, in their separate spaces, grappling with a situation that's suddenly far more complicated than either of them planned. This is the first fight that's mattered and they're both quietly hoping it hasn't shattered everything they've been building.

CHAPTER NINE

Theo's almost done with his Sunday morning cleaning when he hears a knock at the front door to the flat. He's not expecting anyone. Laurie and T are out for the weekend, Ciaran and Gabe left early for some sort of date day around the city, and Lili and Jordan are having a quiet Sunday to themselves, hoping to recover from the master class before tomorrow. So, while he's peeling his marigolds off his hands and untying his apron from around his waist, Theo gives up trying to figure out who it could be just as another quiet knock sounds through the space.

He is wholly unprepared for the sight that meets him when he opens the door. "Emir! What - ?"

On instinct, Theo reaches forward and pulls Emir inside the flat and into a hug. No one can fake the way Emir looks right now: incredibly weak, sallow as if he hasn't slept in days, trembling like he's got a fever. It's borderline frightening.

"Theo, I swear - " Emir takes a deep breath and holds Theo tight. He's so glad to see him, even in this state. Emir doesn't know what he'll do if Theo sends him away, but for now, he's not alone. "I wouldn't be here if it wasn't an emergency. I promise. I'll leave if you - "

"Just come inside and we'll sort this out." Theo reaches out to close the door behind Emir, wondering what in the hell is going on, all thoughts of whatever's broken between them pushed aside because this is clearly something else.

Emir tears himself out of the hug and steps away, shoving his hands in his pockets so he's less tempted to cling onto Theo again. "I know I owe you an apology and I shouldn't be here, but I didn't know where else to go. I promise I thought of every option."

Emir's pacing now, hands pulling at his hair as he wanders around. Theo's never even imagined Emir this upset. "Laurie and T are out of town, Ciaran and Gabe left this morning, and my sister's on her honeymoon. I can't be on my phone to call anyone else, and I'm not saying you're my last choice, but I promised to give you your space instead of fucking that up too, but I can't be alone right now, and you're safe and - "

Theo cautiously steps closer to Emir, setting a hand on his shoulder because he doesn't know what Emir's dealing with right now, but he doesn't want to scare him. "What do you need?"

"Take my phone and hide it from me." Emir holds it out to Theo like it's leaking poison. "And I'm not supposed to be alone, so I'll go hide in T's room while you go about your day. I won't be in your way, I promise. T offered it before, but if you need to check with them first, I understand."

Theo carefully guides Emir to the sofa by his elbow, nudging him out of the way as he almost walks into the table. "Wait here for a moment. Just don't go anywhere, alright?"

Emir nods and sits down, fidgeting with the sleeves of his jumper and biting at his lip. It's bleeding in spots from being chewed raw, so Theo can guess that he's been like this for a while. Theo waits a moment to make sure Emir doesn't get up, takes the phone Emir handed over, and quickly hides it away in his room between a few thick winter jumpers. He'll remember where it is later when Emir wants it back. Once that's taken care of he walks back into the living room, sitting beside Emir and looking him over again.

"When did you last sleep?" Theo doesn't think he's going to like the answer based on the evidence provided.

"I'm fine." Emir mumbles, huddling up inside of his hoodie and bringing his knees to his chest.

"Emir, come on. You don't have to tell me what's wrong, I'm just trying to get a general sense of the state of things so I can help." Theo grabs the blanket off the end of the sofa and lays it across Emir's lap, glad when he reaches out and hides himself inside of it.

"Two days." Emir waits until he's wrapped in the blanket to answer. "But I think I dozed off for a bit last night. Maybe like twenty minutes. I'm fine."

"Christ, Emir." Theo can't even imagine being that tired. He had a hard time sleeping the past few nights but nothing like this. "Have you eaten anything? Tea doesn't count."

Emir doesn't answer that one. He had a few snacks yesterday during the master class, but that hardly counts. He was busy and then he was distracted. And now he's...this. Theo takes Emir's silence for what it is, already mentally making a list of snacks to try and see if he'll eat them.

"Do you need to stay here or could we go somewhere?" When Theo feels the way Emir looks, he only knows one way to deal with it, but that solution can't be found hiding in T's room.

"What do you mean?" Emir rubs at his eyes under his glasses, and the tired bruises beneath them are so dark they look painful.

"Can I take you somewhere? You can't be alone, right? I have a car. If it's alright, let's go for a drive." It's not quite that simple of course, but Theo can take care of the rest rather quickly if it's a safe option for Emir.

"You hid my phone. I can just stay out of your way in T's room until they're back and Laurie can look after me. I know you have your own life and I can be quiet and leave you to it. Just...not supposed to be alone." Emir starts worrying at his lip again until Theo reaches up and gently uses his thumb to stop him, pulling his bottom lip down and away from his teeth.

"How long did you sit at home before coming here?" Theo wishes they weren't in a fight because he knows that's the only reason it took so long. But they are, and even though he's sure they'll figure it out, they're both aware of the situation.

"Since about six this morning." Emir finally looks up at Theo, genuine remorse in his eyes. "I thought through every option, I swear. I really wanted to take the time to give you a proper apology. And I still intend to, if you still want to hear it. But...this was a bit out of my control. I figured you'd be more upset if I...I didn't know what else to do."

"I'm glad you're here, alright?" Theo genuinely means that. Even if he and Emir had never started working together or any of the rest, he would hope to always be a refuge when needed. "You were a dick, and I'll expect that apology later. But we're here now and there's no point pretending I haven't already forgiven you...I forgave you as soon as you walked away Friday night."

Emir glances at Theo again, surprised, but also not in the least. Theo is a good fucking person and Emir's ashamed it took him so long to realise it.

"A drive?" He adjusts to snuggle more completely into the blanket. A drive with Theo doesn't sound too bad.

"Yeah. I'll do the driving, obviously." Theo smiles softly at his little joke, glad to see that Emir's panic seems to be calming down, if nothing else. "Give me about five minutes and we can head out to the car."

Theo stands up but he's stopped by one of Emir's hands on his forearm. Their eyes meet again for Emir to whisper, "Thank you."

Theo nods before stepping away to get what they need, leaving Emir to sit with his thoughts for a few minutes as he stares at nothing with his tired eyes.

***

Emir's been asleep in the passenger seat for a while now. Theo got him to sip some tea and nibble on a protein bar before he huddled up against the window and passed out. Theo doesn't think he's moved since. He's been driving for almost an hour and they're definitely out of the city. He'll probably stop soon, find somewhere that looks interesting and wake Emir up so they can go for a walk.

They pass a sign for Cookham and Theo figures that sounds as promising as he could hope for, finding his way to the edge of town and stopping the car with a sigh. He really hates to wake Emir because it's likely the first rest he's had in days, but he also can't let him sleep all cramped up against the car door like that.

Theo traces his fingers softly down the side of Emir's face, hoping to wake him as gently as possible. He doesn't think he's having any nightmares but he can't be too careful. Emir sighs and burrows further into the window, face squished into his hoodie. "We're here, Emi. Time to get up."

"Sleepy." Emir mumbles, yawning and rubbing at his eyes. His glasses end up sideways and Theo smiles while adjusting them.

"I know. You must be exhausted. But you can't sleep in the car without ruining your back." Theo reaches down for the thermos of tea that Emir abandoned to sleep. He strokes Emir's arm to wake him up a little more, placing the thermos in his palm and watching his cold fingers wrap around it. "Tea's still hot. That should help."

Without opening his eyes, Emir brings the thermos to his chapped lips and takes a sip, humming quietly. He looks calm, which is a noticeable improvement. Emir blinks his eyes open and tries to sit up, wincing at the sun. "Where are we?"

"Haven't a clue. Cookham apparently." Theo looks around them to get an idea of their surroundings. "Looks quaint."

"It's England. It all looks quaint." Emir mumbles. He's slowly waking back up enough to reorient himself. He doesn't think he's been asleep for very long. It's still morning. "Why are we here?"

"Well..." Theo reaches for his own tea and takes a drink, readjusting to face Emir. "The thing is, when I feel lost, I get lost. I go somewhere I've never been and find my way around. It doesn't fix anything, but it reminds me that I know how to figure it out, even when I haven't a clue where I am. So...I just drove until somewhere looked confusing."

Emir isn't nearly well rested enough to appreciate how fond he feels right now. Yes, he recognises that he has it bad for this human teddy bear. But who could blame him, when Theo so casually says something this profound and ingenious. Emir wishes they were in a better place and he'd had time to apologise for the other night, but they're not.

He settles back in his seat and stares at Theo with shining eyes to say, "You might be the smartest person I've ever known."

Theo smiles and looks down at his tea, feeling warm in more ways than one. He knows they still need to talk, and they will, but they're going to be alright. "You up for a walk?"

"You may have to carry me but I wouldn't be opposed to giving it a go." Emir glances out the car window before looking back at Theo. "So we just...wander?"

"Let your instincts guide you. If you feel like finding some place to eat, you find one. You want quiet, either find a cemetery or a body of water. That sort of thing." Theo reaches into the back seat to grab the bag he packed earlier. "Here."

Theo hands Emir a black beanie, a new lip balm, a bottle of water, and another protein bar. Emir takes them carefully, all too aware of his feelings seeing the consideration Theo managed to cram into about five minutes of preparation back at his flat. Now that he's sure of what he wants, Emir would prefer to curl up in Theo's chest and stay there forever.

"I'm new to this. Lead the way?" Emir tilts his head towards the pavement with an encouraging smile while pulling the hat over his exceptionally disastrous hair. Theo grins, and there are those eye crinkles that Emir adores. The churn in his stomach is not from hunger, at least not for anything edible.

They step out of the car and into what feels like another world. The air is crisp and clean, nothing like what they adjust to in London. It's an old town, as most of them are, and it feels both familiar and entirely new.

Theo locks the car and waits for Emir to join him, glad to see Emir unwrap his snack and take a small bite. It's a start. They wander in silence for several minutes, sticking to the main road, not chatting with any of the locals they encounter beyond brief hellos. Theo knows that Emir needs quiet, and Emir appreciates that more than Theo may ever know. The rhythm of their footsteps and the sound of the mid morning is soothing and Emir breathes deeply as they go. It's exactly what he needs.

"I think...can we find somewhere quiet? A churchyard on a Sunday probably isn't the best idea, but aren't we near a river?" Emir pauses in his path to look across at Theo.

Theo looks wonderful, and not fit, just...the flush from the cold reflects how warm he is, and the way the wind blows his loose curls reminds Emir of how it felt to tangle his fingers in them. It's all sentimental and lovely and Emir feels like even if he's in a crisis he's also been given this gift of knowing Theo's heart. He's been so open and trusting with Emir since the first moment they decided to work together. And that trust was essentially what Emir tried to make him feel ashamed about the other night, which is just...he'll add it to the list of apologies.

"I saw a few signs that looked water related. Just pick a direction and if it ends in water, great. If not, we retrace and start again." Theo's wearing the brick red gloves that T knit for him but he still blows warm air onto his fingers all the same and rubs them together.

Emir thinks about it for a moment before making a hard right. He knows it's not back the way they came or in front of them, so that really just left two options and Theo said to go with his instincts. Barely two minutes of walking later, Emir grabs Theo's hand and starts dragging him, excited for the first time in days.

"A bridge!" Emir says, as if that explains everything. But Theo's so relieved to see him smile he's not about to ask questions.

Emir keeps leading Theo until they're standing in the middle of a beautiful stone bridge that crosses the river. He drops Theo's hand and leans over the edge, watching the water beneath them with a tranquil smile as if the current is carrying his worries away. Theo stands next to Emir, pressing their arms together and staring out at the scenery with him.

Emir digs in his pocket and takes out the lip balm Theo brought, uncapping it and applying it carefully to cover the damage he did earlier. The wind is making him even more aware of how sore his lips are right now. The fact Theo even noticed and thought to bring such a simple, but easy-to-forget comfort item is extremely on brand. Emir's in so much trouble, honestly. There's no way in hell he's getting over this crush or whatever it is.

"Can I tell you about this morning?" Emir is the one who breaks their silence, the bridge and the water giving him the confidence to even bring it up. Theo deserves some sort of explanation, but Emir's surprised to find he intends to tell him the whole truth of it.

Theo keeps looking out over the water, watching how the sunlight finds its way through the clouds to glint along the rippling surface. "You don't have to. But if you want to tell me about it, I'm here to listen."

Emir gazes at Theo's side profile for a moment before staring into the river to start talking. "It's a bit of a long story. But...there was a boyfriend."

Theo thinks he's meant to say something, so he asks, "A recent one?"

"No." Emir lets out a sigh. Even if the pain feels fresh, the wound is old. "Before uni. Things...ended the summer before I started at Roseborough. We were together for over a year. I thought he was a good one. Someone I could trust...thought I loved him."

"Hm...did you?" Theo is fidgeting with his gloves, staring at the threads and following the stitches that were so lovingly made.

"Yeah. It would be easier if I didn't." Emir sighs again, pausing to take a drink from the water bottle Theo brought for him. "He knew my family. He was the first boyfriend I had, and I haven't actually dated anyone since. The damage he did took a while to fix...Clearly."

Emir gestures in front of them at the water. He hates that someone from years ago could still affect him, but it's much better than it used to be. Theo's listening quietly, letting Emir talk, only adding thoughts when Emir wants him to. It's strange to think back on all this with the sharp contrast of Theo beside him.

"So anyway, I trusted him. And I was with him around the time I was figuring out my gender. I realised I was bi when I was about 14, but I didn't sort through my gender identity until a little later." Emir kneads his fingertips against his eyes, taking his glasses off so he can rub the sleep away properly. Theo glances at him for a moment, not liking where this story is headed based on what Emir's already shared.

"I didn't talk to anyone about it. Not my family. Not my friends. But once I had a label that fit, I told *him*. I was so nervous, so worried that being genderqueer was going to change every single relationship I had. It was one thing for people to accept that I was bi, but another thing entirely to explain being under the trans umbrella." Emir clears his throat, because this is where it gets really difficult to talk about. "And I was right. Because when I told him...he called me disgusting. Told me I was a freak. Broke up with me and threw me out of his house where we were hanging out that night. He made me walk home in the dark even when I could barely breathe from crying."

"Fuck, Emi." Theo reaches out a hand and tentatively touches Emir's, glad when Emir takes it and laces their fingers together. Theo can feel how cold his hands are through the yarn and the way he's quivering as he talks.

"That's just the start, unfortunately." Emir scoots closer to Theo, hoping it's alright. Theo drops his hand to put an arm around him instead, and Emir feels safe. "He outed me, and not just once. He called my house and yelled at my parents over the phone before I even made the walk back from his place. That was alarming enough for them, but they were lovely, absolutely perfect. Just worried about me and ready to support me. So were my sisters. Safiya wanted to knock him out."

"I'm really glad they were there for you. I can't even imagine what that sort of betrayal was like." Theo kisses the top of Emir's head through the beanie, feeling furious and so fucking upset that anyone would do that, but especially to someone they were intimately involved with.

"It got worse." Emir shifts so he can take another drink of water before continuing. "He went on this bizarre social media rampage. Made a video destroying all the things I'd ever given him or like tickets from concerts we went to, that sort of thing. Started posting my private information everywhere he could think of. Tagging me and being transphobic and outing me to anyone with an internet connection. Turns out he was racist as well, calling me words I won't even repeat. Making sure everyone knew he threw me away like the *deviant* he thought I was...and most people took his side."

"They *what?*" Theo leans away to get a look at Emir's face because there's no way he heard that correctly.

"They did." Emir nods to confirm. Sometimes even he can't believe it. "Every single friend I had from home, every person I had grown up with, even people I'd never met. Then he posted my family's address, all our phone numbers, my email, and all my socials. The calls started that same day. Strange cars started creeping past the house, too. I shut down my email pretty quick and I had to delete all my social media that night. Someone painted a slur on my dad's car while he was at work, and that had never happened the entire time our family's been in Shipley. Even my primary school teacher called and yelled at me over the phone. Said she always knew I was 'sick'. It went on for weeks. Shipley's not that big. News spreads fast. It didn't matter that his posts were reported and taken down in a few days. It was too late. He outed me as both bi and genderqueer, and he doxxed me. And I couldn't do anything about it."

Theo can feel Emir shaking now, shivering with both cold and adrenaline while he tells Theo what happened. The water bottle is trembling so bad in his hand that Theo takes it and sets it aside. Once that's taken care of he folds Emir into a hug, holding him against his chest. He genuinely can't imagine what going through something like that would feel like. And maybe Emir has always been reserved, but it's no wonder he barely keeps any friends around.

Every single person Emir trusted outside of his family, everyone in his town, every friend he thought he had, they were all gone, and he didn't even do anything wrong.

Emir hates talking about this and he hates reliving that time. He's only told Laurie and T, and shared just the highlights with Ciaran and Gabe, but now Theo knows too. Which is huge honestly, because that means he trusts Theo. They only really started getting to know each other a few weeks ago, but he's just shared the worst time of his life with him and he didn't even have to be drunk to do it like he did with the others.

Being semi-delirious after practically no sleep for days is its own drug, but not in the same way. And Theo is still here, after everything, comforting him and supporting him as if there was never any doubt that he would.

But Emir still hasn't explained what happened today and how they ended up here. He doesn't want to. Emir would rather just fall asleep right here inside this hug, but he pulls himself away enough that he can finish explaining. "So, ever since, I don't use social media. I don't use any of it. But I do have one secret instagram account that's just for my family and T and Laurie. Ciaran and Gabe don't even have it. I don't post anything, but I use it sometimes to see my family when I miss them."

Emir picks up the water bottle from where Theo set it aside, finishing what's left.

"My sister mentioned posting wedding pictures, so I thought I'd take a look. I made the mistake of clicking on the profile for one of her friends...and when I did, I saw that just last week, they'd been hanging out with him. And it just...not only did everyone choose his side back then, they still do even now. And then apparently they show up at my family's events and make small talk with me and lie through their teeth about being happy to see me, all while secretly agreeing with what he did and fucking going to brunch with that monster. I've done everything I can to avoid ever seeing his face again, but I can't control what other people post. I just couldn't believe that after everything...it was just too much. It didn't matter that I saw it by accident, because it brought me right back."

Theo has been rubbing a hand along Emir's back, unsurprised to finally see a few tears falling down his cheeks. Emir may feel numb from being so exhausted, but this must be overwhelming. Clearly it is because of how this morning has gone so far.

"That's why I needed you to hide my phone. When I start spiralling, it can make it worse. I went to therapy for a few months after it all happened and they told me I shouldn't be alone if I get triggered for...a lot of reasons. So even though I sincerely planned on making this right before just showing up at your flat, it *was* an emergency. But I'm still sorry I put you in that position with me in this state. If anyone else had been home I would've gone to them. Not because you aren't the most wonderful human alive, because I'm pretty sure you are, but because you are worth so much more than what I've put you through the past few days. And I would never want to take advantage of you or make you think that I'm just using you when I'm emotional or anything like that."

"I don't think that, but thank you for saying so." Theo uses his gloves to wipe softly at Emir's face, hoping they don't chafe against his skin while he smoothes away the tears. "We had a fight. A real one this time. But you don't use people, Emir. If anything, they use you."

Emir nods because Theo's right. His ex used him until he didn't want him anymore, half the time the people he hooks up with just use him to get off or to brag to their friends about their night out, most people don't even bother caring past how he looks. And often it's easier to just...let them.

"Can we stay on the bridge for a bit longer? I've always liked them." Emir listens to the water beneath their feet and lets the rest of his panic flow away, one breath at a time.

"It's whatever you want this morning. We'll stay as long as you like." Theo glances around their quiet space, appreciating the little town they've found themselves in. If they had to get lost somewhere today, this seems a fitting choice. "I know you're a cuddler, but I also know this isn't a normal day. So tell me: cuddles or no cuddles?"

As an answer, Emir wraps his arms around Theo's shoulders and hides his face in his neck, just like their first hug. He breathes deeply and mumbles, "Thank you, Theo. For all of it."

Theo hugs him back, sighing and pushing himself even closer so they're falling into each other.

They stay on the bridge a while longer, watching the water and pointing out little birds and other animals that stop along the riverbank to each other. They even see a swan.

***

"I think I'm hungry." Emir and Theo are back at the car to offload their empty water bottles and thermoses from earlier. They've left the bridge for now and they don't need to carry anything extra as they wander the town.

"Yeah? That's great." Theo leaves his gloves behind as he shuts the driver side door, the day having warmed up enough that he no longer needs them.

"I'm thinking somewhere casual, somewhere we could maybe talk?" Emir walks around the car to rejoin Theo on the pavement, and it's so easy to be here together, leaving behind uni and everything else for the day so they can breathe.

Theo bumps into Emir, putting an arm around his shoulders and giving it a squeeze. "Sounds perfect."

All things considered, Theo thinks it's been a nice day. Emir is still exhausted, clearly, but having told Theo what happened, he seems back to his normal self, joking and smiling and teasing. They wander down the main road again for a while before Emir steers them sideways, but this time one street further from the river.

"Just a feeling. Maybe less...peopley? I figure most people head straight for the water." Emir tugs on his beanie to settle it over his ears again. It's warmer than earlier but there's still a breeze.

"Can't believe we could've been going on adventures together for two years and instead we decided to hate each other." Theo shakes his head with a smile. "This is way better."

"I don't think I ever actually hated you, though." Emir mumbles, staring straight ahead with his hands in his hoodie pocket.

Now that he understands what Theo means to him, it's so painfully obvious that all Emir ever wanted was Theo's attention. He's been so stubborn, but Theo's given him the gift of a second chance. Honestly, he's had about a thousand chances at this point.

"Yeah...me neither." Theo thinks he probably used to hate the idea of Emir, the person he constructed in his mind, but not who Emir really is. He did what so many others do: judge him before they know him, but in a different way. He always thought Emir had what he never could, but that was so shallow of him.

He watches Emir for a moment, admires his impossibly beautiful face that could shame the angels even on a day like today, and he feels that warmth in his chest again, that thing his sister told him to encourage if it kept growing. Even with the mess of their fight, it's still there. Theo still wants that apology, but he's also ready to move on from it and see what might be on the horizon for them.

Theo thinks Emir must have been right about their direction. This street seems to have more places the locals hang out and less of the trendy, albeit very nice, shops and restaurants of the main road.

Emir stops with a smile a few minutes walk down the side road, staring up at a pub before turning to Theo. "This alright with you?"

Theo nods and walks to the door, holding it open for Emir to slip inside ahead of him.

It's clear the place has just recently opened for the day. They left Theo's flat around nine, and they've been in Cookham for only about an hour, so they're definitely early for lunch. But it's been a bit of a morning so far, and they're glad to be ahead of the crowd. They settle themselves at a corner table and chat while deciding what to eat.

"Should we get a Guinness each, send a picture to Ciaran? He'd be so proud." Theo waits for Emir to smile in agreement before ordering two and turning back to the menu.

"How do you feel about sharing? There's too many good options and we can't exactly take any home." Emir is practically starving, and literally everything on the menu sounds like heaven. But he also doesn't want to overdo it and make himself sick. This isn't his first PTSD episode. He's learned to pace himself after.

"I don't mind at all. But I try to be vegetarian, so if you're planning on any meat options, those are all you." Theo leans across to point at Emir's menu. "You want the halloumi to start?"

"Why not?" Emir appreciates Theo's ability to make decisions like this, because sometimes all Emir can see are the options and he gets distracted. He looks over the Sunday lunch menu, grateful it's only about ten items long. "I've never had butternut squash, but today's an adventure. That work for you, princess?"

Theo smiles and tries to hide it by tucking his chin, unexpectedly glad to hear that nickname again after a few days without it. "Yeah...that works for me."

When the waiter brings their pints of Guinness, Emir orders what they've agreed on, checking with Theo as he does. Once they're on their own again, Theo takes a picture of the drinks on the table to send to Ciaran, not providing any context. He wants to keep today's events private, at least temporarily. Especially now that he knows more about Emir's past, Theo wouldn't share a picture of him without asking first, even with their friends.

"So..." Emir pushes his Guinness to the side and puts his hands back in his hoodie pocket. "I was sort of hoping I could give you that apology now?"

"I'd like that." Theo puts his phone back in his pocket and settles his own hands in his lap. He sits back in his seat, not sure that he's exactly ready to go through this again, but they need to.

"Hard to know where to start..." Emir scratches at his chin, Theo noticing a few days worth of stubble growing. It's a good look on him. "There's so much to apologise for, but I'll get to it all. I promise."

"I don't need an essay, Emi. Just be honest with me and we can go from there." Theo pulls his hands into his jumper sleeves, crossing his legs to get more comfortable.

"Right. First, I want to apologise for being really controlling. I have no right to tell you what to do or who to talk to. No one does, and I should never have acted as if I owned your choices. You're more than capable of making your own decisions without input from anyone else, and especially from me." Emir takes a breath, waiting to see if Theo has anything to add, but for now he's listening intently, taking it in. Processing.

"I also told you that you're too trusting, like you should be ashamed of it or something. Which is ridiculous, because that's one of the most wonderful things about you. You have such an open heart, and if someone takes advantage of that, that's not on you. That makes them the problem, and it was borderline victim blaming to imply that if you trust someone you're asking for whatever happens."

Emir scratches at his head through the beanie. "And if I'm honest, I think it was an overreaction based on my own trust issues, which I need to sort out privately and not put that shit on you."

"Along those lines, I owe you an apology too." Theo puts his hands back on the table in front of him and stares into Emir's eyes. "I more than implied that by having casual sex with people that you're just waiting to be assaulted. It's completely unacceptable for me to say something like that. Especially in the context of a fight that started because of Josh, now that I know what he's done."

They both pause, smiling softly at each other as they acknowledge the trigger that started their fight, which brings Emir to his next point. "I also wasn't communicating well because of my panic seeing Josh, and some of the things I said came across as judgements about your inexperience. I didn't intend that, but I more than understand how it sounded that way."

Emir tucks a leg up under himself and puts his hands on the table as well. "You *did* tell me that in confidence, and I understand that the number of people someone has been with has absolutely nothing to do with their ability to make safe choices. That was another one of those times where I was letting my past affect me, and instead of recognising that, I yelled at you. Which...I should never have let that happen. In any context. When we disagree in the future, there will be no yelling. I was being condescending and rude and just..."

Emir trails off looking for the right word.

"A twat?" Theo offers with a soft smile. It seems Emir did actually think about all of this and he recognises where everything went wrong, which is all Theo needed to be sure of.

"Yes, that." Emir sighs and brings his hands back into his lap. "I meant what I said yesterday. I know I crossed several lines. You have every right to stop working with me and to ask that we only see each other when necessary in class. I wouldn't try to change your mind if that's what you decide."

Theo reaches across the table, palms up, asking for Emir's hands. When he brings them back out, Theo's glad to feel they're only slightly colder than ambient, a major improvement from earlier.

"I also meant it when I told you I forgave you as soon as you walked away. I knew you regretted that fight as much as I did, but I also appreciate the apology. I don't know that we would've been able to move on if we didn't talk through what happened."

Emir rubs his thumbs across the tops of Theo's hands, smiling at where they rest on the table. He knows he has a lot to make up for, but it seems they'll be alright. "So, where does this leave us?"

"You're stuck with me, I'm afraid." Theo lets out a dramatic sigh, sliding down in the booth like he's really being put out before breaking into a grin. "As long as you meant everything you said and we both try to rein in the fighting, I don't see why we can't still work together and...everything else."

Lacing their fingers together for a moment before letting them go, Emir feels lighter than he has in days. Now that he sees how wonderful Theo is, he's so grateful that he'll get to keep him in his life. He's grown pretty attached to him, and even if his feelings are unrequited until they eventually fizzle out, he'll have an actual good person as one of his friends. And besides Laurie and T, he hasn't been able to trust someone like that in a really long time.

They go back to sipping their Guinness until their food comes. A few more patrons join their area of the pub, regulars it seems, and they give the two of them smiles but leave them to their own little bubble in the corner. They don't need to rush, so they enjoy their meal, sharing between their plates, laughing about their friends and talking about dance (of course). When it's time to leave, Emir pays the tab for them both, glad he thought to grab his wallet and keys on his way out of the flat that morning. And then they head back outside, not quite ready to go back to uni yet.

***

"You know what I wish I had?" Emir stops across from a beautiful ivy covered house with a tilt of his head, tracing the leaves in his mind. "Literally any of my art supplies. Watercolours would be great, but even just the basics. There's so much to draw and paint and remember here."

"So let's go get you some art supplies." Theo starts looking around them, deciding which way makes the most sense to go. They didn't pay much attention to any of the shops they passed, mostly just wanting to walk around.

"Is there a rule against asking for help?" Emir knows there are some sort of guidelines that Theo usually follows. And while this is his first adventure along these lines, Theo's mentioned exploring like this almost a dozen times before. Emir can understand why. It's refreshing, getting yourself out of your routine and discovering somewhere new.

"The only rule I give myself is that I can't cheat and look things up on my phone. But asking people is fine." Theo shrugs and tilts his head at a few people walking their way. "Nothing wrong with asking for help. Ever."

Emir smiles back and waits for the young couple to approach them, Theo supportive by his side.

"Excuse me," Emir waits for them to pause, glad to see they at least look friendly. "Do you know where I could find art supplies? Or even a stationery shop? We're just in town for the day and I would love to paint some of these buildings."

The couple are more than happy to give him directions to their friend's art shop a few streets away, wishing him luck before they continue on their walk. Emir practically drags Theo there, surprisingly energetic for someone functioning on less than two hours of sleep in as many days. They find the shop as promised, Emir spending almost twenty minutes deciding what he wants and finally ending up with a few watercolour pencils, a small sketchbook, and as a joke (mostly), a colouring book and some crayons so Theo has something to do while he paints. He didn't count on Theo being so excited by it, turning pink and holding it like it's what he's always wanted, excitedly flipping through the pages with his gentle hands. Emir shoves down his feelings as deep as they'll go, but they keep fluttering through his chest regardless.

With their new art supplies in hand, the two of them make their way back to the bridge and settle underneath a tree nearby so Emir can work on a small painting or two to take home.

"I know this isn't real art like what you do, but it's so much fun. So different from the way I usually spend my time." Theo chose a picture of a toy soldier to colour in first, using red for his uniform with little yellow buttons and black boots. Emir stops to watch him colouring every minute or so, knowing he must look embarrassingly fond. Theo's so meticulous, shading as much as one can with a crayon and making sure to stay precisely within the lines.

"Sometimes I worry that you don't indulge your whimsy." Emir comments, finishing the outline of the bridge and adding vague human shapes where the two of them had stood earlier that morning.

"I'm not someone who usually does things for me, you know?" Theo flips through the book, trying to decide what to colour next. "I mean, I love dance, obviously, and our friends are great, but I've never really made room to just, like, have fun."

"We're gonna work on that." Emir glances over Theo's shoulder and stops him on a page with a bridge and a vague nature background. "Look! We can both do bridge art."

Emir can't believe how warm Theo's hands are, even on a chilly autumn day like today, but their fingertips are barely brushing and he feels like he's standing in front of a furnace. That might also be from feeling flustered at the hint of contact between them. He really needs to get this whole feelings situation under control. Emir's seeing red, a blushing, thrilling shade that he's never seen before. Whatever colour it is, he knows it belongs to Theo.

***

Theo drives them back to Roseborough after they spend ample time drawing and painting, Emir managing to paint the bridge, one of the houses along the river, and the booth they shared at the pub. But Emir's exhaustion is starting to catch up to him again so they both decide it's time to call it a day, leaving Cookham in the early afternoon and feeling very much in a different reality than the people who drove into town that morning.

"You should take a nap when we get back. Catch up on some sleep." Theo glances at Emir when they're a few minutes away from uni. "I'll just grab a few things from the flat and then we can walk to yours."

"I can be alone now. I'm done spiralling. You don't have to, like, babysit me anymore." Emir yawns wide and rubs at his eyes. He didn't want to fall asleep in the car again because Theo was right about it being terrible for his back.

"Do you want to be alone?" Theo would rather spend all day together, but he's also noticed that Emir needs alone time. Maybe he wants to get ready for the week or take care of some chores or literally anything else and Theo doesn't want to intrude.

"Not particularly, actually." Emir sighs and leans against the window. "Just...it's safe to leave me alone now, and I'm sure you have a million things to get done. I completely took over your Sunday but you can have it back now."

"I actually don't. It was about to be an incredibly boring Sunday, abandoned by all of my friends to deep clean the loo and faff about until it was time for bed." Theo grins at the giggle he hears from Emir, that little flutter of endearment stronger than ever.

"Well, if you really want to hang around my flat while I nap, you're welcome to it." Emir watches Theo's profile and the way his beautiful smile lights up his eyes. Is that a cheek dimple? "If you get bored and feel like cleaning, start with Laurie's room."

Theo laughs so hard that he's glad he's at a red light so he doesn't cause an accident. "Sounds like a plan."

***

Emir falls asleep only five minutes after the two of them get back to his and Laurie's flat. He plugs in his phone after Theo returns it from its hiding spot and flops onto his bed with a groan of relief. It's good to be home. Emir pulls Theo's hand to sit next to him on the bed, throwing a blanket across his lap and snuggling himself underneath it with his back turned away from the window, facing away from Theo. Since Theo doesn't have any work he needs to get done, he brought one of his favourite books with him, *The Amulet of Samarkand*. Something just for fun, thanks to Emir's encouragement.

Halfway through the second chapter, Emir lets out a sigh and rolls over, the afternoon light catching on his cheekbones. He scrunches his nose as he yawns and settles back into sleep. Emir still has the beanie on from earlier, but it's all askew and it doesn't look comfortable. Theo gently removes it, one fraction at a time so he doesn't wake him up, and tosses it off the side of the bed. He can pick it up later.

Brushing Emir's hair back out of his eyes, Theo whispers, "I like you so much...I promise I won't hurt you."

He knows Emir can't hear him, but he swears he smiles in his sleep. Now that he knows what Emir's gone through, and why he has such a hard time trusting people, Theo feels like it's a miracle they've made such incredible progress together in just a few weeks. Knowing that Emir trusts him with something as important as their dissertation, trusts him enough to tell him what happened back home, trusts him enough to have come out to him as genderqueer, it feels heavy. But not like a weight to carry, more like knowing the ground will be there to catch you if you jump.

Theo goes back to his book, finishing about half of it by the time Laurie and T show up at the flat and the noise of their arrival wakes Emir. Neither Emir nor Theo explain how they've made up from their fight or tell them about their day. Something about it feels private, like it was just for the two of them.

When Theo gets home that night, he finds the painting of the bridge that Emir made earlier tucked inside the book he'd been reading. He stares at it for a solid minute with the easiest smile he's ever known, his chest tight from all he's feeling. It's scary, knowing that there might be something growing between them. He thought he had liked people before, but it was never like this. Theo doesn't even know if Emir feels the same, and he's worried if he says anything that Emir will think he's just like the others, all those people who use him for his looks or his body and don't care about the person underneath.

With a sigh, Theo sets the painting next to the drawing of the teacup from before, on display where he can always see it. He gets ready for bed but texts Emir before he falls asleep, huddled up under his blankets.

Theo: *picture of the drawing and painting side by side on his bookshelf*
Theo: *I like my collection.*
Emi: *just wanted you to have something as a thank you for today <3*
Emi: *it's not much, but i thought you'd like it*

Theo: *It's perfect.*
Theo: *Goodnight, Emi :)*
Emi: *goodnight, princess :)*

CHAPTER TEN

Tuesday mid-morning finds Emir and Theo across from Sean's desk, giving him an update for the first time since they agreed to take his advice and combine their work. They've been respectfully letting the other talk, both only having positive things to say, which is new.

"So…" Sean looks between them, and even though he's been slowly watching their rivalry defrost over the last few weeks, he's still slightly shocked at the easy comfort between them. "It sounds like it's been going well? Lydia said you two barely need her help."

"You been gossiping about us, Captain?" Emir smirks at Sean and nudges his knee against Theo's.

"Course I have." Sean waves a dismissive hand, as if anything else would be laughable. "But that's beside the point. You two need me anytime soon? I can always stop by a rehearsal."

"We probably won't go back into the studio together until next week. We'll finish out this week with Lydia's help and keep doing video research for now." Theo smiles when he catches Emir's eye. "But yeah, it's been…great."

"Emir?" Sean waits for Emir to agree, or equally likely, to disagree and for the two of them to stop gazing at each other like *that*.

"It's only been a few weeks, but I think we work well together. Theo keeps me focused." Emir taps Theo's knee with his fingertips then gives it a gentle squeeze. "But I still have to finalise that extended outline for you. And maybe someone could help me with that, too…?"

"If that's your way of asking for my help, you could've just texted me. Or literally asked anytime that we've been in the same room for weeks." Theo rolls his eyes but he's still smiling. "Not that you'll need much help."

Emir grins wide at Theo's confidence in him. It feels genuine. "Thank you, princess. I'll owe you one."

"Don't just write it for him, Theo. I'll know." Sean had to stifle a snort at *princess*, but he's glad they've got this new dynamic working for them. It's a major improvement on the past two years. Not that either of them was unprofessional or rude in class or rehearsal, but it was clear they never got along.

"So little faith in me?" Emir turns to look at Sean again and sighs dramatically. "I solemnly swear to write at least seventy-five percent of it."

"Eighty-five percent." Sean counters while Theo watches the two of them banter back and forth like a tennis match.

"You're writing one hundred percent of it, but I'll edit and help you brainstorm if you want." Theo doesn't really believe in doing the work for someone else, but he's also not sure how much of this part of the conversation is a joke.

"Ninety percent. Final offer." Emir holds his hand out to Sean who takes it and gives it a succinct shake, like a business transaction.

"Deal." Sean nods before letting Emir's hand drop again with a small laugh.

"Don't I get any say in this negotiation?" Theo leans forward and turns more towards Emir.

"Sorry, deal's been set." Emir picks up Theo's hand in both of his and gives it a shake as well. "You are officially my royal scribe."

"Hang on, when did you enter the line of succession?" Sean was typing an update into the tracking document for these meetings, but stops because these two already have more inside jokes than he can keep up with.

"Princess," Emir ruffles Theo's hair before putting his hands under his own chin to bat his eyelashes, "and Prince Charming. Isn't that the way these crusty old ballets work?"

"I don't want to be princess if that's why you call me that." Theo crosses his arms over his chest and pouts with a furrowed brow. He hates anything resembling cisheteronormativity.

"Relax, pumpkin." Emir taps his finger under Theo's chin with a sparkle in his eye. "We're making it gay so it's different. Better."

"I feel like we've moved past the topic at hand." Sean is typing away at his computer again, unfazed by whatever this is. He sort of figured this might happen. "Feel free to continue, but I'm sure you have places you'd rather be."

"Should I just email you when my writing's done?" Emir picks up Theo's bag for him at the same time as his own. He's supposed to be Prince Charming, after all. Theo gives him a confused look but stands up as well, following Emir's lead.

"Preferably before midnight next Friday?" Sean smiles up at them again, waving them off as they head to the door. "See you in rehearsal."

"Bye, Sean. And thanks!" Theo chases after Emir into the hallway, not used to ending meetings so abruptly. But Emir's joy is a bit contagious and Theo gravitates towards him. "Where are we going?"

"I'm walking you home, obviously." Emir takes Theo's water bottle out of the side pocket of his bag and hands it over. "Here."

"Thanks..." Theo takes his water bottle and finishes what's left. They both have time off before their next class, but they've never spent that time together before. "You're still coming to dinner tomorrow, right?"

It's Theo's turn to cook and he likes to plan ahead. He always makes sure he has enough for everyone to have seconds and leftovers. Then again, anything will be an improvement on Laurie's attempt last week.

"Of course. As long as I'm still invited?" Emir pauses walking to check with Theo. He probably shouldn't assume after their fight, even if they've moved on.

"I'll be sad if you aren't there." Theo answers, which is the most honest response he can give.

"Yeah?" Emir bites his bottom lip and Theo nods, Emir's hands finding their way into his pockets as they step outside the building. It's chilly today, and very overcast. "Do you, maybe...do you have plans for Friday night?"

Emir has an idea brewing, a way to do something nice for Theo to make up for all he put him through the last week. But only if Theo wants, of course.

"Not that I know of. I think Lili and Jordan want to go to the shops on Saturday, which I'm sure you're welcome to join, but other than that my weekend's free." Theo is trying not to feel too hopeful about Emir trying to set up plans for them, but he'd be lying if he ignored the flutter in his stomach at the potential.

"Perfect. We can do some more research, but I have a different location in mind. I'll text you where to meet me then, if that's alright?" Emir pushes his hair out of his eyes with his free hand, seeing a bit of light fade from Theo's expression. Maybe Emir misread their dynamic and he doesn't want to hang out together?

"Oh, right, of course. Work." Theo pushes a smile onto his face, but he's pretty sure it's not very convincing. Faking sincerity is clearly easier for neurotypicals. Emir just wants to get back to work. It makes sense. That's the arrangement they've agreed to and he can't fault Emir for wanting to prioritise that. "That'd be great."

Emir walks Theo the rest of the way to his flat, handing over his bag once they reach the building.

"See you in a bit." Emir gives Theo a fleeting goodbye hug and watches him walk through the entrance with a fond smile. Theo turns before the door closes to wave goodbye, Emir returning the wave before pulling out his phone.

Emir: *T i need your help with something*
Emir: *i'm texting you because i don't want to deal with comments from laurie*
Emir: *i need to know theo's favourite foods or treats or whatever before friday*
T: *ARE YOU TAKING TEDDY ON A DATE*
T: *ARE YOU WOOING HIM*
Emir: *of course not*
Emir: *we're working together but i want to do something nice for him*
Emir: *he's been lovely and deserves to be spoiled for once in his life*
T: *(okay but you like him)*
T: *(it's fine i won't tell Laur)*
T: *(im just acknowledging the obvious and then we can move on)*
Emir: */eye roll emoji/*
Emir: *i like a lot of people*
T: *Shore*
Emir: *hey how's that wedding venue decision going*
T: *Don't be mean*
T: *Theo loves so many foods. He's a vegetarian, but I think you knew that. Bit of a healthy eater, but he also LOVES junk food.*

T: Anything chocolate, but especially jaffa cakes. Chocolate dipped fruit would be romantic.
Emir: *but cliche, no?*
T: I think Theo likes cliche? He definitely likes romance and all that
T: His favourite flower is white roses but like the tiny ones
Emir: *i didn't ask*
T: But you wanted to
Emir: *maybe I should've just asked laurie*
T: Well...
Emir: *I SWEAR TO GAY GOD*
T: He was sitting right next to me when you texted! You know how convincing his pout is!!
Emir: *sigh*
Emir: *just...if you think of anything else he likes, let me know?*
T: Laurie says he likes people named Emir Ayan Shah even when they're being a bellend
T: Oh apparently i wasn't supposed to tell you that
T: But you like him so it's alright
T: Oh and also comics. Big comic book nerd
Emir: *batman his favourite? he has that apron and i think i've seen a shirt or two as well*
T: Laurie says yes
Emir: */eye roll emoji/*
Emir: *if he hates everything i blame the two of you*
T: He won't :)
T: If you do the chocolate fruit i think strawberries are his favourite
Emir: */writing emoji/*
Emir: *go back to laurie*
Emir: *and thanks*
Emir: *bi*
T: byeeeeeeee

***

As Theo's cleaning up from family dinner, Laurie corners him near the sink. It would be less alarming if Laurie ever actually spent time in a kitchen without being bribed.

"Alright, Laurie?" Theo sets a plate aside to dry. He didn't have any plans for the night, so he told the others to leave the washing up to him, even though he also did the cooking for tonight. But they were all stressed with uni and weddings and life, and Emir left to head back to the studio for a few hours, so he doesn't mind. This is what playlists are for.

"Brilliant." Laurie hops up onto the counter and kicks his feet absentmindedly for a minute, hands folded together in his lap while watching Theo scrub away with a soft smile on his face. "What about you?"

"Me?" Theo looks at Laurie, confused. The six of them just had a lovely dinner full of laughs and bemoaned class updates and plans for the weekend. Why wouldn't he be alright? "I'm good, Laur...why do you ask?"

"I just - you seem happy and - " Laurie cuts himself off and clears his throat. "I know you and Emir made up after your fight, but things are alright with him? Like he apologised and you two are friends now or whatever?"

Theo turns off the tap and wipes his hands off on a nearby hand towel.

"We *both* apologised. But yeah, I suppose we are. Bit wild to think so after all these years but we're good. He's really wonderful, actually. We just sort of...it's comfortable." Theo catches Laurie's eye and sees that he's very focused on the conversation. He's probably understanding exactly how Theo feels about Emir without it having to be said aloud.

"I know Emir can take care of himself, but he mentioned that he told you some things about back home." Laurie has this really piercing blue eyed stare when he's in a one on one conversation, and Theo still finds it impossible to ignore. He's entirely sincere, everything he feels flashing from his eyes, crystal clear. "He wouldn't share that with just anyone. That means you're pretty important to Emir, that he intends to keep you around, and he's trusting you with more than just his words."

Theo swallows thickly past the lump in his throat. This conversation went from casual dish-washing banter to best mate talk with surprising haste. "I know he keeps his circle of trust pretty small. And I don't take that for granted, not for one second. I won't hurt him, Laur."

"Just as long as we're on the same page." Laurie hops down from the counter so he can grab Theo's forearm, soft but strong. "I think you both got a taste of how easily you can hurt each other last week. I'm glad you fixed it, but the two of you are brothers to me. And I want to be clear that just like I got on his case for hurting you last week, I'd do the same the other way around. Just...look after each other, alright?"

Theo's positive that Laurie knows, that he can tell Theo wants more with Emir just from the way he acts around him. Laurie always knows, which is why he's getting *the talk* right now.

Nodding in response, Theo lets Laurie bring him in for a hug, strong arms holding him close before Laurie steps away again. "Let me know if you need to chat."

And with that, Laurie leaves to go do some work in T's room and Theo returns to the dishes.

It's good to have something mindless to work on because his heart is on a rollercoaster, moving between hope and anxiety with surprising agility. He just feels so many things for Emir. It's like once Theo let himself open up to him there was no turning off the flood. And he doesn't exactly plan on doing anything about it because he doubts Emir is looking for anything resembling what Theo would want, but the truth is obvious now and it's sitting in Theo's heart, taking up more space than he ever knew was possible. And if he's lucky, his hope will keep its feathers and maybe even leave the perch in his soul.

***

As soon as rehearsals are done on Friday night, Emir rushes back to his flat. He tries to walk at his normal pace, to seem like he isn't bricking himself, but he has a lot to get done and only about three hours to do it. He tried to subtly ask for the flat to himself, which means that Laurie and T are definitely going to be there the whole time he's getting things ready to bring with him.

And sure enough, he opens the front door to an already occupied kitchen, T sitting on the counter with Laurie between their legs where they sit near the hob.

"Knew that would backfire." Emir grumbles, toeing off his shoes as he closes the door behind him. "If you two are going to meddle, you may as well be useful. Start the double boiler for me, T? And maybe warm the milk as well?"

"Already did." T smiles at him from across the room. "And I brought over some cute containers for the aesthetic."

"Oh...thanks." Emir meets T's eyes and gives them a grateful smile. He really is incredibly lucky to have T in his life. "That's perfect."

"What are you wearing?" Laurie turns around and leans back into T whose arms circle around his chest in a hug.

"It's *not* a date!" Emir groans as he drops his dance bag back in his room. Laurie can never leave well enough alone. "I'll just shower and wear whatever's clean…did you pick an outfit for me?"

Emir stands in his doorway, staring at the carefully positioned clothes laid on his bed. If he had to guess, that was also T's doing, because if Laurie chose them, he'd have ended up half exposed and with some sort of glitter. Laurie's just really camp when it comes to fashion, but the outfit on the bed is very comfy casual.

"I was bored." T says, trying not to laugh at the tone of Emir's voice. "It's not too smart, but it'll be a nice contrast to your everyday look. Trust me: I'm almost a professional."

Laurie watches Emir walk back into the kitchen, ignoring the two of them to open the fridge instead. Maybe if he has a snack he won't be too annoyed while these two poke about until he's done. Surprisingly they actually are helpful - Laurie mostly helping by staying out of the way - and Emir ends up with plenty of time to get himself ready and pack everything up to carry to the dance building.

He knows Theo's likely to be early, so he plans for it, trying to set up all the food and the small white roses and attach his own laptop to the screen with at least fifteen minutes to spare before eight. Once everything's ready he scurries back downstairs to the practice studio, waiting for Theo and scrolling on his phone, playing some random game that Laurie added for him a few weeks ago.

"Hey, stranger." Theo is standing in the doorway, beaming at Emir and looking so soft that Emir wants to wear him like a blanket. Fuck.

"Princess." Emir returns his smile easily and stands up to meet him, taking his hand and tugging him along before Theo can even ask where they're going. He pulls Theo up the stairs and down the hall until they're in front of the door to the faculty video room. "You tell anyone I have a key, I'll…I won't do anything but shhhh."

Theo holds Emir back before they go inside because this room isn't supposed to be used by students except with faculty supervision. "We shouldn't be here, Emi. Unless Sean's here too?"

As curious as Theo is, he doesn't want them to get in trouble. But Emir did say he has a key somehow.

"Relax. Sean gave me a key first year. I just have to be quiet about it, but the other teachers all know. And I'm only allowed to use it at night." Emir drops Theo's hands but doesn't open the door yet. He wants to see Theo's reaction and right now he's distracted by *rules*. "I've never once left a mess or been a problem, and it helps me with my dance since I'm a visual learner. I swear I have permission and, if anything, you being with me would make the lot of them even more sure that nothing will happen to their precious media room. Also I checked with Sean and he said we could use it for work, just like I always have."

Theo thinks about that for a minute, deciding that Emir isn't lying. And he does have his own key... "As long as you're sure it's alright."

Emir grins again, pats Theo on the cheek, and opens the door, pushing Theo inside ahead of him. Theo walks carefully, as if tiptoeing would make potential trespass more permissible. He believes Emir, it's just weird for him, forbidden almost.

When Theo looks around, it seems like Emir's been here for a while because there's an entire coffee table full of snacks and a couple blankets and his laptop is already idling on the screen, a picture of him with his family which Theo can only assume is from his sister's wedding.

"Go on then. Sit down, princess." Emir nods his head toward the sofa where he set everything up.

Because it's a university viewing room, it's mostly a collection of old sofas and recliners that people outgrew over the years all scattered about the place. It's cosy and definitely one of Emir's favourite places to hide out on campus. Theo's the first person he's sharing it with. Even Laurie and T have never been allowed here before.

"Emir, what is all this?" Theo scoots one of the blankets to the side so he can take a spot on the sofa, staring at literally all of his favourite foods before looking back at Emir.

"Just a few things. I figured you might want some snacks. And since it's Friday we can stay here a bit later than on a school night. Unless you're too tired of course." Emir carefully sits away from Theo, trying to get his nerves under control. He doesn't usually put this much effort into things that aren't dance or family events. If it's too much he's going to feel like an arse for overstepping.

"But these are like...did you make these yourself?" Theo picks up the container of chocolate covered strawberries and holds them in his lap. He's trying really hard to not assume this is some sort of gesture, but it looks like Emir spent hours on this. And it's probably not a coincidence that there's a few white roses in a bundle at the edge of the table. Flowers don't feel platonic, but maybe Emir's just a really caring person...

"I just...I wanted to spoil you. You're always doing nice things for other people and never for yourself." Emir shrugs his shoulders, picking up a pretzel and chewing quickly, not even tasting it because he's too distracted. "You deserve to be the one that someone does a nice thing for. Plus, I still owe you for like two years worth of being a twat."

"You don't owe me anything, Emi." Theo doesn't even know what to say or feel. Even if this is just platonic, it's possibly the nicest thing anyone has ever done for him. His friends and family love him, of course, but this is thoughtful and pointed and...overwhelming.

"I'm not nice to people because I expect them to reciprocate. I'm not saying I'm not grateful!" Theo adds when he sees Emir looking unusually hesitant. Shit. He's always been terrible at accepting gifts. "This is beyond wonderful! I'm just surprised."

Emir scratches at the stubble on his cheeks, looking down at the ground where his toes scuff at the faded carpet. "If it's too much I can –"

"It's not!" Theo sets down the strawberries so he can take Emir's hands in his own. Emir looks up at him with a tilt of his head, waiting for Theo to continue. "This is just new for me. Like you said, I'm usually the one planning this sort of thing. Turns out I don't know how to act when it's the other way round."

Theo chuckles at himself and he's glad to see Emir's posture relax when he does. "Thank you. Honestly. This is like the nicest surprise. It's perfect."

"Not perfect. Laur fucked up the chocolate on some of those." Emir looks at the strawberries before pointing at another treat, "And I'll never make those as good as my mum, but it's my dadi's recipe so they should still taste alright. And the pre-made stuff was just a trip to the shops. Not a big deal."

"You made these? They're so pink." Theo reaches out to pick up one of the sweets, looking at it closely before taking a bite. Whatever it is, it's covered in coconut, and it's one of the best things he's ever tasted. "Fuck, these are incredible! What are they?"

"Cham cham." Emir smiles and takes one for himself. He feels more than a hint of pride knowing he didn't fuck them up entirely. He actually likes cooking and baking and all that when he has the time and an actual reason. "I know they're not one of your favourites, but they're one of mine. I figured if you hated them, I'd just have them to myself."

Theo takes the entire plate and puts it in his lap. "Nope. They're my new favourite. You can have one more then I'm stealing the rest."

To prove his point, Theo picks up another, humming and closing his eyes as he chews. Emir can't help but laugh, finishing the one in his fingertips while watching Theo glow. He looks so happy, and Emir feels warm all the way to his toes knowing he's the reason. He'll make treats everyday if it makes Theo smile like this.

"So like what's the plan then?" Theo asks through a mouthful of sweets. He wasn't kidding when he said they were his new favourite. Sometimes coconut is a no for Theo, despite loving the flavour, but the way it coats the cham cham is perfect and doesn't trigger his aversion to certain textures. "Let me eat enough sugar for a year and...?"

"I wasn't sure, actually." Emir takes a drink from his Hydro Flask, picking up one of the blankets to snuggle himself up inside. "I didn't know if you would actually want to work since that's what I told you to expect the other night or if you'd rather just have a movie night and relax. I'm happy with either."

"Split the difference?" Theo scoots closer to Emir on the sofa. He wouldn't mind a cuddle. "Get a bit of work done and then relax?"

Emir takes a moment to appreciate Theo, sitting there glowing and eating junk food for once and trusting Emir probably more than he deserves and it just feels like...something. Like he's maybe not entirely daft and there's a chance Theo sort of wishes this *was* a date, too.

But it's not, so Emir brings his laptop closer and opens up an email from Theo earlier this week. "There's no way we can get through all of these, but the list is helpful. Maybe we watch some clips from *Cinderella* tonight? I've always loved the scenes at the ball...don't tell anyone I said that. It's *so* cliche."

Theo laughs and leans into Emir, hiding his giggles against Emir's shoulder. "Your secret's safe with me. Those others can think you're some mysterious tough guy but I know the truth. You're a sentimental softie who's a tad romantic and more dramatic than anyone gives you credit for."

He sits back up and bops Emir on the nose with his pointer finger. He's so incredibly cute tonight and Theo doesn't know what to do with all these feelings.

"Excuse you – " Emir sets the laptop aside so he can have his hands free, tickling at Theo's sides while he gasps through his laughter. "I am *not* dramatic!"

But he knows he is. His family's teased him about it since he was a toddler. Tickling Theo's just fun, watching the way he flushes and squirms and laughs.

"Can we – " Theo starts to catch his breath now that Emir's given up tickling in favour of opening the box of Jaffa cakes. "Can we watch the Brandy version after? Some of those scenes would look incredible on this screen."

Theo feels buoyant tonight, overflowing with bubbly joy. They're just sitting on a sofa about to watch dance, but something about it feels special. Maybe it's just special because it's with Emir, with the way he surprised Theo and got his favourite flowers and brought blankets so they could cuddle up together. It's just really sweet and thoughtful and lovely and Theo thinks he's going to have a hard time hiding how he feels because it must be written all over his face already.

Emir smiles at Theo for a quiet moment, reaching out his hand towards Theo before realising and retracting it. He was about to hold Theo's cheek and do something daft like kiss him and just thinking about it makes Emir flush and avert his eyes. He never fucking flushes. "So...*Cinderella* then."

He pulls up the link Theo attached in the email, sorted alphabetically, then by year under each title. Emir hits play, settling into his side of the sofa and swaddling himself in a brown sherpa blanket. Theo takes out his notebook and happily sits in silence next to Emir, jotting down some thoughts and sharing snacks between them as they watch most of the second act. They really don't need to care about the first act, and act three isn't that interesting to them either.

Emir spends most of the time pretending he's not watching Theo instead of the screen. It's not that he doesn't like this ballet, it's just that Theo's more interesting. Every time Theo tries to sketch something, he furrows his brow in concentration and Emir suppresses a giggle and bites down a smile. He doesn't think he's ever felt this giddy in his life.

"You're leaving?" Theo looks up from his notes as Emir stands from the sofa. They've already been here an hour, but he thought they were staying for a while.

"Just need a wee. Back in a minute, pumpkin." Emir isn't usually so easy with pet names but Theo's eyes crinkle every single time. "Just finish this bit without me and then we can switch to the movie."

Theo nods, watching Emir go before turning back to the screen. He's watching but not really seeing anything right now, so he turns it off and clears away some of the rubbish from their snacks just as Emir walks back in and sits down next to him again. There's this really pleasant way they have of being together where they don't always need to talk, the two of them happy to just exist together. Emir finds a streaming link for the film while Theo refills both of their water bottles out in the hallway so they can relax for the next few hours together.

Emir glows as soon as Whitney is singing the opening notes, face sparkling gold in the reflection from the screen. Theo touches his shoulder softly, waiting for Emir to look at him and Theo wonders if he could burn in the embers of his eyes. Slowly, Theo settles himself with his head across Emir's lap, laying down and facing the screen. He thinks it's alright because Emir made room for him to do so, and as soon as he's settled. Emir's fingers find their way into his hair, tracing gently through the curls at the side of his head while the market scene lights up the room.

They lay like that for almost the entire film, Theo more comfortable than he ever thought possible. It's not a date. He knows that. But it sort of feels like one. And he appreciates that Emir didn't try to force that on him. He just did something nice for Theo because he could, which is so respectful and sincere that Theo feels that hope in his heart fluttering to get out. But not tonight, he doesn't think. He knows if anything is going to happen between them, they both need to be cautious, to take their time and get comfortable with each other and with their own feelings if they decide it's something they want. He thinks about his conversation with Laurie from the other night reminding them to look after each other...

"Emir?" Theo sits up for the first time since the film started, just after Cinderella runs from the ball and back to her kitchen corner by the fire.

"Theo?" Emir already misses Theo's warmth, the way he so comfortably fits into Emir's space, the soft curls he couldn't help but run his fingers through, the times he felt Theo laugh and memorised the sound like music.

"I want to tell you something...if that's alright." Theo crosses his legs and faces Emir sideways on the sofa, very sure that he's ready to have this conversation, and knowing it needs to happen sooner rather than later.

Emir stares back before pausing the movie and turning to face Theo as well with one foot tucked under himself. He takes one of Theo's hands in his own to say, "Go on then."

Theo holds his breath for a moment before letting it out again, releasing the anxiety that started to build as he thought of what to say. Best to just get it over with. "I'm demi."

Smiling softly, Emir watches the hesitation in Theo's eyes, wondering how many people he's shared this with. Probably not that many, and he's hoping that's more for privacy reasons than fear of a bad reaction. "Demi, meaning on the ace spectrum?"

Theo nods, looking down at their joined hands for a moment before continuing. "Yeah. I didn't realise it until a few years ago. It was pretty confusing to figure out actually. Way more confusing than figuring out I was bi. I've never known anyone else who's aspec and I never understood why casual dating was impossible for me and the idea of a dating app makes me feel ill. And I know there's nothing wrong with me, but sometimes..."

"Sometimes...?" Emir taps under Theo's chin until he looks up to meet Emir's eyes again.

"Remember how I told you that I worry I'm too difficult or complicated? That's part of what I meant. I'm pretty vulnerable about it still, even if I wish I wasn't." Theo's glad to see that Emir doesn't seem phased in the slightest, just listening and looking at Theo like he always has. Well, not like always, but the past few weeks. "Are you, um, surprised?"

Emir shakes his head slowly, bringing Theo's knuckles up to his lips for a barely there kiss. It's not the identity he thought they were about to discuss, but he's grateful Theo trusts him with this. "I wondered if you were aspec after some of the things you said, but I didn't want to pry. It's your identity and only you get to decide when you want to share that with people. I hope no one has ever made you feel anything less than wonderful for being who you are."

He squeezes Theo's hand and resettles himself on the sofa, head leaning against the back of it while they talk. "You can tell me more, if you like, or we can go back to the movie. No pressure either way."

"I do want to date, hypothetically. And I like sex. Or at least I think I will when it's right. And I do think about sex and - *nevermind*." Theo flushes again, not wanting to explain that he has no issues masturbating or watching porn or getting off, and sex certainly isn't distasteful to him. Emir doesn't need that many details without asking. "But once I learned about being demi, it fit. I don't feel attracted to people without knowing them. I have to have a connection with someone first and be emotionally involved and really get to know a partner before I want to do anything."

Theo waits a moment before adding, "And I, um, I just wanted you to know that."

Emir feels that tightness in his chest again, that mixture of protection and infatuation and gratitude and excitement that makes it hard to breathe. Theo wanted him to know. Because maybe Theo is thinking about the possibility of them being together, too, and treading carefully. Emir doesn't want to assume, and he's not going to make this conversation about that because that's not fair to Theo. So he holds his own emotions tight for now and opens his arms for a cuddle, glad when Theo settles in across his chest, arms around Emir's back as they lay on the sofa together again.

"Want to finish watching?" Emir, more than anything, wants to make sure Theo knows he doesn't need to worry with him, that he'll never push for something Theo isn't ready for or doesn't want. If all they ever do is work together and cuddle while watching movies and joke around with their other friends, it's still a gift that Emir's lucky to have.

"Yeah." Theo sighs and turns his face back towards the screen, reaching one of his arms out from behind Emir to restart the movie. It really is better on the full screen.

***

"Nap time." Theo grumbles from his spot on Emir's chest as the credits roll on the movie. He even adds a fake snore for dramatic effect.

Emir laughs softly, helping Theo to sit up and ruffling his hair. "It's too late for that. Come on. I'll clean up and then walk you home so you can actually get your rest."

Theo flops face first into the other corner of the sofa instead, only mostly joking about falling asleep right here. Emir's a very warm pillow and now he's very drowsy. Also, it's past his bedtime.

"Am I going to have to carry you?" Emir nudges Theo's foot with his own while closing the snack containers. He doesn't get an answer so he's positive Theo heard him and is pretending to be asleep. Emir takes his time getting everything back into his rucksack as quietly as possible before kneeling next to Theo and sliding a hand up his back under his jumper (but over his undershirt) and rubbing soft circles between his muscular shoulders.

"Mmmmm." Theo hums and smiles into the cushions. If Emir thinks this is going to make him less sleepy, he's about to have concrete proof of the opposite. But then Emir suddenly tickles at his sides, making Theo kick and flail and laugh, turning over onto his back so he can grab Emir's hands and make him stop.

"There we go. Nice and awake." Emir smirks, messing up Theo's hair one more time before standing up and holding out his hand. It's becoming a habit, but not one he minds.

"You don't have to walk me home, you know." Theo knocks his shoulder into Emir's while they leave the building a few minutes later, shivering beneath the October moon. He has his bundle of roses held in his hands, careful not to crush them or lose even a leaf on their walk back.

"I know I don't." Is all Emir says, and they settle back into silence after that.

It's not a long walk, and it's Friday night so they come across other people on their way, but it still feels insular, like they're in their own space together. There's a calm between them that would've seemed unimaginable until recently, and it's like finally being home in front of the fireplace after a day spent hounded by rain.

"Thank you for tonight, Emi. Honestly." Theo stops in front of his building, just like the other day. He turns to Emir with his hands still holding tight to his flowers, a grey beanie pulled snug over his ears.

"I know you're busy tomorrow with Lili, but..." Emir fidgets with the strap of his rucksack for a moment, finding the right way to ask. "If you don't have plans on Sunday, would you maybe want to go on a walk with me?"

Theo smiles down at his feet to control his giddiness, no longer minding the cold or the wind because he feels toasty warm from the inside out. "You sure? I know you like your quiet time, but a walk sounds really nice."

"I'm sure." Emir takes a step closer, not sure what he's doing, just wanting to be near Theo while they say goodnight. "I'll text you, let you know what time. And I'll pick you up from yours."

Theo curls the fingertips of his left hand in the fabric of Emir's jacket, holding onto Emir to keep him close for just a moment longer. He doesn't want this night, that wasn't a date but feels like one, to end.

"Alright...see you Sunday..." Theo finally looks up to meet Emir's eyes, finding him already staring. He's gorgeous, almost too pretty to be real. But he is real, and that makes him even more beautiful because he's right here in front of Theo, walking him home and making him homemade treats and staring at him like he's sort of beautiful too.

Emir nods his agreement, not moving away. God, he really wants to kiss Theo. He's nervously chewing on his bottom lip and he knows it's not subtle. But he also knows it would absolutely be the wrong way to end the night, for both of them. Emir didn't plan all of this just to make a move.

So instead, he blinks to break the stare, shifting Theo's hand from his front and sliding his arms around Theo's waist instead, tucking his face against his shoulder with a sigh. "Goodnight, princess. I should probably go before you turn back into a pumpkin."

Laughing, Theo finally steps away and towards the door. "Night."

He gives Emir another of his little waves as he walks inside, and Emir stops fussing with his hair long enough to wave back. Deciding to take a detour on the way home, Emir walks a loop around campus just to be outside a bit longer, to process how he's feeling and connect with that part inside of himself that craves solitude.

Now that he's being honest about this...he really likes Theo. More than he can ever remember liking anyone. He's had crushes before, and he dated – no, Emir doesn't want to think about him right now. Theo is his ex's antithesis, welcoming where he had been cold, gracious where he was bitter, honest in a way that's so rare he can't compare it to anyone, even in opposition. He's absolutely kicking himself for pushing Theo away all these years.

Emir doesn't remember how their feud started. He doesn't think Theo does either. Emir was in a really terrible place when he came to Roseborough, and maybe he could see the heart that Theo has always worn on his sleeve and in some sort of twisted self-protection, he decided they couldn't be close so they had to be antagonists. Maybe some part of Emir knew that Theo was beyond his reach, in every sense, and instead of dealing with that he just decided to push.

And it's not as if Theo could be expected to react any differently than he always has. Emir knows he can be harsh with his words, and of the fights he remembers over the years, he started more than half.

Sighing, Emir stops near the lake, under the tree he secretly claims as his own. He sets his bare palm against the bark, wanting to feel connected to the world without any layers in between. The water looks black, the sliver of tonight's moon barely visible on its surface.

No one comes here at night. There's rarely people here during the day. Emir memorises how it all looks right now, dropping his hand from the tree and heading back to his flat so he can start work on another painting: the same lake he always paints, but this time at night.

It looks different for some reason, and his art has always helped Emir to work through his complicated feelings. While he paints the ripples on the surface, snippets of choreography start flashing into his mind. But even by his standards it's too late to be heading back to the studio to record himself. So instead, Emir takes a leaf out of Theo's book, writing down his ideas in his sketchbook on the page opposite the painting, promising himself that he'll work it through in the morning when he's rested.

And when he finally does fall asleep, it's with an easy smile and an open heart, thinking of soft brown eyes, gentle hands, and loose curls that fall through his fingertips like a whispered promise of tomorrow.

CHAPTER ELEVEN

Their walk together on Sunday becomes the first of many over the next few weeks. Between rehearsals and classes and working on their dissertation, Emir and Theo are together more than they're apart. But even so, they walk around campus side by side on Sunday mornings, and Wednesday nights after family dinner before Emir spends time at the practice studio, and even once midday on a Tuesday because neither of them was busy and it was a beautiful day.

There's such a shift in them that even people they barely know comment on it. A first year from Emir's book club mentions how happy he looks recently, and Alfie chats with Theo during rehearsal about how he seems so much calmer than usual, more self-assured.

They've started dancing together in the studio again a few nights a week, working through the choreography Emir already created with Theo organising it into a recognisable story. Sean even comes by one evening after *Alice* rehearsal to watch a few minutes of what they think is completed choreo, and leaves with genuine pride swelling his chest.

In between their walks and texting each other as they fall asleep, Theo learns that Emir always wants to be cold so that he can swaddle himself in blankets and hats and hoodies and whatever else is nearby. And Emir says his favourite colour is purple or green or red or pink, and it really all just depends on his mood. So Theo starts asking which colour he likes every so often to find the pattern: when Emir says pink he's feeling cuddly, and if he says dark green he needs to be creative, and he mumbles black through a yawn when he's tired.

Theo also learns that Emir is an incredible cook. The first time it's Emir's turn to make family dinner, he makes one of his mum's recipes and it's the most satiating experience any of the other five have ever had, full of perfectly balanced spices and smooth bites of paneer, and he even made cham cham again for dessert, saving Theo a few extra to keep for himself since he'd liked them so much last time.

Emir spends their time together learning about Theo, too. His heart stumbles every time Theo laughs at one of his jokes, and he's started secretly watching old *Batman* cartoons so he can drop his opinions into their mumbled conversations between classes. He learns how Theo likes his tea (strong and with exactly two dashes of oat milk) so that he can bring him a cup when they go on their walks. Emir draws doodles in the margins of Theo's notebooks and hides note cards with off-hand drawings scattered about Theo's room for him to find and add to his collection. He's started ranking Theo's favourite nicknames, with princess his clear favourite and Theodore only tolerated if surrounded by sarcasm.

Halloween weekend arrives sooner than anyone expected this term because they've all been so busy with their final year that their night out at the gay clubs only gets planned via group text a week in advance. Theo asks if he can invite Lili and Jordan along, and of course everyone agrees. Despite the last minute planning it promises to be one of the most memorable nights of their young lives.

Once he's in his fancy dress for the night, Emir walks to Theo's flat with Laurie and T so they can all leave together as a group. T looks absolutely adorable as Minnie Mouse, a short red polka dot dress, mouse ears, vintage white lace gloves, and whiskers drawn over their cheeks. Laurie is a less adorable, but very gay, Mickey Mouse, wearing a skin tight black vest with teeny tiny red shorts and yellow Vans. The only way he's actually identifiable as Mickey is the mouse ear headband that T made him wear. The fight over whether or not he would wear the oversized cartoonish white gloves lasted three days and ended with a gratuitous amount of makeup sex that Emir was glad to be out of the flat for.

T lets them into their flat, holding the door until they're all inside. They'll probably leave soon, but it'll be nice to spend a few minutes evaluating outfits and joking around before they get themselves lost in their pub crawl.

"You two look cute." T says to Ciaran and Gabe as they pregame in the kitchen. Even when they're just talking, T's voice is melodic and measured, floating across the room. It's one of the first things Laurie fell in love with, and always the way that T gets themself out of trouble. "The love bite really adds to the look."

Gabe slaps a hand to his neck and glares at Ciaran for a moment, but he just shrugs and moves Gabe's hand to kiss the same spot again. He has a bit of a thing for marking his boy, just usually not so front and centre.

"That dress is perfect, T. Really shows off your legs." Gabe gives them a bright smile before shotgunning the beer Ciaran hands over. You can take the boy out of America, but you can't take America out of the boy.

"Ciaran, are you...generically American?" Emir gives Ciaran a once-over, putting together the white tee with rolled sleeves and the distressed jeans. "Or are you dressed as Gabe?"

"I'm fucking Bruce Springsteen, mate." Ciaran cackles, running his fingers through his wavy hair before taking another shot and miming an air guitar. "Absolute legend."

"And young Gabriel? Sports?" Laurie pours vodka shots for himself and T, walking over to them near the sofa so they can take them together.

"Hockey." Gabe wipes the beer from his chin before pulling Ciaran in for a kiss. He always gets a little handsy when the two of them are drinking. Gabe's costume is very low effort, just a Rangers jersey and jeans, no gear or padding to weigh him down for their gay night of debauchery.

"T, could you help me with – " Theo wanders out of his bedroom but stops suddenly the second his eyes find Emir. "Fuck me, I'm so gay."

Something drops to the floor from Theo's hand, but he doesn't even notice. Shocked doesn't begin to describe what he's feeling.

Laurie loses it, laughing into T's shoulder before doubling over, Ciaran joining in a moment later. Theo flushes immediately but he can't look away. Emir is a *vision* and Theo was entirely unprepared.

"Alright, princess?" Emir smiles at Theo from the kitchen. He was hoping for a reaction of some kind, and that was certainly one.

"I – you – fancy dress?" Theo is still standing on the other side of the room, gawping at Emir while the others continue to laugh. They've never seen Theo like this, so clearly attracted to someone and not doing a very good job of pretending otherwise.

"Sort of." Emir shrugs, picking up the vodka to pour himself a shot. "I use gay Christmas as an excuse to do drag. Safest night of the year for it."

He pours a shot for Theo as well, setting the bottle aside to make his way over to where Theo's still frozen in place.

"Think it suits me?" Emir tilts his head and gives Theo a sideways smile. He's not above flirting, especially when he looks this fit.

"Emir!" Theo takes Emir by the waist and pulls him close, only letting go when Emir hands him his shot before downing his own.

"Fucking breathe, Teddy. Can't have you passed out before the night's even started." Laurie calls over T's shoulder, finally recovered from his laughing fit. He's glad these two are getting somewhere, but he doesn't need to witness their first shag on the kitchen floor. They have places to be.

"What's your, um - what's like..." Theo takes the shot, throwing his head back and closing his eyes, trying to remember how words work while the vodka stings his throat. He chokes a bit on the aftertaste, scrunching his nose. "Drag name?"

Emir hides a coy smile, looking down at his kitten heels and black tights before meeting Theo's gaze again. "Don't have one. I don't have a drag mother and it's tradition to get one from them. So..."

"You look...I'm trying not to objectify you but like - " Theo takes Emir's hand and gives him a spin. It's overwhelming. "Smash."

Emir laughs loudly, completely caught off guard because Theo seems to have forgotten every word he's ever learned or that anyone else is around. He likes Theo so much, and he's more than a little happy that Theo's so into this. Ecstatic, actually. He never knows how people will react to seeing him in drag, but this is beyond his expectations. Emir knew Theo wouldn't have a problem with it, but based on his now permanent flush and inability to communicate verbally, he wonders if he should dress like this more often.

Before Theo can drool any further, the front door of the flat opens again and Lili and Jordan walk in together dressed as the gay nurses from *Call the Midwife*. It's not obvious enough as a couples outfit that they have to worry, but it's enough of one to make them happy. They'd even asked T for help finding a few things to complete their look, and T was more than happy to go rummage through the nearest charity shop with them.

"Did you say you needed help with something?" Emir taps Theo's chin to get his attention again. He looks fit as a pirate. The way his beautifully muscular chest shows through the billowy shirt is distracting, despite Emir's best efforts to maintain eye contact. Staring at Theo's boobs wouldn't be good form, and Emir doesn't want to make him uncomfortable. He hopes to woo Theo, not objectify him.

"Oh, um." Theo looks down at his hand where he used to have a pencil between his fingers. He reaches down to pick it up off the floor with a shy smile. "I was going to ask T to do my eyeliner. Last time I asked they said no because it's not '*accurate to the time period,*' but I like wearing it all smokey and smudged sometimes, so I thought I'd ask. I only know how to do proper lines, like for stage."

"Hand it over, princess. I'm an expert." Emir guides Theo to sit in one of the kitchen chairs, taking Theo's face in his hand to apply the liner. He stops himself from running his thumb across Theo's pillowy lips, wondering how they look so impossibly soft. "You have gorgeous eyes, you know that? When you wear green, it really brings out all the background colours. You should wear it more often."

Theo keeps his eyes closed, breathing steadily as Emir's gentle hands guide his face this way and that to get the look just right. His fingertips move carefully over Theo's eyes, smudging the eyeliner until it looks sufficiently smoked out, and Theo feels his stomach swoop from how delicate Emir is treating him. Theo thinks he's mostly recovered from Emir's outfit, but he has a feeling it'll be pretty impossible to pretend he isn't completely infatuated as the night goes on and he sees Emir dancing in that mini skirt. Fuck.

"Look up?" Emir waits for Theo to do so before tight-lining his water line. He barely blinks, so Emir assumes he's had this done before, and not just for stage makeup. Maybe he should ask if Theo wants to play around with makeup someday, just in case it's something he's interested in. "There we are. All done and ready to pillage."

Emir finds himself staring, but Theo's staring right back. Even though he's the one who made the eyeliner happen, it's still a lot to take in. He wasn't kidding about Theo's gorgeous eyes and now they're just...right there. He reaches out a hand and brushes Theo's hair from his face, watching how Theo's eyes crinkle as he smiles. Emir rubs his thumb along the top of Theo's cheekbone, his palm cradling Theo's jaw as they continue to look at each other in silence.

"You two done with your mating ritual, or should we leave you alone?" Lili walks over to them, shoving at Theo's shoulder until he stands up and gives her a hug. Emir gladly steps back, taking a moment to readjust his outfit and make sure he doesn't look as flustered as he feels.

"You two look cute. Love the wig." Theo glances over Lili's shoulder at Jordan. "Let me know if you need me to get you some privacy tonight, yeah? I want you two to enjoy yourselves as much as you can. We'll keep you safe."

"Same goes for you." Lili darts her eyes over at Emir as he brings their used shot glasses back to the kitchen. "You and Emir could use some time alone with these outfits."

"Elizabeth!" Theo mumbles, widening his eyes as if it isn't painfully obvious to anyone around that he and Emir are both ridiculously into each other. No one says anything else, but Emir gifts Theo a smirk, confirming that he heard Lili's comment. Theo might shrivel up and die from embarrassment.

The eight of them leave campus in high spirits, Theo and Laurie racing each other down the street to the first pub (Laurie wins) and letting the others catch up while they continue to rough house, Laurie putting Theo in a headlock and making his hair look even more rumpled than before. They get a drink each, mingling and chatting amongst themselves, but the energy isn't there so they move on after only about a half an hour.

But the second place they walk into is exactly what they're looking for. It's a gay bar, queer couples dominating the space, Beyonce and Janet blaring through the speakers, dancers on the bar, and not enough light to see more than ten feet in front of them. Emir gets a beer for himself before leaning over and asking what Theo wants.

"Just water for now." Theo wants to pace himself since they'll be out all night. Emir nods, making sure to get him a bottle in case he's self-conscious about not drinking alcohol with the group.

"You going to dance with me, Mr. Turner?" Emir has a hand warm on Theo's back as he talks into his ear. It's the only way to be heard over the music, but Emir's blonde wig tickles the side of Theo's face and gives him a chill. It's more intoxicating than anything being sold at the bar.

"How'd you know which pirate?" Theo shouts back, letting his free arm move around Emir's shoulders. He's practically hanging off of Emir, shameless in his flirting. Something about tonight and this bar and their outfits giving him permission to be bolder about his intentions.

"Seems like you'd be good with your hands." Emir gives Theo a wink as he sips from his beer. "But you didn't answer my question. You want to dance?"

"You don't have to." Theo can always entertain himself since Laurie is very occupied with his hands on T's arse beneath their mini skirt. Halloween is one of the few times a year the two of them actually party together, and there is no way in hell that Theo is getting in between them. "If you want to go find someone to like...you know."

"Theo." Emir strokes Theo's back softly, keeping him close. Maybe one day Emir will get Theo to understand that he's not a second choice. "I'm exactly where I want to be. Now, will you dance with me or not?"

Theo grins and nods before leaning in to explain, "I've just remembered that Will Turner's person is Elizabeth Swan."

Emir moves him away from the bar and onto the crowded dance floor, not used to being a few inches taller than Theo because of his heels.

"Are you calling me a swan or am I meant to go find Lilibet and let you make Jordan jealous or something?" Emir starts moving them to the music, currently a Britney song from her third album.

Theo laughs, bringing his other arm around Emir's shoulders and leaving his face tucked against Emir's neck while they move their hips. They dance together all the time now, but this is decidedly different. And it's not like when he dances with Laurie or any of their other friends.

Emir dances in a way that's entirely his own, like the music is coming from inside of him, happening because of his movements rather than the other way around. Theo gets lost in it, in the way Emir moves their hips and tugs at Theo's hair, eventually turning him around so his back is to Emir's front. He likes having Emir guide him, maybe more than he should.

"This alright?" Emir asks as his free hand makes its way to Theo's stomach, fingertips sliding beneath the open fabric of his shirt.

"Yes." Theo breathes, letting his head fall back. His heart drops when Emir's fingers brush just above his trousers before moving to the far side of his waist under the shirt, keeping them fully connected from chest to thigh. "Fuck, *Emir.*"

"Too much?" Emir loosens his grip just in case. He loves dancing with Theo, loves the way he lets Emir take over and move him how he wants, the way he reacts so immediately to Emir's guidance. And he smells indescribable, fresh and warm and just enough aftershave to make Emir want to keep his nose pressed against Theo's neck until it fades in the heat of the club.

Theo shakes his head, bringing his arm behind himself to wind it around Emir's neck instead. "You're incredible. Could dance like this for hours."

He feels like they're merging into one person, and it's not enough. He wants so much more with Emir and this is the most excruciatingly perfect edging, a hint of what it could be like if they were together.

Emir smiles, kissing Theo's neck just below his collar and pulling his hips in closer to keep dancing. They stay like that for an uninterrupted hour, sweating and grinding and completely in their own world until Gabe finds them to let them know it's time to move to the next bar. Reluctantly, they step apart, Emir taking Theo's hand so they don't get separated as they walk towards the exit and their friends, who all look as sweaty and happy as they feel.

Their group makes it to three other clubs that night, one a complete waste of time that they leave almost immediately, but at the others, it's just like the gay club (but unfortunately with significantly less camp). Emir always brings Theo with him by the hand, making sure they're both hydrated and buying Theo drinks when he wants them. Neither of them dances with anyone else, despite multiple people trying to cut in.

Lili and Jordan find another sapphic couple at the last bar and exchange numbers for a potential double date sometime. Gabe and Ciaran end up fully snogging in the middle of the crowd, Ciaran's hands sliding beneath Gabe's jeans while practically swallowing each other's tongues. T and Laurie are plastered, both of them crying about how much they love each other, as if their engagement rings weren't proof enough of their commitment. And when the eight of them finally make their way back to Roseborough, they easily agree it was a perfect night.

Emir isn't really paying attention as he follows all of them back to their building until they're walking inside and Emir realises he should've split off from them to head home a few minutes ago. He's been too comfortable in their group's energy to worry about going home just yet. But everyone else is off to bed so Emir drops Theo's hand for the first time in hours, making Theo turn around with a raised eyebrow. If Emir isn't imagining things, he looks sad about it.

"I should head home. It'll be dawn soon." Emir rubs at his arms, fully feeling the cold for the first time all night. It's not as if he's dressed for warmth in his mini skirt and blouse. His feet have been hurting for hours, but it's worth it. He only gets to dress up like this a few times a year and he's going to savour it.

"You could...I mean just as friends...like, a sleepover, if you want." Theo doesn't want Emir to think he's invited him inside for sex, but he's more than welcome to spend the night. "I wouldn't mind having a cuddle buddy for the night, you know."

Laurie turns to look at them as he heads inside with T, catching Emir's eyes and giving him an understanding smile before following his partner into the building and leaving the two of them alone.

"I kind of want a shower and all that. Always feel a bit gross after a night out and I shouldn't sleep with the makeup on." Emir doesn't want to leave either, but he also doesn't want Theo to feel obligated just because everyone else will be at his flat and Emir would be the odd one out. He doesn't mind solitude.

But he also wants nothing more than to sleep curled up next to Theo for a few hours. Being around Theo is comforting. He feels safe when they're together, knowing he can be quiet and dramatic and cuddly and flirty because Theo understands him, maybe even more than he understands himself.

"I have things you can borrow. Come on." Theo holds out his hand again, hoping that Emir will take it. "I won't even set an alarm and we can sleep in for once. Day off."

Emir hesitates for another moment before lacing his fingers with Theo's again. Theo smiles, opening the door and bringing him inside, and he doesn't process until later that this is truly the first time he's ever invited someone to stay the night with him. Nothing is going to happen between them, but it's still...something. A step that Theo didn't even realise he'd be taking tonight.

As Emir showers and Theo lays out a soft jumper and plaid pyjama bottoms for him, he realises he doesn't feel any nerves at all. He trusts Emir, and Theo knows he won't try anything or cross a line or do something Theo's uncomfortable with. He gets them both another glass of water so they'll be less hungover in the morning and waits his turn for the shower, staring at his collection of drawings across the room. It's grown steadily over the past few weeks, and it's the last thing Theo looks at before sleep each night.

Emerging from the shower with a towel wrapped around his waist, Emir yawns while taking the clothes from Theo with a thank you. He slides them on once Theo's in the shower and sits on top of Theo's bed, waiting for him to be ready too. He's glad that the others were all too tired to shower tonight so they didn't have to fight over it because he feels significantly better now that he's clean and relaxed from the warm water.

Theo comes back from the bathroom, already in an old black t-shirt and another pair of pyjama bottoms. They're too tired to talk, so Theo switches off the overhead light and pulls back the duvet, letting Emir in first and humming happily when Emir pulls Theo to lay on his chest after the lamp is turned off.

"Goodnight, princess." Emir mumbles, arms comfortable around Theo's back.

"Night." Theo yawns, snuggling up to Emir with another sigh. He's never felt more at peace.

They fall asleep quickly and sleep soundly until midday, waking up to the smell of pancakes and coffee (courtesy of T), and wiping the sleep from their eyes to share brunch with their hungover flatmates.

The six of them sit around in their pyjamas and eat their pancakes while they watch *The Nightmare Before Christmas* cuddled up on the sofas. Emir stays over until it's almost night again, promising to wash and return Theo's clothes the next time he does laundry.

He and Laurie walk back to theirs to get ready for class the following morning, and Laurie doesn't even make any jokes about Emir staying the night. He just says he's happy for Emir and leaves it at that. Emir can't help but pull him into a hug before they both head into their separate bedrooms for the rest of the night.

***

Safiya: *EMIR AYAN SHAH*
Safiya: *WHO IS HE*
Safiya: *Or they. I shouldn't assume. She even.*
Safiya: *The beautiful person next to you at Halloween in those pictures you sent us.*
Safiya: *You look so happy /crying emoji/*
Safiya: *EXCUSE ME DONT IGNORE YOUR SISTER*
Emi: *i was in class yaya*

Emi: *his name is theo :)*
Safiya: *THEO AS IN THEO??*
Safiya: *THAT THEO?*
Safiya: *I thought you hated each other???*
Emi: *we used to. it's a bit of a long story. we're doing our dissertation together. sean's idea.*
Emi: *and...*
Safiya: *AND???*
Emi: *well*
Safiya: *I want to meet him*
Safiya: *Can I tell mum and baba?*
Emi: *there's nothing to tell!*
Safiya: *Liar*
Emi: *there's not!*
Emi: *wish there was...*
Emi: *I like him so bad yaya*
Emi: *like...he's incredible but*
Safiya: *BUT?*
Emi: *idk...not sure if he's even interested*
Emi: *we spend practically all of our time together between class and rehearsal and friends*
Emi: *i dream about him, about like going on picnic dates or holding hands or cooking dinner for him*
Safiya: *EMIR*
Safiya: *You haven't even mentioned liking anyone in YEARS*
Safiya: *I'm not talking about your hookups those were randoms*
Safiya: *This seems different.*
Safiya: *Is he nice? Treats you well?*
Emi: *you have no idea. he's the sweetest man i've ever met*
Emi: *i told him about...you know. i trust him*
Safiya: *If I can't tell the parents, can I at least meet him when we're at your show in a few weeks?*
Safiya: *If he means something to you, I want to meet him.*
Emi: *if you scare him away i will steal buddy and never bring him back*
Safiya: *Rude*
Safiya: *Is that a yes?*
Emi: *no funny comments and if you mention the dancing around in my boxers like Hugh Grant i'll tell baba whose weed was in the car*
Safiya: *YOU WOULDNT*

Emi: *i have no idea what to do. i think we've really built something special but i don't want to move too fast and ruin everything*
Safiya: *Trust yourself, Emi*
Safiya: *I know that's hard because of what happened, but from what you've told me, he's close with Laurie, and Laurie wouldn't keep around someone who's like he who shall not be named.*
Safiya: *If you like him and you think it could be more, use your words. You're quite good with them when you want to be.*
Safiya: *And if he's not interested, then you can cry to me about it and we'll watch romcoms and eat ice cream until we're sick.*
Emi: *i'm maybe a little bit terrified*
Emi: *not of theo, just...*
Safiya: *I know, Emi*
Safiya: *Sometimes the most important things are the scariest. I just want you to be happy.*
Emi: *god he would make me so fucking happy*
Emi: *i catch myself smiling like wild just thinking about him*
Emi: *he does this thing where he laughs so hard he almost falls over*
Emi: *he's so open and trusting*
Emi: *and he's so smart like he understands people and he always looks out for his friends*
Safiya: *:)*
Emi: *:)*

***

Theo and T are folding laundry together Wednesday after family dinner, watching reruns of *Bake Off* because T says they need inspiration for their wedding cake. Everyone else is out, Ciaran and Gabe in the recording studio, Emir at the dance studio, and Laurie taking a nap because he pulled an all-nighter the day before.

"I really like that one drawing in your room. It's a really pretty bridge. Looks soft, almost." T folds one of Laurie's jumpers that they always borrow, watching the telly as Mary Berry explains the technical challenge to Paul. "Is it one of Emir's?"

Theo glances at T while folding his joggers into a neat stack. "Yeah. He gave it to me a few weeks ago. All the drawings are from him."

"He's got so many talents. It's sort of unbelievable that he's good at so many things." T pauses to pull their hair off their face and into a hair clip.

"I used to hate him for it but now…" Theo trails off, not sure how much he wants to say. He's sure that T knows how he feels, maybe even more than Laurie does. They're very intuitive and Theo knows they've seen how different things have been lately.

"Have you two like…are you more than friends now?" T still pretends to be folding their laundry, but it's not very interesting and the conversation definitely is. They fold three socks into one before realising and dropping the extra back into the pile.

Theo sighs, setting down the vest in his hands and looking at T. "No. We're friends. But I think he might be my favourite person."

"But you want to be more?" T sits down on the sofa, crossing their leg over their knee and waiting for Theo to sit down as well.

"I don't think I'm what he's looking for. Actually, I don't think he's looking to be with anyone. Emir seems to prefer casual and to keep his friends separate from anything or anyone else." Theo wishes he felt less disappointment at that, but he's glad to be where he is with Emir. He really is his favourite person to spend time with.

"Have you asked?" T reaches for the remote to turn down the volume. This conversation is too important for distraction.

"What would I even say?" Theo glances at his phone and smiles at a text from Emir complaining about the updated choreography from Raphael that he's working through. "I don't want Emir to think I'm just, like, attracted to him and not interested in something deeper. He's gorgeous, but that's not why I fancy him. But then I also don't want him to think I'm *not* interested in him as more than a friend. I'm shit with words, T. I try to think ahead and plan out what I want to say, but then feelings happen and my brain takes an autistic detour to babble town. Or worse, I won't be able to talk at all and he'll think something's wrong."

"Emir knows you're demi, yeah?" T waits for Theo to nod in agreement. "Then I think he understands that if you're attracted to him it means you've already built an emotional bond. I know Emi has. I've never seen him as comfortable as he is with you. Honestly."

"What if I say something and he shuts down? I don't want to hurt him, T. That's the last thing I want, especially now that I know what he's been through." Theo would rather stay exactly as they are and pine in private if there's any chance that being together would be bad for Emir. He doesn't know if Emir is ready or even interested in another relationship after his last one.

"I think you'll know when it's the right time." T tucks their feet under themself and picks up a t-shirt before dropping it again. Laundry can wait. "I think you both really care about each other, even if it's only been a few months that you've been spending time together. You just seem really happy, like you smile so easily when you're around each other. And I didn't really want to bring it up, but last weekend was the first time that I've gone out with Emir and he had zero interest in going home with anyone. And we both know he could've done so about a dozen times if he wanted."

"Maybe he just didn't want me to feel like a ninth wheel since everyone was with their partner." Theo shrugs, because he's been wondering about it as well. He sort of assumed Emir would find someone to take home because over the past few years that's been the pattern. Not that it was a problem, it's just what Theo expected. "Or maybe he just wasn't in the mood and wanted to hang out with me platonically instead of pursuing a casual hookup that night."

"Or *maybe* he feels the same and you're both trying to be careful because of your history together." T reaches over to grasp Theo's forearm. "You're a catch, Theo. Emir would be lucky to be with you."

Theo sighs, putting his hand briefly over T's before letting it drop again. "Does Laurie...does he think it's a terrible idea? I know you two have talked about it."

T snorts, picking up another t-shirt to fold. "Hardly. He's been trying to get you two together since first year. He always wants me to help him come up with ideas. I have to say, getting you jealous at the beginning of the year worked better than I thought."

"...What?" Theo drops the jumper he just picked up, turning to T with his full attention.

"He had Emi dress extra fit for Troy's party, and he figured the two of you would get all up in each other's space like always and, like, I'm not saying it changed anything, because the two of you have done that all on your own, but sometimes the little things help people to see what they've been ignoring." T isn't ashamed in the slightest. Sure, they usually let Laurie meddle all on his own, but they also just want their friends to be happy. "In this case, ignoring their obvious compatibility for over two years while bickering like children."

"T!" Theo tosses a shirt at them, his mouth open in shock. "I can't believe you two! Why didn't you just fucking say something?"

"Oh, because that would've worked so well?" T rolls their eyes, folding Theo's shirt before handing it back. "You two are so stubborn about it. You always have been."

"I could've been spending all this time with Emir two years earlier?" Laurie has always teased them about their rivalry, but Theo didn't know he actually thought they'd be good together. That's an entirely different conversation.

"Wow, you have it *bad*." T giggles, reaching to turn the volume back up for the Showstopper Challenge. "You know how cute you get every time he comes by to pick you up for one of your little dates? You get all squishy."

"I do not! You sound like Lilibet." Theo huffs, crossing his arms over his chest because he's finished folding his laundry. "And they're not dates."

"You do." T folds their last shirt before setting their laundry aside as well. "And they are."

"I wish they were..." Theo mumbles, staring at the telly but not actually paying attention.

T scoots over on the sofa to sit next to Theo, laying their head on his shoulder. "Love you, Theo."

"Yeah. Love you too, T." Theo puts his arm around their shoulder while they watch the last few minutes of the show before getting up and going back to their own rooms for the night. T wakes Laurie up from his nap so they can spend their evening together while Theo puts away his laundry and gets ready for bed.

Theo: *It's getting late. You heading home soon?*
Emi: *just left :)*
Emi: *can we work in the studio friday night or do you have plans?*
Emi: *i came up with a few things i want to try together, but it can wait if you're busy*
Theo: *I'm not busy :)*
Theo: *But only on one condition*
Emi: *oh?*
Theo: *I get to choose the music.*
Emi: *proper diva, are we?*

Emi: *fine*
Emi: *you may choose the music*
Emi: *BUT*
Emi: *only if you bring me tea*
Theo: *I always bring you tea when we're in the studio*
Emi: *:) :) :)*
Emi: *goodnight, princess*
Theo: *Going to bed anytime soon?*
Emi: *i'll consider it*
Theo: *You're grumpy if you go to bed after midnight during the week*
Emi: *excuse you i am a delight*
Theo: *Only if you get at least six hours of sleep. Really, eight or nine hours would be ideal, but I'll accept six.*
Emi: *sigh*
Emi: *fine*
Emi: */gif of a forehead kiss/*
Emi: *that's for you*
Emi: *now go to sleep*
Emi: *see you in tech hall*
Theo: *:)*

***

"Excuse me, I hear music, and someone told me it was my turn today." Theo leans against the doorframe of the practice studio, Emir's tea hot in his hand while he waits for whatever dramatics he's about to get in response.

"Haven't had the tea yet." Emir finishes his pirouette (perfectly) before walking over to meet Theo halfway and taking the thermos in his hands. "Was I supposed to sit in silence until you decided to show up?"

"I'm ten minutes early." Theo crosses his arms after dropping his bag on the ground near the mirror, waiting to be teased. He's learned to recognise the signs.

"Which in Theo Time means you're five minutes late." Emir takes a sip of his tea, closing his eyes and savouring it. There's nothing in the world like hot tea when you're tired and it's late at night. Especially if someone else made it for you.

"Theo Time?" Theo tugs his jumper over his head and folds it to sit beside his other things.

"You're allergic to being late. Pretty sure you'd break out in hives if you weren't at least five minutes early to anything you've scheduled." Emir reaches for his phone to turn his music off. A deal's a deal, after all, and he did promise.

"It's not as if you're ever late to anything." Theo starts stretching out of habit, even though they only left rehearsal about an hour ago. He's pretty sure he could stretch all his waking hours and still have room for improvement.

"There's a difference between punctuality and Theo Time." Emir sits down and pulls his bag towards him, taking out his pointe shoes so he can put them on. "Theo Time takes a while to learn."

"Please, do tell me more." Theo sits down as well, bending forward over his legs and absorbing Emir's teasing. Now that he knows Emir, Theo understands the teasing is reserved for Emir's closest friends, a small group he's grateful to be a part of.

"Punctuality just means arriving on time. Theo Time is different for different activities." Emir ties the ribbons on his left foot, rolling his ankle a few times before switching to the right. "Fifteen minutes early if it's practice with me, ten minutes early if it's family dinner, twenty-five minutes early *exactly* for tech hall, and ironically, two minutes late if I'm coming by your flat. Care to explain that one?"

"How can I be late in my own flat?" Theo laughs, pulling his phone out to find the playlist he wanted to use for tonight.

"You tell me, princess. Seems every time I show up you're flustered and slightly out of breath and flushed that gorgeous pink colour." Emir watches Theo, smirking when he sees that same flush colouring his cheeks now.

"That's not because I'm running late." Theo mumbles, standing up just to give himself something to do. Emir holds his hand out, waiting for Theo to help him up.
"So...music?"

"Just connect to my speaker. It's bluetooth." Emir points out which one on Theo's phone while warming up his feet, steadying himself on Theo's shoulder.

"No peeking." Theo turns his screen away from Emir while he keeps using Theo as a barre to test out a few balances.

"So, what did you want to work on? Anything specific you want to film?" Theo sets his phone aside, smiling as *Cloud 9* starts playing. The Tegan and Sara version with multi gender inclusivity, obviously.

"Not yet. I'm not even sure how it'll fit together, but maybe we can film later and watch it in the media room next week?" Emir loves this song, so he's optimistic about Theo's music choices, even if they're probably mostly Top Forty. Nothing wrong with a good bop. "The section where we first get together. Our characters." Emir clarifies.

Even if he privately thinks of their characters as extensions of themselves, he doesn't know that Theo does. "It's tentative. Careful. A bit superficial at first but overwhelmingly soft, right? I had some lifts in mind and a few transition options."

"Is it harder to lift me when you're en pointe?" Theo holds out his hand again, bringing Emir in closer and picking him up by the waist to spin him around. "Like they're a bit slippery, yeah?"

"A bit." Emir moves behind Theo now, wanting to test out exactly that. "Actually, turn around for a second. Let me just try to hold you and see how my balance changes on flat."

Theo hops up and into Emir's arms, letting himself be carried. Emir does seem a bit more hesitant than usual, but just as strong. When Emir sets him down again, he immediately goes up en pointe, walking back and forth on his toes as if testing something. "I think it's going to be an adjustment. Tonight I'll just let you do the lifts if that's alright? Maybe wait til we have the choreo more solid before I focus on lifting you in these."

"Of course." Theo doesn't mind either way. The nature of this project is that they have to take turns anyway, so they may as well focus on this tonight. "Explain what you had in mind and I'm sure we can fit it together."

Emir walks him through a few different things, demonstrating as best he can on his own, but Theo learns quickly. Thirty minutes in and they've already sorted another section, Theo adding some essential separated movements in between the lifts to make them flow better.

"That third one. Should I be turned the other way? I know it'll be harder to hold me." Emir is slightly out of breath. They should probably take a break soon because sometimes when they work together they move so fast it's easy to forget. But Emir isn't ready to slow down, even if his feet are hurting and his muscles are tired and he can tell he's starting to lose patience, just in general.

They try it the other way, Emir stopping himself at the last moment and stepping away. He's starting to get in his own head about it because he knows Theo won't let him fall, but he's not worried about that. He's worried he won't hold himself well and it won't be Theo's fault if he gets hurt, but his own. And if that isn't the fucking story of his dance career. It might be the story of his life, too.

"What's wrong?" Theo sets a hand on Emir's waist, ready to try again. "I won't drop you."

"I know you won't. That's not the fucking problem." Emir puts his arms above his head and walks over to get a sip of water. Maybe he should've taken a break before Theo showed up and he wouldn't be so tired now. He always pushes himself, but it's the end of the week and his body is pretty close to done.

"Just trust me, Emi. It'll be alright." Theo pauses for a water break as well, wiping sweat off his forehead with the fabric of his vest.

"You say that like it's fucking easy!" Emir snaps and...oops. He's tired but this is suddenly about so much more than a lift. "Fuck, sorry...just...give me a moment."

"...Alright. I'll go refill these, then." Theo tries not to feel hurt by that outburst because he understands it's probably not personal. He knows that Emir has plenty of reasons to take his time trusting people. He dawdles a bit refilling their water bottles to give Emir space, wanders down the hall, turns off the lights in one of the empty studios, and tosses a bit of rubbish left behind by some careless students. By the time he gets back to the practice studio, Emir is sitting by his bag, untying his pointe shoes and looking decidedly upset.

Theo sits beside him, holding out his Hydro Flask but not saying anything. Emir will talk if he wants, and they probably needed a break anyway.

After a sip of his water and a minute drinking his tea (still hot thanks to Theo's thermos), Emir removes the sweat band from his forehead and runs his fingers through his hair before looking at Theo.

"Sorry. I didn't mean that. I'm just getting tired, but that's no excuse." Emir sets his hand on Theo's forearm, hoping it's alright to do so. "I do trust you, Theo."

"I know." Theo's shoulders relax, releasing the tension of his internal worry. "I'm sorry if I was pushing you. Do you want to be done for tonight? It's been a long week."

"Not yet." Emir sort of feels like he wants to cry because he knows where that outburst came from. The music isn't helping. "What's this playlist called?"

"It's a secret." Theo flushes again, stretching his arms while they sit. "Maybe I'll tell you someday."

"It's all love songs. Did you make it for this project? Like an inspiration type thing?" Emir feels better already just from resting and talking with Theo instead of pushing himself and spiralling. Theo's a great influence on him, reminding Emir to pace himself and take a breath rather than using Icarus as his role model like he's become accustomed.

"Something like that." Theo feels shy again. He made the playlist based on all the different pictures Emir's given him, choosing another song to add each time he found a new piece of art tucked away in a sock drawer or inside a book or under the lamp. "You sure you want to keep dancing? We could switch to video upstairs if you'd rather."

Emir stands up with a groan, stretching out his toes now that they're free of the pointe shoes again. "Just a bit longer, but you're right. We should probably call it a night soon."

They get back into it easily, running through the parts they've already decided on, Theo catching Emir perfectly for the third lift, despite Emir's worries. But now that he's been in his head thinking about Theo, he sort of can't stop. The more Emir pays attention and lets himself get lost in the choreography, the more emotional he feels. He can't help but think about how they had separate journeys but now they've come together, found each other, how there's a natural give and take that flows between them and that it's reflected in every moment of their work.

"What about just a basic jumping into my arms next?" Theo is standing with his hands backwards on his waist, catching his breath. "If we're coming back together after dancing apart for a few measures, I think it could read well."

Is the universe fucking joking right now? Just as Emir goes to do what Theo suggested, *At Last* by Etta James starts playing. Emir looks at Theo and it's almost too much. He wants to run to Theo for real, to throw himself into Theo's embrace and feel like he's at home. Theo's holding out his arms, ready to catch him, and the metaphor is fucking overwhelming.

Emir jumps, wrapping himself around Theo's waist, arms around his shoulders and fuck he wants to kiss Theo, relive that moment from *The Notebook* and let himself be carried away and loved and cherished. He wants to hold Theo close and bring him home to his family and make him breakfast in bed and hold hands when they go on walks and kiss him until his pink flush deepens to a fiery maroon. He wants to kiss him and kiss him again and kiss him until he can't catch his breath and -

Theo freezes, "Did you just - " He cuts himself off, setting Emir down slowly because he's sort of in shock. "Did you bite me?"

"No, definitely not." Emir steps away, hands in his hair as he turns the opposite direction, trying to get ahold of himself because what the fuck was that? He's lost the plot, clearly. His chest is heaving while he breathes way too fast, failing at calming down.

"You did, though." Theo rubs at his shoulder. It doesn't hurt, but it sort of stings a little. He can't remember ever being bitten before and his brain is vaguely short circuiting. Did he hurt Emir or catch him wrong and that was how he reacted? "Are you alright?"

"I'm fine." Emir starts pacing, rubbing at his face and trying to blame this on being tired, but even he knows that's a shit excuse. What is wrong with him? Talk about crossing a line.

Theo isn't sure what he's supposed to do, honestly. Emir looks distressed. Theo doesn't want him to be upset when they work together, especially if it's his fault. "Did I hurt you?"

"Of course not." Emir glances over at Theo, feeling awful because Theo looks genuinely contrite. As if he did anything at all wrong. Emir's the one with a problem, and Theo's the one apologising.

"Why...um...why did you bite me?" Theo's just standing there, frozen, watching Emir fidget and pace and feeling pretty lost. He has no clue what's just happened, the sting in his shoulder already fading away, leaving behind a somewhat pleasant ache.

Emir stops pacing to stare hard at Theo, choosing his words carefully. He doesn't want to lie, but... "It was better than the alternative."

What's that look? Theo knows Emir pretty well by now, but that's a new one. It's very intense, and Theo can't look away, trying to decipher the situation. "I'm confused."

"It's fine. I'm fine. I'm sorry." Emir walks over to his belongings, tossing everything carelessly into his bag except for the speaker because it's still playing that fucking song. He wants to scream. Maybe hurl himself off a bridge. That seems more reasonable than what he just did. "You were right, we should stop and head home."

"But..." Theo starts walking closer, cautiously because he really isn't sure if Emir's alright. Is this confusing because it's *actually* confusing, or is it confusing because Theo can't read the context? He doesn't think being bitten is standard procedure. "I'm trying pretty hard to figure out what's going on, and I don't know what I did, but I'm sorry. Can we talk before you leave?"

"I don't know what to say. I fucked up and I'm sorry and obviously I shouldn't have bitten you. My brain sort of misdirected because I'm tired and you should probably get screened for rabies or something I don't know." Emir drops his bag, everything inside clattering around in a chaotic thud. He's panting, his anxiety about what happens next flooding his body.

"Well...what was the alternative?" Theo brushes his fingertips through the side of Emir's hair, wanting so badly to help him feel safe. It's not as if he was hurt, just surprised. But Emir seems more than a little upset.

"No." Emir shakes his head, feeling trapped. Of course Theo would be confused right now. It's not everyday your dance partner fucking bites you like an apple. But it's also not everyday that your dance partner can't focus because all they can think about is tasting you on their tongue, so it's probably best if they just leave it for the night.

"No what?" Theo sets his other hand on Emir's waist. He's always so gentle and Emir wants to melt into him and never let go.

"No, I won't tell you." Emir turns into Theo despite himself, hiding his face against his chest while Theo's arms circle Emir in a hug. He sighs, Theo's comfort soothing him down from the cliff of panic despite his stubborn heart.

"You promise you're alright?" Theo rubs Emir's back, holding him close and feeling more centred than he has in the past several minutes. When they're like this, it's easy. Nothing to puzzle together or translate, just cuddles. "You can bite me again if that'd help."

Emir laughs, bringing his arms up to hug Theo back, relieved that Theo is making a joke instead of pushing him away. It *is* pretty funny when he thinks about it. "Theo?"

"Emir?" Theo's glad that Emir's calmed down, even if his own mind is still far from understanding what's going on. He doesn't want Emir to be on edge around him, especially when they work together, and biting must have been a reaction to something.

"I bit you." Emir laughs again, feeling a release of the tension that's been building all evening. "I fucking bit you like an animal and you're being nice about it."

"Well, maybe I liked it." Theo jokes, leaning back so he can look at Emir again. God, he is fucking pretty. And he's doing that thing where he's glistening instead of sweating and he smells wonderful, some mixture of baby powder, citrus, and cinnamon, and just a hint of what he smells like beneath all that. "Just ask first next time. We didn't even pick a safeword."

He's only mostly joking. Theo got a jolt of *something* when Emir bit him, and it wasn't a negative feeling.

"Theo!" Emir pushes gently at Theo's chest before immediately pulling him back in for another hug. He sighs, squishing his face against Theo's shoulder and relaxing in his arms. That underlying need hasn't gone anywhere, but he feels heaps better than when they were dancing and he couldn't focus. Theo does that to him, helps him feel safe and calm, especially from the storm of his own mind.

Having Emir hold him closer feels right, like Theo's his oasis from a harsh desert storm, someone he wants to be with and get lost in. Theo thinks he might be starting to understand what's happening. He would usually tell himself that this is some sort of misguided optimism, but it's not everyday someone bites him in the middle of a lift just minutes after an outburst about being able to trust them. There's only one conclusion that makes more sense than the others and maybe it's Theo's turn to be brave, to open himself up to Emir and hope for the best.

"Emir," Theo leans back again, knowing he'll be able to tell if he could just see what Emir's holding in his eyes. "Look at me?"

Emir gives Theo another squeeze before loosening his grip, taking his time to stare at Theo from a few inches away. Theo searches his face for a few moments, his smile slowly growing as he does. And there's the eye crinkles, the ones that mean he's genuinely happy all the way to his core. Emir gradually smiles back, Theo's warmth a reassurance that he's drawn into.

"You can, you know." Theo glances down at Emir's lips, wanting more than ever to feel them against his own. He's certainly thought about it often enough, he just didn't know if it would ever happen. But he wants Emir to decide. He's never going to rush anything he isn't ready for.

"What do you mean?" Emir feels Theo's hands shift lower on his back, holding him differently now, less like a friend and more like a partner.

Emir's arms are still around Theo's neck while he closes his eyes to take a moment for himself, making sure he isn't misreading what Theo wants. It certainly feels like they've moved past platonic, but he's not going to change everything based on his own reckless longing. Theo's too important to him, someone he wants to keep in his life for as long as he can, and if he oversteps, that could all go away in the first brush of their lips.

Theo reaches inside for that spark of courage again, leaning forward until his nose brushes Emir's, leaving their lips just a whisper apart. "Kiss me. That was the alternative, right?"

Brushing his nose along Theo's and bringing their foreheads together, Emir groans, fighting both his desires and his fear. "But…"

Emir can feel Theo's breath, warm and sweet just like the rest of him. He wants to, more than anything. He wants to tell Theo that he's the most wonderful man he's ever met and kiss him and remind him that he's never been Emir's second choice and kiss him again and draw his portrait over and over until he has it memorised and kiss him some more and maybe if he's lucky, never have to stop.

"Kiss me." Theo waits, his heart racing because he's never felt more centred in a moment, as if he finally understands what everyone means when they say they feel alone in a crowded room. They are alone, of course, but this feels different, as if the whole world could be there and this connection would be the only thing that mattered, the rest fading to shades of grey while his life warms with the brightest gold, all of it growing from where his heart is cracking open, waiting to either be broken apart or filled with the most heavenly light. "Please."

The delicate whisper is like an autumn breeze, brushing away Emir's last hesitation until he tilts his head and presses their lips together.

Emir swears he feels a spark, but it's cushioned by Theo's soft, pouty lips, electricity buried in comfort. He doesn't want to take anything, just leave Theo with a hint of how he feels so he can decide if this is what he wants.

It's barely a kiss before Emir stops himself, cautiously optimistic but so fucking scared. It's soft and sweet and wary and hopeful and he waits for whatever reaction Theo is going to have. He wants to be happy with Theo, but it feels too easy, like kissing him should come with a cost. But then Theo's hand is on the back of Emir's neck and now Theo's kissing *him*, holding him close and opening his mouth to let Emir in and it's nirvana, the sweetest nectar Emir's ever known and he lets himself fall into it.

Theo doesn't have a clue where his confidence is coming from, but kissing Emir feels more right than anything he's ever done. He doesn't have to overthink, just follow his instincts and land safely with another kiss. Theo doesn't exactly have a wealth of experience, but it doesn't seem to matter. Emir's lips move against his and he knows what he wants. He wants Emir, as his friend, his confidant, his secret keeper, his partner. Emir is his favourite person, and kissing him is like learning to fly, a dream he's chased that always seemed out of reach. It takes him a moment to catalogue his emotions before realising what he's feeling is joy: pure, unrelenting, blinding joy. And once he realises it he breaks the kiss with a giggle, tucking his face into Emir's neck and holding Emir so tightly they might fuse.

While Theo holds him, Emir tries to calm down, but he sort of doesn't want to. He's full of excitement, happier than he can ever remember, and he can't quite believe that just happened. He hoped Theo might be interested in him, but he wasn't prepared for the reality of it. He feels unsteady on his feet so he's glad Theo's holding him so tight. Emir hugs him back, wanting him close and trying to let his dreams catch up to reality because it turns out there's no doe-eyed fantasy that can hold a flame to how it feels to actually be with him.

"No one's ever kissed me like that before." Emir mumbles into their hug, not ready to let Theo go just yet. Maybe they could stay in this hug for another hour or day or maybe even a week. Who needs sleep or food or anything else when you can be this miraculously happy instead?

"Like what?" Theo has a hand in Emir's hair now, kissing his temple before moving to actually look at him again. He's stunning, but that's not new. It's the way he's looking at Theo that's new, with wonder and care, and the awful overhead lighting of the studio has never seemed more beautiful than when it's reflected back at him through Emir's eyes.

"...Like I matter." Emir isn't sure where he finds the words, but he knows they're true. He's done so much more with so many other people, but it's never been like this. Emir knows kisses of utility, of assessment, or as a step on the path to more. He knows how it feels to be kissed by someone who's waiting for it to shift into sex or as some sort of obligation on the way there.

But that's so far away from how he feels right now, it's as if there needs to be a new word for it. It's not that he doesn't want more with Theo, because he absolutely does. But this was a kiss for its own sake, a way to share their feelings and acknowledge the care they hold between them.

Theo doesn't really know what to say to that because Emir matters more than he could ever explain with something as ephemeral as words. So he kisses Emir again, slow and deep and he even leans forward like they're in a movie until Emir laughs and pushes back into him, a steady press and pull, the two of them kissing like they've been waiting for this moment and they're chasing time. They kiss and they laugh quietly between them until they finally rest with their foreheads together, both of them smiling wide with stars held in their eyes.

"I suppose I should walk you home now." Emir has Theo's hands in his, swinging them between their bodies with their fingers linked. "I don't mean, like, *go home* with you...I just like taking walks together. And it's getting late."

"I like when you walk me home." Theo sneaks another kiss and delights in the privilege. "I know it's cliche, but...I think I like cliches."

"You definitely do." Emir runs his fingers through Theo's hair, putting both of his hands behind Theo's neck to kiss him again. Theo sighs into it, and Emir presses the sound into his memory like gold leaf against an illuminated page. "But I like it. I like you."

Theo looks down at the ground for a moment, grinning when he feels Emir press a kiss to the side of his neck. "Alright, I suppose we should go. Clearly, we're done with anything productive."

"Excuse you." Emir steps away for the first time in several minutes so he can gather their belongings and carry their bags. "That was *very* productive."

"How so?" Theo turns off the speaker, cutting off *Vision of Love* partway through the chorus, a crime in any other context. He hands the speaker to Emir who tucks it into his own bag and walks towards the door so they can get dressed to brave the cold on the walk home.

"Now I can stop pretending I'm not ridiculously gone for you every time you laugh at one of my jokes or do something sweet like make me tea," Emir pauses to slide into his shoes, Theo doing the same beside him. "And the amount of time I was thinking about kissing you can be better spent now."

Theo laughs, lacing his fingers with Emir's again as they walk through the corridor. "Better spent how?"

"By actually kissing you, of course." Emir tugs Theo forward for an awkward sideways kiss, and Theo feels a happiness deep within him that he didn't even know he could access. But then Emir suddenly furrows his brow and holds onto Theo's hand a little bit harder. "Um...would it be alright if we just sort of walk quietly? It's not that I don't like talking to you, I just...sometimes I need to be with my thoughts."

"Of course." Theo loves that they're just casually holding hands as they walk outside, another small thing that's changed that actually means the world to him. "We can talk tomorrow if you like. There's no rush, Emi. Not ever."

Emir's happiness swirls through his chest because he knew Theo was wonderful, but he's not used to being able to take things slow and sit in a moment with another person. He likes that he and Theo can be quiet together, spending time with each other just because they can and not because they have to.

They walk the short distance back to Theo's flat in silence, taking their time and looking around at the moon, the trees, the path beneath their feet, and listening to all the sounds that surround them. Theo appreciates how Emir asks for quiet sometimes. He's never known anyone so willing to attach themself to the world without distraction or filter.

Emir lets them into Theo's building, laying a hand on the small of Theo's back as they walk inside. Once they're standing in front of Theo's door, Emir sets his hand on Theo's chest, feeling the rise and fall of his breath beneath his palm.

"Can I kiss you goodnight?" Emir slides his hand up to Theo's cheek instead, waiting for his answer and staring into those gorgeous hazel eyes.

"You can kiss me whenever you like." Theo closes his eyes as Emir leans in, waiting to feel their lips meet like it's already been too long. It's a soft kiss, quick and gentle and perfect. Theo pulls him in for another, smiling against his lips because he can't help it. Emir makes him deliriously happy.

"Talk tomorrow?" Emir steps back to let Theo go, already excited to see him in the morning. But he needs some time to think, and saying goodnight is definitely the right choice. He wants to give Theo space to process, too.

"I'd like that." Theo unlocks the door and adds, "Goodnight," before finally letting himself inside.

CHAPTER TWELVE

Theo shuts the front door to his flat and leans back against it with a grin. He closes his eyes, laughing softly under his breath, the joy bubbling out of him because he isn't sure he's ever been this happy before. He needs to tell someone. Or like maybe everyone in the entire world. Because Emir Shah just kissed him and he kissed Emir back and there was mutual kissing and then they held hands and it's the most wonderful night of his life. Emir also bit him first, but that's just a fun detail they'll tell someday when they're old and reminiscing.

No one else is home. Why is no one else home right now? T and Laurie are spending the night at the other flat and Ciaran must be at Gabe's. Theo needs to shout about it, to relive the past half an hour over and over until he gets to see Emir in the morning and kisses him again. Hopefully cuddle for a while too.

Theo: *Laur*
Theo: *Laurie*
Theo: *Lawrence William Tempest*
Theo: *Love of my life*
Theo: *Wait no*
Theo: *Emir's favourite white boy*
Theo: *Emir :) :) :)*
Laurie: *Busy*
Theo: *IMPORTANT*
Theo: *Fine. Maybe T wants to know :(*

Theo: *T*
Theo: *T T T T T T T*
Theo: *T Brooks*
Theo: *Love of Laurie's life*
Theo: *I have gay news!!!*
T: *Busy*
Theo: *.......oh*
Theo: *You two have fun*
Theo: *BUT I HAVE GAY NEWS*
Theo: *I'll go yell at Lili*
Theo: *You don't get to be mad I told her first*

Theo drops his dance bag in his room, barely taking the time to put everything away properly before scrounging in the cupboards for a bottle of shit wine and three glasses as he dials Lili's number. Halfway through her greeting he cuts her off to ask, "Please tell me you're home right now and you and Jordan aren't, like, *busy* and I can come over please please please."

"Calm your *massive* tits, Theo. We're watching Drag Race – " Lili barely finishes the sentence before Theo hangs up on her and rushes out the front door and over to the stairs. He feels like he could fly right now, as if Emir transferred some of his magic when they kissed and it's coursing through Theo's veins.

He knocks a few times, bouncing on his feet with his arms full and waiting, ready to burst. As soon as the door cracks Theo half shouts, "I kissed Emir on his entire mouth!"

"Shit fuck Theo, Jesus – " Lili finishes opening the door after jumping in surprise and takes him in, everything from the flush on his cheeks to the way he's practically vibrating where he's standing. "You'd better come in and pour me some of that wine."

She grabs his shirt and drags him through the doorway, huffing when Theo pulls her into a crushing hug.

"Lili he's so – he's – Emir kissed me! Like on purpose." Theo lets her out of the hug when she squirms in his arms, grumbling about being squished.

Lili takes the wine and glasses and sets them on the table behind her before smacking Theo across the chest and crossing her arms. "What the fuck took so long?"

"They were in denial, babe." Jordan calls from the sofa, watching them have their moment while muting Drag Race so they can all talk. She's still in the process of gay education, catching up on culture and history and all the rest, which currently means learning about all the Queens.

Theo rushes over to Jordan on the sofa and scoops her into another hug while she laughs against his shoulder. His joy is infectious.

"Thank you for making Lili so happy." Theo mumbles near her ear before letting her out of the hug. "She loves you a lot, you know?"

"I know, Theo." Jordan squeezes his biceps with a smile before sinking back into the sofa. Lili's best mate is pretty great, even when he's bouncing around their flat like he's full of helium. "I love her, too."

"Oi. None of this sentimental shit." Lili digs through their drawers for a corkscrew, the glasses waiting to be filled. "I want the gay tea and I want it now. It's about bloody time, you big idiot."

"Hey!" Theo gently moves her to the side and finds the corkscrew immediately, handing it over with a pout. "I thought we were being happy for me."

"This *is* me being happy for you." Lili pours the wine for the three of them, handing Theo the first glass. "I want every single detail and don't leave anything out. I've been waiting for this since we fucking met. You two are unbelievable."

"Okay but...how long have you known?" Theo and Lili wander towards the sofa together, Jordan scooting over to make room for Lili to fit into her side and for Theo to claim the other corner.

"Known what?" Lili takes a sip of the wine, wincing at the taste. But after about half a glass, none of them will notice. Except Jordan. "How long since I knew you two were into each other? Or since I knew you liked him for real? Or since I knew Emir had feelings for you?"

"Fuck, um..." Theo crosses his legs under himself on the sofa and sits sideways to face them. "All of the above? I guess?"

"Figured you'd be shagging within a few weeks our first year if I'm honest, but then we got to know each other and you told me you're demi and all that, but even so you two have always had insane chemistry. You should see the way you stare at each other." Lili rolls her eyes while Theo flushes. Maybe he shouldn't be surprised because apparently it's always been obvious to everyone else. "And you're always finding excuses to be in each other's space. Honestly, the part that surprised me was you two finally getting along. I figured you might hate fuck and figure your shit out backwards, but it seems you decided to be all healthy and whatever and fix your issues first."

"It's Theo. Of course they had to learn to be friends first." Jordan hooks her chin over Lili's shoulder, setting her glass of wine down because there's just no way in hell she plans on drinking that. She still maintains *some* standards, as much as she tries to shirk her ridiculous upbringing.

"It took me a long time to figure out how I feel. Too long." Theo sighs and stares into his wine with a moony smile. "I got so distracted fighting with him that I never bothered actually finding out who he is."

"I knew he actually fancied you that day he apologised before tech hall. Remember that?" Lili brings Jordan's free arm around to hug her middle, lacing their fingers together across her diaphragm while they cuddle. "I don't think Emir realised it himself then, but everything changed after that."

"*You* remember that?" Theo tilts his head, surprised that was the moment for Lili. It certainly wasn't when he thought Emir had feelings. He wasn't really sure of that until their Cinderella date night, and even then he thought he was just manifesting his own hopes into reality. "That did change everything. I never saw him the same way again after that."

"I didn't know it was mutual until after that fight when I saw you the next morning." Lili softens to give Theo an understanding smile. She never got the details of the fight or the make up, but that's when she knew Theo's heart had been hurt, which only led to one conclusion.

"That was the first real fight we had, you know?" Theo takes a sip of his wine and glances at the two of them. The feeling of betrayal is long gone, but he can still remember the pain. That fight hurt more than every single other disagreement of theirs added together. "I think I knew before then, but you're right. I couldn't ignore it after that."

"And you've been going on these dates, and then there's the way you were during Halloween last weekend so." Lili takes a larger drink, no longer minding the bitter taste.

"God, Emir looked *so good*." Theo grins, his toes curling while he bites his lip. "And the way he danced that night was just...and his eyes!"

"See, there's the face." Jordan laughs, pointing at Theo and glancing at Lili. "The Emir face."

"There is not a face!" Theo flushes deeper because he's starting to realise there probably is an Emir face and that he's not particularly good at hiding it. "I just really like him and he kissed me and it was the best moment of my life."

"Okay yes, back to this kissing business." Lili readjusts and focuses on Theo, Jordan smiling and leaning back into her corner because she loves the way these two are together. They're genuinely like siblings.

"Right, well first of all, he's very good at it." Theo sets his wine glass down on the coffee table so he can gesticulate better. "Or at least I assume so, but like..."

"Stop that." Lili leans forward and slaps him on the side of the head. But, like...lovingly. "I don't give a fuck how many people you've snogged or not. A good kiss is a good kiss."

"Oh, it was a very good kiss." Theo smirks, his confidence growing as he talks. He appreciates Lili shutting his brain up for him.

"Tongue?" Lili waits for the answer with her chin on her fist.

"The perfect amount. He tastes incredible, oh my *god*." Theo rolls his eyes at the memory and smiles, mirroring Lili's posture. "Like honey, and I think he uses some sort of rosemary lip balm which I was not expecting but – "

"How did it happen? Start from the beginning, but not like, creation of humanity, more like tonight." Lili snorts in amusement, knowing she actually did need to clarify or else Theo could talk for hours before getting to the point.

Theo tells her (almost) everything, including how Emir bit him, which they laugh about, and how he actually made the first move, holding Emir close and giving him permission. How Emir gave him a whisper of a kiss before Theo pulled him in for more, reliving it just as he wanted, both Lili and Jordan reacting at all the right moments and practically squealing in excitement when he tells them about being walked home again and their goodnight kiss and plans for tomorrow.

Lili grabs Theo's forearms excitedly with Theo holding right back, Jordan leaning forward as well. "So are you, like, boyfriends now?"

"Not officially. But we're going to talk tomorrow." Theo smiles so wide his face hurts, eyes crinkled almost closed. "And if he doesn't ask me first, I'm definitely going to. I want to be his. Off the market. Property of Emir Shah. And I want everyone to know it."

They sit and drink their wine and share in Theo's joy until after Theo's usual bedtime when Lili shoos him away and back to his own place because, "You need your beauty sleep or else you'll feel sick tomorrow. You know it's true."

And she's right so Theo leaves them to finish their night in peace, walking calmly back to his own flat and settling in. He texts Emir before he falls asleep, not wanting to go to bed without saying goodnight.

Theo: *Can't wait to see you tomorrow :)*
Theo: *Lili mother hen'd me so I'm going to sleep*
Theo: *Goodnight, Emir /kiss emoji/*

He falls asleep with a smile, his eyes drooping closed by the time he hits send.

***

Emir waits outside of Theo's door for a moment after it closes, hand pressed against the wood as if he could feel Theo through the barrier, that he could hold him close a minute longer, stretch infinity into their goodbye so it never had to end. He'll see Theo tomorrow. They'll talk. But this is a beautiful beginning that started a long time ago, and he's worried that with time to think on it, Theo will wake up and ask that they stay friends without anything else. And he would respect that. Of course he would. But the thought weighs his arm down until it falls back to his side, hunching his shoulders while he walks away and back out the front door of the building.

It's really quite early still, especially for a Friday night. He knows T and Laurie are staying at his place tonight, so he's sure they're well entertained, getting out the stress of the week in each other's...arms. Should he tell them? He feels like he should, but he needs time with himself first. Out of habit, he's already on a path around campus, walking the route he's mapped for himself over the past few years, the one his feet know how to follow while his mind freely wanders.

God, he likes Theo so fucking much. Probably has this entire time, like Laurie has always told him. And T. And even Lili once when they were high together at the end of first year. She said he's the only person she trusts enough to get high with after her incident, and that bonded them as much as anything else.

It's not that Theo's perfect, because perfection is impossible and Emir could never expect it from anyone, but Emir's struggling to find a flaw. And the fact he spent years constructing them says a lot more about himself than it does about Theo. He always felt a twinge looking in those warm, chestnut eyes. And when they would bump into each other, Theo's arm brushing against his own, he'd feel the heat of him like a fire in his soul. If they fought he'd feel more alive than he had been in months.

Theo's magnetic, his presence a gravity that Emir didn't feel with his friends, and one that he always pushed against. But Emir's only human, and fighting the laws of physics is above his abilities. The inertia that began with their dissertation could only have led to one of two outcomes: an explosion or a collision. He's glad they seem to have reached the latter.

It's freezing tonight, early November and it certainly feels like it. He's lucky it's not raining because he's wearing layers and he'd be soaked if the skies decided to open up on his path. Emir keeps his hood over his head and his hands in his pockets, listening to the sounds of the night, still but punctuated with moments of life. He remembers the tea that Theo brought to rehearsal and fishes it out of his bag, shocked to taste it and realise it's still warm. Not hot, but enough to bring some awareness back into his body while he walks.

Theo is genuinely the most thoughtful, generous man that Emir has ever known. He has wonderful people in his life, starting with his family and including his uni mates, but he's never known someone like Theo. It's as if kindness is his blueprint, the structure upon which Theo builds his life. And Emir isn't sure he deserves that sort of angel.

Maybe this is what he's always been afraid of, not that he would get hurt, but that he would be the one who wounded someone he cares about. Maybe this is why he's always kept things casual, kept everyone at arm's length or further. He doesn't know if he could live with himself if he ever made someone feel the way he did when everything happened back home. Is this why he never planned on dating again? So he would never know the worst of himself?

But...he failed. Because he wants to date Theo, and he wants more than that too. It might be selfish and maybe he's being daft and greedy and expecting too much from a cold world. But he wants Theo by his side, his warmth in the darkness, his lips soft against his own, his hair falling through his fingertips. And there's a small chance that Theo wants that too, but Emir isn't sure he's ready to ask.

His feet find their way back to his flat around midnight, hours after he started wandering. He spent some time by the lake, walked through the library for a while, even back past Theo's building, staring up at his window and seeing it already dark.

But Emir needs a wee and he's practically freezing, so he's glad to be home even if he's still processing, his mind tumbling and untying the knots of its own design. Which means there's only one thing for it, since going back to the studio tonight is only going to make him miss Theo even more.

Emir unlocks his front door to a silent flat, T and Laurie presumably asleep in Laurie's bed a few feet away. The door's cracked open but the light's off, and if Emir focuses he can hear the fan that T uses for white noise.

He tiptoes to his own room, dropping his things and stripping down so he can shower. Emir's not ready for bed, but he knows he needs to after a long day of dance and a few hours of walking. Maybe it's a good thing Theo can't smell him right now because woof. He towels dry and slaps on some moisturiser, choosing his favourite pyjama bottoms with tiny dogs all over the blue fabric, and a sleep shirt with a minion on the chest to wear while he gets to work.

Emir starts with the kitchen, cleaning and drying every single dish, wiping all the countertops, scrubbing at the limescale around the faucet, organising their fridge and tossing anything expired. And then it's time for their tiny living room. He leaves a pile of Laurie's laundry outside his door (and a bit of T's) that he can gently nudge through the door later, moving his own to his room and into the laundry basket. His room's a disaster, but he's not done with everywhere else yet.

Now comes the best part. The place is tidied, no junk or debris left around, so the furniture can move wherever Emir likes. Nothing major, just a shift of the sofa, a new arrangement for the coffee table, reorganising the shelves they keep their gaming devices on, swapping around the artwork to create a new vibe, whatever will make it feel renewed.

He's nearly done, keeping as quiet as humanly possible of course, and he almost has the sofa exactly where he wants it when he hears a sleepy, "Emir?" mumbled from across the room. Emir turns around and sees a confused, yawning T in an overlarge shirt, rubbing at their eyes and walking towards him.

"Shit. I'm so sorry, T! I didn't mean to wake you." Emir starts pulling at his hair anxiously. He really wants to finish what he's doing, but now T is awake and he feels guilty for disturbing their well deserved rest.

"Are you alright?" T stares at the furniture, by now aware that this is how Emir copes with emotional problems. If he can't dance through them, the flat has to be cleaned and rearranged. It happens about twice a year, on average.

"Fine. Completely fine. Just...thinking." Emir glances around, wondering if he actually should move the sofa the other direction instead because of the way the afternoon sun comes through the windows. "With furniture."

"Do you need help?" T puts their hands on the back of the sofa and gives it a nudge, somehow shoving it exactly in the spot Emir needs it.

"No, I'm just losing it a bit and trying not to." Emir forces a fake laugh, biting at his lip and scratching at the stubble that's starting on his chin. "Go back to sleep, T. I'll keep it down, I swear."

T stares at him for a moment before seeming to decide something, leaving Emir with a nod while he replaces the throw cushions and blankets how he likes. Emir figures T probably went to go get Laurie to deal with him instead, and sure enough –

"What the bloody fuck are you doing? It's the middle of the night." Laurie's annoyed grumble gets Emir's attention this time, not nearly as gentle as T's melodic questioning.

"I'll be quiet I promise." Emir lays one of his blankets over the arm of the sofa, his back to Laurie while folding the extra neatly and tucking it underneath the coffee table. He always has at least three in the living room, and even more in his bedroom.

"Emi..." Laurie sounds exasperated as he walks over to Emir, tugging him to stand upright and yanking him into a hug. "You need to sleep, mate. I'll help you move everything tomorrow."

"Not tired." Emir mumbles, hugging Laurie back despite his mood. "Just let me clean the loo. I'll even save my room for tomorrow."

"No, you won't." Laurie sighs, still hugging him. He knows Emir better than that. T was right to be worried and to wake him up. "Does this have anything to do with Theo texting us earlier about gay news?"

"...Theo texted you?" Emir stills, holding his breath, scared of what he might hear. Shit. Fuck. Dammit. He's an idiot. "What did he say?"

"So that's a yes then." Laurie sighs again, letting Emir out of the hug to tug on his arm instead, pulling him towards his bedroom where T is now scrolling on their phone and waiting for Laurie to come back to sleep.

"In." Laurie points at the bed, T tapping the spot beside them and waiting.

"Absolutely not. No." Emir looks between them, but Laurie's already back in the common areas turning off the lights and checking that the front door is locked.

"Come cuddle with us or else." T yawns through the command, which softens it more than a little.

"Did you change the sheets after?" Emir feels Laurie's hand on his back now, moving him towards the bed. As much as he's protesting, a cuddle sandwich with T and Laurie sounds like maybe the only way he'll be able to sleep tonight.

"No. But don't worry we didn't get anything on the bed tonight." Laurie waits for Emir to climb in the bed before getting in after him, tugging the duvet up to cover them all and turning on his side to face Emir and T.

"Yeah, Laurie wanted to try something in the shower instead. Plus, I don't like to waste it." T yawns again, as if they haven't just confirmed being a cum slut with absolutely zero hesitation. But Emir's well past being shocked by what these two get up to.

"Fine. Guess you two are cleaning the loo tomorrow then." Emir snuggles himself beneath the duvet, T's ankle finding his and wrapping them together while Laurie turns off the lamp so they're in the dark again.

"So are you going to tell us?" Laurie runs his fingertips through Emir's shower damp hair, soothing him from there while T keeps playing footsie with his toes. Maybe it should be weird, but it's not. Not for them.

"We, um...well, I sort of bit him." Emir starts chewing on his fingernails again until T's hand reaches out to stop him. Good instincts as always on their part.

"Like sexually?" Laurie asks, a lilt of surprise to his voice because that would be skipping a few steps.

"No, you animal." Emir laughs softly, thinking back to how Theo reacted to his absolutely unhinged behaviour. "I just wanted to kiss him so fucking bad and we were dancing, obviously, and he was holding me and I just...I bit him."

"Oh, Emi." T scoots closer and smushes their face against his shoulder with a sigh. "You can't just bite people without asking."

Emir laughs again, Laurie's fingers in his hair making him drowsy. "That's what Theo said. But like...he wasn't mean. He made a joke about it and then..."

He stops talking, retracing the memory in his mind as if he can feel Theo's lips against his own if he tries hard enough.

"And then?" Laurie yawns, stifling it behind his free hand before reaching over and laying his arm across Emir and taking hold of T's waist.

"He sort of brought me into him and then he told me I could kiss him. I must've been so fucking obvious if he knew that's all I could think about. But he said I could...so I did." Emir stops when he hears a gasp from T, hoping it's a good one.

"Great kisser, isn't he?" Laurie adds through another yawn. "It's the lips. So pouty."

"Hang on." Emir turns his head towards Laurie, almost able to make him out in the darkness. "How do you know that?"

"They've kissed dozens of times. Just when they're dancing, usually." T pokes Emir in the cheek, trying to get the frown off his face. "Not as if you haven't kissed both of us plenty of times."

"That's different." Emir pouts, suddenly distracted from his story. He's not jealous, but he is surprised. Theo doesn't just go around kissing people, but Emir also knows without a doubt that it's never been more than platonic.

"Relax, you angry little kitten." Laurie sounds both fond and exasperated. It is the middle of the night after all. "He's all yours. T and I are very happy sucking each other's cocks without snogging your boyfriend too."

"Not my boyfriend." Emir grumbles, his arms crossing over his chest. Not that he's actually upset that Laurie's kissed Theo. He's more upset that Theo's not technically his boyfriend and probably won't be either.

"Stop that." Laurie stops playing with his hair for a moment so he'll pay attention.

"Stop what?" Emir glances at him again, already missing the comfort of Laurie's petting. He likes to pretend he's all tough, but really he's a sentimental softie. Emir's not going to complain about the cuddles.

"I can hear your brain spinning." Laurie taps him on the temple before carding his fingers back in Emir's hair, smiling when he releases a happy sigh in response. "If you want him to be your boyfriend, just ask."

"He'll say no." Emir's resigned to it, the obstacles in their way everything from it being their final year of uni to Theo just not being interested. He's spent the last several hours finding all the reasons Theo's going to turn him down, and it's a long list.

"He'll definitely say yes." T lays an arm across Emir too, spooning him from the side like an overgrown koala. "He's in like with you."

"I think...fuck. I think I might love him." Emir admits, swallowing past the lump in his throat and the tears that start in his eyes. "Why the fuck did I let that happen?"

"Shhhhh none of that." Laurie keeps petting Emir's hair, letting Emir's tears fall while the two of them offer their comfort. "Being in love is a beautiful thing. Don't ever be ashamed of that. Especially with someone as wonderful as Teddy."

"Did you tell him that you love him?" T asks, wiping away Emir's tears with the pads of their thumbs.

"Of course not." Emir manages a wet laugh that turns into a hiccough. "He'd be sprinting for the hills. We've just had our first kiss. I'm not about to tell him I'm already in too deep."

"Didn't you say that Theo's a deep well?" Laurie asks gently. "Maybe falling in deep is natural in this case?"

"What if...what if he hurts me?" Emir whispers, ashamed for even asking. Theo's about as dangerous as a puppy, but Emir's also fragile and he doesn't know how to stop being scared of that.

"He might." Laurie admits with a sage nod. "But that doesn't mean you two shouldn't be together. T and I hurt each other sometimes. It's just what it means to be human."

Laurie leans over Emir to give T a peck of a kiss before laying back again. "But if you care about each other and you invest in your relationship, it'll be alright."

"What if I hurt him?" Emir feels the tears start again as he asks, already feeling guilty for something he hasn't done. "I think that would be worse."

"Well, try not to." T shrugs before burrowing further into the cuddle. "If you love him and he feels the same, I think it's wonderful. You two could be really happy together."

"What they said." Laurie slides down to settle in on Emir's other side, one hand still in his hair and the other holding T at the waist. "You think you can sleep now?"

Emir nods, yawning and pulling the duvet up to his chin, hands curled up on his chest while he relaxes between them. "Don't let me sleep too late. Have to see Theo and tell him that...ask him to be my boyfriend."

"Damn right you do." Laurie ruffles Emir's hair one last time before relaxing his hand to fall back asleep.

***

Laurie: *this yours?*
Laurie: */picture of Emir asleep, T curled up beside him, Laurie on his other side squinting at the camera against the light/*
Theo: */side eye emoji/*
Theo: *Is he alright? Or is this a common occurrence?*
Laurie: *He had quite the night apparently. Kissed some fit bloke or something.*
Theo: *...you mean me right?*
Laurie: *Of course I mean you*
Laurie: *Is that what you wanted to tell us yesterday?*
Theo: *YES*
Theo: *But you were both "busy"*
Laurie: *We were. Believe me it's better you didn't come over*
Laurie: *You're lucky you texted before we made it to the shower. We weren't quiet.*
Theo: *Well?*
Theo: *What do you think?*
Laurie: *I think the shower isn't big enough*

Theo: /eye roll emoji/

Theo: I am NEVER showering there. Ever.

Laurie: Not even with Emir?

Theo: No comment.

Laurie: You really like him?

Theo: Honestly...I more than like him.

Theo: I know what you're going to say, but it's true.

Theo: Emir is just... to know him is to love him, I think. And I know him now. The real him.

Laurie: You promise you won't hurt him?

Laurie: If you do there will be consequences, and not the fun kind

Laurie: I would kill for this moody gay boi

Theo: God I hope I never fucking hurt him. Not even a tiny papercut or another stupid argument ever again.

Laurie: In that case

Laurie: You didn't hear this from me, but you're not the only one who's in more than like

Theo: TELL ME EVERYTHING

Laurie: Wow I'm so fucking tired back to sleep bye /snoring emoji/

Theo: LAURIE TEMPTEST

Theo: ANSWER ME

Theo: Fine. Keep your secrets.

Theo: Have Emir text me when he's awake? He said we could talk today.

Laurie: He left his phone in the kitchen overnight. That's why he didn't answer. Sorry I just saw when I went to get the coffee started and decided to plug his phone in while he and T sleep in. I wasn't snooping.

Theo: Don't wake him up. He needs the rest. Always so tired.

Laurie: You're so fucking whipped already

Theo: So what if I am?

Laurie: You two are going to be insufferable

Laurie: Did you tell our international contingent yet?

Theo: Just Lili and Jo. Went over theirs when the two of you were too busy for me.

Theo: Ciaran must've spent the night at Gabe's but now they're here this morning so /shrug emoji/

Laurie: Fine. Next time you can walk in on me balls deep in T while they choke around a dildo suctioned to the shower wall.

Theo: I didn't ask for the visual. I'm glad you two found each other though. Absolutely filthy but in a compatible way.

Laurie: They're perfect and I'll never apologise for our sex life. Perfectly healthy.

Theo: I may not have experience, but I'm well aware that a healthy sex life can be important in a relationship.

Laurie: You haven't...?

Theo: *When would I have possibly done that without you noticing??? You're the only person I go out with. I've always come home alone at the end of the night and there is no universe where I have anonymous sex with a stranger at a club.*

Laurie: *Does Emir know?*

Theo: *He does actually, yeah.*

Theo: *I told him that night the four of you were swapping spit during family dinner.*

Laurie: *We were swapping a lot more than spit...*

Theo: *All four of you?*

Laurie: *Not sure if I'm allowed to confirm or deny that*

Theo: */writing emoji/*

Laurie: *I think Emir might be waking up. I hear giggling coming from the bedroom so i assume gossip is happening*

Theo: *:) :) :) :) :) :) :)*

Laurie: *I'll let them be for a few minutes. I'm glad they have their little moments.*

Laurie: *Oh by the way Emir's jealous that you and I kiss*

Theo: *Not often. And not like real kissing. Fine, the kissing is real, but we're not in love or anything. Platonically in love, maybe.*

Laurie: *A jealous boi is a jealous boi Teddy*

Theo: *I've seen him and T kiss more than once, and I know the two of you have gotten off together before, so.*

Laurie: *I don't mind that they kiss. T is just very affectionate and we have some degree of an open door when it comes to sex.*

Theo: *I don't mind either, but I think Emir and I will have to talk about all that if he wants to be like official. I do, of course, but I have to wait for him to ask.*

Laurie: *Why can't you do the asking?*

Theo: *Just a feeling. I only want him to agree to what he's comfortable with and not feel pressured.*

Laurie: *Coffee's done and I think they're actually awake now*

Laurie: *I'll subtly suggest that Emi check his phone*

Theo: *Thanks, Laur. You're the best :)*

***

Emir knocks on the door to Theo's flat, heart in his throat while he waits. Theo's expecting him of course, but his anxiety is on another level right now. It's not that he dressed up just for this...except he did. T helped him pick out something a little more intentional than normal and he spent at least fifteen minutes fixing his hair before walking over.

The door opens a few seconds later, Theo beaming at Emir and immediately reaching out to him. Emir realises in the instant it takes for their hands to meet that he's been stressing over nothing, that Theo has only ever been entirely open and honest with him, and even though it feels way too easy, he can let himself have this. He melts into Theo in the doorway, allowing himself to be brought in for a soft kiss that he closes his eyes and smiles into before sliding his hands around Theo's waist to hold him the way he's always wanted.

"Missed you." Theo sighs into his shoulder, which is the most endearing, lovely thing he could have ever said after only a few hours apart.

"Yeah?" Emir meets him in another kiss, this one slower and sweeter while they keep each other close. "Been thinking about you all night, princess."

"GABRIEL, GET IN HERE!" Ciaran yells from the hallway that he shares with T, frozen in place while he stares at them.

"WHAT'S WRONG?" Gabe trips over his feet, half naked in just his boxers and one sock as he comes running around the corner. By this point Emir and Theo are turned to face them, laughing with their arms still around each other. "Jesus, Ciaran. You scared me!"

Gabe has a hand over his chest, catching his breath and leaning on Ciaran's shoulder.

"They're kissing!" Ciaran keeps still, wide eyed and unmoving until Gabe nudges him out of his spot and towards the other two.

"We can hear you." Emir has one hand in Theo's hair, the other warm around his waist. Theo's face is tucked into Emir's shoulder, hiding his flush from his friends. He's not sure if it's possible, but he thinks he's even happier than last night.

"And we can *see* you!" Ciaran finally walks to them and immediately throws his arms around them both in a three person hug. "My gay babies are finally kissing. Gabe, tell them how long I've been waiting for this."

"God, for fucking ever, I swear. You should've heard him last weekend when he saw you dancing together." Gabe drags Ciaran away to replace his arms with his own, practically swallowing the two of them in his massive wingspan. When Gabe steps back beside Ciaran they stand there expectantly, staring with wide grins.

"What?" Emir asks, pressing his lips to Theo's temple, knowing that it makes him smile even if he can't see it.

"Go on then. Kiss him." Ciaran puts his arms around Gabe's waist and pulls him into his side, looking bleary eyed and bright as if they've just woken up.

"Only because I want to and not because you asked." Emir turns back to Theo, nudging a finger under his chin to bring Theo's lips back to his own, humming when they fit together. Theo's lips are like a pillow, so soft and plump and comfortable. Emir's hand finds its way back into Theo's hair, holding him close to lengthen the kiss before leaning back again. They still have a lot to talk about before he gets lost in Theo.

"You alright there, Teddy?" Ciaran asks with a laugh when he sees Theo's dazed expression.

"Never better." Theo's eyes glaze over while he tries to take in Emir. He's pretty sure his hair is floofier than normal, but it's always incredible so maybe not.

Emir's hand is rubbing softly along his back and Theo wants to melt into the floor. His insides feel like a toasted marshmallow, warm and squishy and sweet. If Emir can do all that with just a kiss, Theo wonders about the future that might be ahead for them.

"You ready to go? There's somewhere I want to take you." Emir keeps rubbing Theo's back, staring between his lips and his eyes, unable to choose which he prefers. Every inch of Theo is his favourite.

"I should probably grab a coat. Maybe a scarf too." Theo hasn't moved, still smiling at Emir before leaning in for another kiss. He's not especially motivated to do anything else when kissing Emir is an option.

Emir kisses him back, forgetting for a moment that they're in an open doorway and their friends are eagerly watching as he slips his tongue into Theo's mouth and muffles the moan that Theo offers in response as he presses their bodies even closer.

"At least close the door and let us catch up if this is a group activity." Ciaran reaches over for a sofa cushion, tossing it their way as payback for all the times it's been the other way around.

"Maybe later." Emir tosses the cushion back onto the sofa before stepping over and grabbing Theo's coat from beside the door. "For today, I'd prefer to keep Theo to myself."

Theo lets Emir help him into his coat, one sleeve at a time, Emir also reaching for his winter scarf, looping it around his neck and pulling him in for a finishing kiss. Emir tilts his head to ask, "Gloves?"

"Can't you just hold my hand instead?" Theo asks with a laugh, only partially kidding. He loves when they hold hands.

"You two are adorable." Gabe observes from where he's wrapped himself around Ciaran's back. "And pretty. You look good together."

"Not as adorable as me." Ciaran elbows him gently in the side with a scoff before looking back at their friends. "You two have fun and don't do anything I wouldn't do."

"Is there anything actually on that list?" Theo asks over his shoulder as they head out into the hallway. Ciaran shakes his head no and watches them leave, the door closing behind Theo with a soft click as Emir's hand finds its way into Theo's to link their fingers together. "Where are you taking me, then?"

"Secret." Emir presses a kiss to the side of Theo's jaw as they step outside the building, holding the door open for him. He's never really wanted to be like this with anyone else, but he likes to spoil Theo, to romance him and take care of him and walk with him through the world.

"I don't think we've seen that bird on our walks before. What's it called?" Theo stops their progress, pointing into a nearby tree when he spots their new friend, keeping his voice low so it doesn't startle.

Over the past few weeks of walking together, Theo's learned so much about the local animal population that he never knew existed, dozens of birds and rodents and even the trees they inhabit. Emir really is a nerd when it comes to these things and Theo adores it.

"It's a waxwing." Emir stares at the bird fondly, glad that Theo has never minded his fascination with the wildlife they find on their walks, especially when it slows them down because Emir wants to study one of them in silence. "You can tell by the feathers on their heads and their size. And that's a rowan tree which is one of their favourites."

"So pretty. That soft tawny brown and the bluegrey on their wings." Theo glances at Emir, watching the way he focuses on the tiny creature in fascination. After a few moments, the bird flies away to another tree and they continue their walk, falling into the easy rhythm that they've settled into recently. But instead of their hands brushing occasionally and making them startle, Theo has Emir's hand secure in his own and it's the best walk they've ever been on.

When they reach the lake, Emir stops under his special tree and turns Theo around to face him, hands starting on his shoulders before circling around to his back as Theo pulls him closer.

"Surprise." Emir mumbles, letting Theo look around them at the familiar landscape while trying to figure out why they're here.

"You wanted to walk to the lake? We come here all the time, babe." Theo looks back to Emir with a furrowed brow. It's one of the only tranquil spots nearby, and definitely the only body of water they have access to. Every indulgent walk they've taken has included the lake at some point.

"This is my tree." Emir taps under Theo's chin to get him to look up into its branches. "My safe place where I draw and paint and write and cry and sometimes even sleep. And I wanted to share it with you. I've always avoided it before when we came here because it's out of the way, which is why it's my hiding spot. But it can be yours too."

Theo's wondered where Emir wanders off to when he's not in the studio or his flat. Now that he knows that Emir really only spends time with about four people, he figured there must be somewhere like this that Emir thinks of as his, somewhere he could be without worrying about interruptions or distractions. The fact that he's sharing it with Theo feels significant, like he's sharing much more than a location. "Do you want to sit for a while?"

Emir loves Theo's quiet acceptance, the way he absorbs what Emir shares and fits himself into Emir's space like there's the exact right amount of room for him. And he's right. It turns out there's been a Theo Palmer sized hole in his heart for a long time, and it's not that he expects forever or anything as impossible as that.

But maybe if he's lucky, he and Theo can grow together for a little while, keep learning about each other and the world with their hands held tight. He's a sentimental softie for wishing for such bliss, but it's hard not to when Theo's in his arms and in his life, taking up just the right amount of space and filling the cracks in Emir's heart with his gentle laugh and kind eyes.

He reaches into his bag for a blanket, setting it down in his usual spot and tugging Theo down to sit beside him before unfolding a second blanket to lay across their laps. Theo rests with his head on Emir's chest, one arm thrown over his diaphragm while Emir holds him in a cuddle. It's more comfortable than Theo would've thought, but maybe that's because he has Emir beneath him instead of the cold ground.

"What're you worried about?" Theo asks after a few minutes of listening to the birds chatter overhead.

"How'd you know I was worried?" Emir runs his fingers through Theo's hair and stares up at the sky, thinking the metaphor was more apt than he initially realised that day in Theo's room.

"Because I know you. I'm pretty sure you walked around for hours last night before cuddling up with Laurie and T." Theo extricates his phone from his front pocket, unlocking it to show Emir the picture that Laurie sent. "You're cute when you sleep."

"I'm always cute." Emir smirks down at the picture, remembering how cosy he was when he woke up this morning. Maybe if he's exceptionally lucky, he'll get to snuggle Theo tonight instead.

"Deflecting." Theo puts his phone away and settles back on Emir's chest, prodding his stomach with his fingertips and making him chuckle. "Come on. Tell me what you're worried about so we can get back to the kissing and et cetera."

"Et cetera?" Emir lets his own hand wander onto Theo's side and under his coat, tickling where he knows Theo's most sensitive. "And what could that possibly mean, hm?"

Theo giggles and gasps until he manages to get Emir's hands away from the danger zone, nuzzling his face against Emir's neck and sighing happily. "I'm not going to make you talk if you don't want to, Emi. Just leaving the option open."

"Can I be honest? Like actually tell you what I'm worried about?" Emir's fingers still in Theo's hair, his breathing shallower than before. "And before I do, you're not the problem. Not for a single moment. I'm more worried about...circumstance."

"While I appreciate the reassurance, it'd be alright if you are worried about me. You've been hurt before and it's reasonable to be cautious." Theo presses a kiss to Emir's chest where his heart lies beneath many warm layers of fabric. "I might not want to hear it, but I'll try not to take it personally. It's not as if I have experience to point to that could reassure you about me."

"Hey." Emir's voice is like velvet, soft and soothing as he sits up so he can look at Theo fully. "It doesn't matter if you've been in a dozen relationships or none at all. A shitty person is a shitty person, and in your case, an angel is an angel. I may have spent most of last night having a small crisis that you didn't actually want anything to do with me, but I think I'm over that now."

Emir finishes his consolation with confidence, very sure that Theo wouldn't be snuggling up to him and giving him sweet kisses today if he wanted as much space as possible between them.

"Alright then...I'm glad to hear that." Theo smiles as Emir leans down, rubbing their noses together before giving him another soft kiss and pulling Theo back onto his chest.

"It's not a fun list, princess. You sure you want to know all this mess?" Emir would feel better if they talked about it, but he also doesn't want to ruin Theo's peace.

"Well, it's my mess too. If...if you'll let me." Theo turns his head to catch Emir's eye. He may not have been in a real relationship before, but he knows that honest communication is important.

"It's our last year, Teddy. We only have a few months before we're done here. Starting something now could be setting both of us up for incredible pain in a few months. It's already November." Emir brushes a strand of Theo's hair away from his eyes. This is one of his main worries: that they'll have an unbelievable year of falling in love only to be ripped apart when they have to leave this place behind.

"Well...I can't decide for you, but I would rather have the best eight months of my life and have it hurt at the end than not have it at all." Theo's thought about this too, of course. But it's his own fault for fighting with Emir all these years when they could've been together instead. "And for what it's worth, I don't have solid plans for after we leave here. I doubt I'll get hired on full-time by any of the professional companies in the city unless I'm extremely lucky. I've been talking to Sean about it and my options for after graduation are flexible. So if an inevitable end is something you're worried about, maybe it doesn't have to be so inevitable?"

"I suppose we'll have to talk about that one again later." Emir sighs, kissing Theo's forehead and cradling him against his chest. "I haven't a clue what's going to happen next year either. I hope I get an offer or two and I'd love to stay in London if I can. But...I don't know. I just...I think if I knew what it was like to be with you, and then that was ripped away, it might break me. Especially if it wasn't because we decided it was for the best, but just because of life. I'm not trying to be dramatic, and I'm not going to pretend that long distance will work, because I know that I can't do it. I'm just being honest so you don't think more of me than I am. I wouldn't want to hurt you by trying to be someone I'm not."

"Alright what else? I don't think we're going to solve the paradox of time this morning." Theo starts running his hand along Emir's front, not moving below his waist, but it's so naturally soothing and Emir wishes there wasn't a single fibre of clothing between Theo's hand and his skin right now.

"We're working together. What if it all goes wrong and we can't work together anymore and then we're both fucked for our dissertations? Or if we're together but it's so distracting that our work is a disaster because we were too focused on being together to do anything besides kiss during rehearsal?" Emir feels Theo laugh against his chest before sitting up to stare down at Emir.

"You can't possibly be worried about that." Theo laughs again, wondering where in the world Emir got that from. "We worked together when we hated each other. There's no way on earth it could be more tense than that. And as for the opposite problem..."

Theo pushes the blanket off of himself so he can straddle Emir's lap and lean forward on top of him. "We'll just have to stick to a schedule. An hour of work, five minutes of fooling around. I'm, like, *really* good at schedules..."

He kisses Emir, way past chaste this time, hand moving into the hair at the side of his head and tongue pushing past his lips, licking along the roof of his mouth. Theo's never been like this before, with anyone, but he's hungry for Emir and he's not going to hesitate now that he knows it's mutual.

"Seems a bit unbalanced." Emir grumbles between kisses. That's not nearly a good enough percentage. "Shouldn't it be an equal ratio? Thirty minutes of work and thirty minutes of hands in each other's pants?"

Theo's right of course. They're both great at respecting boundaries and staying focused where dance is concerned, always putting it above their personal drama, good or otherwise.

"I'm open to suggestions." Theo counters, kissing Emir a minute longer before moving back down his body to lay on his chest again. "Anything else?"

"What about around other people? Do we kiss hello and goodbye? Hold hands? Touch each other when we're in the hallways or when we're in class together?" Emir laughs when Theo chokes at the thought. "Not like that, princess. I think I can manage not to grope you in public."

Emir pretends to be exasperated, but he's grinning. Why was he so worried that Theo didn't feel the same? "I meant more like intimate, nonsexual touching. Like how I like to put my hand on your back or run my fingers through your hair. That sort of thing."

"I'm completely fine with that. I honestly don't have any issues with PDA around our friends, but in public I'd rather keep it to quick kisses and the intimate nonsexual stuff you mentioned, at least at the start, if that's alright." Theo lets his hand beneath Emir's jumper, fingers only separated from Emir's abdomen by the shirt he's wearing underneath. "You?"

"I think I'm of the same mind, but I'm a private person. I'd rather we keep intimacy between ourselves unless we have a conversation about it beforehand. Like if we go to a party together...crowds can be hard for me, the past few years. I might be anxious and not ready to kiss you. That sort of thing." Emir catches his breath as Theo's hand rests on his lower stomach. It's not sexual, ironically given the conversation, but it's so familiar. Like Theo's comfortable with him and in his space. Emir loves it.

"Have we run out of things you're worried about now?" Theo's glad that Emir shared what kept him up all night. If they're going to be together, difficult conversations are a must, especially with their history. They know what buttons to push too easily.

"Not quite." Emir sits up again, fiddling with Theo's fingers until he sits up as well. "I was sort of hoping..."

Emir makes the delicious mistake of looking into Theo's eyes and he can feel himself heat all the way to his toes while his stomach does a nice cartwheel. Best to just rip off the plaster, and if Theo turns him down, they'll have to figure it out together.

"Go on then." Theo links their fingers and kisses the side of Emir's neck, breathing in the smell of cinnamon and citrus that he's pretty sure comes from Emir's soap. Maybe his shampoo. He'll know soon enough.

"I don't want to be with anyone else. And I'd rather you weren't either, but that's up to you." Emir scratches at his hair before remembering all the effort he put into it this morning and dropping his free hand back to his lap instead. "And you don't have to be my boyfriend if you don't want to be but we're already mostly dating and I'd like to take you on a proper date soon and more, if you're interested. So like...boyfriend?"

"I thought you'd *never* ask." Theo tackles Emir back onto the blanket and kisses every inch of his face while Emir laughs and squirms against him. "I'm literally one impulse decision away from buying a shirt that says: *Property of Emir Shah*, so yeah, I think being your boyfriend sounds alright."

Emir takes Theo's chin in his hand to hold him still for a full kiss, glad that they're hidden by his tree because he doesn't want to share this moment with anyone else. They lay in the cold morning air, warming each other up while they kiss beneath the branches, sheltered from the almost constant drizzle of the sky.

"You make me so happy, Theo..." Despite the panic of its truth, that important phrase sits on the tip of his tongue, but Emir's not going to say it. Not now. It's too soon and he doesn't want to ruin the moment by adding another milestone. The last twenty-four hours are already heavy with those.

"I'm glad." Theo kisses the bridge of Emir's nose and cradles the back of his head. "I've never known anyone as interesting and beautiful and determined and intelligent as you. And if I make you happy, then that's the best thing I've ever heard...But wait - "

Theo searches Emir's face, suddenly very serious because he doesn't want to fuck this up already. Emir's said in the past that he's fine with gendered terms but still. "Are you alright with being my boyfriend or is there, like, a better word or something else you prefer?"

"Boyfriend is perfect, but I love that you asked." Emir kisses Theo again, his darling princess, his thoughtful boyfriend, this generous heart he's fallen for. "You see me, and remembering to ask means the world."

"Boyfriend." Theo's eyes crinkle as he smiles again, rubbing his nose against Emir's just because he can. "You're *my* boyfriend. Can't believe it took two years of fighting to get us here."

"Can I...is it alright if we tell people? Our friends already know but like," Emir props himself up on his side, resting on his elbow while he fiddles with Theo's scarf. "My family's coming to see *Alice* and I'd really like for them to meet you, if you're alright with that."

Theo lays beneath Emir and stares, eyes wide with surprise. Emir asking that means he's really serious about this. He wants to be with Theo, and introducing him to his family isn't even close to casual. Emir's met Barbara, but that was mostly by accident. Of course Theo wants to meet the Shahs, but he's sort of shocked that Emir's ready for it. Maybe that's on Theo for assuming he would need to take things slow after what happened because apparently he was very wrong. "You...want me to meet your family? Like properly?"

"Only if you want." Emir stops fidgeting to stare at Theo, worried he's overstepped. "If it's too soon, just tell me and I'll back off. I don't want to make you uncomfortable."

"No! It's not that at all." Theo sits up on his elbows, close enough that one of Emir's errant strands of hair brushes his cheek. "I just...I didn't know you liked me that much. Your family is so important to you and meeting them would be..."

Emir watches Theo's lips, pink and swollen from how much they've been kissing, like he can see evidence of their connection left behind. "I've had a lot of time to think about this. I don't just mean last night. I've been wanting to be yours since at least our day in Cookham. But you've never been my second choice, Theo. All these years, you're all I was looking for. I don't think I was ready before. And I was busy being a knob to you."

"We both get the blame for the last few years, babe." Theo kisses Emir's cheekbone before resting their foreheads together. It's becoming one of his favourite habits, to share Emir's space and know he's right there. "I honestly wasn't looking for anyone and I don't want to pretend I'm some gothic poet who was just waiting for *the one*."

He presses his lips to Emir's jaw, nosing along it until finding his mouth and kissing just his bottom lip, Emir's breath stuttering against him. "But just because I wasn't looking doesn't mean I'm not radiantly happy to be yours. You surprise me every day, and you've shown me a joy that I didn't even know existed. So maybe I wasn't waiting for you, but I think that means you're remarkable enough that I couldn't deny this once being with you became an option. It's been a slow burn, but that's sort of the only way for me. And I hope that's alright with you because once I'm in, I'm in. So like...you have me. And you can introduce me to whoever you like and I'll feel lucky to meet them."

"How are you real?" Emir holds Theo's head while laying him back down, kissing him again because his heart might actually stop if he lets himself fall into those words. Maybe later. Because there's no chance in hell he's forgetting that monologue anytime soon. "You want to stay over tonight? I know we're both busy this afternoon, but dinner at mine? I'll cook, but I know you like to help."

"Can we make one of your family recipes?" Theo loves that they're still in this quiet space together, under Emir's tree, as if they're in their own world. "And maybe watch a movie and cuddle up on the sofa?"

"I am definitely calling mum after I walk you home. I need to tell her about you and have her help me decide what to make. But mostly brag about you." Emir kisses behind Theo's ear, settling in to lay beside him again, the blankets he brought with him tangled up around them.

Theo smiles bright, knowing he'll be calling his own mum as soon as he's home. It's a day before their usual weekly call, but he can't wait. He wants to tell her as soon as possible. And if he's spending the night, he's not sure how early he'll be up tomorrow anyway. "Emir?"

"Princess?" Emir's toying with Theo's scarf again, thinking of how soft Theo's skin is, just waiting to be kissed.

"I'm not ready for sex. I figured I should tell you so you're not surprised when I come over and don't...when I can't...it's not that I don't want to, just not yet." Theo flushes, but this time it's out of embarrassment.

Theo struggles sometimes with expecting things from himself that he's just not ready to give. Understanding his demisexuality and being comfortable with it in the context of a relationship are two different things, and he's still learning to navigate the latter.

"I'm not ready either, to be honest." Emir presses his lips against that butter smooth skin hiding beneath Theo's scarf, hoping he can feel how in love he is even if he's not ready to say it. "There's a difference between casual sex for its own sake and sex with feelings. I'm, like, insanely attracted to you, but I don't want to rush into anything. Kissing you is already so overwhelming I'm not sure I could handle anything else so soon."

"You're not just saying that?" Theo can't help the insecurity that laces his words.

"I'm not. But I'm happy to remind you if that's what you need." Emir unties Theo's scarf, needing to be nuzzled up against him even closer before he has to walk him back home. "I'd much rather we take this slow and work up to when it feels right for us...but I can't promise I won't be tugging one off in the shower thinking about you."

"Emir!" Theo laughs while Emir cuddles up into his space, his face chilly against Theo's neck from the autumn winds.

"What? Have you seen yourself?" Emir nips at Theo's birthmark, already planning to bruise it with his mouth. "Pretty sure you were my wet dream for all of first year. Especially after we'd fight."

"I, um..." Theo clears his throat, flushing again, and Emir can feel it against his face. It's so intimate, to know Theo's body in this way, to feel his emotions skin to skin and realise he's the reason. "I might have..."

"Theodore - *I don't know your middle name* - Palmer. Have you been wanking while thinking of me?" Emir sits up and tickles at Theo's sides again. It will never stop being fun to watch him giggle and squirm and smile like that.

"It's George!" Theo yells between choked off laughter. "My parents are very white."

Emir's the one laughing now, unable to keep tickling Theo while he falls against his chest to laugh together.

"You're my favourite person." He admits, splayed on top of Theo like a tired blanket. "Also, I'd like the details of those thoughts some day. For research."

"I don't think sticking your hand in your trousers counts as research, babe." Theo teases, hand finding its way to Emir's spine to trail his fingertips up and down.

"See that's where you're wrong." Emir takes Theo's free hand with his own, lacing their fingers together while he stays on Theo's chest. "I plan to memorise every inch of you. Learn what makes you tingle. Discover your mysteries and unravel all your secret pleasures. I'd like to take care of you, court you and romance you and waste my days spoiling you. If you're my princess, I want you to feel like one."

Theo hums, wrapping his arms around Emir and holding him close while the wind picks up around them. They'll have to leave soon and make their way back, but it's been a perfect morning. "I'm going to sleep so well tonight. You're the best cuddler in the world."

"And don't you forget it." Emir kisses Theo's neck again, relaxing against him until it's time to walk home. His mind is a broken record of *I love you I love you I love you* to the rhythm of Theo's heartbeat. He's still scared of what it means to fall like this, to be weightless in the arms of the person you love, but he's learning to adjust, to stop second guessing and remember that Theo is safe and good and kind, and if he was going to fall for anyone like this, he's really glad it's Theo.

CHAPTER THIRTEEN

"They look so happy."

"We should wake them up."

"Absolutely not! It's way too early."

"It's after eight. I'm shocked they're still asleep."

"Maybe they had a long night."

"You think they shagged?"

"Laurie!"

"What? It's a fair question."

"I don't think they're there yet."

"Well that's why I want to ask."

"You can't just ask people if they're having sex."

"Sure you can: watch me."

"Laurie, no!"

"Mph. Get off me, you giant!"

"Shhhh you'll wake them up."

Emir groans, rolling over into Theo's space and nuzzling his chest below his throat. Theo sighs, arms going around him and one leg moving over his thigh to hold onto him.

"Look, they're moving."

"Doesn't mean they're awake."

"They're at least a little bit awake."

"Oh god, what if they want to like - their first morning together…"

"We can hear you." Emir grumbles, moving his arm just enough to flip their friends off over his shoulder.

"See! Told you we were being too loud." T smacks Laurie's shoulder with a scoff, Laurie taking that as his cue to walk fully into the room and join them on Emir's bed.

"Laurie!" T follows after him, climbing on the foot of the bed as well, as if they've been invited. As much as they try to keep Laurie's chaos in check, they usually end up reluctantly joining in. It's hard to resist an excited Laurie Tempest, especially while engaged to him.

Theo cracks his eyes open, catching Emir already staring back with a gentle smile and adorable bedhead. Theo moves even closer to whisper, "You think they'd leave even if we asked?"

"Probably not, no." Emir sighs, still not looking at T or Laurie despite their weight near their feet.

"Oh good, you're awake." Laurie interrupts, at a normal volume this time. "How's my favourite new couple doing this morning?"

"Be doing a lot better if I could kiss my boyfriend in peace, thanks." Emir glares at Laurie, moving himself even closer to Theo because if there's anything he loves first thing in the morning, it's sleepy cuddles. Theo presses his lips to Emir's forehead, happy to have woken up still in his arms.

"I told Laur not to wake you up. But he insisted." T sounds genuinely contrite, laying a hand on Theo's calf through the blanket in apology.

"Oh, we heard." Theo breathes out a laugh, one of his curls hitting Emir's cheek as he does.

"So like…did you - " Laurie doesn't even finish his question before Emir interrupts.

"No we did not, and if and when we do is none of your fucking business." Emir hides his face against Theo's chest and breathes deep. Theo smells incredible first thing in the morning, like sleep and clean laundry. The sun is way too bright.

"I'm just curious. I want you two to know that you have our support and all that." Laurie shrugs, laying himself sideways at the foot of the bed and putting his head in T's lap where they're sitting cross-legged in the corner. "And lube if you need it."

"I appreciate your very odd form of gay support." Theo says, running his fingers through Emir's hair and burying his nose in it. Waking up with Emir is clearly superior to the alternative, despite the interruption. "And we're not sharing your lube."

"Can you two go have morning sex or something and let us wake up properly?" Emir mumbles, not even bothering to move off of Theo's chest. He's more than comfortable exactly where he is.

"We absolutely can." T moves Laurie off of their lap and stands back up, pulling on Laurie's arm until he starts to follow. "Just remember to be back at ours to set up for the party around three. And bring whatever you signed up for on the spreadsheet. Oh! And we invited a few more people, so there should be almost thirty of us."

"Goodbye, T." Emir catches their eye and waits for them to leave, dragging Laurie along behind them and finally shutting the door to Emir's bedroom.

"So...you want to kiss your boyfriend good morning, is that it?" Theo rubs his nose along Emir's with a smile, feeling a flutter in his stomach with the first brush of their lips.

"Sleepy morning cuddles are my favourite." Emir admits, leaving warm, slow kisses all along Theo's jaw and finally reaching that beautiful birthmark that he adores. He spends a few moments leaving a bruise, Theo groaning softly in response, hand in Emir's hair encouraging him to continue.

"I'm never waking up alone again." Theo breathes heavily, Emir's mouth moving away from his throat to meet his lips again.

***

"Emir!" Theo looks at himself in the mirror, dried off from his shower and just about to get dressed.

"What?" Emir's voice is almost immediately outside the door. "What's wrong? Is the spider back? Don't hurt him!"

Theo spins around to open the door, towel around his waist and right hand covering his neck. "What the hell am I supposed to do with this?"

Emir stares in confusion for a moment, gets distracted by Theo warm and pink and in a towel, then finally remembers the panic in Theo's voice to meet his eyes again. "Do with what? I told you, we just put Peter outside whenever he crawls back in. Bit determined for a spider, but he seems to like it here."

"I can't believe you named him Peter, you absolute nerd." Theo moves his hand away from his neck so Emir can see what the issue is. "But I was talking about this. Care to explain yourself?"

"You taste good." Emir smirks, reaching out his fingertips to brush against the bruise. It looks incredible, in Emir's very humble opinion. "And your birthmark has a friend now."

"I've never had one of these before, but I'm assuming it won't be gone before class tomorrow?" Theo crosses his arms over his chest, the towel falling deliciously low on his hips.

"Not if I did it right." Emir bites his bottom lip, eyes shining with mischief. Theo looks so good fresh out of the shower, inspiring thoughts of all they could get up to in there together some day.

Theo sighs, resigned to the comments that he knows will inevitably follow once he leaves the flat. "Do I at least get to return the favour then?"

"Have I mentioned that you're my favourite?" Emir winds his fingers into Theo's wet hair, Theo's arms falling open to let him in and hold Emir by the...lower back. "Mmmm handsy this morning?"

"That alright?" Theo closes his eyes, Emir's fingers like magic against his scalp.

"More than alright." Emir tilts his head to the side, encouraging Theo to get started on his promise to mark him up in retribution. "I like love bites, both giving and receiving."

"Is that a vers joke?" Theo giggles from his spot on Emir's neck, nosing along his jaw and pressing his lips behind Emir's ear.

"Not intentionally, but you're also not wrong." Emir moves them so Theo is pressing him against the doorframe, the new position doing incredible things for his already interested dick.

"I don't know what I'm doing. Do I just...?" Theo pulls back enough that he can ask Emir for guidance, and his earnest question goes straight through Emir's heart, further solidifying Theo's place there. Theo trusts him so openly.

"Just um...put your mouth on my neck. I bruise easy near my collarbones. Right there." Emir catches his breath as Theo kisses exactly where he wants it, his lips warm and wet with just a hint of a scratch from a day or two of stubble. "Little bites, kisses, a bit of sucking. Use your tongue if you want. You'll see it start to turn red."

Emir is very into giving Theo instructions while letting him mark his neck. It's delicious and dirty and everything he loves. For someone who's never done this before, it's probably the hottest necking he's ever had.

"I - " Emir clears his throat as his voice goes hoarse. "Make it dark. I like the reminder. I like when it hurts for a day or so."

Theo finishes what he thinks is a sizable love bite, enjoying the way Emir's fingers grasp in his hair while he groans in response to Theo's mouth. For a first try, he doesn't think he's done too poorly based on the very obvious hardness against his hip. Theo brings their mouths back together, Emir's lips parted until Theo captures a withheld groan with his kiss.

"Need to - I should shower." Emir blinks his eyes open, pupils wide while he stares at Theo, still fresh and sweet from his own shower. He smells like Emir, his soap and his shampoo and his moisturiser, and it's all going straight to Emir's dick.

"Got a little something you need to take care of?" Theo smirks, hand dragging down Emir's front and stopping just above his waistband. He steps away, leaving Emir sweaty and hard, and in a sudden moment of inspiration, Theo unties the towel around his waist, letting it fall to the ground as he walks away, positive that Emir is staring at his bare arse.

"I'm just going to...yup." Emir's rubbing himself through his boxers, staring after Theo with his mouth gaping open. Who knew Theo could be such a fucking tease? This is the best morning of his life.

"Have fun, babe." Theo calls from Emir's bedroom, already reaching into his overnight bag to get comfy cute clothes for the day.

Emir locks himself in the bathroom, not even letting the shower warm up again before he settles beneath the water and gets himself off, one hand pressing against his new love bite. He comes embarrassingly fast and loud, shouting Theo's name as he paints the wall. Theo hears him yell, turning pink with something like pride while he makes Emir's bed and tidies, waiting for his boyfriend to come back to him.

***

Laurie: *Emi you are an ANIMAL*
Laurie: *You have no room telling me and T off ever again*
Emi: *what did I do this time?*
Laurie: *Have you seen Theo's neck??*
Emi: *you haven't seen mine*
Emi: */picture of the pound sized love bite on his collarbone/*
T: *Ooooo nice one Theo. Very purple*
Ciaran: *Oh so we're having that sort of party tonight /wink emoji/*
Ciaran: *Maybe one of us should go stock up*
Gabe: *I'm still at the store. I'll take care of it :)*
Theo: *In my defence, Emir bruises easy. Told me so himself.*
Laurie: *Did he now? /Baby Yoda sipping tea gif/*
Gabe: *Any special requests? They have a bunch of flavours.*
Ciaran: *Condoms or lube?*
Gabe: *Both /picture of the options on the shelf/*
Laurie: *T and I have plenty just get what you need*
Theo: *Wait...*
Emi: *DON'T SCARE MY TEDDY*
Theo: *Not scared, just curious.*
Laurie: *Great they've taken it to a private chat /crying emoji/*
Laurie: *LET US WATCH YOU BE HORNY*
T: *Laur you can't just ask people that*
Ciaran: *It'd be rude not to ask. Can't watch without permission.*
Gabe: *They have holiday flavours. I'm getting them.*
T: *Actually, we're running low on lube. Just checked my room.*

Gabe: *Already got peppermint for you. It's tingly. I'll grab the boring shit too, just in case.*
Ciaran: *Did you get us more of the fun colours?*
Gabe: *What am I, an amateur?*
Laurie: *Emi, do you have enough weed or should I text Tim?*
Emi: *i'm good for tonight*
Emi: *i have enough for me and theo if he wants to share*
Emi: *thanks for checking though*
T: *I'm starting to worry about all of us being able to attend class tomorrow...*
Ciaran: *This is what they get for having class the day after a holiday.*
Theo: *Emi and I will be fine. Or at least I will. I won't be drinking tonight.*
Emi: *yeah probably just weed for me tonight*
Emi: *last week of rehearsals and all that*

***

Theo: *Is it alright to ask you questions?*
Theo: *Or is that like a dick softener?*
Emi: *BABY I YELLED*
Emi: *DICK SOFTENER*
Emi: *ask me whatever you want, princess*
Theo: *Do you like the flavoured stuff?*
Theo: *I might have...bought a few things. Just in case.*
Theo: *But none of it's like fancy or flavoured or anything like that.*
Theo: *And I wasn't sure about like fun toys or anything so I just scrolled a few websites to get ideas.*
Theo: *I already have a few of my own things of course. But I think you already know that.*
Emi: *...i may need another shower*
Emi: *i'm sweating*
Theo: *Only because you're at the studio.*
Emi: */selfie with his vest discarded and abs on display, arm over his head/*
Emi: *this sweat is NOT from dance*
Emi: *it's all you, pumpkin*
Theo: *I've never wanted to lick someone so bad.*
Emi: *that could be arranged...*
Theo: *We're both supposed to be focusing.*
Theo: *You can't just send me pictures like that. I'm easily distracted.*
Theo: *But I need to know if I should ask Gabe to get something else while he's there.*
Emi: *i think we should start by tasting each other and decide together*
Emi: *and since i've been busy simping over you for the past few months i'm well stocked on anything we might want*

Theo: *Okay :) sounds perfect :)*
Theo: *I just...I really like you. So much.*
Emi: *can't wait to see you in a few hours*
Emi: */gif of minion kissing the screen/*
Theo: *Back to revising :(*

Emi: *it's been enough minutes that I know you're away from your phone, but when you get back and see this*
Emi: *you should know i like you so much it scares me*
Emi: *that when i think of you i feel safe*
Emi: *when you smile at me with your eyes all crinkled i want to cry*
Emi: *your joy moves me somewhere deep down that i'm only learning to access*
Emi: *and when you reach for me i feel special*
Emi: *like i matter to you not because i'm pretty or talented or anything*
Emi: *but just because you actually like me for who i am*
Emi: *and i could cuddle you every morning and every night and be the happiest person alive*
Emi: *you're so wonderfully precious to me, Theodore George Palmer, my princess, my pumpkin, the baby to my johnny*
Emi: *i'll see you soon, i just...wanted you to know*

***

The party's been going strong for over an hour already, Ciaran and Gabe making sure the music keeps up with the vibe while T wanders around socialising and checking that everyone has what they need. Lili and Jordan are dancing with Laurie and it's the gayest thing Emir's ever seen.

"How are you feeling?" Theo leans in to ask Emir, kissing his cheek for good measure while waiting for an answer.

Emir tilts his head and looks at Theo, arms draped over his shoulders while they dance near the kitchen. All of their regular furniture is pushed to the side, their sofas draped in sheets that T keeps for when they have parties, and whatever seating they have available moved away to make room for everyone to mingle. Laurie hung a banner on the wall that he found on the internet, reading: *Please Leave By Nine.* And they're not going to kick people out, because it's just their friends and everyone has class tomorrow anyway, so it's more of an inside joke than anything.

"Lots of people in a small space." Theo mumbles, just loud enough for Emir to hear. He squeezes Emir's waist beneath his loose black t-shirt, his fingers warm against Emir's skin. Theo's doing fine for now, but he knows Emir sometimes has a hard time with parties, too. He and Emi haven't had that talk yet, but he's sure Emir has noticed his stims and his routines, teasing him about Theo Time and letting Theo know, in his own way, that Emir understands. Theo knows that Emir's trauma isn't the same as his own autism, but they have similar strategies for interacting with the world, including needing breaks from environments like this party.

"I'm alright." Emir gives him a grateful smile before leaning in for a kiss and resting their foreheads together. "I might want a break soon though."

Theo nods, brushing his lips against Emir's before turning himself around so his back is to Emir's front. He loves this song but has no idea what it's called. Theo only knows that moving himself against Emir to whatever Reggaeton beat Ciaran picked is perfect.

Emir's hands slide down Theo's front, eventually holding him by the hips so they can move together deeper, fully flush while he grinds into his boyfriend and leaves hot kisses on the back of his neck. Laurie glances over at them with a grin, making a rude hand gesture that has Emir rolling his eyes. When the song ends, Emir moves Theo back around to face him, one hand on the back of his neck for a rough kiss that Theo leans into immediately.

"Go dance with Laurie. I can tell you two miss it." Emir turns Theo away and pats his bum to get him moving. "Go on. I'll get us something to drink."

Theo hesitates, pulling Emir in by the shirt for another kiss before walking the few feet it takes to reach his best friends, squeezing himself between Laurie and the girls.

"Oi!" Lili grabs Jordan to dance by themselves nearby, glaring until Theo leans over and kisses her cheek. She can never stay annoyed with Theo for very long.

Emir watches Theo and Laurie dance for half a song, immediately finding themselves in their own rhythm, and Emir sort of loves it. Two of his favourite people with a bond all their own. Theo is glowing so pretty tonight and he and Laurie always have a great time together at parties. But Emir needs a break anyway, so he walks towards the fridge to get some cool water for them to share. True to their word, neither of them is drinking tonight, but they still need to stay hydrated.

"So, you and Theo?" Emir hears from his side, turning around to see Alfie walking into the kitchen to join him. It takes a moment to adjust to seeing Alfie in something other than dance tights.

"Oh...yeah." Emir feels himself smiling wide, one hand on the water jug, the other brushing his fringe off of his forehead. "We're together now. Boyfriends, like."

"I figured." Alfie reaches past Emir to grab a beer from the fridge, cracking it open and closing the door to lean against it. "You happy?"

"Beyond happy." Emir takes a glass down from the cupboard, pouring from the jug and drinking half of it down in one go. "Kinda wish I wouldn't have been a dick for two years but...we figured it out."

"It's banging, you two being together." Alfie opens the fridge for Emir to replace the water jug.

They've known each other for years, but they've never really spent time together socially. Emir isn't entirely sure how to continue the conversation, never having had a personal moment with Alfie before and not knowing where to start. He's always been shy, and moments like this remind him of being that kid in primary school who would play alone because he was too scared to say anything to the other kids. It was when he started ballet that he learned how to make friends. And now, a decade and a half later, it brought him Theo.

"Cool to see you outside the studio." Emir absentmindedly tosses a crisp into his mouth from one of the bowls on the countertop, aiming for casual because Alfie is a very relaxed, very chill sort of person. "Did Theo invite you?"

"Oh, did you not - I figured they would've..." Alfie flushes maroon all the way to his ginger roots and sets his beer down. "Ciaran invited me."

"Oh! That's great. He and Gabe are two of my best mates." Emir isn't sure what all the embarrassment is about, but Alfie's already making his way out of the kitchen again.

"Yeah that's what he told me." Alfie gives him a painful smile, hurrying away and moving over to Ciaran, whispering something in his ear that makes Ciaran cackle and look at Emir. Ciaran winds his fingers into Gabe's hair to whisper something, looking between Alfie and Emir before kissing Gabe and retracing Alfie's steps.

"Ciaran, what the bloody fuck have you done to Alfie?" Emir asks once he's in ear shot. "He's about to shit himself."

"This one's my fault. I was supposed to tell you before he came tonight on account of how you're my mate and all." Ciaran sidles up beside Emir so he can talk to him privately. They're alone in the kitchen but this isn't information to be broadcast. "We met him on Grindr. Gabe and I...well, you can put the pieces together."

"Like dating or just shagging?" Emir's a little surprised, but not much. Ciaran and Gabe have always been open to inviting others into their bed, if not their relationship. The surprise is more about two completely separate parts of his social circle colliding.

"Just casual, but we have incredible fun together." Ciaran smiles over at Alfie and Gabe talking near the telly, which for some reason has a display of a fire crackling in the background. Maybe that was the compromise after they all vetoed Laurie's suggestion of playing *V for Vendetta* on a loop until the party ended.

"Is that where you were on Friday?" Emir smirks, remembering how Theo told him that they were mysteriously gone from the flat all night, but there when he woke up the next morning.

"Yeah. We've been meeting up about once a week. Whenever it works for all of us." Ciaran shrugs, casually sipping his own beer. "It's not too weird for you, is it? Since you know him from dance?"

"You're good." Emir pats Ciaran on the cheek with a smirk. "But you made poor Alfie run away. Go on and tell him I'm fine with it. Your sexcapades are none of my business, but I appreciate the heads up so it's not awkward when I inevitably walk in on you three at some point. Be safe and have fun and warn us if you're being loud."

"Will you tell Teddy for me?" Ciaran asks, already walking away so Emir can't argue even if he wanted to. "Thanks, mate."

Emir grins, refilling his water glass and making his way over to Theo and Laurie, their bodies intertwined even more completely than Emir and Theo had been before. Emir catches T's eye, sharing a knowing smile before switching his gaze to Laurie who tilts his head in invitation. How Emir ever thought Theo was straight is beyond him because...wow, he is zero percent heterosexual. Once he's next to the two of them,

Emir reaches out and grabs a handful of Laurie's arse. He gives it a squeeze to get his attention before sidling up behind him, hand grasping the front of his thigh instead.

"Alright if Theo and I share you for a dance?" Emir asks quietly, close behind Laurie but leaving enough room that he can move away if Laurie says no.

As an answer, Laurie pushes his bum back into Emir while tugging Theo by the hips to grind into his front. He throws his head back, exposing his neck and leaving room for Emir to meet Theo in a kiss around him. While snogging his boyfriend, Emir sets the too-full-for-dancing water glass down on the windowsill and fits one arm around Laurie's waist while the other plays with Theo's hair.

Laurie waits for them to finish their kiss then brings his lips to Theo's for just a moment, making sure it's alright with both of them. When Emir kisses the crest of his cheekbone Laurie takes that as permission, Theo tilting his head and letting Laurie kiss him back, Emir still grinding against Laurie's arse from behind and toying with Theo's hair. Laurie has a remarkable arse, probably the best Emir's ever seen, and getting to rub up against it - with permission of course - is more than a little hot.

Laurie breaks the kiss to ask, "Thoughts?" He leans his head back against Emir's chest, waiting for Theo's verdict.

"Great kisser, but Emir's my person." Theo shrugs, turning Laurie around so he's facing Emir instead. "Sorry, Laur. Nothing and no one can compete with that."

Emir smiles at Theo, pulling Laurie onto his thigh so he can manhandle him, Theo following gladly while the three of them keep sweating on each other to the beat of the music. Laurie's tongue finds its way into Emir's mouth, exploring and leaving a taste of Theo behind beneath the layers of alcohol Laurie's consumed. Emir kisses him back, but they don't have a very compatible sexual dynamic most nights. They both prefer to be dominant, and the kiss doesn't last very long.

"You're fit, but I think I'll leave you to this one instead." Laurie winks at Emir, his delicate hand reaching behind himself to hold the back of Theo's neck and body roll between the two of them like a fucking porn star.

"Nice bum though." Emir reaches a hand between Laurie and Theo's writhing bodies and he's definitely not *not* into it. He can feel Theo's dick beside his hand, Theo purposely moving so Emir *can* feel it, and Laurie letting Emir's hand slide between them as he pleases. Emir's not groping, just encouraging them and enjoying the game.

"Sorry, this fantastic bum belongs to only one penis." Laurie grins over Emir's shoulder at T who's talking with one of Laurie's guests. Laurie has a small group of lesbians that, when he's not hanging out with these five, he can usually be found leading around the campus. Since Laurie works on sets and interior design with a fairly steady gig managing the various stage productions, it's not much of a surprise that he'd spend a lot of his time surrounded by gay ladies. And T adores every single one of "Laurie's lesbians" as they call themselves.

Emir and Theo keep dancing with Laurie for another two songs, Theo making his way into the middle so he can be closer to Emir, and that arrangement works better for the trio. Both Emir and Laurie guide Theo, who follows them effortlessly, letting himself be pulled and moved and touched however they like. Laurie never crosses a line, and he never would. They're just having gay fun and putting on a bit of a show, for themselves and whoever feels like watching. But Laurie gets restless and wanders away to find T for a dance, leaving Emir and Theo to be on their own again.

Theo reaches for the water that Emir set on the windowsill earlier, drinking the whole glass in one go and pulling Emir into his front for a cuddle. Emir wraps his arms down and around Theo's back, hands holding tight to his shoulders from underneath while he places soft kisses along Theo's neck. They're both done dancing for the moment and Emir needs a break. A real one this time.

"I was wondering..." Emir bites Theo's earlobe then noses along his jaw. "I'm ready to go outside for a bit. Sort of want to get high. You want to join? You can stay here if you want."

"Take me with you." Theo kisses Emir hungrily, one arm strong around his back while he keeps Emir on the tip of his lips. "Please."

Emir smiles, biting Theo's bottom lip before soothing it with his tongue, just one more filthy kiss before they leave the party behind. "We should grab something warm from your room. Can I borrow something?"

"I love seeing you in my clothes." Theo means that wholeheartedly. The night they went out for Halloween, he memorised the way Emir looked cuddled up in his pyjamas. "But I get to wear my Batman jumper."

***

Being outside in the fresh air after the sweaty, hot flat full of people feels like being reborn. Emir keeps Theo tucked against his side while they walk to his tree. It's honestly the best spot on campus for getting high, besides safely in his and Laurie's flat.

"I've never...like, it's not that I don't want to, but no one ever seems to invite me." Theo watches Emir take two pre-rolled joints out of his pocket along with a lime green lighter, and he's equal parts curious and turned on by the sight. Emir can pull off the bad boy vibe extremely well.

"Not even Laurie?" Emir has Theo mostly in his lap with his back against the tree, the lake spread out before them from a fair distance away.

"Laurie usually smokes with you, and until recently that meant I wasn't included." Theo shrugs, not meaning to make Emir look like *that*, as if he regrets his entire existence just because Theo wasn't invited to get high with them.

"Do you actually want to? Just because I smoke sometimes doesn't mean you have to." Emir forgets the weed for a moment, arms holding Theo in his lap as he kisses his neck. "And I'm sorry. If I could undo all of it I would. Sometimes I forget how much our fighting got in the way of our lives."

"It's alright. No one else ever asked me either. Maybe I seem like a prude or something." Theo sighs, laying his head back against Emir, smiling as a kiss lands on his cheek.

"You do sort of seem like one because of how put together you are. But everyone assuming that you're uninterested because of that is just a judgemental prick, myself included." Emir tucks one of the joints back into the bag in his pocket for later. "But if you do want to smoke tonight, you're sharing. I'm not having you overdo it your first time. Let me shotgun you for now and you can decide if you like it."

"Is that when we sort of kiss and you teach me how to breathe it in or something?" Theo turns his head so he can look at Emir, not wanting to move from his spot between his legs. He likes sharing Emir's lap.

Emir laughs, kissing the side of Theo's mouth before confirming. "Something like that. And then we can just sit here and look at the lake and each other."

You're prettier than the lake, Emir thinks, knowing it's too ridiculous to say aloud.

Theo watches Emir's every movement, from the way his lips hold the joint, to how his fingers catch on the lighter, his lungs moving as he takes his first drag, all while staring right back at Theo. On his second drag, Emir teases his fingers under Theo's chin until their lips meet, releasing the smoke into his mouth and guiding him with softly mumbled instructions while he inhales for the first time.

"Alright?" Emir asks, carefully watching Theo for any reaction, positive or negative. So many first times for Theo, and Emir gets to be there for all of them. Knowing how safe Theo feels with him, to be honest and vulnerable and naive...maybe he's already high because he feels like he could cry. Staring into those big brown eyes and viewing himself through Theo's perspective is like nothing else.

"Kiss me again?" Theo whines, waiting for Emir to move so he can cuddle him face to face.

Emir takes another hit, letting it out into the night air and away from Theo this time before pulling Theo in for another kiss. They alternate between kissing and smoking until the joint burns out, Emir watching Theo slowly unfold as he feels himself relaxing too. They giggle, pressing their joy into each other's skin and lips and the minimal space left between them. Emir's not sure how much time has passed since they left the party, but Theo's on his chest and everything feels right.

"What are you thinking about, princess?" Emir presses his lips to the top of Theo's head, arms cradling him protectively and one leg holding him from below.

"You know how you kissed me?" Theo takes a moment to answer, clearly processing even more information than usual.

"Which time?" Emir stares at the sky, and he might be imagining it, but he thinks he sees a few stars peeking through the haze. "I'm lucky enough to have kissed you dozens of times by now."

"The first time..." Theo sighs, his eyes closed against Emir's neck and his eyelashes fluttering across his skin in a butterfly kiss. "Remember how you told me that I was the sky? I think about that constantly. That conversation changed my life."

Theo's almost whispering, more even and calm than Emir has ever heard. "When you kissed me it was like you were the earth and I was the sky and we were meeting at the horizon. And then I remembered that story about the ancient gods, and how the Sky and the Earth created the world with their love. And when I kissed you back, it was like I wanted you to reach for me, like how the earth makes mountains just to marry the sky. I needed you to pierce me, to take whatever you wanted and let us create something new from the exchange. Like if we worked together, we could invent the sunrise."

Emir feels the tears on his cheeks before he realises he's crying, sniffling and wiping them away with his nearest hand. What did he ever do to deserve the angel in his arms who speaks poetry and holds him like glass? Theo might be magic.

"I think I'm going to marry you someday." The words are out before Emir processes thinking them, but...they're true. Maybe more blunt and honest than he would want to be tonight, but true nonetheless.

"I'm not saying no, but if we elope before Laurie and T have their wedding they might actually kill us." Theo loves how he can feel Emir laugh beneath him, their bodies shifting together because of his joke. The sky laying against the earth, moving in harmony.

"I'm not proposing, Theo." Emir strokes his fingers through Theo's hair, burying his nose at the crown of his head and leaving it there while they cuddle under the tree. "That was the most beautiful thing I've ever heard. You say the things that confuse my soul in a way that makes sense, like some sort of translator for my heart. So maybe someday, if we decide it's what we want, we can talk about something as permanent as that...but for tonight I think we should just kiss for a while before we head home and cuddle up in your bed."

They stay under the tree until Theo starts to fall asleep on Emir's chest, snoring softly while Emir pets his hair. Emir wakes him up to walk home, glad to see that the party's over so they can shower in peace and go to bed. They both have to be up early for their usual class schedule, but they sleep better together, with their legs intertwined and Theo's head on Emir's heart. The flat is still a bit of a mess, but they'll help the others clean it up tomorrow night. And who cares about a messy flat when your new boyfriend is cuddled up in bed with you, warm and soft and sleepy?

Theo falls asleep first, again, and Emir spends the few minutes before he follows thinking about their night and the weekend they've had. They only shared their first kiss two days ago. It feels like a different reality that he spent Friday night scared and trembling with T and Laurie reassuring him that everything would be alright. Because now he has Theo and he feels secure, like they've found solid footing and they're both better off moving forward together. He kisses Theo once more before settling in to sleep, happier than he could have ever dreamed.

CHAPTER FOURTEEN

Theo's alarm wakes him early Monday morning, significantly before dawn. And it's just like every other Monday morning, except in every way that matters. Before he can turn off his alarm, a sleepy grumble from Emir breaks the stillness, and when it's quiet again, Theo lays his head back over that steady heart, letting its rhythm start his day.

He knows Emir will be awake soon enough, his own alarm set for only fifteen minutes later than Theo's. They haven't woken up together on a weekday morning before, but they know each other's schedules by now. While Theo begins his day in the studio before visiting the gym, Emir will spend a few hours outside, running and thinking and letting the world share its poetry through the morning.

Allowing himself to indulge for a minute, Theo cuddles up against Emir, trailing his fingers through his hair and watching him sleep. He's so peaceful and warm, his chest Theo's favourite pillow, especially when he sleeps shirtless like last night. Moving his hand down, Theo runs his fingers through the short hair covering Emir's chest, laying his palm flat to rub slow, soothing circles across Emir's sternum until he hums happily and nuzzles his face into Theo's hair. Emir pulls Theo closer with both of his arms, one leg moving around Theo's hips while he resettles and falls back asleep. And Theo really should get up, but five minutes won't be the end of the world. In this case, it might actually be the beginning.

But among other things, Theo's bladder requires attention. He regretfully peels himself away from Emir, a delicate smile warming his face as Emir pouts and reaches out for him when he moves. "I have to get up, Emi, but you can sleep for a few more minutes."

"Mmmm...alright." Emir pouts again until Theo leans forward to press their lips together, Emir smiling immediately then yanking the duvet up and over his head, creating a cave to sleep in for the next ten minutes until he has to pull himself out of bed.

Theo brushes his teeth, swipes his deodorant under his arms, washes his face, has a wee, and by the time he's ready to get dressed, Emir's alarm goes off, the sound of birds chirping through the space while Emir groans and flops his hand out of his cocoon to turn it off. Theo sits beside him, watching Emir stretch and squirm around in his bed, hoping it'll become a regular occurrence.

Emir blinks his eyes open, grumpy at needing to be awake, but better rested the last few nights spent with Theo than he can ever remember before. He sleeps soundly when Theo's there, no waking up in the middle of the night or struggling to fall asleep.

"Morning." Emir's voice is low and gentle, holding out a hand to Theo and waiting for him to lace their fingers together.

"You getting up?" Theo asks, his heart melting when Emir uses his free hand to wipe the sleep from his eyes. He's *adorable* and Theo can hardly believe this moment is real.

"I give myself one snooze in the mornings. Helps me wake up." Emir yawns, curling himself back onto his side while staring up at Theo. Waking up early isn't so bad if Theo's there to spend time with. "Do you need me to get up so you can leave?"

He really hopes Theo says no, but it's his room so technically he can kick Emir out whenever.

"Of course not. You could stay all morning if you like." Theo reaches out to run a hand through Emir's hair. He's not exactly worried about leaving Emir behind in his space. "What's your favourite colour today?"

Emir pauses for a moment, breathing deep and thinking about Theo. "Red. Definitely."

As red as Theo's lips when they kiss. The colour of roses and blood and passion and life. Red for love, because Emir is in it, so deep he may never find his way out. He's barely awake, and his brain may need a moment but his heart is sure. This is what love is supposed to feel like: warm, safe, fun, interesting, comfortable, so many things that he never knew before. But now that he's experiencing it, he understands. He knows why T and Laurie fight over practically every little thing for that wedding, but never once consider calling it off. He realises what Safiya meant about trusting another person more than yourself. He understands how Gabe and Ciaran can open their relationship without a single doubt about their commitment to each other. He gets it: the breadth of love that he's always seen around him.

Theo is love. And love is bright, beautiful, blushing red.

Tucking Emir back in for his last few minutes of sleep, Theo kisses him once more before getting dressed, sneaking out of his own room so that he doesn't wake him. He sort of loves knowing that Emir is so comfortable in his bed that he can't drag himself away a moment before absolutely necessary.

While Theo walks into the practice studio, he thinks again about their first kiss, how it was just feet away from where he's warming himself up for the day. And instead of being distracted by it, he feels a new layer of fondness for the space and for the work that brought them together. They never would've been in each other's lives without dance. If they hadn't both been so passionate and committed they wouldn't have found themselves where they are now: boyfriends, collaborators, partners, and so much more.

He'll have to remember to tell Emir later, that what he's feeling is the opposite of what Emir had been worried about. Theo's not struggling in the slightest to keep focused or to practise. Instead, he has an entire new source of inspiration.

***

Emir sneaks up behind Theo, sharing a look with Lili so she won't give him away while the two of them chat at the barre before tech hall. It's their first day of class as boyfriends and he hasn't seen Theo since he woke up. He'd prefer to get Theo back in his arms, even if only for a stolen minute before class starts.

Theo gasps, jumping and turning to grab Emir when he tickles his sides without warning, Emir laughing and falling into Theo's front while composing himself. Theo knows he's flushing, surprised but always glad to have Emir nearby, even when he's being a tease...maybe especially then.

"You should see your face." Emir keeps giggling, poking Theo in the side just because and winking at Lili while she laughs into her side stretch.

"You're too quiet!" Theo pouts, arms crossing over his chest defensively. "Like you've got ninja feet or something."

But he unfolds his arms and lets his face fall into a smile. It's pretty impossible to stay grumpy at Emir.

"Come on. Got something I need to ask you." Emir tilts his head toward the hallway, brushing his fingertips against Theo's palm without actually catching his hand. Theo follows close behind, waiting until they're out the door to give Emir's bum a smack, a small retaliation for surprising him at the barre. And he looks fit, tight black dance tights beneath running shorts and his usual oversized vest that shows flashes of skin as he moves. Emir just grins and winks at Theo over his shoulder, as if they do this everyday.

"What did you..." Theo trails off as Emir guides him against the wall in an alcove near the stairwell, one of his hands sliding up underneath Theo's shirt, smoothing across his stomach and over his waist. "What're you...?"

"Shhhh, I just needed to kiss you." Emir waits a beat in case this is too much for Theo. But Theo grins, his own hands grabbing at Emir's bum and giving it a squeeze while he brings their lips together. They kiss quietly to keep their privacy, Emir wrecking Theo's hair with his fingers while getting a taste of his tongue, Theo pushing his hips up and against Emir before stopping suddenly and pulling back.

"Um – I..." Theo flushes, letting his head drop back and thunk against the wall. "I think I need a minute before we go back in there."

Emir uses his thigh to nudge at Theo's semi, leaning in to kiss under his jaw instead, the bruise from yesterday still visible beside his birthmark. "We've got time. Catch your breath, princess."

"Lili's definitely going to notice." Theo groans, running a hand over his face, but pulling Emir back into his front for a cuddle. "And I'm blaming you."

"Please do." Emir tugs at Theo's shirt to get his attention, the reason he had to pull Theo aside for a kiss blaring cherry red from his chest. "Now I know why you asked what my favourite colour is today."

"Oh..." Theo bites his lip nervously, looking down and avoiding Emir's eyes. "I just thought...I want you to be happy. I've been doing it for a while but I'm usually better at asking which colour without it being obvious."

"How long is a while?" Emir's chest feels tight again, his eyes doing something ridiculously close to welling up. Will Theo ever stop being the most thoughtful person in the world?

"A few weeks. It's not always my shirt though because I don't actually have that many colours." Theo shrugs, still looking down at where their bodies meet while fiddling with the hem of Emir's vest along his back. "Sometimes I make you stop near a yellow patch of leaves on our walk, or send you a picture of my morning green juice, and there was that time I wore those purple socks and put my feet in your lap on the sofa. I don't do it so you'll notice, I just think it's nice to make sure you have something nearby that makes you happy."

Emir sniffles, making Theo look up in concern. But then Emir laughs, wiping at his eyes and shaking his head to clear it. Now is *not* the time to be weeping over juice and socks.

"There isn't a person alive who deserves you." He gives Theo a wet, lingering kiss, breathing him in and hoping Theo understands everything he can't say right now. Class starts in about five minutes and they should really get back in there. "And today is *definitely* red."

***

Sean sits across the desk from them, waiting expectantly while leaning back in his chair.

"You know usually when you ask for a meeting you do most of the talking." Sean had an email from Theo, with Emir cc'd, in his inbox early Monday morning, asking if he could set aside time during their usual Tuesday meeting hour for the three of them to talk. Of course Sean had agreed immediately. These two never ask for anything.

"Emir and I...well you see – " Theo clears his throat, a pretty pink flush already warming his face. "We've sort of..."

"You changed your minds? But I thought it was going so well." Sean frowns, clearly disappointed. What he's seen so far has been exceptional and it's nowhere near their final work. But if they've decided to split their project it's not too late, just inconvenient.

"No! I love working with Emir!" Theo panics, not sure how to say the thing that needs to be said for his own peace of mind. He doesn't think Sean *technically* needs to know, but it seems like one of those unspoken rules. "Wait, you don't want to stop do you?"

He turns to Emir with panic in his eyes. Theo hasn't even thought about that since Saturday when they talked, but –

"Of course not." Emir knows that Theo wanted to handle this conversation, but a few sentences in and it seems he should step in. He puts his hand on Theo's thigh to comfort him, accompanied by a reassuring smile.

Theo's shoulders relax as his hand gently lays over Emir's on his leg, giving it a squeeze as if asking him to take over the conversation. Emir makes him nervous, and he's positive that's obvious to anyone within a ten metre radius. No, not nervous. Flustered.

"The thing is," Emir grins, turning to Sean and getting to the point, "Working together was just the beginning and to be up front about the situation, we figured we should tell you that we're together now."

"Together as in…" Sean has a smug look growing as Emir continues. He figured this might be inevitable, especially once they started getting along and spending significant amounts of time alone together. They agree about all the important things and their passions are the same.

"Boyfriends, like." Emir pulls Theo's hand up to his mouth to give it a small kiss. "We didn't plan for it to happen, and we've already had all the grown up conversations about keeping work and our relationship separate, but since you're an important part of the process, Theo figured we should let you know sooner rather than later."

Sean smirks, watching how Theo stares at Emir while he's talking, the fixed point of his attention, and Sean can tell he absolutely adores him. Not that Emir's much better, but he's at least able to stop staring long enough to talk to Sean. "Can't say I'm surprised."

"You along with the rest of the world, apparently." Emir giggles, lacing his fingers between Theo's before resting their hands back in Theo's lap. "Turns out Theo's undeniable."

"But we're not going to be a problem, I swear." Theo finally looks at Sean again, almost pleading. "If anything we're more committed than ever to making this work. It means even more now because it's sort of our story together instead of just our separate narratives."

"I'm not worried about that. Not with you two." Sean runs a hand through his hair and chuckles, thinking that he's probably won the pool between the dance instructors because his guess was that the two of them would finally get together during the

Alice performances, so they're just slightly ahead of schedule. "But thank you for telling me. Honest communication and all that."

"Well...that's sort of all we needed to tell you." Theo glances at Emir, waiting for him to chime in again. There isn't an obvious transition away from the news they needed to share and back to what these meetings usually are like.

"Are you free to come watch again this week? The rest of November there's just no way." Emir has gotten better at this whole planning ahead thing, thanks to Theo. It's not that he's ever been disorganised, but still. "And we're probably about halfway through the choreo now."

"Thursday? I know you two have other commitments Wednesday nights after rehearsal." Sean's heard vague mentions of family dinner over the years, and he's very glad they have that. He wouldn't want them to reschedule something that important.

"Perfect." Emir stands up, taking Theo with him by their joined hands. "Thanks, Sean."

"Not sure what you're thanking me for, but you're welcome, I suppose." Sean smiles and waves as they walk out of his office, Theo tugging Emir backwards so he can lean through the doorway and shout, "Thanks!" for himself before disappearing around the door frame again.

***

Lili: *Can you ask Theo what I'm supposed to bring to this thing?*
Lili: *Jo says I signed up for something*
Emi: *you live in his building and have his number*
Emi: *he's literally your best friend*
Emi: *you're lucky i even saw this*
Emi: *also he says to check your email he sent the spreadsheet again*
Lili: *This is why I asked you*
Lili: *Mrs. Shah doesn't even notice his phone when you're in the room*
Emi: *excuse you, that's his royal highness princess theodore shah-palmer to you*
Lili: *I said what I said*
Lili: *Tell him the spreadsheet is too many things*
Lili: *Nevermind Jo says we're bringing a crudite whatever the french fuck that is*
Emi: *you're as dramatic as laurie*
Lili: *Only T is as dramatic as Laurie*
Emi: *true*

Lili: *Apparently I'm also supposed to ask when we're having a double date*
Emi: *ew why*
Lili: *Do I look like I know why*
Emi: *this sounds like a theo question*
Lili: *But you're the one I'm already texting*
Emi: *added him to the chat so you can ask princess yourself*
Theo: *What'd I do?*
Lili: *Hold on I'll add Jo*
Jordan: *Hi?*
Emi: *jordan what the french fuck is a crudite*
Theo: *It's like raw vegetables and stuff.*
Lili: *Hello Mrs. Shah can you please set up a double date with Jo because apparently I was supposed to ask you last Saturday*
Theo: *Is that me? What if I want to hyphenate?*
Emi: *told you*
Theo: *You and Lili talked about that? /side eye emoji/*
Emi: */running emoji/*
Jordan: *Right so party on Saturday night, tech all next week, shows the next two weekends. I'm thinking this Sunday is our best chance.*
Jordan: *Thoughts?*
Theo: *Is the weather too shit to have a picnic?*
Lili: *You and your fucking picnics*
Emi: *leave him alone he's cute*
Lili: */eye roll emoji; vomit emoji/*
Jordan: *It's London so the weather is...weather.*
Emi: *could use my place on sunday*
Emi: *laurie and T are busy with lucy most of the weekend*
Emi: *but i'm not cleaning up before. you get gay chaos or nothing.*
Theo: *That's fine, babe. It's just casual.*
Jordan: *But what are the activities?*
Lili: *See this is why the wives need to plan this and not me and Emir*
Theo: *I would've been such a good housewife like sixty years and a different assigned gender ago.*
Emi: *my thoughts are inappropriate for a groupchat*
Emi: */french maid outfit gif/*
Lili: *I HAVE SEEN ENOUGH*
Jordan: *I'm giving you options, everyone veto what you don't want:*
Jordan: *1) spa day*
Jordan: *2) baking*
Jordan: *3) mock film festival where we pick a theme and like a half dozen movies*

Jordan: 4) board games and jigsaws

Emi: veto board games. last time i played monopoly i ended with the dog up my nose. T had to use tweezers to retrieve the poor thing.

Theo: Maybe you shouldn't have told Laurie he was a fascist class traitor an hour in.

Emi: he bought all the railroads and utilities AND he was the banker. i stand by it /painted nails emoji/

Lili: Veto film festival. I don't want to use my attention span this weekend.

Theo: Can we do baking AND a spa day?

Theo: /begging kneeling gif/

Emi: theodore. people can see this.

Theo: I DID NOT MEAN IT THAT WAY

Theo: But...

Emi: /smirking emoji/

Lili: Brb I'll be bleaching my eyes

Jordan: So spa day and baking?

Jordan: Theo, I'll talk to you tomorrow about what we can bake. I don't want any of us to have to buy anything so we can just compare what's in the cupboard and figure something out.

Emi: i'm not sharing my headbands when we do face masks

Theo: Not even with me? /crying emoji/

Emi: i have something special for you to keep your hair back

Emi: not like that

Emi: bought it years ago but never used it

Lili: What. The. Fuck.

Lili: Theo is not using sex rope to hold back his hair while I'm in the room

Emi: behave yourself elizabeth or i'm revoking your right to ask sex advice

Theo: Excuse me what the fuck is going on?

Theo: Do I need to research how to be a good rope bunny?

Lili: Who told you what a rope bunny is???

Jordan: Wait a minute...

Jordan: You're Lili's "friend from back home"?

Lili: Emi didn't want people to know he's like a sex guru so I lied. Also we didn't grow up that far apart...

Emi: it's called shibari and you should research whatever you're comfortable with

Emi: like i said, never had a chance to use it

Emi: but that's definitely not what i had in mind for spa day

Theo: I have access to the internet, Lilibet.

Theo: But also we're wildly off track. Sunday? Baking and spa day?

Emi: i want to paint my nails but we can't because of tech week /crying emoji/

Jordan: We can paint them however we like and just remove it by Monday afternoon.

Lili: *What if Alice is just really into black nail polish?*
Theo: *I say yes, but I think Raphael says no.*
Lili: *Gay sigh*
Emi: *princess can i paint your toes purple?*

***

"You *really* didn't have to come with me." Theo keeps his eyes on the road even though he's very aware of Emir watching him from the passenger seat. "You can still be my boyfriend without running tedious errands with me."

"But then how would I spend all day staring at you?" Emir takes out his phone to snap a picture. There's just something about the way Theo's hands flex on the wheel...

"But you're not even going to the party." Theo hosts these parties the weekend before tech week for every production.

With the exception of the spring show last year when he was in Boston, he's done so since his first show first year. Nothing elaborate, of course. They're uni students and it's in the student lounge of the dance building. But it's still a way for them all to socialise before a rough few weeks of tech and performances. And Emir's never been to a single one. He's never even responded to the invitation emails.

"I'm not?" Emir already decided on his outfit. He purposely matched what he saw Theo lay out last night before he spent the night at Emir's. He's trying to be a good boyfriend. "Pretty sure I was invited. Or did you mean to invite a different Emir Shah?"

"You're coming?!" Theo snaps his head to stare at Emir before panicking and looking back through the windshield. "You can't just tell a man that while he's driving in London traffic!"

"Why wouldn't I be?" Emir grins and takes another picture of Theo, the mid morning sun glowing in his hair. His boy is just stunningly pretty. "You expect me to spend my Saturday night alone at home while you're busy taking care of the whole world again?"

"There's only sixty of us in the dance programme. And plus ones for those who have them. Or plus twos potentially, but I don't actually think anyone told me they're bringing a polycule, just a partner added to the spreadsheet here or there." Theo turns into a car park next to the charity shop where he needs to look for a few decorations. Once he's safely parked, he shifts to actually look at Emir, cuddled up in a purple hoodie from his time abroad. "Also, I know you need quiet time. I don't expect you to change your entire personality to support me, you know."

"Being alone with you isn't the same as being really alone, but it's better in some ways. You let me be quiet *and* I get cuddles." Emir leans forward so he can kiss Theo across the centre console. The car is private enough for them to be comfortable in their affection. "But I can have quiet time tomorrow morning. I'll go sit under my tree and you can call Caroline and George. I planned on it, actually."

"Caroline and George?" Theo smiles, tugging on the strings of Emir's hoodie. "When did you learn my parent's names?"

"Ages ago. After I met Barbara." Emir laughs at the memory. "That was so embarrassing I decided instantaneously that it could never happen again. And it'll be a good first impression to know their names when I see them at the show...unless you don't want me to meet them, which would be fine. I guess I shouldn't assume."

Emir frowns, scratching at his chin. Just because he asked Theo to meet his family doesn't mean it's automatically reciprocal.

"Of course I want you to." Theo caresses Emir's thigh, his palm warm through the joggers. "They're going to *adore* you, babe."

The show runs for two weekends, and while Emir's family is coming to opening night, Theo's family will be at the second week's Saturday show. It's going to be a very busy few weeks.

"Good. I'd like to meet them." Emir tugs on Theo's jumper to crash them together and lands with his lips against Theo's. "I have a feeling I'll be keeping you for a while, and they're important to you."

"A while?" Theo smiles against Emir's lips before leaning back in his seat so they can actually go into the shop and achieve a few things on that to-do list burning a hole in his pocket. "That sounds vaguely like you've thought about it."

Emir ignores him, smirking while he gets out of the car and huddles into his hoodie against the cold. Theo doesn't need to know just how much he's thought about it. "Let's see the list, then. Can't help if I don't know what's on it."

***

"Do you think people are having fun?" Theo mumbles to Emir, glancing around at almost the entire dance programme mingling in the lounge. "Maybe I didn't decorate enough...What if we don't have enough food?"

Emir keeps rubbing his hand on Theo's lower back, sipping on his tea while keeping Theo tucked into his side near the edge of the room. "It's perfect and so are you. You should try to enjoy yourself."

"I'll go talk to people. I just want to make sure everything's alright, you know?" Theo catches Emir's eye. He's not nervous, but it's a different group every year and he's never sure if it's a terrible idea to have these or not. What he does know is that he was left out often enough growing up and he's determined to ensure that no one at Roseborough will ever feel that way while he's a student here. "Will you walk around with me? Or do you need Emir time? Lili looks done already, doesn't she?"

"Nah, she's just stuck near Georgia right now." Emir kisses Theo's jaw and squeezes his waist, walking them over in that direction. He's marginally upset with himself for never showing up to one of these before. Theo hosts these out of the goodness of his heart, just wanting everyone to have a place to get to know each other outside the studio and relax before a stressful week.

"Yo. Mind if we join?" Emir drops his hand from Theo's back once they reach Lili, Georgia, and Alfie by the drinks table, but brushes Theo's hand with his own so he knows Emir's still right there with him.

"Georgia thinks we should be doing *Coppelia* instead of *Sleeping Beauty* in the spring. But we just did that first year. It's too soon to drag it around again." Alfie looks genuinely relieved to see them, his tolerance for Georgia waning as the year goes on. They have to work together twice a week for pas de deux, which means he's basically in the trenches.

"It's more interesting. Everyone knows the story of *Sleeping Beauty*, but *Coppelia* is almost unique to ballet students." Georgia crosses her arms over her chest defensively. She's clearly alone in her argument, as in most things. "And I've always wanted to dance Swanhilda."

"Not this again." Lili rolls her eyes before walking away to go find Jordan.

The spring ballet is usually where the first years get their chance to dance the principal roles, as the second years are studying abroad and the third years are in supporting roles to focus more time on their dissertations. And in their first year, Lili had danced Swanhilda's part beautifully, with Georgia relegated to one of the village girls.

"I didn't say it was her fault." Georgia looks at them as if they'll back her up. "But we all know why she got the part."

"I recommend you drop it, Georgia." Theo is not about to let Georgia make more of her microaggressive racist comments about his best friend (or anyone else), especially not where other people could overhear and be hurt by association, making the situation even worse. "And I'm not talking about your issues with this year's spring ballet."

Georgia has this sick idea that Lili keeps partnering with Theo and being given the lead roles because she's the only Black dancer in the programme and the choreographers want to appear progressive. Which isn't only dismissive of Lili's incredible talent, but also completely missing the reality of the world they live in. The fact that she's the only Black dancer in the programme should maybe give Georgia a clue and yet...

Emir takes a different approach, completely ignoring Georgia and turning to talk to Alfie, hoping she'll make herself scarce before he has to be rude to her. Theo is good at showing restraint. Emir...not as much. "Is your family able to come to one of the shows, Alfie? I know it's not an easy trip from Cardiff."

"Mam and Tad still aren't talking, so I'm glad they decided on different days. I don't need the stress of mediating while trying to make it through these four show weekends." Alfie sighs as if the weight of the world is compressing his lungs, his parents' recent divorce a constant stress since the summer. Theo rests a hand on his shoulder momentarily and offers an understanding grimace. "Mam'll be at opening night and Tad's coming to the matinee the same weekend."

"My family's coming to opening night too." Emir smiles wide, tugging Theo back into his side to continue. "I finally get to introduce Theo to them."

Georgia scoffs and walks away, her barely concealed homophobia saving them from any continued conversation with her, at least for now.

"So you two are really in this then?" Alfie looks between them with a huge grin. "I wasn't sure with your history, but I think it's tidy, you two together."

"I can't predict the future, but he's sort of my favourite person." Emir tickles at Theo's side until he giggles, leaning into Emir. "Someday I'll forgive myself for being a dick for two years, but yeah. We're happy."

"I know that Ciaran..." Alfie keeps his voice low, not sure how much he can say with other people around. "Well, I spend more time with him and Gabe now, and you all seem like really decent people. We're just having fun, we are, but maybe someday I'll find what you all have."

"Don't feel like you need to rush anything." Theo rests his head on Emir's shoulder for a moment. "If you're having fun and everyone's in a good place, just enjoy it. And if you want to find someone, or more than one someone someday, you will. It's not like I ever could have predicted where I am now."

"Everyone else could." Alfie snorts, grabbing himself a sparkling water from the table and deciding to leave them to it, more grateful than ever that they saved him from another moment dealing with Georgia. "I'm going to chat with the boys for a bit. Thanks, Theo. Lush party."

After Alfie walks away, Theo turns to Emir and squishes his cheeks between his hands, staring at him very seriously while Emir scrunches his eyebrows in confusion. He's the most adorable pouty boyfriend and Theo needs him alone immediately.

"It's our one week anniversary and I didn't even realise." Theo keeps Emir's cheeks squished, giving him a forehead kiss. Remembering things like anniversaries is his specialty and he probably should've made Emir a cake or something. "Bad boyfriend behaviour. I'll make it up to you."

"I don't think most people celebrate one week anniversaries." Emir tries to say with his lips smushed together, the words coming out muffled. Theo drops his hands from Emir's face to grab his forearm instead, walking him out into the hallway and finding a dark corner away from the party. He wants privacy with Emir and no one needs him in the lounge right now.

"I like celebrating anniversaries and things." Theo leans back against the wall, waiting for Emir to crowd into his space. He always does when they're alone.

"Well, what did you have in mind?" Emir figured they might celebrate their one month, maybe a six month, and god willing a year. But he didn't know there were rules about a one week anniversary. "Bit late for me to go out and get you flowers, but I'll draw you one if you'd like."

"Kiss me." Theo trails his pointer finger slowly along Emir's jaw and down his throat, retracting it as Emir pushes him against the wall with a hard kiss. Theo opens up to him, letting Emir fit himself between his legs and into his mouth, groaning as Emir presses into him and tugs at his hair. Emir takes control easily, sliding his hands on and around Theo and relishing this private moment in the dark, with their friends only about a hundred feet away and completely unaware of where they've gone or what they're doing.

"I was thinking," Theo groans again as Emir bites near his birthmark. It's definitely one of his favourite spots to bruise. "Maybe we could...try some things tonight. If you're up for it."

He's breathless, wishing they were already back home and could make progress in a sexual direction. He's ready for more, and he's hoping Emir is too.

"I'm ready for anything with you, princess." Emir kisses him again, pulling Theo's tongue into his mouth and pushing his semi against where he can feel Theo's own through his trousers, hoping Theo understands exactly how much he means that. Anything. Theo could ask for the entire world and Emir would give it to him.

"Stay the night at mine? I think I'll be more comfortable." Theo hasn't gotten this far with a partner before, light snogging really all he's had experience with. If he's in his own bed he thinks it might be less intimidating. Only one way to find out.

"Try and stop me." Emir grins, pausing to run his fingertips gently through Theo's hair and staring adoringly into his soft hazel eyes. They haven't spent a night apart since getting together last weekend and Emir wouldn't have it any other way. "Do I get to kiss you for another minute or are we expected back inside?"

As an answer, Theo reaches down and grazes his fingers along Emir's dick, cautiously letting Emir grind against his hand while kissing him a while longer. It's delicious, letting Emir use him like this to work himself up. Theo's learning so much about himself through the way Emir is with him, understanding what he likes and wants, and discovering new desires he never knew he had.

"Fuck, we have to stop." Emir leans their foreheads together, lacing his fingers through Theo's and moving his (very warm and very talented) hand away from his dick and around his back instead. "We already look wrecked and we need to stay here a few more hours."

"Did you give me another mark?" Theo brushes his fingertips along a spot under his ear, feeling a familiar tingling left behind.

"Is that alright?" Emir kisses the purple bruise that's starting, proud of his handiwork. He made sure it was light, nothing that would last past tomorrow with their performances so soon.

"Yeah, I like when you do that. I feel like I'm...yours." Theo flushes somehow darker, already pink and turning the most beautiful fuschia. He doesn't know what it means, really, but there's something that feels so safe when he thinks about Emir claiming him. Not in a possessive way, more in a protective way. Like he's Emir's to take care of and watch over, and he gets to do the same. "But until *Alice* is over, we should maybe only bruise in places that won't show onstage."

"Fuck, princess. You've no idea what you do to me." Emir wraps his fingers around Theo's neck and strokes the back of his head, caressing him while they both calm back down. The idea of marking Theo's skin on his chest or back or *fuck* maybe even his thighs is not helping his dick to calm down. "I can't wait to watch you be the perfect host for a while longer before you take me home and we can get back to this."

"Thank you for coming tonight." Theo kisses Emir's temple and hugs him close. Hosting is definitely more fun with his person by his side. "I like having you here."

"You're very welcome, one-week-anniversary boyfriend." Emir mumbles, trailing his fingertips beneath Theo's shirt to tickle at his abs. He's always so squirmy like this and Emir loves to make him giggle, watching his eyes light up and catching the music of his laugh. "Now, back inside with you. We have people to entertain."

Emir teases and tickles Theo all the way back to the party, pushing him through the doorway and sneaking in behind him.

"Look who's back." Lili snarks from somewhere to their left. "Enjoy yourselves?"

The people nearby all chuckle, glancing at Emir and Theo with a knowing look. They didn't exactly make an announcement about their relationship, but word spread fast.

"We, um…" Theo flushes again, glancing at Emir as if he'll save him. "We needed to have a private conversation."

"And your hair was involved because…?" Lili stares back, unimpressed, until Jordan not so subtly steps on her foot. Theo starts flattening the back of his hair, wondering if he should go fix it in the loo or just leave it be. Maybe the damage is already done.

"There was a spiderweb." Emir shrugs, walking back to the drinks table to pick up the tea he left behind. It's in Theo's thermos, but at this point it may as well be Emir's with how often he uses it. "I had to help get it out of his hair. Took a while."

"At least you lie better than your boyfriend." Lili sighs, dragging Theo over to stand with her and socialise with some of their classmates. Emir winks at Theo and leaves him to his best friend time with Lili, looking around and deciding how he wants to spend his own time. He doesn't really hang out with these people. Most of them are perfectly fine, but he prefers his small group of friends.

But then he looks over to the card table where Theo created a little teacup display and laid out a few decks of playing cards, both to match the *Alice* theme and to give people an activity if they wanted. Emir sees the shy first year sitting alone, the one that he's watched in rehearsals, always giving 100% and clearly the most talented of his year. Emir's mind is made up immediately. There's a kindred soul alone at a party, and Emir thinks it might be good for both of them to talk to someone new.

"Alright if I join you?" Emir takes the seat opposite the kid, his head jerking up in surprise as soon as Emir sits down.

"You're…you're talking to *me*?" He looks behind himself as if he's not obviously the only person nearby. Half the dance students are either piled up on the sofas or else loudly swapping stories in groups along the walls, the stragglers standing near the snacks while they bemoan the week ahead.

"Of course I am. I'm Emir." Emir holds out a hand for a fist bump, waiting for his new friend to respond. He knows to expect this when he talks to people since he's so quiet in group situations.

"I know who you are." He bumps his knuckles against Emir's, still staring, slightly confused. "I'm Samuel. Sam, if you like."

"Sam, then." Emir smiles, leaning easily in his seat and picking up a deck of cards to give it a shuffle. "You mind if I sit for a while? It gets a bit loud for me being around this many people."

"I don't mind." Sam tilts his head as if asking a silent question, watching Emir sip at his tea before shuffling the deck again.

"You want to play a hand?" Emir holds up the deck and waits for an answer, very glad that he chose to come over here and make a new friend. "*Go Fish* so we don't have to think too hard?"

He offers a kind smile and waits, glad to see Sam return it.

"Go on then, why not." Sam shifts in his seat, readjusting his trousers and leaning with his elbows on the table. "I don't think I've ever heard you talk before."

Emir laughs, dealing them seven cards apiece before setting the remainder in a stack between them. "I'm a pretty quiet person. Introvert, I suppose. I hang out with my mates and talk with them, but otherwise I prefer the quiet. Take a lot of walks. That sort of thing."

"Same for me." Sam takes the cards Emir offers with a smile, fanning them out in his hand with his tongue between his teeth. "It's easier, in some ways."

"You make friends with any of the other dancers yet?" Emir asks, looking around the room and seeing most of the other first years sort of hovering around, still not sure how they fit in with the older students and none of them sparing Sam a second thought.

"Not really…" Sam trails off, eyes carefully trained on his cards. "Got any sixes?"

Emir hands over a card, realising that Sam's sitting alone tonight might be about more than his shyness. "I really only talk to Lili and Jordan, and of course Theo now, too. But that's all new. I didn't really talk to anyone besides my flatmate and his partner for a long time."

"But you and Theo…aren't you, like, together?" Sam looks at Emir expectantly, like it's some sort of test. Emir's familiar with that look, having worn it often enough himself. Trying to judge how safe the person you're talking with will be.

"We are, yeah." Emir holds up a five, silently asking if Sam has any before fishing from the top of the deck. "But we used to hate each other. Well...not really. It's a bit complicated. We used to fight constantly. Couldn't even be in the same room, even though we had the same best mate and went to all the same social events."

"Wait, really?" Sam's distracted from his next move, surprise written across his face. "But Theo's, like, the nicest person I've ever met and you're...well you're nice as well, but you just seem to get along so easily."

"We were nice to everyone except each other. Here." Emir hands over a two in response to Sam's card in the air, both of them seemingly agreeing to play silently so they can continue their conversation. The game is giving them something to do with their hands and it's not complicated. "Have people not been kind to you? I know it can be intense joining a new dance programme, especially at university. Takes a while to settle in, I think."

"I think it's..." Sam glances at Emir before darting his eyes away again and lowering his voice. "I told the first year lads that I'm trans because I figured they'd notice soon between the packers and taping my chest. I pass well enough, but changing in the dressing room and backstage and all that, they would have asked if I didn't tell them. And they weren't, like, mean to me...I think they just aren't sure how to act around a trans person. Like I've got some sort of taboo or something."

"Have you talked to Sean about it?" Emir lays down a trio of eights, waiting for Sam to continue. Even as a first year, Emir would be surprised if Sean's reputation of overt acceptance and advocacy for the dancers hasn't reached Sam's attention.

"You're the only person I've explicitly told so far besides the first year lads. But all the teachers know from my audition tape." Sam sighs, taking another card from the deck. "You seem like you'll keep it quiet, and I don't exactly want to find out which people hate me on principle so I don't broadcast it."

"I'll keep it private. But I don't want you to think you should hide yourself away because of who you are." Emir tosses his hair out of his eyes.

He glances over at Theo when he hears his distinctive laugh and watches him and Lili reenacting something that looks suspiciously like *Dirty Dancing*. Did Emir just discover who Theo's been practising with all these years? God, that's adorable.

"I know what that isolation is like, and a bit of the gender situation. Not the same of course." Emir pauses waiting for Sam to settle after the revelation, his eyes having gone wide the moment Emir said the word gender. "I'm genderqueer, but the only person in this room who knows is Theo, and I'd appreciate it if it stayed that way."

"Absolutely. I would never - I'm just - " Sam sets his cards down to run his hands down his face. "God, that's so good to know. I've been feeling like such an outcast. Honestly, they haven't been mean, but I know I'm alone. Well...maybe not anymore."

"You read books, Sam?" Emir holds up a queen, tucking it back into his hand when Sam shakes his head no in response.

"Of course I do. Always been an active reader." Sam scratches at the hair on his neck. "A bit of writing when I have time, but always reading."

"I'm in a book club with Jordan and a few other students." Emir glances her way, seeing her watch Lili from across the room while stuck talking with Georgia and a few second years. He hates knowing how this world that claims to be so open is still so closed, and he sees the evidence of that all around him. It's how he and Theo started working together in the first place. "We're very low key and it could give you a few people outside of the studio to get to know. No pressure of course."

"That's so...I'd love to." Sam startles Emir by standing up and throwing his arms around him in a hug. "Thank you. So much."

"Don't worry about it." Emir holds Sam carefully until he steps away again and flops back into his seat, looking like an entirely different person that just a few minutes ago. His smiles seem genuine now, his laughter no longer withheld as he and Emir keep trading cards and jokes, playing several rounds of *Go Fish* before trying their hand at *Snap*. Emir's not exactly an expert at this whole mentorship thing like Theo is, but he feels responsible for Sam in a way.

Sam reminds Emir so much of himself at that age, hiding himself away and thinking he should. But Emir deserved better then and Sam deserves more than being socially ostracised for his existence. Plus Sam's, like, a really cool person, as Emir realises when he learns about his hobbies and interests the longer they sit together. He'd probably be the most popular kid in the programme if the other dancers would just talk with him for a few minutes and get over their shit.

Theo watches them fondly from afar, letting them have their space. He's not surprised that Emir managed to find the other introvert at the party and made a quiet bubble for the two of them to be comfortable while the others were loud around them. Theo keeps himself near Lili, knowing it's killing her to keep this much distance from Jordan. Maybe if it was a smaller group they could get away with sitting together or something similar, but since being out isn't an option for them, the least he can do is keep Lili company.

But when he looks at Emir, his heart could melt. He has a quiet grace, this gentle fire that he shares sparingly. But Theo knows firsthand what it feels like to be illuminated by his light. He knows it isn't easy for Emir to branch out and make new friends, even if he's fine in casual social situations. He's quiet and gentle and so incredibly kind, and watching him bring the joy out of Sam the longer they sit together makes Theo proud. Emir is a wonderful person, and Theo gets to be his boyfriend. He really thinks they bring out the best in each other.

Lili nudges Theo and raises a judgemental eyebrow, always catching him when he's drooling over Emir. She's incredibly happy for them, but she's still going to tease Theo like any good sibling would. And the way he melts into a pile of goo when Emir's around is definitely worth annoying him about.

The party lasts for a few hours until all the snacks and drinks are gone and everyone is ready to head back to their flats or out to the bars for their last night of freedom before the shows. Lili and Jordan stay to help Theo and Emir clean up, but almost everyone tidied up after themselves, and only a few minutes later, the four of them are walking amiably back to Theo's building, each arm-in-arm with their partner to huddle up against the cold.

***

"Have to stop kissing me long enough to open the door." Emir isn't helping his own argument as he pushes Theo back against it, hoping he manages to find his keys and unlock the door to his flat with Emir's tongue in his mouth. Emir's always admired his ability to multitask.

"Mph." Theo pushes forward against him, trying very unsuccessfully to get his keys out of his pocket, but refusing to stop kissing him. "You get them. Front right pocket...the other right."

Emir takes his time exploring Theo's front, hands wandering on their way to his destination. The keys are very well hidden on account of being attached to Theo. They only left Lili and Jordan behind about thirty seconds ago so Emir's basically starving for another taste of him. He has been ever since they had to separate in the hallway and return to the party.

He finally untangles the keys and shoves them into Theo's hand, giggling as they fall backwards through the doorway together when Theo manages to open it. And without even turning on the light they immediately notice that they've stumbled into a scene they weren't expecting.

T, Laurie, Ciaran, and Gabe are all in the living room, spread across the sofas, and there's not a stitch of clothing in sight. It takes Emir and Theo a moment to reorient themselves and figure out what's going on, never having walked into something quite this...

"Should we, like, turn a light on?" Theo curls himself around Emir, not really sure what the protocol is when you walk in on all of your best mates shagging in your flat while you were away. To be fair, he and Emir hadn't specified where they were staying tonight and the door was definitely locked.

"I think no." Emir is keeping his voice low because he's not even sure they've noticed the interruption yet. But they weren't being quiet in the hallway and they practically broke down the front door. "Do you still want to..."

"Only if you do." Theo turns his face to Emir, eyes wide but not uncomfortable. He's not actually bothered at all. If anything he's...curious. Theo feels his palms starting to sweat, his whole body heating in response to the situation they've encountered added to the anticipation of taking things further with Emir. "I um..."

Emir raises an eyebrow, watching Theo try not to stare at their friends while simultaneously holding Emir against him and moving his hands along his back. Is Theo into this? Emir's not against the concept of group sex in the slightest, but he and Theo haven't had sex together, never mind introducing other people. But if Theo's reaction is anything to go by, he's at least interested.

"Did you want to..." Emir trails off, nodding his head in the direction of the sofas while Theo's hands find their way beneath Emir's shirt. They both kick their shoes off in the entryway while mumbling to each other, no longer bothering to be very quiet about it.

"I want *you*, babe." Theo mouths along Emir's neck, pressing against him and starting to walk them towards his bedroom. He's not ready for anything like what's happening a few feet away from them, but he'd be lying if he pretended it wasn't making him hot as hell. It's not really that he wants to watch or to have them watch him and Emir, at least not tonight. He's not sure he knows how to explain what about it he's so interested in, but he can worry about that later. Emir probably knows.

"You two joining us, or..." Ciaran's the one who finally acknowledges their presence, seemingly the spokesperson for the group. The others' mouths aren't exactly available for conversation at the moment.

"We'll be in Theo's room." Emir groans as Theo sucks a mark into his neck, using his teeth just enough to sting. But that gives him an idea. "Mind if we keep the door open?"

Theo stills for a moment before picking him up and carrying him instead, Emir gasping in surprise then burying his head in Theo's neck and starting work on Theo's shirt. He wraps his legs around Theo's waist and tries to make good use of his hands. Too many fucking buttons.

"Be our guest." Ciaran manages to give them a salute before being pulled back into the activities at hand. Literally. It's only a few more steps into the bedroom, Theo pushing the door all the way open as he carries Emir inside.

"So does that make me the Beauty or the Beast?" Emir asks, fingers tangled in Theo's hair before they fall backward on his bed together.

"I was sort of hoping you'd be both." Theo lets Emir move up to lay against the pillows before crawling over to lay on top of him, Emir finally undoing the last of Theo's shirt buttons and shoving it roughly off his shoulders.

"I need you to talk to me first." Emir pulls Theo forward to fit between his legs so they can grind against each other, the sounds from the other room bordering on obscene already and they just got here. "I don't want to take this too far."

"I don't even know what I want..." Theo rolls over to pull Emir on top of him instead, hoping he'll take control. "I just know I want to get off with you."

"That's fine." Emir shifts so that he's kneeling across Theo's hips, hands on his bare chest. "One thing at a time. You want clothes on or off?"

"Yes." Theo's staring at the hint of Emir's collarbone that he can see where his jumper falls forward as he leans over. He can't stop thinking about whether biting him in that exact spot would show up on stage...

"That wasn't a yes or no question, Teddy." Emir laughs softly, giving Theo a sweet kiss then pulling his own jumper off over his head. Theo's eyes stare harder, fixated on Emir's bare skin. "Trousers?"

"Off. Definitely off." Theo cautiously slides his hands beneath Emir's waistband but over his boxers, waiting for Emir to get the hint and strip down. But he wants Emir to undress him too so he waits, watching Emir's body in the grey light from the window. His muscles move like water beneath his skin, poetry in motion. He's seen so much of what Emir's body is capable of, but this new context is revelatory.

When he's down to his boxers, Emir lays back with Theo to kiss him slowly, waiting for Theo's hands to find his back again and hold him close. Theo falls so easily into Emir, lets his mind go blank and just lives in this moment, knowing that he's safe with him without a single doubt.

"I think I'm a bottom." Theo mumbles completely unprompted, his mind making connections between everything from how he likes when Emir manhandles him to how desperately he wants Emir to explore his body.

Emir giggles quietly against Theo's lips, pulling back to brush Theo's hair away from his eyes. He has such a beautiful mind and open heart, able to share something like that with complete sincerity. Emir knows he loves Theo, but sometimes it's painful to hold back from confessing it in whispered kisses against his skin.

"Yeah?" Emir presses his lips against Theo's forehead beneath the curls, wondering why it's scrunched in concern. "Do you need to talk about it?"

"I just..." Theo pouts until Emir gives him a kiss. He didn't plan to even mention it tonight, but he *feels* so much more than he thinks when Emir's around. And sharing how he's feeling with Emir seems important. "I like when you tell me what to do or when you sort of get rough with me. I want you to undress me and move me around. It feels nice..."

"That sounds more like a sub thing, but if you're a bottom or a sub or both there's nothing wrong with that." Emir gets momentarily distracted by a very loud slap from the other room that's followed by an unmistakable moan, so that's a thing he knows now. But Theo's still under him and this is a vulnerable moment. "But...you probably do lean towards both bottoming and subbing just like...based on what I've noticed."

"You think so too?" Theo sighs, his eyes falling shut while he smiles.

It's almost a relief to have it confirmed. Not that he needs to know as like a foundational part of his identity, but he thinks it's been a sort of mental barrier to letting things move forward between them. Theo didn't know how to have that conversation because he thinks Emir prefers to top, but would it all have ended before it really started if they were both strict tops or strict bottoms?

But if Emir already thought about all this, then Theo doesn't have to worry about it anymore. Maybe it doesn't need to be a big conversation, but rather a quiet acceptance. Sure, he wonders about fucking Emir, but most of his dreams and fantasies have definitely been the opposite. Emir fucking him in the shower, or tying him up (honestly, learning about that rope was a gift), or letting Emir finger him open before pushing inside. Fuck.

Theo's growing hard just thinking about that. "So, like, could you please ravish me now?"

"Excuse me?" Emir laughs louder this time, hiding his face in Theo's neck. How can he be so bashful and then immediately confident in his needs? A deep well, indeed. "I'm absolutely planning on it, but not tonight, princess."

He bites Theo and starts a new bruise on the back of his neck, hoping that someday he'll find Theo's favourite spot to be marked. They've got time for Emir to test every inch of his skin.

Theo takes Emir's hand and moves it to his jeans, hoping that Emir will get the message and fucking take them off already. He needs them off and he wants Emir to do it, but he doesn't know how to say so.

"Want me to undress you?" Emir mumbles near Theo's ear, keeping his hand on Theo's stomach until he tells Emir to do more. He wants to be careful with Theo, to treat him and their relationship with respect and err on the side of caution rather than assuming too much. If Theo ever wants him to fill some type of dominant role they'll need to discuss it first, and not when they're already mostly naked and sloppily snogging in Theo's bed.

Theo nods and shifts his hips, biting his bottom lip as Emir unbuttons his jeans and opens the zipper, fingertips slowly pulling them down and off. "Leave my boxers on?"

Emir's certainly taking his time and Theo watches every second of Emir's fingers trailing along his legs, his mouth leaving soft kisses along his thighs that make Theo shiver.

Emir tosses Theo's jeans off the side of the bed to join his own, both of them looking towards the doorway as someone clearly starts getting railed in the other room, the sound of the sofa shifting back and forth unmistakeable. It's hard to tell who's doing what but it certainly sounds like the four of them are enjoying themselves.

Theo caresses Emir's chin to get his attention again, bringing him in so their lips can meet, this time with barely anything left between them. He takes Emir's hand from his chest and guides it, stopping just above his waistband.

"Touch me?" Theo asks, his breath catching as Emir's fingertips slide beneath the fabric.

"I'll stop the moment you tell me to, alright?" Emir waits for Theo to nod before actually taking him in hand, going slow and soft and just barely grazing Theo's dick at first.

"Oh my GOD." Theo throws his head back, arching up into Emir reflexively. He's never had another person's hand on him before and it's overwhelming.

Emir keeps his touches light and leaves Theo's boxers on, watching his reaction and biting his own lip so he doesn't do something embarrassing like moan at the look on Theo's face. And he knew Theo was well endowed - dance tights don't hide much - but fuck does it feel nice in his hand.

"You can - more - whatever you want, just *please* don't stop." Theo places his right hand on the back of Emir's neck, pulling him forward so they can kiss while Emir gets him off.

He's already close to his climax, but instead of being embarrassed like he may have been otherwise, he just lets it happen, lets himself feel everything, every tug of his skin and breath against his lips, Emir trying a few different things until he finds how

Theo likes it. And once he does, Theo just gives up entirely, letting Emir take over while he jerks up into his hand.

A minute into watching Theo come undone Emir stops and removes himself, Theo opening his eyes wide and breathing hard.

"What – ?" Theo feels like he's on fire and he definitely didn't tell Emir to stop. He's pretty sure he said the opposite, but the details are hazy.

"Trust me." Emir smooths his dirty hand along Theo's chest before helping him sit up. Carefully moving the blankets out of the way, Emir guides Theo under the duvet, laying his head to rest on the pillows again and sliding himself back on top, this time under the sheets together. "Easier to cuddle this way."

Theo stares at Emir, not sure what to say. Knowing that Emir wants to cuddle after they get off shouldn't be a surprise, and yet Theo feels ready to scream *I love you Emir Shah* until his voice goes hoarse. Emir is everything he's ever hoped for in a partner, all those nights spent dreaming up an impossible person, a combination of wit and warmth, and here he is, cuddling up to Theo and waiting to make sure he's comfortable before continuing. "You're everything I've ever wished for and I was rather enjoying that so if you don't mind I'd like to continue."

Emir laughs and feels his cheeks heat, his hair falling in Theo's eyes as they kiss again while Emir's hand wanders back down Theo's chest and into his boxers. "So formal, princess, but give me a moment and you'll be moaning again."

Sure enough, within seconds Theo is gasping into the next kiss, pushing himself up into Emir's beautiful fingers while he slowly lets go. Emir seems to know every trick there is, and Theo is grateful for his experience. He's so confident in how he moves and that confidence is getting him off as much as Emir's hand.

"If you're loud enough, they'll hear you all the way in the other room." Emir mumbles in the space below Theo's ear, words accompanied by the rhythm of each stroke of his hand. "And if they find it half as hot as I do, they might all come on the spot."

And that's it for Theo, Emir's dirty talk and his perfect handiwork making him come harder than he can ever remember. By the time he's done he's seeing stars, his forehead and back covered in sweat while Emir wipes his hand off on the inside of Theo's boxers so he can use it for other things. Like cuddling Theo.

"God, Emir. You're - I'm - " Theo snuggles up into Emir's chest, hands holding firm around his back while he calms down inside of the hug. He feels weightless, like nothing he's ever felt when he's masturbated. Not that he didn't enjoy those times, but it's so different sharing his body with someone he loves.

And even though Theo's completely sated, he can feel Emir's very obvious hardness against his stomach and he wonders if Emir expects him to return the favour. It's not that he doesn't want to, but his arms feel entirely useless at the moment.

"Can I watch?" Theo noses beneath Emir's jaw, pressing himself against Emir and feeling the wetness in his boxers. He should probably do something about that soon before it becomes a sensory nightmare. But first, Emir.

"You want to watch me...?" Emir tilts his head back as Theo kisses the base of his throat, nuzzling like some sort of overgrown puppy. Theo's mentioned liking when he lets his stubble grow, but he's not usually so affectionate about it.

"Please." Theo tugs on the waistband of Emir's briefs and snaps them against his hip with a devious smile. "And these can go too."

"Just to be clear: you want me naked and you want to watch me get myself off?" Emir figured he would have to go take care of himself in the shower or something. Not that he'd mind, because helping Theo moan through his orgasm was enough wank material for a century.

"If it's agreeable." Theo nips at Emir's collarbone and gives his bum a squeeze. He needs Emir right here, under his touch and perfectly within kissing distance. Which reminds Theo that it's been a minute since he's felt those beautiful lips against his own, so he readjusts again to press their lips together, tangling their ankles inside of the sheets.

"You some sort of Victorian gentleman now?" Emir giggles, letting Theo feel him up and keep snuggling against him. Did Theo get high without him noticing? It's like he's trying to make human origami by reorganising their limbs over and over until he's comfortable.

"Words are hard." Theo sighs, the hot air cooling as it flows across Emir's chest. "And so are you."

Theo's hand finds its way into Emir's hair, twirling it around his fingers while he pushes his tongue back into Emir's mouth, lazily snogging while he waits for Emir to decide what he wants next.

Emir does his best to strip out of his boxers while Theo's wrapped around him, giggling when he has to kick and flail his legs to finally free them from around his ankles. He likes to take his time when he's alone, and even though Theo's here, he doesn't want to rush. Once he's naked, he doesn't immediately reach down to touch himself. Instead, he starts moving against Theo, his dick occasionally meeting bare skin and sending shivers through his body, Theo gasping in response the first time it happens.

Glancing down, Theo gets distracted because that's the first dick other than his own that he's seen on purpose. The first dick belonging to someone else that he's felt. He's not some blushing virgin - well, maybe he is a blushing virgin, but not in the connotative way - but it's different having someone naked and in his arms.

"Oh..."

Noticing Theo's change in attention, Emir follows his line of sight to his very hard dick as it rests between them.

"Not what you were expecting?" Emir smirks, rutting up against Theo's upper thigh and letting him watch. If Theo wants a show, Emir's more than comfortable as a performer.

"No, not at all." Theo's known he likes cock for years, but being faced with the reality of wanting that specific one in his hand and his mouth and definitely in his arse is all hitting him at once and he feels dazed. "Changed my mind. I don't want to watch, I want to help."

Emir laughs, laying his face against Theo's chest and feeling way too fond for a mutual wank session. Theo doesn't pretend and he doesn't hide, sharing what he wants and thinks so freely and Emir is infatuated. "Want me to guide you?"

Theo nods, kissing Emir again and intertwining their fingers. Emir goes slowly, making sure they're both laying comfortably as he brings Theo's hand down to touch him.

"What if I'm bad at it?" Theo mumbles quietly, hand resting beneath Emir's on his lower stomach, and he can feel the short curly trail that will lead him where he wants to be. Every moment of this is a revelation, and Theo soaks it in like the sun, letting each hair and breath and tremor imprint in his memory.

"I'm ready to come already and you haven't even touched me." Emir reassures him, and he's not lying. There's been more than enough foreplay and he's been wanting this with Theo for years if he's honest with himself. "Just do what you would to yourself and take your time. I like when it's drawn out."

Moving his own hand this time, Theo slides it out from beneath Emir's and cautiously takes his dick in his hand, trying a few slow tugs to see how Emir reacts. If the groan he immediately releases is any indication, he's on the right track. The mechanics are familiar, but he's not able to feel it through his own body.

"So different..." Theo mumbles, not sure why he feels like he needs to talk right now, but it'd seem strange *not* to share with Emir.

"You can stop if you're not ready." Emir's eyelids flutter, his pretty eyelashes batting up at Theo who speeds up instead with a determined look as he meets Emir's eyes. "Not too fast. I want you to kiss me, princess."

Theo grins and Emir swears he hears angels singing behind the sound of someone coming hard the next room over. But Theo kisses him and moves his hand and even stops for a minute to pay attention to his inner thighs, trailing his fingertips like a whisper across his skin, and Emir feels like he might cry. Theo's being so delicate with him, taking it slow just like he asked and kissing Emir with his perfect pouty mouth that he loves so well.

It's not until Theo's free hand gets involved that Emir really starts to lose it, jerking and chasing Theo's touch with his hips as he feels another hand spreading his legs further apart. When Theo's fingers start moving featherlight between his cock and his hole in rhythm with his other hand's glide he knows he's seconds from coating his own chest.

"Theo, wait - " Emir bites the inside of his cheek to distract from his almost orgasm, Theo's hands stopping immediately and falling off his body. "No, it's alright. Just wasn't sure if you want it on you."

"Oh..." Theo brings his hands back to Emir's body but to his hips instead, pulling Emir to kneel across his waist while Theo lays flat on his back. "Paint me? Sort of been dreaming about it."

"You're joking." Emir sits back on his heels, hard dick smacking against Theo's bare stomach and sending a jolt through both of them. Feeling Emir's dick against his skin is a thrill for Theo, and he's absolutely not joking. He wants to watch Emir from below and have the evidence of his release striped glossy across his chest.

"What? I'm into it." Theo grins sideways, eyes darting down to Emir's dick where it's resting on his stomach. "I like feeling used."

"Shit. Alright then." Emir takes a moment to brush Theo's hair off his forehead and leans forward to give him a kiss before sitting up again and taking himself in hand. No one's ever asked him to do this before but he's always wanted to. "Touch me. My thighs."

"I love your legs, babe." Theo slides his warm hands along Emir's thighs as he pulls himself off, quick and messy this time and hardly any restraint left with one hand holding Theo's waist. "Bet you could ruin me with thighs like these, pounding me into the mattress and scratching my back with your pretty fingers."

"Theo!" Emir can't hold it back anymore, his spunk landing all across Theo's torso and even a bit on his chin, Emir stroking himself through it while Theo watches on in wonder.

It's the most beautiful thing Theo's ever seen, Emir's mouth gaping open and his eyelashes fluttering in pleasure. When he's spent, Emir falls to the side, laying on his back and partially off the edge of the bed, breathing hard. That orgasm hit him like a wall, shoving itself through his body in a rush.

Theo stares down at his chest, curiosity getting the better of him. Emir watches as he swipes his finger through Emir's spunk and brings it to his lips, dabbing a bit on his tongue and testing it like a gourmet spread, thoughtful consideration furrowing his brow.

"You were right." Theo turns his face to Emir, wiping up a bit more for a second taste. It's just as Emir described it: a bit gloopy, sort of metallic and some flavour he can't identify. And now he wants to know what it feels like fresh from the source, a curiosity about having Emir's dick in his mouth that he knows is going to give him wet dreams for the foreseeable now that he's familiar with the feeling in his hand.

"You're going to kill me someday." Emir stops Theo from tasting a third time, not sure he'd be able to process Theo discovering yet another kink today. It's already been a whirlwind. "I'm still not convinced you're real."

"But you bit me and everything. That has to count for something." Theo's teasing. He's not as exhausted as he was just after he came, able to hold a conversation better now. "I feel like we should maybe clean up though."

Emir groans and rolls off the side of the bed, grabbing his jumper from the ground to cover his crotch while he sneaks to the bathroom. It sounds like things are slowing down in the living room as well, but there's still activity happening. He wets a flannel in the bathroom sink and tiptoes back into Theo's bedroom where he sees Theo with his hands behind his head and a relaxed smile across his face.

"Can I take off your dirty boxers or is that still a no?" Emir sits on the edge of the bed and waits. He knows that being naked is a different boundary for many people and he doesn't want to assume.

Theo looks shy for a moment, reaching down to peel off his sticky, wet boxers and waiting for Emir's reaction. "I've never shown anyone my dick before. But I trust you."

"Can I clean you up?" Emir doesn't stare at what is admittedly a very pretty penis (yes, he's very aware of how gay he is), instead holding up the flannel and waiting.

Theo nods, arms gradually floating back above his head as Emir brings the wet flannel to his chest. He's careful to swipe up each remnant of spunk, gingerly cleaning around Theo's dick as well in case there's any of his own left behind. He likes looking after Theo, and it shouldn't feel so romantic to be cleaning his partner's body, but it does. It's like showing Theo that he respects him and wants to look after him, always.

"Would it be weird to cuddle and watch something on my laptop until we fall asleep?" Theo snuggles into bed as Emir tucks him in under the duvet with a kiss. Emir tidies up after them, carefully folding their clothes from earlier, not because of his own need, but because he knows Theo will appreciate it.

"Just give me a minute. Be right back." Emir kisses Theo's forehead, walking to Theo's desk and handing over his laptop so he can pick something for them to watch.

Pulling on his boxers, and thankful they're still clean, Emir walks quietly into the kitchen, ignoring all four of their friends in the living room. It seems they're done as well, but they haven't yet reached the cleaning up and going to bed portion of their evening.

Emir grabs them each a water from the fridge and a banana, knowing that it's one of the best post orgasm snacks. He catches Laurie's eye as he walks back to Theo's room and they share sideways smiles, T falling asleep on Laurie's chest with their curls a sweaty disaster around their face.

He closes Theo's door this time, quietly letting it click into place before setting the snacks down on his bedside table and shoving his boxers back down his thighs. Theo laughs from under the blankets as Emir slides in beside him, letting his cold toes find their way between Theo's calves.

"Eat, or no more fun for you." Emir kisses Theo's temple and hands over the banana, throwing an arm around Theo's shoulder and holding him on his chest while they watch *Gogglebox*.

They sit quietly for a few minutes until Theo gets up to throw away their rubbish, stopping before he gets to the bedroom door to say, "Thank you."

"For what?" Emir pushes himself upright in bed and waits for Theo to put on his joggers to venture bravely into the common area. He likes when Theo borrows his things, even if it's just for a minute. It's why earlier, when he was getting dressed for the party, Emir left the joggers folded where he knew Theo would notice and, hopefully, wear them.

"You just...you're so sweet to me." Theo shrugs and rubs a hand along the back of his neck. Is this oversharing? He's never done anything like this before to have a reference. "And that was as domestic as it was fun. It was...nice. Comfortable."

Emir smiles and Theo feels his chest swell with pride. That's his boyfriend laying in his bed, watching shit TV with him and cuddling after sex. He never thought he'd be so lucky.

"Hurry back." Emir loves this silly man more than he knew was possible, from the tips of his curly hair to his calloused feet. In a way, he understands why younger Emir pushed Theo away so hard, like he knew he was too good for Emir's broken heart.

Emir couldn't love himself back then, and he never would've let Theo love him the way he wants to let him now.

They make a warm nest in Theo's bed after that, snuggling and laughing together while watching whatever they feel like until Theo falls asleep on Emir's chest. Emir carefully turns off the lights and plugs in his laptop for tomorrow, making sure both of their phones are charging. Theo bought a phone charger for when Emi stays over, and Emir didn't cry about it...except he did a little bit. Theo's so thoughtful.

He doesn't fall asleep right away, listening to the sounds of Theo's sleep sweet breathing as he lays on Emir's bare chest, brushing his fingers through Theo's hair and letting himself be with his thoughts. He plans to sneak away to the studio in the morning after a walk to his tree and before their double date. But for tonight, having Theo asleep on him while he settles in to rest is perfect.

CHAPTER FIFTEEN

Theo: *We're planning to stay at Emir's tonight, but I'll have to stop home and grab a few things even though we're here now. I brought things for our double date with Lili and Jo that I don't want just laying around for no reason.*

Laurie: *We're staying there too*

Laurie: *Do I need earplugs?*

Emi: *don't think we were the ones spanking each other last night*

Laurie: *You weren't exactly silent*

Gabe: *So what I'm hearing is that Ciaran and I get this place all to ourselves tonight? /fire emoji/*

Ciaran: *I'll text Alfie /three eggplant emojis/*

T: *That was nothing. Be glad we had company*

T: *Laurie didn't even use a paddle*

Theo: *I did not need to know that.*

Theo: *But good for you.*

Ciaran: *I don't remember any complaints about your company last night*

Emi: *any of you lot know shibari?*

Laurie: *Yes, but I'm not teaching you*

Emi: *not even if i ask nicely?*

Emi: *the books were too...straight.*

Theo: *Let me read them. I'll figure it out and explain it to you. I'll be a willing test subject. /covering eyes emoji/*

Gabe: *Why is that so cute?*

Gabe: *Ciaran and I learn sex stuff together too*

T: *I let Laur take care of that*

Emi: *cough pillow princess cough*

T: */gif of putting on a crown/*

Theo: *I thought I was princess?*

Emi: *you're my princess /heart emoji/*

Laurie: *So are we going to talk about last night or?*

Emi: *what's there to talk about?*

Laurie: *T fancies an audience sometimes and those two like to share. We have clear boundaries and all that. Not the first time it's been discussed/shrug emoji/*

Theo: *We weren't worried, honestly.*

Theo: *If you want to have fun together, maybe just let us know and we'll stay at the other flat next time.*

Theo: *Not that we didn't...enjoy it?*

Emi: *theo's still figuring out what he likes and why*

Emi: *but yeah you four do whatever you want just let us know so it's not a surprise next time*

Gabe: *To be honest last night wasn't planned. Like we'd all talked about it before but it just sort of felt right.*

Ciaran: *And you weren't home so we didn't break the rules*

Emi: *honestly it's fine*

Theo: *And we should be better about telling you where we're staying each night. It's only fair.*

Laurie: *Is my red tracksuit in my room?*

T: *It's not here I've checked everywhere*

T: *We keep this flat tidy so it wouldn't have anywhere to hide.*

Theo: *Can't check now. Face masks are happening.*

Theo: */selfie with Emir wearing green tea face masks, Theo sticking his tongue out at the camera/*

T: *Awwwww Theo that headband is adorable*

Emi: *i gave it to him*

Emi: *he's so cute i could cry*

Ciaran: *On that note /waving goodbye gif/*

Ciaran: *Time for my midday kip*

"Who are you two texting this much?" Lili's mask crinkles on her forehead, the pink bandana that's holding back her hair complimenting the pale green of the skin treatment oddly well.

"The gays." Emir sighs and takes Theo's foot in his lap again. He's only done one coat of purple polish so far and it definitely needs another. "Ever since we started a group chat, it's been almost nonstop."

"Is that why you keep your phone on *Do Not Disturb?*" Jordan asks, her toes being painted orange by Lilibet's careful hands. She's one of the only ballerinas that Emir's met who will paint their toes and dance en pointe. Pointe isn't exactly a recipe for pretty feet.

"Nah, been doing that since sixth form." Emir hopes he doesn't need to elaborate. They're having a nice time and he doesn't want to even think about the reason why right now.

"I think purple's my colour." Theo wriggles the toes on his free foot, staring at them in awe. His sisters used to dress him up and put him in makeup and such growing up, but he's never had his toes painted. At least not that he can remember. "Do I need more purple to wear?"

"You absolutely do." Lili recaps the orange polish, scratching at her hair beneath the bandana while she still can. She wasn't kidding about wanting black nails for herself, but she wanted to do Jordan's toes first in case it got messy. "Also purple is very gay. The most homosexual. The limp wrist of colours."

Emir sneaks another picture of Theo in his teddy bear headband, two little bear ears poking out between his curls. He bought that headband at a pound shop a few years back and never wore it. It looks made for Theo and he hopes he'll wear it again. It's almost too adorable. Teddy bear accessory for his Teddy bear.

"Remind me where we got this mask idea from?" Jordan scrunches her nose and gives it a wriggle since she can't itch her skin without ruining the whole situation. "It almost seems too easy."

"Tan France." Theo answers, sticking his tongue out at Emir again as he takes even more pictures. If Emir wasn't covered in green yoghurt, Theo would see how flushed with delight he is just from watching his boyfriend be cute. "The gayest person to come from Doncaster, only rivalled by our beloved rebel Yungblud."

Lili carefully removes Jordan's feet from her lap and starts filing her own fingernails instead. "Didn't even have to get anything from the shops. Just some plain greek yoghurt and Emir's green tea."

"Oooo will you make me tea after we rinse it off?" Emir sets his phone aside again and holds Theo's hand while he begs. Sure he likes to spoil Theo, but he's not above asking his boyfriend to make him tea. "I like when you make it. It tastes better."

"Does not." Theo giggles, shoving at Emir's shoulder playfully. "You just like staring at my arse while I reach into your cupboard for everything. Don't think I didn't notice you moved the honey to the top shelf."

Lili scoffs but Emir turns to her with a grin. "What? It's a great arse."

"Why didn't I think of that..." Jordan sounds genuine and Emir wonders how their kitchen is about to be rearranged when they get back home. Then again, Lili is already significantly shorter than Jordan, so things might not need to move too far.

"When will the apple crumble be done?" Lili cranes her head to try to see the timer, but it's hidden from her view.

"I'd guess another twenty or so." Theo sniffs the air experimentally. He can usually tell by smell alone, but the nail polish is too strong. "But we'll have to let it cool about an hour before we can eat it."

"Twenty minutes." Lili counters, she and Theo starting one of their sibling spats while Emir and Jordan watch on with fond smiles. "Can't wait an hour. I'm starved."

"Forty-five." Theo crosses his arms over his chest with a huff. He'll not have the crumble ruined because Lili's impatient. They have snacks if she's hungry.

"Thirty-five, and I get a corner." Lili mirrors him, arms firm across her sleeveless hoodie with a worn out Rebel Alliance logo on the front.

"Fine. But no complaining when it's not properly set." Theo pouts but Emir distracts him with a chaste kiss, their face masks safe from how far they purse their lips. Just as they lean away again, Jordan's phone alarm goes off, meaning it's time to rinse off the yoghurt and moisturise with their product of choice before finishing their nails.

"Race you." Lili springs up, shoving Theo into the sofa, and Emir along with him, Jordan chasing after her until they're both squealing and laughing as they crash together in front of the sink.

"Are we that cute?" Theo turns to ask Emir, helping him sit back up after being so rudely knocked over.

Emir shakes his head, eyes twinkling beneath his black cotton headband. "We're cuter."

***

It's already been a long tech week and it's not quite over. Thursday afternoon finds Emir in the wings watching Theo and Lili block their pas de deux to adjust the lighting for what must be the tenth time.

"You ready for tomorrow's show?" Sean walks up beside Emir and lays a familiar hand on his shoulder before letting it drop. He shouldn't be surprised to find Emir here because he always hangs around the stage whenever possible, even before having a boyfriend to watch.

"I think so. Still not a hundred percent about my first solo, but Raphael seems happy with it." Emir turns to Sean, rabbit ears flopping slightly as he does. Because it's their final night of tech, with a final dress rehearsal scheduled to start in about an hour, they're all in full costume.

"It's brilliant. Your execution has really come a long way in the past few weeks. Especially the turns." Sean and Emir both have their attention fixed on the stage where Theo has Lili above his head while the lighting technicians make sure the angles work for all the choreography that's planned. It's surprising how many tiny details go into each production, but they're all used to it after so many years. "Have you eaten anything since we broke for lunch?"

"Too nervous." Emir's honest with Sean, even about this. "Haven't been hungry all week."

Emir starts stretching out his arms, still sore from when he had to hold a specific pose for almost five minutes while they made adjustments. "My family's coming to opening night."

"Yeah? That's great, Emi. I'm glad they can make the trip to support you." Sean sincerely means that, knowing that family support isn't always guaranteed for students who choose to study dance at this level. "You know, I'd bet Theo's going to be hungry when they're done in a few minutes. Why don't you go grab something for the two of you?"

Emir glances at Sean, seeing through his suggestion immediately. He knows Emir pretty well by now, and he definitely knows that Emir would always rather look after someone else before himself. "Suppose I could go grab us tea and a snack. You think Lili's good?"

No one else is around the backstage area, all the other dancers relaxing in the dressing rooms until a few minutes before curtain.

"Jordan's got her covered." Sean adds casually, and Emir wonders how much he's noticed about Jo and Lilibet without being told. "Don't forget to throw on your joggers and a jacket so the costume department doesn't have your head."

Emir nods, leaving Sean with one final glance at Theo before shuffling away. He avoids the dressing rooms (way too many people being way too loud) and heads instead for the lounge inside the theatre where they all keep their snacks and games and anything not allowed in the dressing rooms for the remainder of the production schedule. He grabs two granola bars, two bananas, an apple, a jar of peanut butter, and tosses it all in one of the tote bags he hid behind his things before making a cup of tea for each of them. It's not going to be too many more hours, but having something warm to sip on helps.

Hurrying back up the stage side stairs, Emir makes it to the wings just as Theo and Lili are walking offstage, Lili groaning about her feet being sore and Theo rubbing at his arms.

"Babe!" Theo re-energises immediately and picks Emir up in a hug, Emir doing his best to keep the tea out of harm's way. Theo doesn't care how sore he is. Emir waiting for him is like tiger balm to his entire existence. "You didn't have to wait for me. You should've relaxed."

"I like watching the whole process. Always have." Emir kisses Theo's cheek until he's set back down on his feet, holding Theo's thermos out for him to take. "Too many people in the dressing rooms, you know?"

"Come with me to throw on some warmups and then we can go hide somewhere and have our tea?" Theo holds Emir by the waist, no longer caring that he's tired or hungry because now he doesn't just get a break, he gets quiet time with Emir before they're needed back on stage.

Lili finally gets her shoes off, groaning from her seat on the floor beside them.

"Did you see where Jo got to?" She asks Emir while gathering her shoes and lambswool from the mess of a backstage floor. It doesn't have any of the supple Marley of the stage, only painted black boards that are sanded just enough that splinters are less of a concern.

"Think I saw her studying with Alfie and Eric on my way upstairs." Emir smiles as Theo's hand weaves its way into his own and tugs him towards the stairwell he just left.

"Don't forget your brace." Theo calls over his shoulder while leading Emir away. "Her knee's acting up again and it's already swollen. Sean wants her to elevate all night and wear her brace whenever she can, especially for full dress."

"What about you?" Emir follows along, keeping his hand linked with Theo's while they rush back to the dressing room, if only temporarily. "We were up an hour past your bedtime and I know you need your sleep."

"Can we sleep early tonight? You're right about being behind." Theo pauses at the bottom of the stairs to finish talking before they run into everyone else. "Sorry if I'm high maintenance. I'm probably not a very fun boyfriend."

Emir quiets his worry with a sweet kiss, pulling Theo into his front and cradling the back of his head. "I'm putting you to bed at nine thirty. Try and stop me."

Theo smiles and rests their foreheads together, glad that Emir's white rabbit face paint is transfer proof.

"Thanks, babe. I'm so fucking tired and I just want to be home, cuddled up in your bed with all those extra blankets you love." Theo sighs at the thought, giving Emir another kiss before stepping away. He's starting to understand Emir's constant need for blankets the more time he spends sharing them with his boyfriend. "But first tea, then dress, *then* we can finally go home."

Emir feels his heart warm at the way they've taken to referring to both of their flats as home, sharing their space easily because they're both considerate and respect each other's boundaries without having to be asked. And while Emir loves dance with his entire soul, like Theo, all he wants right now is to be snuggled up in his blankets with his boyfriend, resting before opening weekend.

And before Theo meets his family tomorrow night. They haven't talked about it much, but it's on both of their minds. Emir isn't worried, but he's sure his family will be at least apprehensive given what the last boyfriend put him through. Theo's definitely nervous, his heart racing every time he thinks about how important these people are to Emir and how everything could go wrong in the blink of an eye.

But that's tomorrow's problem. They still have to get through dress rehearsal, classes in the morning, and then opening night of *Alice in Wonderland* before they can focus on boyfriend stress. So they huddle together on the floor at the back of the auditorium, behind the seats, sharing snacks and leaning into each other in their own private bubble.

Emir thinks vaguely of all the shows before this, how he would hide out here alone, and he's positive this is better. He still gets his quiet *and* he gets to be with Theo. And Theo thinks it grounds him, the way Emir makes time and space for quiet, something Theo's rarely done for himself before. Being with Emir is bringing out the best in him, and he hopes it's reciprocal. Because if Theo could spend every tea sharing an apple and peanut butter with Emir for the rest of his career, he thinks that sounds perfect.

***

Theo dials Laurie's number Friday morning, tucking the phone into his ear while lacing up his trainers at the gym. He knows it's early and Laurie hates to be awake before he needs to be, but this is sort of an emergency. He's spiralling a bit and he can't go back to the flat in case Emir's there and –

"You better be fucking dying, Teddy." Laurie's voice is raspy, clearly having woken up because of the call. "The sun isn't even awake."

"It's an emergency." Theo mumbles. He does feel slightly guilty about waking him up, but this is what best mates are for.

"Fuck, really?" Laurie is suddenly completely different, voice soft but focused, big brother mode fully activated. "What's happened?"

"No, sorry, not like a medical one. I'm alright." Theo winces because now he does feel bad. He knows how seriously Laurie takes that sort of thing. "Unless I pass out from anxiety or something. Then I may require a doctor."

"Theo, what the fuck?" Laurie closes the bedroom door behind himself, walking into the living room so he doesn't disturb T, bare feet shuffling along the cold floor of the flat. "Just...I'm awake now. Talk."

"Right, so I'm at the gym and our first show is tonight and Emir is out running around campus like he does everyday and everything's completely fine except my relationship is probably over on account of how I'm meeting his family for dinner." Theo's pulling at his hair nervously, shoes untied and abandoned for now.

Laurie audibly sighs and Theo's positive he's sitting on the sofa with his fingers rubbing at his forehead. "Have you talked to Emir about this?"

"Of course. He knows I'm meeting his family." Theo sits on the nearest bike, no one else in the gym to yell at him for it right now. The privacy is one of the many benefits of his gym routine being so early in the day.

"That's not – " Another sigh from Laurie. He didn't phrase his question clearly enough. "Does he know you're this worried?"

"Oh...that would be a no." Theo didn't want to show Emir how nervous he is. Between opening night stress and how exhausted they are from this week he didn't want to add yet another thing to Emir's plate.

"I don't mean this to sound...I'm fucking tired and it's too early, alright? So just...this is a boyfriend thing." Laurie's voice is evening out, less raspy than when he first answered the phone as he starts to wake up. "I'm not saying to panic him. But you have to tell Emi when you're nervous like this. He'd want to know. Wouldn't you want to know if he was this worried?"

"Of course." Theo's so itchy, his nerves making his skin crawl. He scratches at his arms, his chest, then his neck until he remembers the show tonight and stops. He can't have visible scratches all over, especially when he and Emir have already displayed their fair share of love bites recently. "But he doesn't have anything to worry about. He's incredible and my family's going to love him. Like...probably more than they love me."

Theo smiles to himself at that, already hoping that Emir and his mum are going to be fast friends.

"Why do you think it'd be any different meeting the Shahs? I've met them plenty of times. They're decent, Teddy. Real decent." Laurie's in the kitchen now and Theo can hear coffee being made. Before university, Laurie was a tea drinker, but the late nights and long hours converted him, even if he still loves Yorkshire in the evenings.

"I'm not Emir. I'm not lovely and creative and warm and...I'm not Emi." Theo knows he isn't wording anything well, but even with the extra rest last night he's still tired today. "I've said it before and I meant it: to know him is to love him. He's got nothing to worry about."

"Don't make me feel things before the sun is up, Teddy." Laurie groans, dropping his head against the counter, the thunk heard through the phone. "You're not Emir but Emir's not you. You're kind and empathetic and all that good shit people try to be and you're my best mate for a reason. If the Shahs don't love you, I'll go vegan for a month."

Theo finally laughs for the first time all morning, grateful as always to have Laurie in his life. "I should talk to Emir, shouldn't I?"

He thinks Laurie might be right because yes, he would definitely want to know if Emir was panicking like this. Boyfriends are supposed to communicate properly, not anxiety-dial their friends at the crack of dawn.

"Before class, probably." Laurie confirms, yawning again. "And don't forget I'll be at every show. So will T. If you really need us, we're around."

T is helping with the costumes for the Hatter and a few background characters, and Laurie always has a hand in the stage design, on top of doing most of the stage managing for student productions. Their hours aren't as long as the dancers, but they've been around for much of tech week as well. Hence Laurie's exhaustion being more acute than usual.

"I'll grab him before tech hall." Theo stands back up, staring at his shoes as if wondering how they untied themselves. "Thanks, Laur. Sorry I woke you up."

"Consider it payback for all the times you've done the same for me." Laurie has woken Theo up in the middle of the night more than once, so he's not wrong. Especially their first year. "I'll check in backstage before the show with T."

Theo hangs up and returns to his morning routine, going easy at the gym so he doesn't tire himself out before the weekend. He sort of coasts through the rest of his morning, still worried but no longer frantic like he had been before. He waits patiently for Emir before tech hall, glad that he shows up just a few minutes after Theo so he can grab his hand and drag him down to the practice studio. Emir doesn't question it, following Theo gladly and without hesitation. He had a quiet morning and he's in a wonderful mood heading into the first show.

Once they're alone and Theo's shut the door he pulls Emir into a crushing hug to mumble in his ear, "I'm really fucking nervous about meeting your family. And Laurie said I should tell you because that's what boyfriends do and he's right and I'm sorry I didn't tell you but also I'm sorry to worry you."

Emir's arms have barely circled Theo by the time he's finished his confession, throwing the words out as fast as possible while Emir tries to catch up.

"What are you worried about?" Emir rubs his back, Theo sighing in his arms and snuggling into his hold. Emir's hugs make everything better.

"That they're going to hate me and then you'll hate me too." Theo's face is squished against Emir's shoulder, but his words are clear enough, as is the anxiety behind them.

"They're not going to hate you, princess." Emir can't help but smile a bit. He thought something was up this morning when Theo left, squeezing Emir extra tight in their morning cuddle before he left for the studio. "You're a wonderful person and they just want me to be happy. You make me happy."

"But...you deserve the whole world. And I'm just...me. Just Theo." Theo sighs, resigned to the knowledge that Emir's family may spend one dinner with him and decide Emir can do so much better. Which is likely true.

"I thought we went over this months ago, baby." Emir leans back before cradling Theo's head for a lingering kiss. "You're not *just* anything. You're an incredible person and my family will see that, alright? I'm more worried about them behaving for you, if I'm honest."

"What do you mean?" Theo fusses with Emir's shirt, flattening it against his chest with a loving hand.

"They can be a handful. Three sisters plus my parents, and they're all very protective. And very sarcastic." Emir rolls his eyes, already planning for Saima to say something that makes their mum scold her, and then Safiya will play big sister and ask Theo all the *questions* until their baba tells her to be nice. He misses them every day even though they can be a lot ™.

"So that's where you get it from." Theo teases, hugging Emir again, but less like a vice this time. He's so incredibly relieved that Laurie gently scolded him into talking to Emir about this because now he can focus on getting through the day and their show, which is just as important as dinner. "You promise I don't need to move to France and change my name?"

"Can't promise that until after tonight." Emir giggles, Theo swatting him on the chest and crossing his arms.

"I think you owe me a proper kiss for that one. Rude." Theo keeps pretending to be annoyed until Emir pulls him forward by his t-shirt and smashes their lips together uncomfortably. But within seconds they're kissing softly, Emir playing with Theo's hair because he honestly can't help it.

"Suppose we should get to class." Theo kisses across Emir's jaw and down his neck, leaving one gentle bite at the edge of his collarbone so Emir knows he wishes they had more time. So much of their communication is nonverbal, but it works for them.

"They'll love you." Emir takes Theo by the hand and reopens the door to the practice studio. "And if they don't, we can run away to France together...but you'll have to teach me French."

Theo laughs all the way back to class, cheeks pink and eyes bright. He really loves his boyfriend.

***

They're crowded around a very small table in a dimly lit restaurant, and the only thing keeping Theo from completely panicking is Emir's constant pressure against his side.

The show was nearly perfect. Emir pulled Theo into a congratulatory kiss the moment the curtain was down, then after the kiss and the mini celebration on stage, they headed back to the dressing room to remove their costumes and for Emir to take a quick shower to wash off the body paint.

It was a short walk upstairs once they were presentable, Emir pulling Theo by the hand towards his family who were at least as intimidating as Theo had imagined, all bright smiles and easy laughs and the sort of intimacy that only comes from genuine familial love. And now here they are: in a Pakistani restaurant that Theo never got the name of, and apparently Safiya knows the owner and everyone who works there because it's near her flat. Theo is absolutely thrilled to be here, but he didn't get to read a menu ahead of time and it's very loud. Overall, it's *a lot* to process.

"You're doing great, princess." Emir whispers in his ear, giving his thigh a squeeze beneath the table. Theo's being unusually quiet and he keeps holding his hands in his lap while hunching his shoulders, like he's worried about being in the way.

"I'm trying to follow along but...what's everyone saying?" Theo whispers back, eyes darting around, unable to decide what to focus on.

There's about a dozen dishes on the table and it's family style so everyone's meant to be sharing. They're all talking over each other but not to him because they haven't all been together since Safiya's wedding and they need to catch up. Theo's plate is still empty even though everyone else is gladly eating whatever they like from the feast before them, but he isn't sure if it's worse to just start grabbing food or to wait awkwardly for an invitation.

"Shit. Sorry. Should've warned you." Emir lays his forehead on Theo's shoulder momentarily with a laugh. "We usually use Urdu when we're all together like this. Even mum."

He presses his lips to Theo's shoulder through his shirt before moving back, wishing he felt comfortable enough to kiss him for real right now.

"I don't, um - I only learned a few words and I don't think I know how to pronounce them right." Theo flushes, staring down at his hands in his lap and wondering if he's already failed the boyfriend test. "But, like, I can definitely learn, I just don't know it yet."

"You learned Urdu for me?" Emir scratches under Theo's chin and focuses his attention completely on him for the moment. He's with his family, but Theo's important, too. Especially when he looks so ridiculously worried and nervous while fidgeting with whatever he can find nearby.

"Well you gave me that note with the thermos, and a few others with little inscriptions..." Theo flushes under his attention, not sure what the rules are with Emir's family. Are they allowed to hold hands under the table? He's not even sure if that would help him at this point. He's fine in social situations, a natural extrovert, but he's never been someone's boyfriend before, and he's never been introduced to a partner's family. Theo wishes there were some sort of manual. "And, like, you're important to me. I tried learning online, but it was shit ,so I sort of gave up until I could find something better."

Emir squeezes Theo's thigh, turning towards him and whispering in a way that lets his hair fall in Theo's face, the intoxicating smell of citrus and cinnamon fresh from his quick after show shower distracting Theo's senses for a moment. "I wish I could kiss you right now. I wish I could *more* than kiss you, but we'll have to save that for Monday. You're so lovely, Teddy."

"What are you two whispering about?" Amina asks from across the table. Theo's on the end for his own comfort, but Emir has his mum Natalie on his other side, happy to be between them. Theo knew Emir was close with his mum, but watching their easy interactions feels like watching Emir be at home. It's sweet and soft, the two of them communicating less with words than with micro expressions that only they can understand.

"Mind your business." Emir says, reaching out to start filling Theo's plate.

Theo had no idea where to start, so Emir taking over that decision is a relief. He's introduced Theo to plenty of these foods during the past few months, but he didn't want to make some sort of faux pas just by filling his plate incorrectly or with bad manners. Better to let Emir do it, and now he doesn't have to awkwardly wait anymore.

Emir serves both himself and Theo, knowing that Theo devours anything with paneer, and he makes sure they both have a healthy helping of saag because it's a clear favourite. He doubts Theo will eat as much as he normally would because he's so nervous, but both he and his mum would be upset if Theo left dinner starving because he felt so out of place. Emir's hoping he can at least tempt Theo with a few bites of paneer and naan, and take home some of what's left in case he gets hungry back at the flat.

"So, Theo." Safiya stops talking to her new husband for a minute, Emir rolling his eyes because he already knows what's coming. "What're your plans for next year? You staying in London?"

"Oh, um..." Theo stares wide-eyed, not entirely sure how to answer that question. He sets his fork down after just one bite and clears his throat, settling his hands in his lap again. "I'm honestly not sure. I'd love to join a company, but it's rather unlikely for me to get a contract in the city. I study business as a backup just in case, and it depends where Emir ends up of course."

"Does it?" Safiya tilts her head, her eyes darting to Emir because this is brand new information to her. "Isn't that rather fast?"

"Yaya, please." Emir runs his fingers through his hair with a sigh. "Nothing about this was rushed or irresponsible. I'm pretty sure Theo's incapable of being irresponsible for a single moment of his life. And it's just different with dance. Our careers are so ephemeral. We'd both like to stay in London, but we won't know until June."

Safiya knows a bit about their time getting to know each other as friends before becoming more, so she really shouldn't be judging. And Safiya's only known her husband for about two years and they're already married, so.

"Why business?" Saima asks, sitting between her baba and Safiya. So far she's been too focused on talking about the costumes in *Alice* to be asking rude questions. "Sounds boring."

"Well, I am a bit boring." Theo smiles softly, not embarrassed to admit that. Emir's shown him that it's just part of who he is and he doesn't need to apologise for it. "I figured it should be something that could make me a living in case I have to dance for pennies at some independent company. And the courses didn't interfere with my dance training at all."

"You're not boring, princess." Emir adds, arm going around Theo's shoulder protectively. "Theo's very practical and grounded. And I really like him, so be nice."

"What's your favourite colour?" Amina asks out of nowhere, staring Theo down like this is the most important thing he'll ever have to answer.

"Oh, well mostly it's purple." Theo catches Emir's gaze to finish his answer, knowing he remembers that Theo's toes are currently lilac. And then Theo gets distracted by all that Emir is. "But sometimes it's honey-sweet brown, or midnight black, and occasionally, a perfect brick red that no paint could ever replicate."

Emir's eyes are doing something that Theo can't decipher, but they're staring right back at Theo as if giving him the chance to figure it out. Theo clears his throat, then adds, "Someone taught me that you don't need to have just one favourite colour, and they really opened my eyes. To a lot of things."

Emir lays his face against Theo's chest, arm still around his shoulders while he hides his embarrassment. How could Theo possibly have been worried about meeting his family when he says lovely things like that and admits that he's tried to learn Urdu and lets them tease him like one of their own. He's so fucking gone for his human teddy bear, and he knows his family can tell.

"Alright, he can stay." Saleem says, smiling wide at his son and his new boyfriend. Anyone who loves Emir so clearly and respectfully is fine with him. And Theo's friends with Laurie, so he already gets a pass.

"He loves you." Natalie whispers to Emir when he sits back up, for Emir's ears only.

"*Mum.*" Emir flushes even deeper but he thinks she has a point.

Neither of them has said the words aloud, but he can feel it in the way Theo is with him. Theo still brings him tea, months after that first time, and he proudly displays all of Emir's little drawings and notes like they belong in a museum, and he holds Emir like he's important, never taking their physical intimacy for granted for a single moment.

"So, um, does this place have cham cham?" Theo asks, finally taking a bite off his plate with a grateful smile to Saleem.

They've barely spoken two words to each other, but Theo can tell how much Emir loves his dad. It's different than the way he is with his mum, but no less loving. Emir has told Theo how much his family supports him, but seeing it for himself makes him grateful to know that Emir's always had them, and vice versa. Emir's been through so much, and having the family he does must have made a world of difference.

"You know about cham cham?" Saima asks, her mouth full of biryani. She's clearly surprised that Theo would know enough about their desserts to even ask.

"Emir makes it for me sometimes." Theo answers proudly, cheeks glowing as he settles in. They seem to have approved of him, at least temporarily.

"Is that right?" Safiya smirks at Emir, knowing very well that in most cases he only "cooks" toast or reheats leftovers from their mum. Her new husband has been silent practically the entire time, but Theo thinks he's rather like Emir, preferring the quiet rather than ignoring Theo for any reason. Since all three of Emir's sisters seem rather loud, it would make sense to have some balance around the house.

"I made it for a special night and Theo fell in love with it." Emir shrugs as if it's insignificant, even though he knew from the moment he decided to make it that he was already in too deep. Especially since he used his family recipe.

"That's not the only thing he fell in love with." Saima mumbles to Amina, but definitely loud enough for everyone to hear.

Theo chokes on his food, Emir patting him on the back while he swallows down an entire glass of water and tries to recover. Emir knew this teasing was inevitable, and it sort of means they've accepted Theo into the family so he's not upset. He remembers this same process when Mihir was first introduced a few months after he started dating Safiya.

"Yes, Theo, they do have cham cham." Natalie hands an extra napkin to Theo, which he takes gratefully. Theo notices a secret smile that's almost identical to Emir's. "Not as good as mine of course."

"Could never be like yours, mum." Saima confirms before getting back to quizzing Theo. She's the youngest and her attention span is definitely the shortest. "Who's your favourite Spice Girl?"

"Me again?" Theo checks before answering. "That's a tough one. I think I'm most like Baby, but my favourite is probably Posh. I've always been tangentially interested in fashion. Like, not for me to wear necessarily, just as an interest, I suppose."

"Is that how you became friends with T?" Amina asks, also joining the conversation. It seems they've all decided Theo is more interesting than whatever they were talking about before.

"No, actually." Theo settles against Emir's chest. Emir's hand is resting easily on Theo's collarbone as they get more comfortable, sliding from its former position atop his shoulder. "Laurie is my best mate, and they're soulmates, so...but they're brilliant! Like, I'm really proud to be their friend. Laurie too, when he behaves."

Saleem laughs loudly, covering his mouth with his napkin. "He's a riot, that one. Best friend my Emi's ever had, but pocket-sized chaos, definitely."

"Theo and I are both going to be in the wedding. It was nice of them to include us." Emir takes his arm back to eat more of what's left on his plate, Theo following his lead and starting to eat again. "Now if only they could decide on a venue..."

"The wedding's early summer and they haven't chosen a venue?" Safiya looks scandalised, hand covering her mouth in shock while she sets down her fork. "They'll be stuck using a barn soon."

"I think they wouldn't mind that, actually." Theo scratches at his cheek thoughtfully, his short stubble irritated by the constant application then removal of stage makeup this past week. There's only so much calming that moisturiser can do. "Laurie still wants to use his mum's house, but T is into the rustic, vintage situation. I should mention a barn..."

Dinner's easy from there. Saima continues asking Theo wildly random questions, but it seems he answers all of them correctly. Safiya's protective, but by now she can see that Theo is lovely and very smitten with her brother. Amina just seems content to be there, getting to know Theo and spending time with her family. Saleem gives Theo a hug before they part at the end of the night, which shocks him before remembering how cuddly Emir is and realising he must have learned that comfort at home. And Natalie...

She pulls Emir aside to have a private moment while the rest of the family is fussing around. Her voice is quiet, a conversation just for the two of them.

"He's spectacular, Emi." Natalie doesn't need to say any more for Emir to understand, but she does. "I can see you love him, and he loves you too. That's a rare thing to find in this world. Share your light with him. He understands you."

"Thanks, mum." Emir hides his face on her shoulder and hugs her close, sniffling while he wipes at his eyes and holds her for a sentimental moment. "I think he might be my person."

Natalie keeps her voice low while answering, rubbing his back. She really does miss him when he's so far away, even if she knows he's doing what he loves. "You glow around him. I'm a very proud mum, alright?"

"Love you." Emir kisses her cheek before stepping away, wiping his eyes on his jumper as they join the group again. Knowing his mum not only approves but can see that it's more than just casual is really important to him. He knew his mum would like Theo, but it's still nice to have it confirmed.

"Back to uni?" Theo asks as Emir pulls him into his side and presses his lips to his temple. The two of them drove in Theo's car, but Emir's family is staying with Safiya tonight and can easily walk to her and Mihir's flat from the restaurant. They'll stop by the flat and say goodbye to Emir in the morning, but it's goodnight for now.

"Take me home, princess." Emir mumbles in Theo's ear while tickling at his side, making him giggle as he waves another goodbye to the Shahs.

Theo's pretty sure he's done alright, passed whatever boyfriend test he was given sufficiently well that he doesn't think their relationship is in imminent danger. He drives them back to campus with an easy smile, laughing as Emir sings along to whatever Top Forty is playing on the radio, completely in love with his life. They stay at Theo's that night, Emir snuggling up under the two blankets that he's brought from his own flat for nights like this, Theo's red blanket shared between them. There's never enough blankets for Emir, but Theo on his chest always makes up for it.

Emir's quiet after dinner but Theo's not worried. He's never worried when Emir's quiet, especially when Emir keeps his hands and his eyes on Theo like he's the centre of his entire world. The only exception is when they have to shower separately, but as soon as they're back in the same space Emir is cuddled up in his bubble, enjoying his companionship. Theo settles into the feeling of quiet warmth and gentle partnership that they're building together. He falls asleep on Emir's chest, like always, more at peace than ever before, knowing that Emir is there, loving him and keeping him. He rather likes being Emir's.

CHAPTER SIXTEEN

"Thanks again for taking care of dinner this week." T says to both Ciaran and Gabe in that slow, considerate drawl that they're known for. It was supposed to be their week for family dinner, but Ciaran had volunteered himself and his boyfriend instead.

"Family means helping each other." Ciaran shrugs and shovels another mouthful of pasta onto his fork. "You four are way too busy this week to worry about cooking."

"You're not wrong there." Laurie is practically inhaling his food. He had to skip lunch to finish a project for his *21st Century Interiors* course, and then it was straight back to the auditorium with the others for more tech work. You'd think after an entire weekend of shows everything would be perfect, but of course not. It didn't help that Georgia managed to shatter one of the set pieces during Sunday's matinee.

"I'm not even going back to the studio tonight." Emir gives Theo a grateful smile. "Theo talked me into resting instead. We stayed late working on our dissertation last night, and I stayed even later."

"You have five minutes to look at a few designs for your costume?" T asks Emir from a seat over. "I already showed Theo but I want your input before I start finalising anything."

T is helping with their dissertation costumes, of course. There's no one that either of them would trust more.

"Ooooo babe, you have to see. They're brilliant." Theo wraps his ankle around Emir's under the table to snag his attention again. "T is a genius."

"They absolutely are." Laurie stops eating long enough to kiss the side of T's mouth and run his fingers through their hair. But then it's immediately back to consuming carbs at an alarming rate.

"What about you two?" T directs his question at Gabe and Ciaran, always great at making sure everyone's sharing updates during family dinner and that no one feels left out. "It seems things have settled down with classes?"

"I think so, yeah." Gabe agrees easily while running a hand through his curls and flashing a brilliant smile at T. "But we're looking more into if we actually want to move to New York next summer. So that's...I was going to say exciting but it's actually really stressful."

"Gabe's being nice. It's a bleeding nightmare." Ciaran leans his face in his hand and starts rubbing at his forehead. "America is complicated. There's so many forms, and if I don't have a job, I have to go on a travel visa and hope to get one, like, right away and do different paperwork. Then if I don't get that sorted, we've wasted all our money and time and everything for nothing. And you know how America is with immigration, especially these days."

"What if you stayed in London for a while, or even went to your parents in Kildare? You'd at least be around us and maybe it'd be easier to find a job after uni's over?" T asks, trying their best to be supportive. As much as they'll all miss Ciaran and Gabe, they want them to live their dreams. Which unfortunately means New York or LA. Probably.

"Ciaran's worried that if we stay in London after we're done, we won't leave." Gabe sets his fork down so he can talk more animatedly. "Which isn't a bad thing, but it's not New York."

"No, it's not." Ciaran sighs, his other hand joining in the forehead massage. "I love London and all of you, and we could probably tolerate my family for a while, but London just doesn't have as much of a music industry, and Kildare has essentially none, so like...what would we even do?"

"Grow into the boring old queens we're destined to be, I suppose." Gabe doesn't seem nearly as stressed as Ciaran, but Ciaran is very much a Virgo and Gabe's a laid back Leo. Their relationship is built on balance and it shows, especially in stressful situations.

"How soon do you have to decide?" Theo asks through a mouthful of broccoli, covering his mouth with his hand. He'd somehow managed to create a portion for himself that was 80% vegetables from a very well balanced serving dish. Not that anyone else is complaining.

"Probably by mid-March." Ciaran leans back in his chair as Gabe stands up to massage his shoulders for a minute. He hums, eyes closed while Gabe's hands work their magic.

"I don't think there's much we could help with, but let us know if there is." Emir is usually quiet at these dinners, as he is everywhere else, but his offer is genuine. "We just want you to be happy, wherever you end up."

They finish dinner between their usual weekly updates, everyone going back for second portions because they're significantly more tired and hungry than usual. Where they would ordinarily have leftovers there's a serving bowl scraped clean and six very content uni students.

"Emi, with me?" T asks, gentle hand on Emir's elbow as he goes to follow Theo to his bedroom. They were planning to watch some telly together before getting ready for bed in a few hours, and reviewing costumes with T already slipped Emir's mind.

"Sorry. Forgot." Emir leans over to give Theo a quick kiss before following T to their room. "Be back in a few, princess."

Theo nods and watches them go, catching T's eye and hiding a smile when they wink at him.

"I attached fabric samples with each sketch, of course. Gives you an idea of what it'll really feel and move like." T hands Emir a few cardstock pages that are exactly as described while Laurie flops face first onto T's neatly made bed. "Theo already told me no feathers so I repurposed that sketch for a class project. Oh, and all the fabric is deadstock because we have no budget and also I care about the planet."

"Don't hate me." Emir sits cross legged on T's floor with the sketches in his hand. They're ethereal. He has no doubt that some day, T is going to be a brilliant designer. "I had an idea last night and I didn't even mention it to Theo yet, but I may want you to change our colours. No greys or blacks or that sort of thing."

"I think I need more information." T tilts their head and tucks a curl behind their ear, joining Emi on the floor. Being friends with two dancers, they've grown used to a lot of floor sitting and stretching at random times in inopportune locations. "I don't mind changing the colours, but you know it helps me to understand why when I'm designing. And I still need to find a time to come watch a rehearsal or two."

"Theo and I sort of have this…story. About us." Emir is already anticipating the comments from Laurie once he knows this, but he truly doesn't care. He might even welcome the teasing. "I don't want to tell you the whole thing because it's private, but…a while ago, I told Theo he was the sky, and when we got high together he gave me this little speech about how he was the sky and I was the earth and when we're together we make the sunrise."

"What the actual fuck, Emir?" Laurie mumbles, face still muffled by a pillow. "I expect this behaviour from Teddy."

"I love him, alright? And I think adding that element of our actual story to our work would make it more real, for us and for the audience." Emir huffs, setting down the drawings that T made in front of them. "I want to look at these regardless, but I figured I should let you know that we might have to update the colour palette. And Laur, if you're still helping with the staging, I'll want to talk to you about how the lighting could be like a sunrise behind us at a specific point."

"Do *not* give me work while I'm still sore from building your *Wonderland* set." Laurie grumbles, tossing a pillow halfheartedly in Emir's direction that he catches easily.

"I'm positive Theo has it written into his calendar when we're supposed to meet with you about it, so I'll bother you then." Emir tosses the pillow back, Laurie barely even reacting when it hits the middle of his back and settles on his bum. Under normal circumstances they'd already be brawling, but everyone's too tired, and it's only Wednesday.

Meanwhile, Theo is in his room, scrambling to get it set up in the few minutes that T agreed to distract Emir so he could put together a sort of date night for them. Nothing extravagant, and definitely nothing close to their *Cinderella* night, which they've both agreed by now was definitely a date. But he wanted to do something cute and romantic and maybe a little exciting to help both of them relax between their very busy show weekends.

He really likes Emir and he wants to be soft and sexy and *everything* with him. And part of that is planning dates. He'll definitely do something more involved after they're past the *Alice* shows, but for now, he thinks Emir will like this. They'll get to be quiet and Emir gets to draw and Theo can show off his body. Theo's a little proud of himself for thinking of this.

Once he has everything in place, he puts on his dressing gown and turns off all of the lights, leaving the room illuminated only by the unscented candles that he scattered around, and he waits. Longer than he anticipated...

Just as Theo's about to ruin the surprise and go check on where Emir got to, the door creaks open and Emir stops before he's fully inside, staring around the transformed space with wide eyes until he finally finds Theo sitting on the bed.

"What's this?" Emir asks, barely above a whisper, slowly shutting the door behind himself. He doesn't need details to know this is private.

"A sort of date type thing." Theo shrugs, the front of his dressing gown almost slipping off his shoulders before he recovers himself. Emir nearly swallows his tongue.

"*Not sex!*" Theo adds when he sees the confused but interested look on Emir's face. "Sorry, I just figured I should clarify."

"Right, so..." Emir waits, arms at his side and face illuminated by candlelight. Theo finds him even more gorgeous than usual, if that were possible. Something about the way the glow dances, illuminating as it goes, hiding then revealing different angles of his face as if by magic.

"So you know *The Titanic*." Theo waits for Emir to nod, but instead he stares at Theo even more confused than before. Maybe this isn't as obvious as he thought.

"Are we heading into the bath to shiver in some cold water then?" Emir isn't sure what else to think with Theo already in a dressing gown. He saw enough when the gown slipped to know that Theo's naked beneath it.

"Babe, no, oh my god." Theo starts laughing, clutching his stomach as he falls back on the bed, careful to keep the gown closed this time. "Not like the actual boat. The movie."

"I'm not sure that changes my guess..." Emir finally sits on the chair from the dining room that Theo placed near the wall, wondering how much longer it'll be before he understands what's happening. "You planning to push me off a floating door or something?"

"Yes, perfect. You sit there. And just...wait a minute. You'll see." Theo stands up from the bed and picks up the sketch pad and pencils that he keeps here for Emir, handing them over while Emir gets comfortable in the chair. Hopefully, he's thought of everything Emir will need.

"No laughing." He adds, knowing that Emir is a giggly person. Theo doesn't think he could handle it once he strips down.

"Princess, are you about to..." Emir nervously flips open to a fresh page in the sketchbook, hands fumbling in anticipation because he thinks he's finally figured out the activity. And while he's a moderately talented artist, his boyfriend is sculpted perfection. Michelangelo would struggle to capture his beauty.

"Shhh." Theo climbs up on his bed, realising that he'll be laying the opposite way as Rose, but it'll have to do. He bats his eyelashes and lowers his voice, slightly overdoing the bit. "Emir...will you draw me like one of your French girls?"

Emir's mouth falls open as Theo kneels away from him with his legs spread apart, letting the dressing gown shimmy down his spine, leaving his beautiful back exposed as Theo smiles over his shoulder. He stays like that for a few moments, letting Emir take him in, on his knees and coquettish before he lets the gown drop the rest of the way to the bed. Emir's left admiring the way the fluttering gown reveals Theo's bum, round and firm at the bottom of his muscular back. He groans, pressing his hand against his dick and hoping it behaves.

"I may not have a blue diamond to wear, but I have this gold chain, and it'll have to do." Theo brings his knees back together, carefully arranging the dressing gown beneath where he's going to lay before actually doing so, propping himself up on his arm and hoping the way he's posed is at least artful in some way. Being a dancer means he has a sort of natural grace, but he's never modelled for a nude portrait before.

"And I have to stay here and actually draw you?" Emir's already started an outline of the bed, but only as a distraction tactic. If he has a pencil in hand, it's practically instinct. "I'm not allowed to come over there?"

"Not yet." Theo teases, letting his free hand lay gracefully over his hip bone. He actually wants to see how the drawing turns out. Watching Emir show restraint like this is more than a little amusing. "And if you behave, I have dessert. For later."

"Do I get to eat it out of your arse?" Emir asks, realising after it's already said that it's maybe too forward considering they're taking their time. But Theo flushes and laughs, not offended in the slightest. He's glad his boyfriend's so obviously attracted to him.

"Not tonight, but maybe someday soon." Theo sighs and settles into his pose, his eyes watching Emir's hands move as the sound of his pencil fills the air. He already warned the others that he and Emir are having *private time* after dinner, so Gabe and Ciaran left for Gabe's flat, and T and Laurie are in T's room across the flat, promising to give them space.

"Stay still, shehzadi." Emir tsks as Theo resettles on the pillows. He looks gorgeous, and Emir isn't even focusing on how completely naked he is. Every inch of him is coated gold by the candles, softened and defined at the same time. He looks edible, but in the way that Emir knows one taste would ruin all other sustenance. "Can't have you moving about if I'm meant to draw you."

"Shehzadi?" Theo finds a comfortable spot and vows to do his absolute best to stay still. He's not great at that, but he wants to do what Emir needs for the drawing. "Does that mean princess?"

Emir doesn't answer right away, tucking his face down into his chest and smiling while biting his lip. How is Theo always so fucking adorable?

"See, you're already learning." He believed Theo when he said he was trying to learn Urdu, but it seems he really meant it. No one's ever done that before. Not even his friends.

"Did I say it right? Shehzadi?" Theo's brow furrows while he focuses, staying still like Emir asked. Repeating it again to be sure, he mumbles, "Shehzadi...shehzadi?"

"Sounds perfect." Emir starts adding shading to Theo's legs, appreciating how toned and muscular they are and anticipating the feeling of them beneath his fingers, between his own legs, having them wrapped around him, pressing kisses to every inch, feeling Theo shiver against his lips...

"You alright?" Theo notices Emir's flush even in the dim light, Emir shifting in his seat and readjusting his trousers. Theo's never been tempted towards vanity, but he's always hoped to be fit. Who hasn't? Emir never wastes an opportunity to remind him that Theo's the most beautiful person he's ever known, and somehow it never sounds like sarcasm.

"I'm fine, you're just - " Emir fusses with his hair and goes back to his drawing. "You're really fit, alright? Getting me all hot. It's those legs, Theo. They're unbelievable."

The person attached to the legs is the real issue. Emir's never desired someone in the way he does Theo. It's been a discovery, to know he could lust for the person he loves, and have those motivations share space rather than compete for dominance. He's learned so much from being with Theo, about love and about building a real relationship. They're partners in the true sense of the word, balancing each other along the way.

"Maybe next week you can draw my bum." Theo laughs as Emir fully drops his sketchpad, cursing while he leans down to pick it up. He was joking, but he makes a mental note. If Emir has a thing for his bum...

***

"I was promised dessert." Emir's finally done with his drawing, so naturally he's on the bed, Theo beneath him while he kisses him hungrily. "And I choose you."

"I'm not on the menu tonight, babe." Theo pulls Emir's hoodie off, interrupting their moment. It's worth it when he remembers that Emir didn't wear a shirt underneath. He loves having his hands all over Emir, feeling him move beneath his fingertips, scratching and massaging and using his hands to know Emir's body one graze at a time.

"But I behaved. I even drew two different sketches, just in case." Emir undoes his own joggers, shimmying out of them and pressing himself against Theo. Too many layers in the way. "The first one was too focused on your massive cock."

"Emir!" Theo giggles, said dick happily nudging against Emir's through his boxers. He's glad Emir's not completely naked yet because he had a plan for the rest of the evening and it's already close to being derailed. Emir has that effect on him. "Shower first then dessert."

"Shower like...together?" Emir stops to stare at Theo, his eyes on the verge of shining with hope. They've never been fully naked together...

"That was the plan, yes." Theo runs his hands along Emir's back, scratching gently at the skin there until Emir melts on top of him. He makes this little noise when Theo finds a sore spot, and it might be Theo's favourite sound. "Tense?"

"Course. We're both stressed." Emir hums as Theo keeps rubbing his back, even massaging his bum, but not in a naughty way, just to relieve tension. He wouldn't be mad if Theo was managing to do both.

"Good. Then a shower is perfect. I want to wash you and help you relax." Theo pauses before admitting the next part. He doesn't want to be weird or too emotionally invested already and scare Emir. "I just thought it might be...domestic. Sort of soft and boyfriendy."

"You know, you make it really difficult to be anything less than in love with you." Emir sits up, pulling Theo with him and shoving his dressing gown into his hand. "Cover up so we don't make the others hungry."

"Emir!!" Theo scolds, even louder than last time, covering himself as his entire body flushes red. "I think they can behave at the sight of a bit of muscle and a limp dick."

"Not so limp, last I checked." Emir helps Theo tie the gown closed, leaning in for another kiss before patting Theo on the bum. "Now, lead the way to our domestic, boyfriendy, relaxing shower, please and thank you."

They scurry across the hall, shutting the door behind them only a moment before Emir has Theo pressed up against it, shoving the dressing gown back off of him. It's really just in the way at this point.

"Lemmegetthewateron." Theo mumbles against Emir's lips, turning them around and fumbling with one of his hands until he finds the shower knob. He's pretty sure it's turned to the right temperature, but they'll find out soon enough.

"Is the shower just for getting clean?" Emir hopes not, but he'll always respect Theo's boundaries. Always.

"I hope not." Theo's in a bit of a *specific* mood, and he's pretty sure he knows how to help them both relax. "I'm not ready for anything like *in* me, but I want you to get us off. Both of us. If that's alright?"

"What's off-limits?" Emir reaches around Theo to adjust the water, noticing it's turned way too high. He doesn't want to scald their delicate skin.

"Penetration." Theo tugs Emir forward by the hips, fussing with the waistband of his boxers which he'd really like to be gone by now. "No hands or anything else inside me.

But like...you can touch my bum or even lick it I guess. But that seems difficult in a shower."

"First of all, don't doubt my abilities. We're both very flexible." Emir smirks while finally removing his boxers, tossing them to the floor for now. "I know what I want, but you can stop me whenever, yeah?"

Theo nods, hand bravely brushing the inside of Emir's thigh and sending shivers through him, ending with a jump in his stomach. Emir's never been as sensitive as he is with Theo. The way Theo makes him feel is unlike anything he's known before, and he's very aware that it's not just on a physical level. "If you had any idea, baby..."

"Hm?" Theo trails that same hand around his thigh to hold his lower back, and his innocence is anything but crafted. He trusts Emir and he knows, without a doubt, that Emir won't cross a line with him. He knew that even back when they still hated each other. That era seems like a lifetime ago now.

"Just the effect you have on people. Me, specifically." Emir steps back into the tub, shoving the curtain aside while his hair gets plastered to his forehead. Theo follows him in, guided by the hand, the hot water hitting him like a wall before he adjusts.

"Kiss me. Get used to touching me naked." Emir suggests, making sure they're both warm beneath the water. Theo's hands explore him carefully, running over his chest and across his back and even down to his bum.

"You can touch all of me." Emir clarifies, realising that Theo is intentionally avoiding his dick.

Theo pauses with a hand on Emir's stomach, looking like a wet puppy as he watches Emir's reaction. Carefully, he moves his hand down and presses against Emir's dick, Emir's head falling back, eyes closing while he holds Theo easily in his arms.

"I don't think it'd be safe to kneel. Might slip." Theo decides to say, and Emir can't help but laugh. Theo never hides his thoughts, always letting Emir into that beautiful mind of his.

"You don't have to use your mouth, just get used to being like this together." Emir purposefully meets Theo's eyes, making sure he's alright. He looks fine, just a little nervous. "Or we can stop and I'll get out."

"No!" Theo's hands are back on Emir's waist, moving them so his own back is against the wall instead. He's immediately more comfortable. "Just...sorry. I'd rather you, um...I like touching you, but could you...I like when you – "

"You can tell me, Theo. I won't laugh." Emir runs a hand through Theo's wet hair, giving him a careful kiss of encouragement. He knows that Theo has a hard time verbalising what he's into, especially if he's already worked up.

"Use me? Like my body?" Theo looks down at where they meet, both of them half hard and soaking wet. He feels bashful but confident somehow, like he knows this is what he wants but he's shy about needing it. But then he sees something he wasn't expecting. "Is that – Emir, is that a tattoo?"

Last time they were naked together it was dark and they were under many blankets. But even with the water coating them, it's clear: a black mark that moves with his skin, like Emir could write novellas through the air with his hips.

Emir laughs again, taking Theo's hand in his to press against the ink. He wants Theo to know he's comfortable with him touching wherever he likes. "It is. Only spot I could get one for now. When I'm signed with a company, hopefully I can get more, but..."

"Can I look?" Theo realises it'll put his face directly next to Emir's dick, but it's genuine curiosity he's following.

"You can do whatever you like." Emir watches as Theo kneels, so carefully you'd think he was made of glass, but Theo's caution and care is part of why Emir loves him.

"Is it...does it say Emir in Urdu?" Theo looks up again, water splashing against his face until he wipes it away with his hand, fingers leaving Emir's skin momentarily, but his other hand holds tight to Emir's hip like an anchor. This sharing of Emir's other language has been almost constant ever since the dinner with his family, and it's like Emir's letting Theo into a side of his life that only those closest to his heart have access.

"I wasn't sure what to get, I just knew I wanted something. I felt so out of my body at the time, and this was a small way to reclaim it, I guess. It was back when I wasn't entirely sure who I was. First few months here at uni." Emir runs his fingers through Theo's hair again, pulling on his shoulder until they're eye level. "My name in a language that belongs to my family and not to...well, this whole mess of a society. It just seemed right. I don't regret it."

"How did the tattoo artist even..." Theo brushes his fingers over it again, letting the back of his hand graze Emir's dick. It's hard not to. "Like, because of the placement."

"She'd seen me naked before, so she wasn't exactly fazed. And tattoo artists do penis and vulva tattoos sometimes, if it's something they're comfortable with." Emir shrugs, shaking the water out of his eyes. It's not the best use of hot water, but also not the worst.

"Oh, did you two have sex before you got it done?" Theo doesn't mind mentioning Emir's sexual past. It doesn't bother him who he's been with or when, and it's not as if they talk about it frequently. He knows they're committed now, and anything before is just part of Emir's path to being here.

"The week before. She mentioned what she did for work when we met. I think she was an apprentice at the time." Emir presses his own fingers against the tattoo, not really paying much attention to it nowadays. He'd had to put it somewhere purposely hidden a majority of the time but it also felt more private that way. Theo's the only person who's noticed, or at least the first to ask about it.

"I like it. Like...not sure I can explain it, but I like seeing it, especially knowing that it gave you meaning when you were in so much pain." Theo leans against the shower wall again, glad when Emir crowds into his space and kisses the corner of his mouth. "I don't like thinking of you all alone, but I know you had your family and it's so...*you* - to validate yourself when no one else could."

"Why are you so sweet to me?" Emir asks, nuzzling under Theo's chin and letting their bodies fall together. If Theo wants to feel used, Emir has a few ideas. The emotions Theo's pulling out of him aren't dampening his desire in the slightest.

"I don't know any other way to be. Even when we were fighting, I usually felt so guilty I'd try to do something nice for you without you knowing to make up for it." Theo should've expected the way Emir would stare at him in surprise. It's definitely the first time he's mentioned it to him. Or to anyone.

"I need to hear a lot more about that." Emir caresses Theo's cheek, wiping a stream of water away from his eye, feeling once again like he has an angel in his arms and not entirely sure how to process what it means to love Theo. He's his actual boyfriend and he's still learning new things about him every ten seconds.

"Just like…I'd ask people to move away from the spot you like at the barre. Keep Georgia away from you during downtime so you wouldn't have to deal with her. Correct people who would say that your family was Indian when even I knew you're half-Pakistani. Nevermind that those conversations were borderline problematic just from the bits they'd let me overhear." Theo scrunches his forehead in frustrated hindsight until Emir brushes his fingers across his cheek again. "Once I left extra tea in your cupboard at your flat when I saw you were almost out. That one was after that huge fight we had at the beginning of last year when I actually came by to apologise for once before changing my mind…"

Theo sighs and hides his face against Emir's neck. "I'm pathetic, I know. I just didn't know what else to do when I felt like we were being so nasty to each other and I wasn't even sure why. Like, of course I was jealous of your talent, and I used to hate the way you drew attention without even trying, but…I never liked fighting with you. But I also didn't know how to stop."

Emir really isn't sure what to say to that. He never did anything of the sort before they became friends and then eventually more. But of course Theo did. Of course. "You're definitely too good for me. But I suppose you've chosen me for who knows what reason, and I respect your choices."

Theo laughs, eyes crinkling while he stares at Emir. Emir's realised over the past few weeks that Theo doesn't look at anyone else that way. And if it were anyone else staring, it would aggravate Emir, itching at his subconscious while they stare and gossip and admire. But not with Theo. Theo doesn't look at him like the others do. He admires him but without the expectation. He stares but without the gossip. Theo just…likes him. But he likes the real Emir that almost everyone else misses.

"You know, I said essentially the same thing to Laurie before I met your family." Theo smiles at the memory, that dinner having gone so much better than he ever thought. "So I guess we're both too good for each other and we should just give up now. Sorry, no dick for you tonight."

Theo lets out an exaggerated sigh, and while he's not a very talented actor, he's very good at being adorable.

"Excuse me, I believe my boyfriend requested that I use his body." Emir bites at Theo's birthmark, careful to keep it light. He loves marking Theo, but not when they have to worry about stage lights. "And I was looking forward to it."

"Promise I'm not...too much?" Theo pauses Emir with a hand on his chest. He still feels too high maintenance or like he's asking too much of Emir because of his lack of experience. They've been taking things slow by the standards of what he would consider a "normal" relationship (at least based on the few he knows), and he still worries that it's an issue. Even though he knows logically that there's nothing wrong with the pace they've taken.

"Baby..." Emir hasn't called Theo that very often, but sometimes it just feels right, especially when he's feeling protective, like now. And Theo's reaction to the term every single time has been one of acceptance and comfort. "You're never too much. You know I never expect sex with you, but I'm always excited if it happens."

He kisses Theo, slow and deep and yearning, hoping that he believes Emir because he's answering in earnest. He knows that sex means something different to Theo, maybe something more, and he's never resented that.

"If you promise..." Theo lets himself be vulnerable now, relaxing against the wall and waiting for Emir to take over. He just needed reassurance. Maybe someday he won't, but this is all still so new to him: new boyfriend, new intimacies, new things about himself that he's discovering along the way. It's an adjustment, even if he's loving every moment they're together.

Emir lets his hand move down Theo's torso, stopping at his waist and waiting for Theo to nod his permission. When he gets it, Emir starts with a careful hand on Theo's dick, moving slow and adjusting him to the sensation. "Can I try something, princess?"

"Whatever you want. I'm yours." Theo's head is leaning back against the wall, but he meets Emir's eyes to make sure he knows it's alright before falling into the moment again. He's a hundred times more comfortable like this than he was a minute ago, grateful for Emir taking charge of the situation, and of Theo.

Emir scoots himself closer, more glad than ever that they're basically the same height. He's never done this in a shower, or without lube, but he'll be careful and go slow. Lining up their dicks in between them, he moves his hand around both of them, holding Theo's back to keep him close and kissing him at the same time.

"What's - first of all I love this - but what are we doing?" Theo vaguely wonders if he isn't supposed to be moving his hips up into Emir's hand but it just feels *so good* and knowing what exactly he's feeling through his skin is doing something to him mentally. Emotionally. Some combination of the whole of him. It's overall the most interesting thing he's ever felt. He doubts Emir will be done with him after this, but he's imagining Emir shooting his release onto his dick and just the thought has Theo moaning before Emir can even answer his question.

"Give me your hand." Emir takes it, letting Theo use his admittedly larger hand to get them off. He noticed Theo squirming more than he anticipated, so he wants to give him a bit more control over how their bodies move. It'll be good to let Theo figure this out for himself, too. And he's...very good at it. Theo doesn't have any preconceptions or hesitations, he just knows what feels nice and what he likes. His honesty is beyond refreshing. "It's called frotting and you're incredible at it."

But as Theo suspected, Emir doesn't want this to be the end of it. They have at least a little more time before the water runs cold, and Emir's only getting started. Just as Theo feels his knees getting weak and that tightness building from inside, Emir moves his hand off to intertwine it with his own, bringing Theo's arms above his head and pinning him to the wall.

Theo feels helpless and empowered all in one.

"Oh." His eyes fly open to watch Emir barely a moment before he's pushing into Theo again, holding his arms up and out of the way while grinding up against him and kissing him like they're running out of time. Water, maybe. Theo's gasping in anticipation, this whole Emir holding him down situation is exactly what he was hoping for.

"Rope?" Theo asks, maybe a little too eagerly, because he's actually wondering if Emir somehow thought that far ahead.

Emir takes a break from kissing Theo to turn him around instead, hands tracing across Theo's skin to warm up the parts of him that haven't been under the hot water. "Rope is for later. Lots of things we have to talk about before you can be a bunny, baby."

"I like when you use pet names." Theo admits with a sigh, his back to Emir's chest while Emir soothes him beneath the water for a soft moment. "And when you hold me."

"I've never cared much about any of that before you, but I like being sweet with you: leaving you drawings and making you flush and giggle and calling you every pet name I can think of." Emir rubs his arms up and down Theo's front in a lazy massage. "Now, bend forward for me, princess. I won't hurt you and I won't put anything inside you, alright?"

"I trust you, Emi." And Theo means that, maybe even more because of their past. They had to work through a lot to get to this point, and he might trust Emir more than anyone else by now.

He leans forward, facing away as Emir bends his arms to have him hold himself up against the wall on his elbows. "Oh..."

With Emir still flush behind him, this is definitely the closest he's been to being fucked from behind, or in any position. It's sort of overwhelming.

"You alright?" Emir asks, face near Theo's while laying on top of his back. This is probably a lot for Theo to process. It's a lot for Emir to process and he's been with dozens of people.

"I'm fine. I'm good - I just..." Theo thinks for a moment, relaxing when Emir hugs him, arms around his chest, face laying on Theo's back. It's new, but it's Emir. He's good. "Better now. Just, um, could you give me a warning before you do anything?"

"Like asking if I can touch your cock?" Emir grins when Theo laughs beneath him, still holding him tight as the warm water falls down around them.

"Yes, that's great. Just enough so I'm not surprised. Not ready for surprises." Theo feels Emir's hands moving down his chest and resting on his stomach, and now he's excited instead of nervous because he knows what's coming. "You can, if that was you asking."

Emir kisses his back, once, twice, then a few more times, tasting Theo's skin somewhere beneath the sheen of water. He lets his fingertips graze everywhere except Theo's dick, caressing his thighs, tickling his stomach, all while slowly and softly thrusting behind him to get him warmed up to the idea, essentially just grinding like they would while dancing at a party. "I'm about to touch your bum, just on the outside. If it's too much, I'll stop."

Theo nods and lets his head drop forward between his shoulders as Emir moves back enough for his hands to start rubbing across Theo's arse cheeks, spreading them carefully in slow, sensual circles. He knew it was happening, but he still gasps when

Emir's thumb drags across his hole, just barely there before moving back to rub his bum. "Do it again. More. That wasn't enough."

Emir smiles but doesn't laugh at how demanding Theo sounds. He doesn't want Theo to think he's laughing at him when what he's really feeling is fond and protective. He knows this is a moment for Theo and he wants it to be safe and comfortable. But Theo said more, so Emir keeps rubbing, letting his thumb start at the base of his spine and trail all the way down until it reaches his perineum before detaching again. Theo shivers each time, his legs shaking while he tries to control his body's reaction.

"You ready for more, baby?" Emir moves his hands to rest on Theo's waist instead, Theo still obediently leaning on his elbows and letting Emir have his way.

"God, yes. I didn't know my body could feel all this at once." Theo's panting, trying to catch up to all the sensations between the water and Emir's hands and his dick whenever it taps his bare skin and he's overall very glad he's not also dealing with prostate stimulation today. Not that he isn't aware of it, since he owns a few toys and he's done his own exploring. But he knows it'll be different letting someone else engage that part of him. Someday, but dear lord not today. He's barely standing as it is.

Emir leans forward over Theo again, massaging his arms to get some feeling back in them, and knowing that Theo's about to have elbow bruises that they'll have to sort tomorrow. Whispering in his ear, he asks, "Can I use your bum to get off, cock between your cheeks, while I use my hand to make you come?"

Theo groans, pushing his hips back into Emir needily and wishing it was already happening. That sounds exactly like what he wants, even if he didn't know to ask for it. "Will you come on my back? But don't wash it off right away. I want to know if I can feel it through my skin."

"You're such a wet dream, babe." Emir kisses the side of Theo's mouth since it's all he can reach right now, then down his neck and across his shoulder as he stands up and gets himself in position. Gently, he nudges Theo's legs apart then rubs his cheeks again, eventually holding them open so he can slide his own dick between them. Theo moans as it happens, and Emir is more sure than ever that Theo has sensory sensitivities. It's not the first time he's noticed, because Theo is generally incredibly responsive, especially in these situations. It's a conversation for another time.

Emir tests a few slow thrusts to make sure Theo's comfortable, Theo moving his hips to meet him each time, so he thinks he's found a good position.

As he gets into his own rhythm, Emir grabs Theo's hip in his left hand and trails his right along Theo's side until taking him in hand again, slow and matching his thrusts to his wrist as Theo groans, moving back and forth between Emir's hand and his hips.

"More, please. I am *begging*. You won't hurt me and my legs are ready to fucking collapse." Theo has his eyes closed, hands balled into fists where he has them clenched together on the wall above his elbows. "I said use me. Fucking *use me*, please."

"So bossy. Can't be having that." Emir bites his lip as he speeds up, doing exactly as Theo asked. He's never done this before, not exactly, but he's spent way too much time figuring out ways to ease Theo into this whole sex situation, and creative ways for them to play intimately on days when they can't deal with the potential physical consequences of penetration. This was top of the list. "Bossy, bossy, bottom baby."

"I swear to god Emir if you don't - " Theo moans when Emir pinches his side with his left hand, enough to get Theo's attention.

Emir's starting to understand just how much Theo wants him to take charge. If he wasn't having so much fun with this, Emir would be coming already because having Theo bent in half while he fucks him (albeit nontraditionally) is...it's incredible. His dick has never been so happy.

"Thought you didn't believe in god." Emir teases, and he knows it's maybe a bit unfair to play with Theo like this, but Theo definitely likes it, his hips losing their rhythm for a moment while Emir changes his pattern right in the middle of the sentence, catching Theo off guard.

"Don't be clever right now. I've never felt more stupid." Theo grinds his hips against Emir and squeezes his cheeks together, proud when he hears Emir swear in response. "Head empty, dick full. You want a chat, you'll have to get me off and wait a while."

"So mouthy. To think we used to fight when we could've fucked instead." Emir changes the position of his hips so that when he shifts back his dick will rub against Theo's hole. The first time it happens Theo shivers violently that Emir genuinely worries his legs will give out. Maybe Theo's not ready for that today.

He wants Theo to finish first, so he focuses on him, moving his hand the way he's
learned Theo likes and holding his waist a bit harder, Theo's head dropping again
while he starts to shake, but this time Emir knows it's because he's on the edge.

"If you want my spunk on your back, you have to come first." Emir moves his hand
from Theo's hip to scratch at his back instead, his fingernails leaving angry red trails
behind, but Emir's careful not to scratch too deep. Not this round. He knows Theo is
so close that it's like a game now. He just needs him to let go. "Maybe next time we
could even use that rope, let me gag you so you have to scream to be heard, tie your
hands so I can really use you, maybe even let you get a taste of me in that bossy
mouth of yours."

And sure enough, that does it. Theo yells as he comes, his whole body shaking
beneath Emir who's stopped thrusting, using his hand to bring Theo all the way
through his orgasm, watching as the water washes away any evidence as it drops,
except for the bits that stay on his hand. Which gives Emir an idea. "You want to taste
yourself, baby?"

Theo nods somewhere in his orgasm haze, opening his mouth wider and waiting for
Emir to push his fingers inside. There's not much on them, but he carefully pushes his
index and middle finger past Theo's lips, letting him suck and satisfy himself as he
keeps coming down from his high until he finally opens up again, gasping for air and
chest heaving while he catches his breath.

"You taste better." He gasps out, and Emir finally does laugh. It's subjective obviously,
but it seems Theo is very interested in tasting him again sometime soon. Emir is very
much looking forward to that day. Those lips are just...the dreams that Emir's had...

"Stay there. I'll use you a minute longer and then you can feel me on your back, just
like you asked." Emir rubs Theo's chest and kisses his shoulder before standing back
up and praying the water stays warm for another few minutes. They still have to get
clean after all this, too. "You've been good, so you get what you wanted."

"What happens when I'm naughty?" Theo turns his head and catches Emir's eye, his
own still glossy and half open from his recent orgasm. Emir's surprised he's still
standing. Must be those gorgeous muscles he always admires.

"Then I get to punish you. Now turn around and focus on standing up because I'm not going to be gentle." Emir squeezes Theo's bum before pushing himself back where he was, but this time he holds Theo's hips in both hands so he can really thrust properly.

It doesn't take Emir long to reach his own climax, and Theo must be purposely clenching and unclenching like he is because it's exactly in rhythm with Emir. He'll get a nice reward for that later, but for now Emir chases his high, pulling out from Theo's cheeks just as he shouts Theo's name so he can paint his skin, making sure to keep the water off Theo's back with his own body so he can feel every drop. He's aware that Theo's back is so warm that the effect will be minimal, but Theo sighs as Emir comes, feeling or imagining the spunk on his back and liking how he really feels *used*, but not in a bad way at all. Theo knows enough about basic kinks to know it's common enough. It's extremely validating for him to experience, and he's not entirely sure why.

"Rub it in." Theo doesn't care where these desires are coming from. Once Emir's done dripping on him, it's all Theo can think about. It'll get washed off in a moment anyway.

Emir takes a beat, but Theo feels his hand start massaging it into his skin soon enough, hesitant at first but eventually turning it into a massage while he lets the water re-enter the situation so he's washing it off as he does.

"Can we maybe clean each other?" Theo finally stands up from the wall and faces Emir, bashfully reaching out for him but happy when Emir pulls him into a hug, one hand on the back of his neck, cradling Theo in his space.

"Of course we can." Emir kisses the side of his neck then pulls back enough to give him a real kiss. Emir looks softer right now. Sweeter. Like being in this space together meant as much to him as it did to Theo. "But we'll have to be quick about it before the water runs cold."

They've barely finished shampooing before the temperature starts to drop, but Theo insists they keep washing anyway. Theo soaps and scrubs and loves on Emir, every inch of his skin taken care of like Theo's trying to anoint him. And even though they're shivering, Emir can't hold back his fondness. He feels cherished, and he understands what Theo meant about this being domestic and boyfriendy. He returns the favour, using Theo's soaps and scrubs to clean his boyfriend like the angel he is and making sure he feels as loved as possible.

By the time they're out of the shower the water is like ice. They shiver through their smiles while they towel off together. Theo's insistent that they have to moisturise each other as well, not content with the bathing and the washing. Emir takes a moment and shows Theo his elbows in the mirror, not wanting it to be a surprise tomorrow when he wakes up.

"Well...they won't be able to see my knees to know if they match, so it'll be a fun mystery." Theo shrugs, poking one of the bruises experimentally before pulling Emir into another kiss. "I'm not ashamed of having marks, babe, but thank you for telling me."

They finish getting ready for bed but Emir stops himself before brushing his teeth, remembering what Theo said back before their shower. "Didn't you mention dessert?"

"French ice cream. Well, french vanilla ice cream, which I've decided is close enough." Theo smiles wide, tying his own dressing gown around Emir and securing his towel around his waist so they're both decent to head out of the bathroom. "They had all these fancy desserts on The Titanic, but most of them were complicated and I'd rather just share a tub of ice cream with you instead."

"Two spoons. We're boyfriends, not animals." Emir tosses his hair dramatically, a drop of water smacking Theo in the face and making him giggle.

"Deal." Theo opens the door and lets Emir stumble ahead of him to the kitchen. "But we're eating it in bed so we can cuddle."

***

It's very late that night, probably past one if Emir were to glance at his phone, and it's perfectly quiet. There's no blinking reminder of time passing in this room because Theo has this fancy clock that turns off the light display when told and only turns back on when the alarm goes off. Emir loves it, just like everything else about Theo. He's intrinsically thoughtful, even when it's just a clock to most people. Theo took the time to research and decide how it would fit into his life. He doesn't do anything without consideration.

Theo's fast asleep beside him, eyes covered by a satin eye mask that he'd picked out once they started sharing a bed. Apparently, the lamp that Emir needs for drawing and reading and all the rest keeps him up otherwise. It was an easy compromise.

Emir's still wide awake, catching up on reading for his book club which meets again next weekend. It's definitely later than Emir should be up on a school night, but *House*

In The Cerulean Sea is too endearing and full of found family for him to put it down with only a few chapters left. Theo can't lay on Emir's chest like he's used to, so he's on his lap instead, face nuzzled on his thigh and arm thrown over his legs. Emir has no idea how he looks so comfortable, but Theo insists he is every time Emir's woken him up to sleep more...normally.

He's almost to the end of the book when Theo's hand finds his. His fingers hold tight to Emir's, a gentle smile on his face, and Emir wonders if he's dreaming or just comforted by his grasp. Either way it makes Emir irredeemably happy to know that Theo reaches for him, even in his sleep

Emir finishes the last chapter that way, setting it aside with a sigh and rubbing his thumb across the back of Theo's hand. It's domestic, boyfriendy, all those things Theo loves best about their relationship. Emir carefully picks up his phone and takes a picture of their hands like this, and then another where he can see Theo's sleeping face beside it, the last one just for him.

But now that Emir's really looking at their hands, he needs to draw. It's like an itch sometimes, like the way he gets about dance but less intense. His need to dance is more like a compulsion, fighting with the rest of him until he's able to move through space the way he needs. He knows he won't be able to sleep tonight until he draws, so he presses a kiss to Theo's hand before carefully dropping it from his grasp, leaning over to exchange his novel for his sketchbook instead, flipping past the pictures of Theo from earlier, but taking time to appreciate them.

He couldn't capture how beautiful Theo looked laying out on the bed like that, but he still looks gorgeous, and Emir definitely got the posture right. Emir spent several minutes on just his eyes, hoping to showcase their warmth with graphite, but it's just a shadow of what they truly hold.

Theo snuffles and readjusts on Emir's lap, arms circling his waist to hug him instead. Emir makes sure he's asleep again before starting to draw.

To anyone who glances at the drawing, they could be anyone's hands. But Emir knows those knuckles, the ridges and dimples and veins that cover the landscape of Theo's hand as it dances across his skin or holds him firm in its grasp. And he knows his own hand, the corners that clay clings to when he shapes pottery and the curve of his thumbnail that used to fascinate him for hours as a kid, the half moon buried beneath the pink shell, and that freckle that's just above his pinky finger. So maybe to another eye it's just a set of hands, but to Emir it's comfort, their individual beauty coming together to make meaning. It's Theo finding him in the dark and holding tight, and Emir holding right back.

It only takes Emir about half an hour to be happy with the drawing, smudging and shading and fussing until he's done. Before he sets it aside he takes another picture, this time of their hands but as he's drawn them, the lamplight softening every angle and giving the stark white background some warmth.

Then Emir makes another choice, one that's unplanned but sure. Keeping his phone out, for the first time in several years, he posts a picture to his private instagram account. Emir doesn't tag Theo and he doesn't post a caption. He only has seven followers between his family and friends, but it's still a step. He didn't know that he'd ever be ready to share any piece of himself with the internet again, but this feels safe. It's a private moment, but he's only sharing what he's comfortable with, with who he trusts, and it's nothing identifiable.

Emir plugs his phone in to charge, finally turning off the lamp and setting everything aside so he can scoot down the bed to snuggle Theo properly. As if on instinct, Theo resettles on his chest, sighing and pressing a kiss against his shirt and mumbling something incoherent until Emir pets his hair and he falls back asleep. Emir carefully lifts the mask from his eyes, setting it with the other things on the side table since Theo won't need it the rest of the night. He kisses his forehead and nuzzles his face into Theo's hair, feeling truly happy.

***

Theo's brushing his teeth the next morning when he checks his phone for the first time since waking up. Nothing surprising. A few notifications from his sisters, a text from his mum confirming which restaurant for dinner with Emir and the family this weekend, and of course a few things from Laurie and Ciaran after he fell asleep last night. Gabe and T are on their phones more during the day, but Laurie's a night owl and Ciaran's been up late recently stressing about the move.

Once he's fresh and clean, Theo opens his Instagram notifications. At first he thinks Emir's sent him a random picture. They do this sometimes: send each other posts that make them happy or videos they should watch, but it only takes a moment for Theo to realise the post is from Emir's own account. His private account. His secret, hidden, impossible-to-find-without-Emir-typing-it-in-your-phone-for-you account. The one without any posts.

Theo doesn't even open the picture to look at it, panicked already because how dare anyone hack into Emir's personal account like this? After everything he's been through? And pretend to be him for what? Why would someone violate Emir's privacy like this?

"Emi!" Theo drops his deodorant and sprints back across the hall to his bed, grasping Emir's shoulder to wake him up. He always rolls into Theo's spot once he gets out of bed to get ready, but Theo doesn't have time to feel fond about that right now. "Emir, wake up. It's important."

"Too early." Emir grumbles, extra sleepy because he stayed up late the night before reading and drawing and feeling. He pulls the blankets back over his head and hides his face in Theo's pillow instead of his own. "Come cuddle."

Emir knows Theo won't, but a boi can dream. Morning cuddles are already over, sadly.

"Emiiiii." Theo turns his phone around and shakes Emir's shoulder again until he looks up at Theo through one half opened eye. "Someone hacked your Instagram. And I don't want you to panic but I know how important it is to you to have privacy and it must've been while you were asleep last night because it was posted so late and they sent me something from your account but you don't have anything posted which means they stole your password or something and I know how much trouble you went through to set this one up so maybe we could change the password and set up two factor authentication if you haven't already or make a new one for you and text your family so they know what happened and I could cut my time at the gym to help you because this is way more important obviously - "

"Baby." Emir's sitting up now, rubbing the sleep from his eyes and confusing Theo with a soft, sleepy kiss. The pet name silences Theo immediately, Emir taking the phone from his hand and opening the picture to show him. "I didn't get hacked, princess. Look again at what I sent you."

Theo shuffles back into bed with Emir as he holds up the blanket for him to make room.

"I don't understand." Theo's shirtless but wearing joggers, halfway through getting ready, his eyes wide while he processes what he's looking at through a fog of panic. His hand finds Emir's forearm to hold his attention, trying to make sense of the situation. Why isn't Emir panicking, too?

Emir reaches across Theo, flailing his hand around until he finds the sketchbook then opening it to the page with the hand drawing, showing it to Theo and waiting for it to click. He's too tired to find good words right now, so he's hoping the visual will suffice.

"It's...you drew this? And posted it?" Theo looks between the phone and the sketchbook and Emir's face where he's fallen back against the pillows, one arm covering his eyes. "I don't understand."

He keeps saying that, but it's true. Emir doesn't post anything anywhere after what happened. He barely even uses his phone at all.

Groaning, Emir pulls Theo to lay back with him, flopping himself on top of Theo and joining their hands together just like in the picture. "You were sleeping and you grabbed my hand and held it for like an hour while I finished reading. And I'm in like with you, so I drew our hands because I'm a ridiculous softie. And then, because you make me believe in things like trust and decency, I posted it to my secret account and messaged it to you so you would see how in like with you I am. Which clearly backfired."

Emir waits for his explanation to register, thinking he probably should've included a message beneath the picture when he sent it so Theo wouldn't panic.

"You...drew our hands. And posted it. As the only picture on your secret account. Because you're in like with me." Theo stares at the sketch again, the one in the book rather than his phone, and now that he's looking, that's definitely their hands. Then he notices the time stamp on the post. "How late did you stay up?"

"You're soooo pretty, princess." Emir knows it won't work, but Theo still softens into a smile at his attempt. It was worth a try.

"Yes, we've established my visual merits." Theo squeaks when Emir's fingers manage to find one of his tickle spots before his hand falls back in the blankets. "How late, babe?"

"Late. I don't know." Emir grumbles, hiding his face against Theo's chest and getting comfortable. Maybe today's his lucky day and he'll get extra Theo time. He smells all fresh and clean, his toothpaste and deodorant already making him fragrant, even if he hasn't gotten around to his aftershave yet. Emir buries his nose in the smell and sighs. Theo's always his favourite pillow.

"You're going to be tired all day. Why don't you sleep a little extra this morning? I can change your alarm to be like forty-five minutes later. Maybe just a shorter run this morning?" Theo carefully sets the picture aside and moves his phone out from beneath him, holding Emir on his chest where he clearly wants to be. While Emir resettles, he opens his alarm and does exactly that, adding a heart emoji to the notification at the same time.

"Can I have ten minutes of cuddles to help me go back to sleep?" Emir mumbles against Theo's warm skin, leaving a kiss above his heart. He's secretly hoping for fifteen, but he'll settle for ten. And Theo hasn't had time to put a shirt on yet. What a beautiful morning.

"Normally I would say no, but you earned them with the hand picture." Theo wraps his leg around Emir under the blankets, folding him into a full body hug. "I know I can't tell anyone about the picture, but it means a lot to me. Not only because you posted it. I understand that's a big step...Just that you wanted to draw something of the two of us together. It makes me happy."

"Good. I always want you happy. Now shhhhhhh." Emir's hand moves up to place a fingertip against Theo's lips before resettling next to his head. "Quiet in bed, please."

"I thought you liked it when I was loud." Theo smirks at Emir's immediate groan, his whole hand finding Theo's mouth to cover it this time before patting his cheek softly and falling back to his chest.

Emir mumble whispers against Theo's chest again, hiding those words he's not ready to say out loud. He does love Theo, so incredibly much. But if posting that picture was a step, saying those words is like jumping a flight of stairs. And he's glad Theo doesn't ask, hoping he assumes Emir's just grumbling about the noise.

But Theo knows. He's absolutely not going to push it, but he knows and he understands why it needs to stay a mumble for now. So he keeps quiet and holds Emir to his chest until he finally falls back to sleep, whispering those words himself into the crown of Emir's hair before finally getting up to leave for the morning.

The first thing he does when he gets to the studio is add *I Want To Hold Your Hand* by The Beatles to his special playlist. That playlist is the only thing he's listened to for weeks. The latest addition is extremely literal, but it'll always make him think of this morning, and of last night when he slept through Emir's moment of inspiration.

The lyrics keep him smiling through his warmups, *"It's such a feelin' that my love, I can't hide..."* and yeah. He thinks he knows what they were singing about all the way back in 1964. He couldn't hide his love for Emir even if he wanted to. Every day with him is a revelation. Even when he's tired or sore or frustrated or just in a bad mood, he can look at Emir or hold his hand or kiss his neck as he settles in to cuddle and it makes his world brighter.

Maybe that's what he meant that night when he told Emir they could invent the sunrise, not that they would blaze a trail, but that they would illuminate their path. A steady momentum to their days, a natural beauty to remind them to take this all one solemn kiss, one sweaty rehearsal, one hour of fun in the shower, one day at a time. Nothing's promised but they'll find their way by creating their own light.

CHAPTER SEVENTEEN

Safiya: Emir.
Safiya: Don't ignore your sister it's rude.
Safiya: Are you in class? You're probably in class.
Safiya: When you're done with class call me
Safiya: What's your schedule? Besides always in the studio
Safiya: Also I love you and if you don't answer soon Buddy says he's mad at you

"Buddy would never say that. I'm his favourite." Emir cuts his sister off before she can even start talking when the call connects.

"Not if you keep ignoring me. I called you three times already." Safiya huffs through the phone even though she knows that it's a Thursday and Emir's in the studio more than he's not. "Buddy knows when his Emi is too busy for him."

"I'll just have Theo email you my schedule. He even added the days I'm most likely to stay late in the studio and my bookclub times on the weekends. It's colour coded." Emir turns to see Theo leaving through the door of the dance building, catching his eye to give Emir one of his little waves. Theo has a free period so he's headed back to his flat for a while, but Emir has another class in twenty minutes so it's his only break to call Safiya like she asked. "Also, I just saw Buddy last weekend. Think you might've been there too."

"Very attentive, that boyfriend of yours." Safiya ignores his sarcasm, rolling her eyes while walking Buddy through the park. When the Shahs visited campus to say goodbye to Emir last Saturday morning, she'd brought Buddy along for a quick visit. Emir would never have forgiven her otherwise. Theo had been in Emir's flat when they stopped by so Theo got to meet Buddy too. "Buddy told me Theo's alright, so I guess you can keep him."

Emir smiles, wandering up the stairs that lead to the lounge so he can have a bit of privacy. They can't talk for long but he's positive that he knows why she called. "And what does Buddy's mum think of him?"

"Do you want my protective big sister answer or my sarcastic annoying answer?" Safiya didn't get a chance to talk to Emir alone after last weekend. He had three more shows after they visited, then went right into another week of class and everything else.

"Both. But since he and Buddy bonded, I don't think you get much of a say." Emir giggles when Safiya sighs through the phone. She knows he's kidding...probably.

"I think he's perfect for you, and if he hurts a single cell in your body, I will hunt him down and feed him to Buddy for tea." Safiya's voice is even and calm, no teasing or dramatic flair. She absolutely means that.

Emir knows she's serious, both about approving of Theo and of watching him closely. Safiya's been protective of Emir their whole lives, but after what happened with the last boyfriend, she's on high alert. Completely fair, given the circumstances.

"I really like him, Yaya." Emir flops onto the tired orange sofa in the lounge, the old cushions deflating beneath him. "Like...I know it's sort of fast and I'm young and all that but he's...kind. And he's brilliant. He makes me laugh and he wears my favourite colour and he's trying to learn Urdu so he can understand that side of me and I just...I want to keep him. Like maybe forever."

"And you drew a picture of you two and posted it?" Safiya asks, Emir well aware that this was what prompted the call. She and Saima are the most active on social media, so he knew she'd see it soon enough.

"Just our hands..." Emir shrugs as if she can see his pretend nonchalance. "I didn't tag him and there's nothing that identifies either of us."

"I know, Emi. I'm just surprised?" Safiya's voice raises at the end while she thinks, choosing her words carefully. "I'm really happy for you and Theo seems wonderful. I'm just worried. Not because of Theo, just at the idea of you loving someone again. I want you to be happy and I wish I could keep you safe because I didn't last time."

"I'm scared too." Emir admits, covering his eyes with his free hand. It's not as if she's saying anything he hasn't thought a thousand times himself. "But I'm also so fucking in love and I don't regret it for a single second. Last time wasn't like this. I didn't know him like I know Theo. *Everything's* so different this time. *I'm* so different."

"You are. You've...grown up." Safiya sighs through the phone again, and Emir's positive that she's kneeling down next to Buddy and pressing her face against his fur. He's seen her do it often enough. "I like Theo and if he's good to you...that's all I want, Emi. I hope he deserves you but I don't think anyone ever will."

"I used to think the same, but Mihir's alright." Emir smiles when she scoffs on the other side of the call. "I have to get to my next class in a few. You back to work after your walk?"

"How'd you know I was walking Buddy?" Safiya laughs through her question, Buddy already pulling her forward to the next interesting smelling tree.

"Sounds like you're being dragged around by a polar bear." Emir remembers how Theo first reacted seeing a picture of Buddy just after the wedding. It's sort of amazing that a few months later they've met and he even has a picture on his phone of Buddy giving Theo a full body hug on his sofa. "Love you, Yaya."

"Love you, Emi." Safiya promises to send a picture of Buddy on his walk before she hangs up.

Emir stays on the sofa for another minute, smiling to himself and staring at that picture of Buddy and Theo. He may as well have Theo's full name tattooed on his forehead to share with the world how entirely taken his heart is.

Emir: *we need a dog*
Theo: *Don't you have class in seven minutes?*
Emir: */picture of Theo and Buddy from last weekend/*
Emir: *teddy look*
Emir: *don't worry i'll be on time*
Theo: *I know. You're never late.*
Theo: *Neither of our flats allow dogs though, and moving in the middle of the year doesn't sound fun.*
Theo: *And we both like our flatmates.*
Theo: *And Lili and Jo live in my building and we like them too.*
Theo: *Secret dog? But they bark, so maybe not.*
Theo: *My parents have a dog. Maybe they could bring him when they come visit this weekend?*
Emir: *excuse me this sounds like you think i don't already know about bruce*
Emir: *don't ask them to bring bruce he can't watch alice and it seems mean to exclude him*
Theo: *Five minutes til class babe.*
Theo: *Can we wait to talk about dogs when I see you after?*
Emir: *that reminds me can i send that calendar you made to safiya?*
Theo: *Of course. I'll just...remove a few things.*
Emir: *should i be looking closer at this calendar... /side eye emoji/*

Theo: *Please go to class. I'm getting worried.*
Emir: */selfie with Lili in studio 2/*
Theo: *I'll make a duplicate without my special notes and send you a link to give to whoever you want. I'll send it while you're in class. Shouldn't take long.*
Emir: *thank you princess /kiss emoji/*
Theo: *I want a real kiss /sad emoji/*
Emir: *i'll make it up to you. promise*
Theo: */three orange heart emojis/*

***

"Hurry up hurry up hurry up hurry up." Theo is visibly vibrating, waiting for Emir to finish getting dressed after his post show shower. Tomorrow's their last *Alice* show, but tonight Theo gets to introduce Emir to his family. The anticipation is killing him.

"Don't think the restaurant will let me in without clothes, pumpkin." Emir pauses before buttoning his trousers to take Theo's hands in his own. He's never seen Theo this excited. "They already know we need time to get ready and the reservation isn't for twenty minutes."

"Eighteen. But I'm *really* excited." Theo lets Emir fold him into a hug but doesn't relax like he normally would. Between the show and the amount of energy they've been using the past two weeks he's not great at regulating his emotions right now. "I've never had a boyfriend before and you're my favourite person and only Barbara met you already and you thought we were on a date which was weird but then you were jealous and Barbara told me I should let myself like you – "

"What was that?" Emir pulls back from the hug with a smirk, finally buttoning and zipping his black trousers while waiting for Theo to explain. This is the first he's heard of it.

They're the last two left in the "men's" dressing room since Emir's the only one who *has* to shower before leaving after each show. The white face and body paint can't be removed with a cursory makeup remover wipe. Sam and Alfie got to chatting with Dan but even they left three minutes ago. Emir's been really glad to see Sam opening up to the others ever since their talk, and he's unsurprised that Alfie's extended a friendly hand to him, so to speak.

"Barbara told me you were jealous and pretty and I should give you a chance." Theo shrugs it off because that seems like a world away right now. "I was already going to, honestly, but she did help me realise I wasn't imagining that you liked me."

"I have a lot of questions, but I think I should finish getting ready before you drag me out of here half naked." Emir slides his arms through his shirt while kissing the side of Theo's mouth. "And I'm pretty sure we were the only two who didn't know this whole fucking time."

"God, you're pretty." Theo's staring now, hands reaching out to Emir, hoping for...he isn't even sure what. "If we're staying at yours tonight, does that mean we can have fun since Laurie will be at my flat? We'll have the place to ourselves."

"We still have a show tomorrow, so nothing new." Emir finishes buttoning the blush pink shirt and tucking it into his trousers, hoping that he looks smart enough for this restaurant they're going to. He knows Theo's family is a bit posh even if he doubts they would judge him for something as personal as his fashion. "But if you think I'm not going to kiss you silly before we fall asleep, you're *very* mistaken."

"Kiss me before we go upstairs? It'll be the last one for a few hours." Theo watches as Emir puts on his belt and ties his shoes, already gathering their phones, wallets, and keys so they can dash as soon as he's done. "Please."

Emir stands up, fully dressed and glowing with a fire in his eyes. He takes Theo by the hips and backs him up against the wall of the dressing room, Theo setting everything he just picked up aside so he can hold Emir instead. Emir leans in, hands keeping Theo still, smirking when Theo's breath catches. "Just one kiss then..."

They don't make it upstairs for another five minutes.

***

The restaurant is just beside the university, which meant they were able to walk over as a group and enjoy the busy Saturday night around them. Theo hugged Emir from behind while introducing him to his family, chin hooked over his shoulder as Emir shook hands with all of them, ending with Barbara. Theo's grandad hadn't been able to make this performance because his sister, Theo's great aunt, just had surgery, but he'll introduce Emir to him at the next one.

Theo held Emir's hand the entire walk over, smiling brighter than Emir has ever seen. Theo even started skipping at one point. Where he finds the energy after a two show day, Emir may never know.

Emir holds the door open for Theo when it's their turn to enter, and Theo pauses to give him a sweet kiss on the cheek before brushing past him to follow his family inside. He and his mum had chosen *Al Forno Putney* for several reasons, mostly because it's where they usually go after his family comes to watch him perform and he wanted to include Emir in the tradition.

"You take your time looking at the menu, Emir. We've all been here half a dozen times, but Theo said you haven't been here before. There's no rush." Caroline is sitting across from Emir at the table and Emir likes her already. She has the same kind eyes as Theo and there's just something about her that's genuine. All the Palmers seem really lovely.

"Teddy told me the mushroom pasta's his favourite, so I might have to give it a try." Emir glances at Theo's menu to see what he's deciding between, but it's already open to the desserts. "You know what you want, princess?"

Theo flushes that perfect pink that Emir adores before answering, "I think I'll get my usual, but I can't decide on dessert. Do you have a favourite?"

"I'll just share with you. I'll probably be pretty full after the pasta." Emir gives up and closes his menu, knowing he'll devour whatever he gets at this point. He really likes this place, warm and cosy and sort of homey feeling, and he can see why Theo likes it here.

No one talks much until after they place their order, but once that's taken care of they settle into their conversation. It's much quieter than it had been with the Shahs. Theo's sisters are both older and George seems like a rather quiet person in general, so Emir's not worried about needing a break or feeling like he's being too introverted. It's only been a few minutes, but he can see how he might fit in with them already.

"So, Emir," Jayna is seated across from Barbara at the other end of the table, but it's tight quarters and he can hear her just fine. "Have you always wanted to be a dancer?"

"Sort of, yeah." Emir gives her a smile, clearing his throat to keep talking. "I love books and animals, and I even thought about being a teacher, but dance is in me all the way to my core, right? I love a lot of things, but dance is just...who I am."

"You're very talented, but I'm sure people tell you that all the time." Caroline nods her head knowingly, as if Emir's talent is world renowned. "Theo sent us that *Firebird* video last year and you were just wonderful. And of course, you both were darling in *Alice*."

"How did the ears stay on so well?" George asks, giving Emir that same intense stare that Theo has when he's curious about something. "You were spinning around like anything but they never did more than wobble."

"Oh well they're not very heavy. Just thin fabric over a wire and braided into my hair. T would know more, to be honest." Emir glances at Theo and sees that he's still smiling so wide, looking at him with those puppy dog eyes. He can tell Theo wishes they were cuddling right now. It's a specific body posture he gets when they're around other people and he can't help but lean into Emir subconsciously. God, Emir really loves him.

Leaning in to match him, Emir whispers, "You can hold my hand if you like."

Before he shifts back to sitting upright, Theo's fingers find his beneath the table and bring Emir's hand into his lap. Theo sighs in contentment and gets lost in Emir's eyes for a moment, the warm light of the restaurant giving them that amber glow he fell in love with. He's been so excited for this night for so long, and Emir is fitting right in with his family just like he hoped.

"Barbara," Emir gives Theo's hand a squeeze before teasing him, "Theo said that when you were visiting you may have given him some...encouragement in my direction. Which – I need to thank you if that's true."

"Please." Barbara literally waves him off before taking a sip of her wine and glancing at her sister. "Jayna and I have been hearing about you for years. I know you two didn't used to get along, but once I saw you together it was *painfully* apparent."

"Give me a little credit." Theo interjects, turning to face his sisters. "You know I can't just...that it's not easy for me to...I just needed a little time."

"They're only teasing, Theo. Barbara's very happy for you." Caroline gives her daughters her sternest mum look. "She and Jayna both told me how excited they are. Emir, we're very happy to officially meet you."

Emir rubs his thumb along Theo's knuckles, letting his free hand rest on the table while answering. "It's a big deal, getting to meet you all this weekend. Theo talks about you constantly and I know how important you are to him. He met my family last Friday, and they *adored* him, but I'm sure that's no surprise to you."

"What did they say?" Theo asks, but Emir ignores his question with another squeeze to his hand. For another time, when they're in private.

"I...I want you to know that I care about Theo and I'm hoping to be in his life for a very long time, if he'll have me." Emir feels Theo heating up beside him. He doesn't need to see him flushing to know it's happening. "Getting to meet you all is wonderful. You've helped make Theo into the kindest, most honest man I've ever known. Thank you for letting me join your family dinner. I know how precious these get-togethers can be and I don't take it for granted."

It's silent for a moment before Jayna breaks the quiet. "Hell, Teddy. You didn't tell me he was so eloquent."

"Pretty sure I did. I have an itemised list of all my favourite things about Emir, and his beautiful words are definitely on there." Theo is trying very hard not to grab Emir and rush him away somewhere they can be alone, because that wasn't just a lovely thing for him to say, it was incredibly brave. Theo doesn't think he could be so vulnerable like that in the same situation, and knowing Emir's past, it means even more.

"I never did understand what you two were always fighting about." Caroline sets her chin in her palm and smiles at them. "Not that Theo really complained much but I knew you weren't friends before this year. I'm sure you were never like those horrible kids growing up or we wouldn't be here now."

"What do you mean?" Emir tilts his head, looking between Caroline and Theo, confused.

He's not heard much about Theo's childhood outside of the cute family memories he's shared occasionally, so he assumed it was fairly standard. There was that incident with Theo studying pointe, but he loved the new studio he ended up with and he didn't mention any issues once he got there.

"You know what it was like for him at school. The bullying and harassment and all that." George is the one who answers, surprisingly. His eyebrows are scrunched together in annoyance at the memory, and Emir can tell that the Palmers haven't moved on from whatever it is they're talking about. They are also clearly under the impression Emir knows all about it.

"Kids can be horrible but they have to learn it somewhere." Jayna crosses her arms over her chest, expression matching her dad's. "My kids will *never* act that way."

"Little Ron's already dealing with it and he's only four. He's the same build Theo was. Lots of baby fat, especially in his cheeks. They still use all the same names for things they don't understand." Barbara is the definition of *if looks could kill* right now while talking about how her kid's been treated. "It used to make me mad as your big sister, and it's a hundred times worse as a mum."

"Heard a kid use the F-slur the other day when I was picking the boys up." Jayna adds with disgust. "I thought maybe that'd calmed down since we were in school but he was only about six. I wish I knew who the parents were."

"It wasn't, um..." Theo's starting to not like this conversation. He's intentionally not shared this with Emir because what would be the point? He grew up and he grew out of the bullying and started new at University. Sure, some people are still homophobic, and the bullying was worse because of his obvious neurodivergence, but he'd lost the baby fat a few years back (not that it was ever alright that he was bullied for it) and now all his friends are queer.

But most relevant to the current conversation: his mum is right. Even when he and Emir were arguing it was never like that. "It's better now than it was, I think. And it was worse for me because of ballet, so maybe it's not as bad for other kids. Not that it's ever acceptable, but..."

Emir hasn't said anything since this conversation started, but he feels absolutely sick. He had *no idea* that Theo was bullied growing up, and from the way they're talking about it, it was bad. Like, *still worth talking about as an adult* bad. He's only seen one picture of Theo as a kid and he was adorable, his eyes warm and intelligent just like they are now, his cheeks perfectly squishy while he smiled at the camera with a plush dinosaur in his hands.

But now Emir knows that Theo came to Roseborough hoping to put that all behind him, only for Emir to be mean to him from the very start. He's a monster, and Theo never deserved any of the way he's been treated.

"I don't care the reason, there's no excuse for what happened to you, Theo." George readjusts in his seat, giving his son a gentle look. "Those kids were homophobic and bigoted and violent and I'm still upset that the school never stepped in. It was appalling."

Emir flinches because did George just say violent? He feels himself flushing with anger at the possibilities that unfortunately opens. Who hurt Theo and how dare they? Theo's the gentlest, kindest person he's ever known, which is even more remarkable if he was put through that sort of pain.

"Could we maybe, um, talk about something else?" Theo shrugs and runs his hand through his hair, shoulders caving in like Emir's recognised as a sign of his discomfort.

"My fault, Teddy, of course we can." Caroline reaches across with her hand out, waiting for Theo to take it in his right. "So sorry. We're here to celebrate your performance and to get to know Emir."

"Do you know what Lilibet plans to do after uni?" Jayna asks, and Theo is relieved at the subject change. Jayna's always been good at recognising when he needs a distraction.

"She wants to stay in London like us. Lili's finishing the year and hoping to land with a company contract." Theo sits back and leans into Emir, keeping their joined hands in his lap. Emir feels stiffer than usual, not melting into Theo like he's grown so used to. "She's been exceptional as Alice, and I'm sure her dissertation is going to be stunning."

Before they can talk further, the waiter comes back to the table with their shared appetisers and Emir jumps at the opportunity for a break. He feels trapped, desperate for a moment alone to process before he can keep talking. Honestly, he's worried he's done for the night, but that's unfair to Theo and to the Palmers who've done absolutely nothing wrong. Emir's the problem.

"I'll just...bathroom." Emir mumbles, standing up and pressing a kiss to Theo's temple but not meeting his eye as he practically runs away. He has no fucking clue where the loo is, but he knows how to get outside, so he tries to move as quietly and discreetly as possible to get to the front door and back into the night. He's not running away, he just needs a minute or ten. That was a lot of complicated information all at once, and they all made it sound like he should've known, which...maybe he should have.

Theo watches him go, confusion and hurt swirling together in his heart. Emir's never run away from him like this before. He knows Emir well enough by now to recognise when he needs a break, so he doesn't want to just chase after him. Usually he tells Theo that he needs quiet or alone time, but this time he just...left.

But Theo's genuinely worried and nervous, because maybe Emir heard them all talking about the way he was treated in school and realised that Theo's too much. A lot of baggage that he doesn't want. Too complicated and too insecure to bother with. Theo knows he isn't exactly easy to be with, between his daily schedules and his sensory differences and his sexual inexperience, but Emir didn't even say if he was coming back this time...he could walk back the way they came and go home. Theo knows he won't be checking his phone if he did.

"He probably just needs a minute." Caroline gets Theo's attention with a gentle hand on his wrist. The others are talking amongst themselves, having bought Emir's excuse of a trip to the bathroom, but Caroline's sitting across from them and she sees the truth in Theo's face plain enough.

"I'll...I'll go look for him in a few minutes." Theo stares at the empty space beside himself, flexing his fingers which were intertwined with Emir's only a minute ago. He feels guilty, like Emir's been ambushed by a new revelation that he probably feels Theo should've told him a long time ago. And it's not the only information that Theo's been keeping private.

"It can be hard to hear sometimes." Caroline tries to get Theo's focus again, knowing that he's upset but doing his best to give Emir space. Theo always respects a boundary, but she can tell that all he wants is to go check on his partner. It's always been his instinct to take care of the ones he loves, and she can clearly see that includes Emir now. "When someone loves you, it's not easy to know that you were hurt."

Theo glances at his mum, finally, eyes wide and frowning. "Maybe it was too much. Maybe he thinks – "

"Let's give him a minute." Caroline repeats, reaching instead for the caprese and putting it between his and Emir's plates for them to share. "Tell me about the show. Only one left tomorrow and then you're done with that role. How'd you like it?"

Theo tries his best to make small talk with his mum and the others, talking about *Alice* and how Gabe and Ciaran are coming to tomorrow's show, telling them about how Laurie checks in with them before each curtain, just because he can. But Theo keeps checking his watch and after five minutes he can't take it anymore. His family tells him to hurry back as he leaves the same way as Emir, carefully manoeuvring through the tables and chairs to the front entrance and praying to a god he doesn't even believe in that Emir is somehow still just on the other side of the door.

He glances around in a panic, heart falling until - "Emir!"

Theo finds him at the end of the building, holding onto himself in the cold because he left his jacket inside. He runs to Emir, wrapping him up in his arms, alarmed to feel him shaking. "I thought you left!"

"I'm sorry, Theo. I'm so, so, unbelievably sorry." Emir hides his face against Theo's chest and holds him close, crying and shaking from the cold. "I owe you a thousand apologies and I'm the one crying. Fuck, just give me a second."

Emir sniffles and wipes at his eyes, trying to get himself under control. His emotions are not the priority right now. He has to make this right.

"Thank you for not leaving." Theo keeps holding him in a hug, not sure what Emir thinks he needs to apologise for, but he's so relieved to see him still here that he doesn't think about it too hard. He doesn't even need Emir to talk right now. It's enough just to know he didn't leave.

"Why are you even friends with me? After the way that I treated you?" Emir steps away from Theo and rubs at his eyes with the palms of his hands. "I was *horrible* to you. You never did anything to deserve it. I just didn't know how to be a person and I made it your problem. God, what the hell is *wrong* with me?"

"But...we're not friends?" Theo doesn't understand what Emir's talking about. "We're boyfriends and dance partners, and I guess we're friends too, but like...I'm confused, Emi."

He takes a step towards Emir again, glad when he doesn't step back, but he keeps his hands to himself for now. "We were both rude to each other until this year. I wasn't nice to you either."

"But baby you – " Emir catches a sob in his throat and pauses to calm down again. He takes a deep breath and wipes his hands down his face, trying to reset. "People hurt you. Your dad said they were *violent*. And then you came here and I was *awful* to you. How were you not terrified of me? I was just like all those bigots who did – I don't even know what – to you and you've never once called me out for what I put you through. I can't believe you even talk to me."

"No, Emir, that's not what happened." Theo thinks Emir's rather misunderstood the situation. It's not even comparable. "I should've told you about it so you wouldn't find out like this, but you were *never* like them. Even during our worst fights I was never scared of you. Annoyed and frustrated, but never scared. And you and I were just unpleasant. Neither of us ever crossed a line. What those kids did..."

Emir sees a flicker of something cross Theo's face, and he has Theo in his arms before he even processes the fear taking over Theo's eyes at the memories.

"I am so incredibly sorry for every single way I hurt you. I can't even explain how much I care about you and how ashamed I am for how I acted all that time." Emir's no longer crying, both because it's better talking about it instead of shivering in the cold, and because he sees that Theo needs him now and that absolutely takes priority over his own guilt.

"It was really bad, Emi – Not you, I mean, like, as a kid." Theo admits, mumbling his words against Emir's shoulder. The hug helps. "When I was little, they made fun of me for being the fat, weird kid who didn't understand their jokes and made odd noises, and when I got older and they found out I was queer they – "

Theo pauses before finishing the memory. "It wasn't just the slurs and the harassment. They would toss me around at school, and I didn't have any friends so they never got caught, even when I got hurt. And they would, like, break my stuff just because they could, and one time they stole my dance bag and they all took a piss in it before giving it back. Things like that."

Emir doesn't really have any words for what he's hearing, the specifics at least as bad as he'd been imagining the last few minutes since he found out about this part of Theo's past. So he just holds Theo tight and kisses the top of his head while they stand in the cold together.

Theo feels more vulnerable than he expected, the relief of finding Emir still out here waiting for him having worn off, replaced by an old pain. He meant what he said about it never being anything like that when he and Emir were fighting, and he really didn't need an apology from Emir. They went through that weeks ago after the fight at the party. What he needs is to know that Emir learning this part of his life isn't going to make him leave.

"I didn't like that you ran away like that." Theo says, arms holding tight to Emir's back and sighing. He always feels better when he's honest. "Not because you needed space, I understand that. I just thought you left and you weren't coming back and it hurt. I thought I was...too much."

"Baby, no. Absolutely not." Emir keeps rubbing Theo's back then starts trailing his fingers through his hair, both hands busy comforting his beautiful partner. Theo hums and turns his face to hide in Emir's neck. "I wasn't running away from you, I just needed a few minutes. I was always going to come back inside, but I'm sorry I made you think I left. You and your family are perfect."

"You always tell me you're coming back, and I know you don't owe me that, but it scared me." Theo's voice is getting even quieter. "If you need to go home, I'll go with you. I can walk you and then come back. It's not that far."

"Shhhhh, shehzadi, I'm not going anywhere." Emir coos, soothing Theo until he feels relaxed again. He sways them together in the still night air, and after a minute, Theo is closer to seeming like his usual angel boyfriend. "We'll go home together later, but for now, your lovely family is waiting inside for us, probably thinking we snuck away to be naughty."

"Mum knows." Theo shifts and Emir kisses his forehead between his eyebrows, holding his face between his hands. "She knows me too well. She knew that I was nervous you left."

"Either way, we probably shouldn't keep them waiting. Also it's freezing." Emir gives Theo a dulcet smile, staring into his eyes and brushing his thumb along his cheek. "Kiss me?"

Theo grins back, meeting Emir in a simple kiss then pressing their foreheads together. Sharing space with Emir has felt progressively more like home with each day they've been dating. "You're really cold, Emi."

"That's on me for running outside without my jacket." Emir tickles Theo under his chin, tugging Theo into his side to walk back towards the restaurant's front door again. "After you, princess."

***

"Teddy, go walk with your dad." Caroline nudges Theo away from his boyfriend and loops her arm through Emir's elbow to walk with him instead. "Give me a moment to get on Emir's good side before we leave you two back at Roseborough."

"Be nice to him." Theo hesitates before walking over to join George, staring between Emir's very amused expression and his mum's teasing smile. "And no embarrassing stories."

"Well now I need to hear all the embarrassing stories." Emir giggles, walking along next to Caroline as casually as he can. He's not nervous because the night's gone well, besides the temporary detour to cry town. Emir hopes Caroline doesn't think he needs some sort of lecture about taking care of her son and treating him well and all the rest. He fully intends to do all of that and so much more.

"You know how he loves *Batman*?" Caroline squeezes Emir's elbow and grins, waiting for him to nod in agreement. "When he was three, he looped one of Barbara's skirts around his neck as a cape and pulled a black beanie down over his eyes, then jumped off all the furniture in the house to test out his superpowers. I still have a video of it somewhere."

"Did he get hurt?" Emir is smiling like the sun, looking over at Theo where he's walking with his dad and picturing a tiny version of him hopping around in his homemade outfit. It's easy to picture, even with Theo all grown up.

"No, he was always a good jumper. Still is. That's why we got him started in dance lessons." Caroline laughs with Emir, thinking back on those early years with such fond memories. "Before *Batman* was the love of dinosaurs, but that one never really went away."

"Theo showed me a picture from when he was about five and he had a little triceratops. It was the cutest thing I've ever seen." Emir leans into Caroline for a moment as he laughs, whispering, "Don't tell him, but I'm already working on his Christmas present and it involves *Batman*. If I have time I could do something with a dinosaur, too. Does he have a favourite?"

"Usually the triceratops, but he always liked the pterosaurs too because they could fly." Caroline sighs, looking over at the rest of her family where they're walking ahead of the two of them. "Was Theo wearing a red shirt in the picture he showed you?"

"He was, yeah." Emir has to think for a moment, but he's pretty sure. "He was cheesing at the camera and holding the dino like he was showing it off. It looked brand new. And Theo looked really happy."

"That was the day we found out he's on the spectrum." Caroline readjusts her glasses and gives Emir's elbow another squeeze. "We gave him the dinosaur for being such a good kid at the doctor's office. That was his favourite shirt that year. He told us he wore it because it made him brave. Theo didn't like the doctor much as a kid, but I suppose most kids don't."

Emir very intentionally does not react to Caroline's words because she just dropped that information like he already knew. Does he already know that? He's wondered, sure, but he hasn't had Theo's neurodivergence confirmed. Theo's not mentioned it that he remembers, and Emir's pretty sure he would remember that conversation.

"That must have been a memorable day." Emir adds, keeping his voice even.

He can't think of anything she could possibly have meant besides telling him (inadvertently) that Theo's autistic. There's many spectrums in the world, but given the context of Theo's age at the time and the conversation they're having about things that Theo's loved since he was young...

But Emir's not surprised. It's not as if it's a bad thing, and it actually explains quite a lot. Theo's still the remarkable man that Emir's fallen in love with, and now he knows another thing about him. Emir wishes he would've learned it from Theo himself, but he's sure Theo has reasons for not sharing that information with him, at least not yet.

In the ten seconds since having confirmation, Emir realises he doesn't actually need to process this hardly at all. He loves Theo. Theo's autistic. He also laughs like music and hugs like a teddy bear and smiles like sunshine and gets cuddly when he's tired. He loves sweets and dancing in the rain and spending time with his friends and learning about everything he can. He's Theo, and the more Emir knows him, the more he loves him.

So even if Emir's mind is spinning, he's not about to rush over to Theo and ask him about it. Theo will tell him if and when he chooses to. It's obvious Caroline thought Emir already knew, and he's not going to make her feel guilty for talking about an important memory with her son. It's very clear that Theo's entire family loves him to his core.

"It *was* a memorable day, but only because of what came after." Caroline glances at Emir and sees him watching Theo with the purest, sweetest gaze. It seems Emir truly loves her son, and he's not very shy about it. "They set us up with parent support groups and that sort of thing, but Theo was still our sweet, sensitive boy. Sometimes those groups scared us more than they helped. So much misinformation was going around back then and it felt like everyone told us that Theo could never have friends or find love or live a full life. Always talking about that dangerous anti-vaccination rubbish and making it sound like we hurt our son, or that we should be trying to 'fix' him. I'm glad we stopped going to those groups after only about a year."

"That sounds really scary, for you and for Theo." Emir meets Caroline's eyes and gives her what he hopes is an understanding smile. "I can't imagine Theo any other way than exactly how he is. You know how much our friends rely on him. He's like the glue that holds the world together some days. I'm sorry people told you that he could never have that."

"I always had faith. I know every situation is different, but I was never worried about Theo. He had a hard time at school, but not because of who he is. It was the other kids who were the problem. And sometimes the teachers, unfortunately." Caroline pauses and gives Emir a knowing smile. "But I didn't even have to wait very long for him to fall in love."

Emir flushes and looks at his feet for a moment, taking a moment to himself before he can answer. "Does that mean I pass the test?"

"Flying colours." Caroline can see how Emir feels plainly enough, and Theo's been open with her about his own feelings during their weekly phone calls. Since Emir's close friends with Laurie and T, she knew even before meeting him that he must have a good heart. "Did Theo show you pictures from the last time he was in an *Alice* production?"

"He absolutely did not!" Emir looks back up at Caroline, giddy excitement making him glow in the early winter night. "He mentioned he was in *Alice* when he was about ten, but I didn't know there was evidence."

Caroline takes her phone out of her pocket, disconnecting from Emir so she can scroll through her photos. "Here. I made sure to look them up before we all came this weekend so we could reminisce."

"He was a Playing Card, *of course*. Impressive as a ten year old, but I'm sure he was ahead of his years." Emir asks for permission before swiping to the next pictures, gasping when he does. "He was The Caterpillar?!"

"I helped make the costume myself." Caroline zooms in on Theo's little face in the caterpillar head piece. "The tail was full of old stockings so it wouldn't be weighted down, and Theo helped me paint it all blue. There's a couple videos too, if you keep going."

"This is incredible. Can you send these to me?" Emir keeps switching between the pictures, adoring every second of Theo as a squishy, dancing caterpillar. His dance technique was incredible for a ten year old, and in the videos he's clearly younger than all the other dancers. Advanced for his age, just like Emir had guessed.

"Go ahead and text them to yourself. I don't mind." Caroline watches as Theo walks over to them, George following close behind. "But hurry before Theo stops you."

"You two look like you're way too excited about something." Theo falls in step beside Emir, George finding his spot on Caroline's other side. Jayna and Barbara are still twenty feet ahead, cackling about who knows what.

"Your mum has pictures from when you were The Caterpillar." Emir is still waiting for the pictures to send, the service not exactly exceptional in this spot. "You were so *tiny*, princess."

"Mum!" Theo flushes, trying to grab the phone from Emir's hand, but he's too slow. What are the chances Emir hasn't seen the video of him shaking his caterpillar bum yet?

"Too late, I already memorised them all." Emir starts dancing out of Theo's grasp, phone held high while Theo keeps trying to reach it. "And she said I could have them, so I sent them to my phone."

"They're embarrassing!" Theo's fully chasing Emir now, the two of them sprinting in circles, Emir laughing so hard he can barely breathe and Theo wishing Emir wasn't so bloody fast. Those morning runs are clearly paying off.

"Caroline, catch!" Emir flies past her, dropping the phone in her hand while Theo closes the distance. "And thanks."

She tucks it away into her purse, George chuckling beside her. He's never seen his kid so happy.

Theo finally catches Emir, picking him up from behind and spinning him around while Emir squeaks and tries to get free. "You can't show those to Laurie. He'll never let me live it down."

"They're getting framed and put on my wall." Emir reaches around until he finds Theo's tickle spot in retaliation. It's an impressive feat while dangling in the air.

"Emir!" Theo drops him harder than he'd like, but still gentler than anyone else could manage in his circumstance. He's squirming and trying to catch Emir's hands, but failing spectacularly. "I'm - I can't - "

Barbara's been surreptitiously filming their...whatever this is on her mobile. When Caroline and George catch up to them, with Theo and Emir mostly just tickle-wrestling nearby at this point, Barbara grins and says, "I am *definitely* showing this at their wedding."

CHAPTER EIGHTEEN

Theo's backstage watching Emir's Act One solo for the final *Alice* show and he's struck by the moment, by watching Emir perform, seeing him inhabit this character and fly around the stage like it was crafted just for him. How did he possibly become so used to working with and being with Emir that he let himself get complacent in his appreciation for his gift, for the talent he works so diligently to explore and expand?

Emir's feet are swirling around themselves, hopping and gliding while he moves counterintuitive to his body's direction, en manege but reverse of the way he would've trained his whole life, all while looking graceful and poised. Theo's thought this before, that Emir moves in a way that seems like the music is following him or created by his presence, and it's mesmerising. Of course Theo recognises his boyfriend, but he wears the character and not the other way around. Emir's absolutely stunning.

There's no reality where the audience can appreciate what they're watching unless they themselves are trained dancers. They won't notice the minute details of immaculate rotation and silent landings after every single jump. They won't see the way Emir regulates his breathing to be in rhythm with the music. Emir works harder than any dancer Theo's ever known, but watching him, it looks beyond effortless. It's as if Emir was born with this choreography in his body and he was just waiting for his chance to share it.

But his solo ends after only a minute, the ballet moving on from one part to the next with Emir and Lili in every scene in some capacity, Theo watching from the wings whenever he isn't under the lights. Theo loves every beautiful second of it. He loves performing and he loves dance and he loves telling a story with his body. But he's never been one of those performers who can "get lost in it". He's more present when dancing than any other time, fully focused and in alignment between his body and mind. If other people get lost, he finds himself instead.

With intermission comes Theo's first chance to pull Emir aside. It's a sharp fifteen, and Theo has to change. Even Emir has to change his waistcoat, but they have a minute for Theo to pull Emir back to the furthest upstage wing, hands warm on Emir's forearms.

"What's wrong?" Emir tilts his head, rabbit ears wiggling before settling again. Theo usually races him down the stairs at intermission, which Sean has gently scolded them for more than once. But not today it seems.

"Nothing's wrong, I just…" Theo glances around to make sure they're mostly alone. T is fussing with a costume about ten feet away but they won't mind. Theo darts forward to give Emir the quickest kiss known to humankind, surprising Emir into a smile before his posture softens to gaze back at Theo.

"We have a minute, baby. What's going on?" Emir takes Theo's hands instead, giving them a gentle squeeze. It seems something's on Theo's mind, and Emir can make time. What are they going to do, start up again without two of their leads?

"You're my favourite dancer." Theo says it with the seriousness one would usually reserve for a funeral, or maybe a court appearance. Something requiring an oath before god. Maybe Emir calling him the sky wasn't hyperbole.

"You've already told me you think I'm talented, princess. What's – ?" Emir can't finish his clarification before Theo firmly shakes his head, so Emir pauses to let him talk.

"No, you're my *favourite* dancer. *My favourite dancer.* Do you understand?" Theo is still holding Emir's gaze like this is the most important conversation they've ever had. "I don't care about the Royal Ballet or Trockadero or ABT or Rambert or anyone else. You're it. My absolute favourite. You have more technique than half the professionals and you have qualities that can't be taught. You're graceful and instinctive and nuanced. You dance like it's your purpose on earth and somehow it seems humble, like I can feel your work ethic without seeing the strain of it. People tell you that you can fly, but that's not what it is. You're part of the air and the lights and the floor *intrinsically*, because you take the time to be quiet in the world and learn its truths. You're not just dancing. It's not just choreography. You're painting your soul for everyone to see, and I can't believe I haven't stopped to tell you before. Am I making sense?"

Emir thinks he left his body halfway through the words *you're it*, Theo's earnestness like glue to his feet, keeping him enthralled and connected to the moment. He knows he's staring, that he's searching Theo's eyes and his lips and looking for the sarcasm or the dramatics to start, but they never come, because that wouldn't be Theo.

"Shit, I'm sorry. That was too much." Theo drops Emir's hands and starts scratching at his own arms, suddenly very nervous. Emir hasn't moved since he started talking and he looks scared. His eyes are wide and his mouth is open and *why isn't he saying anything?* "Forget it, I was just trying to explain how much I admire you, like, separate from us dating or working together or anything else, because you're a really incredible person and I don't want to take you for granted, so I figured I should tell you, right?

You should know how unique you are because you're the only person I'll ever know who can dance like this and I genuinely look up to you as an artist, but maybe that's too much pressure or - "

The spell breaks for Emir when he hears the panic in Theo's voice. He has nothing to apologise for. He's standing here, being an absolute miracle of a person, opening his heart and being vulnerable yet again. Emir takes Theo's face in both of his hands and just holds it for a moment, Theo finally stopping his ramble as Emir's thumbs brush across his cheeks.

Bringing Theo's lips down to his own, Emir meets him in a kiss, closing his eyes and trying to share the depth of the moment. He keeps his hands on Theo's face, cradling him while they kiss, Theo's arms trailing to Emir's lower back to hold him close. Who cares that they're backstage and they don't usually kiss in public and they're a few minutes into intermission now?

Theo lets Emir move him as he slides his hands around Theo's shoulders like in a movie, rubbing their noses together when they need a breath before colliding again. They're in harmony, and not just physically. Emir never would've expected Theo to say something so important to the core of his identity, yet here he is, beautifully open and trusting and honest. Only another artist, and specifically another dancer, could appreciate the true depth of that compliment. That Emir's his *favourite* dancer when there's literally thousands to choose from? Theo understands the hard work and the long nights and the injuries and the way that no one else ever comprehends the incredible commitment of a lifetime that was made when he chose his path.

There's a clunk from the direction of the door that leads to the stairs and they break their kiss to glance over, Laurie looking apologetic while holding a croquet mallet. He has to spend intermission helping the stage crew set props for the rest of the show, but since Emir and Theo are normally in the dressing room at this point they didn't expect to see him until after the final curtain.

"Shit, sorry. Back to your necking." Laurie picks up the prop and covers his eyes for some ridiculous reason. "Not that we can see you or anything."

At least it's only T and Laurie on this side of the stage, so Theo's only mildly embarrassed. Emir couldn't care less who sees them right now, which is new, but not unwelcome.

"Theo, you have Emir paint on your nose." T is helping Laurie, which is very much not their job, but they aren't needed until the next quick change two scenes after the show restarts. They point at Theo's face, then at their own nose, laughing and turning to hide their smile against Laurie's shoulder. "But we weren't watching."

Theo sighs, wiping at the tip of his nose but smiling bright. Emir taps under his chin and gives him another peck of a kiss, rubbing his painted nose against Theo's again just to make him giggle.

"Can you help me clean it off before we're back on stage?" Theo grabs Emir's hand and holds it against his own cheek again. He likes when Emir does that, running his fingers down Theo's face like he's memorising his features to recreate them in his art. It makes him feel cherished, like Emir finds meaning in his dimple and peace in his eyes.

"Of course I will. You're my princess." Emir thumbs across his cheekbone once more before letting his hand drop to find Theo's fingers instead. He walks them over to the stairs, stopping to say, "You two can have the flat all next weekend if you give us an extra five before curtain."

"Done." T and Laurie respond at the same time, Laurie with a smirk, T with wide-eyed anticipation.

Emir tugs Theo to race him down the stairs, only a few minutes behind schedule. They still have half of a show to do, so they rush through their usual intermission steps, changing clothes and fixing makeup and chatting with the other dancers. But Emir knows that tonight, when they're alone, things will be different. Every day with Theo has been a new level of love, an added layer of companionship and comfort for both of them as they settle into their relationship. They have plans with their friends after the show, but after that he gets quiet time with Theo. He hopes to cuddle and kiss and love this beautiful angel for the rest of his days. Especially tonight.

***

Theo: *Don't leave yet! I want to catch you before you and Jordan head home.*
Lili: *We're going out buttercup, but we can wait a few*
Theo: *Meet me in the hall while Emir finishes showering and all the rest?*
Lili: *Two minutes. Jo's busy with Esme. Apparently someone has a crush /side eye emoji/*
Theo: *ESMERELDA HAS A CRUSH TELL ME EVERYTHING*

"I need the tea and I need it now." Theo rushes up to Lili in the hallway, grabbing her by the shoulders while she holds tight to his forearms. Before she answers, they shuffle off to the side to let everyone else move around the hallway as needed. It's always a bit of a mad rush after the last show with everyone hurrying off to whatever celebration they have planned.

"You first. You said you needed something." Lili knows that Theo's very tired, and when he is, it's harder for him to concentrate. They're all exhausted, honestly. Thankfully the dance programme cancels all classes the Monday after their last performance each season so they can get some much needed rest.

"Oh, that." Theo moves his hands from Lili's shoulders and leans against the wall, waiting for her to do the same. "I just realised I hadn't properly congratulated you on *Alice*. You did exceptionally well and I'm so grateful to be your dance partner every time the casting works out that way. Oh! And that periwinkle dress is a stunning colour on you. Jordan agrees. I asked her. So maybe we should find you another leo in that colour or even a hoodie or something. Not tomorrow though. I'll be sleeping in."

"So you'll be awake by eight?" Lili pokes him in the cheek, making him scrunch his nose and bat her hand away.

"I'm serious!" Theo pulls her into a hug and sways them on the spot. She's so much shorter than him that her head is level with his sternum. "We only have two shows left together in February and May to share the stage. I don't know that we'll ever get to partner again, even with those. And I'm sad about it because you're my best mate and I'm going to miss you so fucking much next year."

"Oi, none of this." Lili sniffles and wipes at her eyes, holding onto Theo with a vice grip. "It's not even December yet. You're not allowed to make me cry about leaving. I love you too fucking much to even think about that right now."

Now Theo's starting to tear up as well, holding on just as tight and burying his face in her hair. "You're like my sister, Lili, and I don't know what I'm going to do when you're not a stairwell away. I don't even know if we'll be in the same city next year."

"Shut up and hug me, Teddy." Lili keeps holding Theo tight until Jordan finds them, crying and mumbling about their favourite memories the past few years like this is goodbye. Ridiculous honestly, because like Lilibet said, it's only November.

"Whose fault are the tears?" Jordan sighs, arms across her chest while looking at the pair of them. "We're meant to be celebrating."

"Theo said we might not ever dance together again and now I'm depressed." Lili wipes at her eyes and throws herself into Jordan's arms instead, tugging Theo to join them in a group hug. "What am I supposed to do without Theo on the weekends? Or when I need a patient person to explain things to me? Or a Teddy hug? Theo, I need your hugs."

"You two are ridiculous." Jordan mumbles, but then she starts getting choked up as well. She's uncertain about her own future, maybe even more than the other two, and she tries not to think about it too much. "I come over here to share gossip about the first years and I find you crying over something that may not even happen. Chances are we'll all be sharing a tiny flat in Soho this time next year and then I can remind you about this."

"Share the gossip and maybe we'll stop crying." Theo suggests, clearing his throat, but he doesn't step away from the hug right away. Lili said she needs Theo hugs, and Theo hugs she will get. But maybe later. Jordan's right: it's gossip time.

"Right, so apparently Esme has it bad for one of the first year boys. And she wanted advice because obviously." Jordan gestures vaguely at herself and flips her hair, Lili rolling her eyes and crossing her arms, leaning back against the wall next to Theo.

"I won't state the obvious, but know I'm thinking it." Lili gives Jordan the least subtle head-to-toe scan possible, because the irony of the most lesbian person she knows giving boy advice is almost too much. Especially when it's her girlfriend. "Continue."

"Well, I thought I knew who it was, but she still wouldn't actually say until I told her that my advice wouldn't be specific enough without knowing who she fancies, right?" Jordan's eyes are shining with excitement. She loves playing matchmaker, especially now that she's so happy in her own love life.

"Please tell me it's Sam." Theo nudges Lili, both of them having noticed Sam's subtle interest in Esmerelda growing over the past few weeks. Shows always heighten emotions, and the number of new couples after each production is statistically notable. Emir may be the one closest to Sam in their group, but they all look at the first years with a nostalgic fondness.

"Oh, it's definitely Sam." Jordan leans in and lowers her voice. "And Esme said all the first years are going out together tonight, and she isn't sure that he likes her. So I said she needed to find somewhere quiet for the two of them to talk, alone but not, like. cornering him, right? Because he's shy. And she said she already knows they both love those home renovation shows, so if she's getting good vibes, she's going to ask for Sam's number to invite him over for a night of telly next week. Good, right?"

"Oh my god, they would be so cute together." Theo glances around to make sure they're still far enough away from everyone else. "But how do we know if it worked?"

"Esme's going to text me before their date to make sure she keeps it casual enough. Low pressure but cute, and I'll help her pick her outfit." Jordan looks at her nails with a smirk. "Seems the first years think I'm the go-to for boy advice."

"Are we allowed to comment on the irony of that?" Theo laughs while Lili swats him gently on the shoulder. "What?"

"Jordan's the straightest, most heterosexual woman I've ever met." Lili scoffs and does her best to hide her smile. "Obsessed with cock."

"Only if it's silicone, pink, and strapped to you." Jordan mumbles, all three of them finally cracking and laughing so hard their stomachs hurt.

"Oi, are you stealing my boy?" Emir's annoyed voice floats over from the door to the men's dressing room, but he's smiling wide. Whatever they're laughing about, he loves to see Theo happy. "He's taken."

"Eugh." Lili cringes, crinkling her nose and crossing her arms again. That's literally her brother.

"Hey!" Theo pouts, looking between the three of them with sad eyes. "You told me I was a catch."

"You are, and I caught you. Now come here and help me, princess." Emir has a towel around his waist, and now that Theo is paying attention, Emir's still wet from his shower and...mostly naked. Oh.

Theo doesn't even bother saying goodbye to Lili and Jordan until he reaches Emir who turns him around and picks up his arm to wave for him, both of them giggling and waving back as Theo gets pulled inside.

"What's...you're, um...you need help?" Theo literally averts his eyes, staring down at his feet because they're very much not alone and he can't be thinking about Emir like that right now.

Emir knows exactly what he's doing, lifting Theo's chin with his fingertip until their eyes meet. "I want your help getting all pretty. It's just dinner, but I assume there will be pictures. I want to look good."

"You always look good." Theo's eyes are wide and he's very intentionally keeping his hands to himself. If he touches Emir's shower damp skin, it's over. He'll have Emir's tongue in his mouth almost immediately. Hands in pockets might be best.

"Then I guess I just want you here to keep me company." Emir stares at Theo for a moment, watching him flush and start to fidget. Leaning in to whisper for Theo's ears only, he adds, "And I know you like seeing me fresh from the shower. Enjoy."

Emir kisses Theo's jaw before stepping away, nosing along his neck for only a moment and gently shoving Theo into a seat. The rest of the dancers file out around them with cheerful goodnights, heading out into the night to celebrate. Alfie grins at a text on his phone as he leaves, which Emir assumes is from either Ciaran or Gabe. But Theo's focus is clearly on one glistening torso and limber frame as Emir innocently gets himself dressed and fixes his hair. Emir knows how to put on a show, and Theo is his perfect audience of one.

***

"Took you long enough. Come here. You were incredible!" Ciaran's waiting for them upstairs, Gabe by his side with a collection of little gifts for each of them, T and Laurie included, of course. His arms are wide open, waiting to give them both their congratulatory hug as they get closer.

Theo reaches him first, hugging Ciaran tight before being handed a single white rose, a milk chocolate bar, and a Batmobile lego set.

Ciaran and Gabe have been doing this since first year, bringing each of them their favourite flower (or as close as they can find), a treat, and something random from the charity shop next to Roseborough. The others take turns doing the same for Gabe and Ciaran's performances, of course, but those are less frequent.

Once Theo has his rose, Gabe folds him into a hug to share his own celebratory moment with him.

"Emi, these are for you." Ciaran holds out a lilac peony, a mars bar, and a giant sketchbook before latching on to him for his own hug. It's different this year, Emir being part of their group celebration instead of scurrying away so that Theo could spend time with them and without him. He can't believe he pushed all of this away for so long, because it wasn't just Theo he kept at arms length, it was a deeper friendship with all of them.

As the four of them finish their round of embraces, Emir realises there's two people conspicuously absent.

"How are we upstairs before T and Laurie? Especially T, because they were done, like, halfway through the courtroom scene." Emir glances around as if they're hiding behind Gabe's back or something. But almost everyone else has already left for the night, the crowd in the foyer thinning by the minute. "The crew's coming back tomorrow for tear down, so Laurie should be done too."

"We figured you knew." Gabe shrugs, hands full of the items they picked out for their other friends, two more flowers with small, but meaningful gifts that both Laurie and T are going to adore. "Thought maybe they got caught up with something."

Emir thinks for a moment then sighs and runs a hand down his face, taking Theo by the hand and turning back around the way they came. "I might know where they are. Come on."

T told him about this once, early in their second year, but since this is the first show where they've all been together afterwards, it's the first chance Emir's had to see if it's true.

Theo goes with Emir happily, the other two following as Emir leads them backstage through the performers' entrance, eventually ending up in the wings where they all watch as T and Laurie dance on the abandoned stage to an empty theatre. They're not very graceful and there's no music so you can hear every step on the marley, but they are stunning to observe, absorbed in each other while they smile and twirl and have their moment.

T giggles occasionally when Laurie makes one of his jokes, and Laurie is staring at T like they're his own personal miracle. It's such a private moment, and Emir thinks he understands why T likes to sneak away to do this. There's something reverent about an empty theatre, like the room is witnessing their love story for them while they shuffle around in circles.

The four of them left in the wings silently agree not to disturb them, instead sitting in pairs just off stage and waiting until they're done. Theo sits between Emir's legs to lean back against him and Gabe lays down with his head in Ciaran's lap. They glance at their friends occasionally but mostly they're absorbed in their own partners, the vibrant love being shared on stage making each of them look at their own person with renewed appreciation. It's dim and quiet, the only light coming from the ghost light at the front of the stage.

Theo, for his part, closes his eyes and lets Emir play with his hair, listening for Emir's heartbeat beneath the ambient noise. If he concentrates, it's barely audible, Emir's fingertips following one pattern and his heart another, like a melody and its bass weaving together. Theo wonders if his own heartbeat's synched with Emir's but he can't hear it to find out.

He's noticed before how their breathing will match up when they're laying together, especially when they're sleeping. Theo's realised it often enough to start anticipating it each night, waiting for them to breathe as one, their bodies connecting subconsciously. That's usually the moment just before he drifts off on top of Emir's chest.

It's one of those things that Theo never knew about before. Before Emir, before their relationship, before he had someone to experience the gift of love with. He never knew that your breath could keep pace with your companion, that you could learn to sense their presence even in your sleep, that they become familiar to you but never mundane, that you start to see them unfiltered and unguarded and it doesn't lessen your infatuation.

It's only been about a month together, but it's been a glorious month, and Theo wouldn't change their story for anything. This, lying here together with their friends nearby on a stage they've both danced across, and the peace of a Sunday evening while they float inside of love is just...it's everything that Theo's ever hoped for.

"Emi?" Theo opens his eyes and glances up at his boyfriend. His hair is doing that artful swoop away from his forehead. It's dimly lit backstage so his eyes are a warm ebony, and when he catches Theo's gaze, his rosy lips soften into a smile.

"Baby?" Emir mumbles, leaning down to give Theo a sideways kiss. He's adorable and warm and Emir loves few things more than feeling his smile when they kiss.

"This is perfect." Theo keeps staring, waiting for Emir to respond. He could stare for hours and never be bored.

Emir nods his agreement, kissing Theo's temple and holding his head against his chest again. "You're perfect."

He keeps petting Theo's hair and occasionally kissing the top of his head, loving the sighs and hums of happiness that Theo gives him in response. How does Theo always know exactly what to say?

T and Laurie notice them hiding themselves away in the wings after only a few minutes, sitting on the floor but entirely in their own worlds. They laugh, T hiding their face against Laurie with embarrassment at getting caught. Laurie figured it was only a matter of time because they've been here a while and someone was bound to come looking for them.

"Family dinner?" Laurie asks, walking hand in hand with T and watching as their friends stand up to join them.

It seems they weren't the only two having a moment just now. Theo was half asleep on Emir's chest and Gabe was nuzzled into Ciaran's lap like an overgrown puppy. It's sweet to see them all so happy and at peace with their partners. He gives T's hand a squeeze, bringing it up to his mouth to kiss their fingertips in adoration, wondering how lucky they've all been to find such genuine, kind, gracious love, and to expand their lives through it.

"Here. Sunflower for T and daffodil for Laurie." Gabe holds their flowers out to them, T's accompanied by some Freddos and a vintage scarf, Laurie's by a chocolate orange and a folded England jersey for his collection. T ties the royal blue and pink scarf around their neck immediately, twirling while everyone agrees that it suits them perfectly well, and then they're off on their way home together.

***

Their after show family dinner ended a few minutes ago, when everyone was clearly too tired to continue. Theo and Emir are walking quietly to Emir's for the night, hand in hand, shivering against the cold, but neither of them is speeding up to shorten their journey. It's one of those nights that feels elastic, as if they could stretch more life into their hours if they just pay attention a little harder, feel their emotions a bit deeper, ignore time and absorb their world instead.

"You didn't have to carry my overnight bag." Theo glances over at Emir, loving how Emir always feels the need to carry his things while also hoping it's not becoming an expectation. He never wants to take Emir for granted.

"I know." Emir gives him a sweet kiss, not a single soul around to see them, and he wouldn't care if there was. "I like doing it, but I'll stop if you'd rather."

"No! Not at all, I just…" Theo searches for the right words while Emir waits. "I'm still learning how to be someone's boyfriend. I don't know the rules or expectations, and I don't want you to feel obligated."

"I don't, princess. I promise." Emir watches as Theo takes his hand back to readjust his beanie before reaching for Emir again. "I like spoiling you. It's the little things that I like best, you know?"

"Me too." Theo lets Emir redirect him away from the path and towards their tree. It used to be Emir's secret, but he's started saying it's *their tree* and Theo is absolutely not going to stop him. It's past midnight, but they don't have class tomorrow, and while Theo may wake up feeling hungover and a bit out of it, he decides this is well worth a few hours of discomfort.

"Are there nocturnal animals in London?" Theo wonders aloud as they settle beneath the tree together. They won't stay for long, but ever since Emir shared it with Theo, they stop here on every walk. Emir sits with his back against the trunk, Theo between his legs as they face the lake looking out through the night together.

"Of course. Bats and owls and mice. Foxes sometimes." Emir wraps his arms around Theo from behind and kisses the side of his neck. "And hedgehogs apparently. Never seen one though."

Theo quiets for a moment, staring out across the water and imagining all the wildlife hidden in the shadows as Emir lists them off. "Is that why T calls Laurie a hedgehog? Because he's practically nocturnal?"

Emir laughs, squeezing Theo tighter and pressing his giggles against his shoulder.

"No one appreciates how funny you are, princess, but I do." He nips at the side of Theo's neck then gives it a kiss, an echo of that moment that finally got them here. "Laurie is absolutely a hedgehog, all grumpy and spikey and scurrying around at night looking for snacks."

"But then what are you? You're a bit nocturnal too." Theo turns to stare at Emir instead, fingers finding Emir's across his waist to keep him close. He's definitely diurnal, but Emir's sleep schedule is borderline chaos. They've made it work well so far, mostly because Emir likes it quiet and Theo sleeps better with cuddles. And the sleep mask definitely helps.

"I think I'm more like a cat." Emir looks off into the water now, Theo's gaze on him like a summer breeze despite the late November chill. He can feel him staring, like Emir's his moon among the stars, or maybe a constellation that he's identifying through the haze.

"Crespecular? No that's not it..." Theo's eyebrows furrow as he thinks back. Emir taught him the word a few weeks ago when they came upon that family of rabbits spread out across the lawn near where they're sitting now. "Crepescular? No...Means they're active at dawn and dusk...crepuscular!"

"Exactly." Emir grins, pride fluttering in his chest at Theo's accomplished memory. Most people couldn't care less that he knows insignificant details about all the animals and plants around them. But Theo doesn't just care, he listens and remembers and brings it up again because he knows it's one of Emir's interests. He really is the most wonderful partner. "Crepuscular. Like me. Lots of naps and I like to be awake at weird hours."

"You sort of act like a cat too. Quiet and cuddly, but secretly fierce." Theo teases, laying his head back against Emir so they can stare out at the lake together.

Silence settles over them, but Theo knows it's not exactly silence. There's the city noise not too far off, and the hidden animals nearby are having their own conversations. It's ambience, and not the kind that heightens anxiety or adds chaos, rather the kind that gives cadence to their thoughts and keeps them company on their path.

"There's a phrase I've been thinking about recently." Theo starts fiddling with Emir's hand, nervous that this might be too much too soon, but it's a way of saying the words without literally saying them. "From Antoine de Saint-Exupery. He wrote that *Love does not consist of gazing at each other, but in looking outward together in the same direction*...it reminds me of us. How we work together, but also moments like this. Where we share space and just sort of exist, looking together like we did on that bridge in Cookham. Like, of course I want to stare at you. You're gorgeous. But it's more than that. We have the same vision for the future, we share the same passions, the same values. It's not that we see the world the same or that we have the same perspective, but we're looking together in the same direction. Two paths converging instead of diverging, to rephrase Frost. And it's not that we merge, but that we're choosing to walk alongside. Hand in hand, even."

Theo breaks his gaze to look down at their still joined hands, something so simple that still feels like a grounding revelation each moment it happens. "And I'm glad to see the world with you for as long as you'd like."

Emir listens and he smiles and he absorbs Theo's words, letting him talk and explain his heart. What he shares is always so thought out and beautifully arranged. Theo quoting like this used to be one of the reasons that Emir assumed he was pretentious, not understanding that it comes from Theo's natural desire to communicate as deep and as true as possible with the people in his life.

All these years, Theo was giving Emir chance after chance to see him and be part of his circle, and instead he judged and intentionally misunderstood because of his own bias and preconceptions. To love someone who quotes Frost and Saint-Exupery, and instead of making it academic, having it be contextualised in a conversation about their relationship is rare, and maybe unique. Theo said he didn't want Emir to feel taken for granted, but once again, Emir is reminded that Theo almost always is. Even his closest friends and family forget how important Theo's kindness and warmth and generosity of spirit have always been.

"You're definitely the whole sky, Teddy." Emir finally answers, remembering how much that conversation meant to Theo. "And I'll gladly see the world with you for as long as you like. I'll keep reminding you that you're special and important and lovely and intelligent and so many other things, because no one else seems to. And you should know. People should tell you that."

"I think you're exaggerating. I just want people to be loved and know that they matter. Isn't that what everyone does?" Theo looks up at Emir again, twisting in his arms and glad that Emir doesn't want to let him go.

"I'm not exaggerating, baby. You're not like anyone else." Emir kisses Theo's forehead, across his eyes, along his cheekbones, and finally his lips. Theo's nose is cold against his cheek, but he's still wonderfully familiar. "Thank you for loving me."

"Oh – I..." Theo's eyes flutter open again while he decides what to say. He sincerely does not want to push a conversation that Emir isn't ready or willing to have. But he also thinks it must be obvious that he loves Emir because, as he keeps repeating, to know Emir is to love him. "You're welcome?"

"And thank you for letting me take my time. It's not that I don't...you know. I just can't...I'm not ready yet." Emir hopes Theo understands that his own hesitation in making those words form across his lips has nothing to do with him and everything to do with Emir's own past that he's steadily working through.

"It's alright, honestly. I can tell without you saying the words." Theo gives Emir a warm and understanding smile before turning back around and resettling against Emir's chest. He smiles remembering all of the times that Emir thinks he gets away with mumbling it when Theo is almost asleep. "Especially when we're alone. Like how you only call me baby when no one else is around. And you still leave me little drawings or paintings to find around my room, and you open doors for me and bring me tea and teach me things about animals and laugh at all my jokes. Even the bad ones."

Emir grins and hides his face against the top of Theo's head, smitten and grateful that Theo notices all of that and understands it for what it is. He really does love Theo. "So is that what you want? Like...for us?"

"Which thing?" Theo has a hard time following Emir's train of thought sometimes because he's almost always thinking about a hundred things at once, and every single one of those thoughts is important. They're important to Theo, at least.

"Looking out at the world together?" Emir thinks that Theo's absolutely right, that the reason they work so well is that they are so different in so many ways, but that their priorities and values are aligned. They both use those values to determine their individual paths, meaning that walking together creates very little tension.

"I've always thought so. You're my first boyfriend, but that's how I've always imagined it. I don't want to lose who I am to be with you, and vice versa." Theo thinks about all the things he loves best about Emir, and how most of them are his idiosyncrasies and personality quirks, things that are so *Emir*. "I like you, and I don't want you to change for me. I'd rather we grow together but keep our independence."

"So is this like – " Emir feels like he already knows the answer, but he's still insecure about it sometimes. He'd rather clarify instead of assuming. "Is this a long term thing for you? Us being boyfriends?"

"Well since we've already met each other's families and you technically proposed a few weeks ago, I'd say yes." Theo hides his honest answer inside of his joke, jolting and laughing as Emir tickles him in response. He thought it was rather obvious that he's already factored Emir into his future plans, but maybe he forgot to tell him. Sometimes he has a habit of thinking something so often that he misses actually saying it aloud.

"I'm being serious!" Emir smirks, knowing that Theo is trying to keep the mood light for his sake. He knows Emir so fucking well, but it's important they have this conversation. "I like you, Theo, and I want to make sure we're both getting what we want out of being together. Best if we talk about it so no one gets hurt."

"Oh, sorry." Theo stops laughing and turns around to face Emir, sad to be out of his hug, but they can't have this conversation if he's being tickled and making jokes. "Okay, serious mode again. Yes, I'd like to consider this a long term relationship and you're right it's important we talk about these things, and I'm sorry I was making a joke because I know you didn't actually ask me to marry you, and we met each other's families but that doesn't mean you're, like, *obligated* to keep me or whatever, but yes I want to stay together as long as we're both fulfilled and being loved properly by the other person, and we should have regular check-ins about this, maybe on Wednesdays after family dinner? No, that's the middle of the week and I go to bed early. How do Saturday mornings work for you? Maybe every other week?"

Emir's never been as good with words as Theo has, so he holds the back of his beanie covered head and presses their lips together again in agreement. Theo sighs and kisses him back, hands finding Emir's waist as they both kneel under their tree in the middle of the night. It's like something out of a movie, where time is suspended and all they can focus on is the places where they meet and the space they share, everything else fading away as they fall into love together.

But it's cold and the wind is picking up around them, and Emir's missing his nest of blankets waiting for the both of them back at the flat.

"Every other Saturday sounds perfect." Emir tucks a piece of Theo's hair back under his hat then helps him to stand up. He throws Theo's overnight bag back over his own shoulder and waits for Theo to resituate his clothes to start walking again.

"If I actually add it to the schedule will you laugh at me?" Theo tugs his coat back down over his bum and resets his shoulders before grabbing Emir's hand again and walking away from the lake together. They'll be back tomorrow.

"Only a little. But I think it'd be good for us. I'm very serious about wanting to build this into something that lasts." Emir swings their hands for a moment before they drift back into the space between them. "You know before that party at Troy's when Laurie called me and you were there trying to stop him?"

"Before term started?" Theo almost trips on a rock, Emir steadying him with a smile. He gets a bit clumsy when he's tired, and Emir can see the exhaustion weighing him down. Best he gets them both to sleep soon.

"That one." Emir thinks for a minute before continuing, appreciating how Theo always gives him that mental space. "I was walking this exact path on the way back to the flat and thinking about how this was my last year and how autumn's always been my favourite."

"I thought you didn't have a favourite season? You told me summer's not great because you can't use as many blankets or hoodies, but then you also said you've always wanted to go to Miami and walk on the beach, so now I'm not sure." Theo subtly tries to hinder their progress. He's not ready to be done with their walk yet.

Emir notices the change and slows his own steps to keep pace. Sometimes spoiling Theo looks like giving him extra time, and they've got plenty to spare tonight...but they should still sleep soon.

"I don't. But I love this time of year, where autumn fades into winter and everything gets quiet and sleepy and cuddles are encouraged." Emir makes his point by dropping Theo's hand to slide his own into Theo's back pocket so they can cuddle while they talk. "But now I think it'll be my favourite because it's the season when I found you. I didn't know you before. I didn't let myself know you. But now, I'll always remember November as the month we had our first kiss, and the first show we were together for, and the first time meeting each other's families. I'll never look back on November the same. Each year, I'll wait for it to come and I'll grab your hand to walk you through the leaves and remember right now. Even in ten years, I'll see you in the yellow path as one year fades into the next and think about where we started."

"I know it's planning ahead, but maybe we could plan to keep walking together?" Theo has his arm around Emir's waist, giving it a gentle squeeze as he asks.

He likes to think that a decade from now they could still find peace in each other's presence, that they could be quiet and soft and happy together. And sure, it's only been a month. But sometimes you just know when someone is safe. Sometimes you can be sure for reasons you can't explain that you found a person who will be in your life, even for an imagined future that doesn't yet exist.

"I'll consider it. You're a pretty perfect walking companion." Emir pauses them as they get closer to his building, giving Theo another kiss beneath the stars. He definitely hopes Theo will be holding his hand and walking through the world for whatever version of the future they build. "Time to head home?"

"We probably should. We'll both be tired tomorrow." Theo sighs and rests their foreheads together, trying to keep them here a moment longer. But his bum is getting cold through his many layers, which is the true sign that they've been outside a few minutes too long.

"We're not saying goodbye, shehzadi, just going home to cuddle in bed and get some rest." Emir rubs Theo's lower back through his coat, understanding why Theo isn't ready for their night to be done yet. It's been a beautiful one.

"Race you there?" Theo distracts Emir with another kiss before taking off running, Emir needing a moment to realise he's serious before sprinting after him. He loves that they can go from earnest conversations about their future to running through the night with reckless abandon.

"Caught you." Emir's panting as he grabs Theo just before the door, his breath drifting up into the air like steam, Theo's starting to mingle with his own. He presses Theo against the door for a moment while he finds his keys somewhere in his many pockets. "You're all mine, princess."

Theo giggles, breathless from the run and from Emir so perfectly close to him. "All yours."

Acknowledgements

The titles for each individual book, as well as the series title, were inspired by the song *Latch (Acoustic)* by Sam Smith, from their *In the Lonely Hour* album. Back in my days as a dance professional, I once choreographed a performance to this song. The story I imagined behind that choreography has stuck with me ever since. While it's expanded from a short dance to a three book series, the heart remains the same. Thank you to Sam and to everyone else who created that song.

Thank you to my editors, J and Hayley. J helped with clarity and consistency, while Hayley helped me sound less American for the sake of my British and Irish characters. Both of your work has been invaluable to the final product.

Thank you to Hannah for the incredible cover art. From the first sketch, you drew Theo and Emir exactly as I pictured. Thank you for giving them life in an entirely new medium.

Thank you to Ashley, who has been the first reader for this series, almost since its conception. Your encouragement has been more necessary than you will ever understand. There were days I wanted to give in and shelve the entire project, but your faith in my writing, and my characters, saw me through.

Thank you to Shriya for having dozens of conversations about Emir's character, including, but not limited to, his use of Urdu and his experience as a Desi individual in England. Your feedback, and your friendship, have been integral to the process.

Thank you to my other early readers and sensitivity readers. Your feedback and commentary were extremely valuable.

And a last thank you to every single reader who has supported my work, in any format. I would not be the writer or the person I am today without the online communities who have shaped me, and for that, I will always be grateful.

BT

About the Author

Briar Townsend is a writer, a reader, and about a dozen other things. Mostly, they are a human who is doing their best. Briar is unapologetically queer and neurodivergent. They find value in writing the stories they always wished to read and representing identities that often go unacknowledged by the mainstream.

Contact: briar.townsend.official@gmail.com

Website: briartownsend.com